THE DARKNESS

Bill Kirton

For Kate, Jo and Simon.

My thanks to Dr Gary Ritchie for his time, patience and expertise and for recommending:
Milestones – The Diary of a Trainee GP, by Peter Stott, Pan Books, London, 1983
and
Doctors Talking, edited by Hellen Matthews and John Bain, Scottish Cultural Press, Edinburgh, 1998.

Also thanks to Caitlin
Anneke and Marcel

ONE

Tommy Davidson was in his study, kneeling on a prie-dieu which he and his wife had been given by some French friends in Rennes. He was thirty-five years old. In his time, he'd played rugby, tennis and golf, managing to get his handicap down to plus four. But he hadn't bothered with any sports for nearly two years. Work took up all his time nowadays. He practised law, specializing in corporate finance, and was very comfortably off.

His head was bent forward, his arms hung loose and the front of his shirt was covered with the blood that had pumped from his carotid artery. It had pooled stickily on the blue and cream carpet and made the job of the police much more difficult as they moved carefully around him.

'Why the bloody hell didn't he think to put a bucket there?' said DCI Jack Carston. 'Selfish bugger.'

'Yes, he's got all my sympathy, too,' said his sergeant, Jim Ross.

'Why bother. It's no good to him where he is.'

'You mean in heaven?' said Ross with a smile.

'I mean kneeling on a bloody chair on a ruined carpet, stone dead. That's a perfectly good Wilton. Somebody would've been glad of that.'

'You reckon he did it himself then, do you?'

'What do you think?'

When they'd arrived, alerted by colleagues at work after he'd failed to turn up for three consecutive days and hadn't answered either of his phones, they'd found the place locked from the inside. On top of that, there were no signs of a fight or anything out of the ordinary.

'If somebody else did it, he must've helped them,' added Carston. 'Just kneeling there and letting them carve away.'

'Hamlet,' said Ross.

Carston looked at him.

'Eh?'

'Hamlet. Sees Claudius praying. Comes up behind him

and …'

'You taking an Open University course or something?'

'No.'

'Just taking the piss, then?'

'I do my best.'

The prie-dieu was facing the bay window of Tommy's detached house which looked out across one of the valleys in the Cairngorms. On the window seat was an empty Edinburgh Crystal tumbler and a hand-written note. 'Sorry, Andrew. I've had enough. You know why, don't you? No point. I love you, though (although it's embarrassing to write it). Take care.'

Beside it, in a silver frame, was a photograph of a woman and two little girls. The woman was in the centre, the girls' faces close to her, their cheeks almost touching her own. The smaller girl had crossed her eyes, stuck out her tongue and opened her mouth as wide as it would go.

Ross pointed at the photo.

'Bet that's why he did it,' he said.

Carston bent to look more closely at it, straightened up and nodded.

'Yes, more than likely. Poor bugger.'

'The doc reckons he's been here since Friday at least.'

'Classic. Pick a time when you won't be disturbed.'

Ross nodded.

'Aye. It's hard to see past suicide, isn't it?'

There was nothing much they could do there so they left the scene of crime boys bagging up various bits and pieces, taking their photos and videos and quietly making a detailed record of the whole room.

'I'll go and see his brother when we get back,' said Carston.

'You want me to do it?' asked Ross.

'No, it's OK. I will. He'll have to ID him anyway. There are no other relatives. Not any more.'

Ross remembered the photo of the woman and the girls and felt a pulse of anger. He'd been on duty when the report came in. A car had mounted the pavement and crushed Tommy's wife, Tara, and their daughters, Penny and Sally, against the wall of the Post Office. The children were lucky. They died instantly. Tara's pelvis had been splintered and pushed up into her intestines. It took her eleven days. They were on their way home from shopping. The shreds of a new skirt from Next were found wrapped around the car's fan belt and Penny's green plastic handbag was full of birdseed.

Listen to this. Listen properly, I mean. To all of it. Maybe your psychiatrists can make something of it. I certainly can't.

I suppose it started when I was doing that house call. Jerry Donald. He's only fifty, but his circulation's so bad it's a miracle his blood moves more than a foot away from his heart. His veins keep blocking. Not many working valves left in them. Home, hospital, the surgery, he's back and forth all the time. I was doing the usual checking and prodding.

'I've thought of it,' he said.

'What?'

'The answer. My blood.'

'Really? What then?'

'A wheel. Like that one you see on telly. Big wheel, bloke inside it, arms and legs stretched out.'

'Is it a game show?'

'No. That drawing. Artist's thing. Used to be World in Action or something.'

'Ah, Leonardo da Vinci. Vitruvian man.'

'If you say so.'

'What about it?'

'That's the answer. You get me one of those, strap me in it, wheel me along and gravity does the rest. Saves my heart trying to pump the stuff up and down. It all just flows downwards as I'm rolling along. Legs, one arm, head, the other arm, legs again and on and on.'

'I'm not pushing you round inside a bloody wheel.'

'So much for the NHS.'

I pulled back the covers to look at his legs. What a mess. Varicose veins, discolouration from the knees downwards. Skin mostly a dark brown, some bruising just above his ankles.

'What's that greeny colour?' he asked, pointing at a bruise.

I brushed my fingertips across it. The skin was tight with the blood that was seeping out of the capillaries into the tissues.

'It's nothing,' I said. 'Normal bruising.'

'Not gangrene, then?'

'No, Jerry, not gangrene.'

'Because I don't want my feet just coming off. Me sitting up in bed one day and finding them still sticking out from under the sheets at the bottom.'

'If that happens I'll come and push them back up.'

He nodded and looked again at his ankles.

'Pity about the colour though,' he said. 'I mean, green, for Christ's sake. There's no team I fancy that wears that. Celtic, Hibs, Plymouth Argyle. Nobody else. If they went red, I'd have Man United, Arsenal, Liverpool ...'

'Aberdeen,' I said.

'Canna win them all,' he said. 'But fucking green.'

I bent and looked at the bruise more closely.

'Chelsea,' I said. 'Everton.'

'Eh?'

'It's not green, it's blue.'

'Blue. Oh no,' he said, as if that was really bad news. 'That's bloody Rangers.'

Gently, I felt the blood vessels in his calves, then his feet.

'Mind you, I should stay away from football altogether,' he said. 'That's what got me here.'

'You played, did you?'

He laughed.

'No. Got caught one Saturday night. Hearts supporters – no, not supporters, hooligans. They thought I'd said something to them. I didn't but it made no difference. Dragged me outside the pub and kicked the shit out of me. That's when I got the first clot in my leg and lung. Been downhill ever since.'

It was just a throwaway remark, but it reminded me ... I'd been talking to Tony Murray earlier. He runs the intensive *care unit at Aberdeen Royal Infirmary. One of his patients had the same thing, mugged by hooligans. He's got a wee daughter and he'll never see her again. He's lying in his bed, hooked up to drips and monitors, brain functions more or less non-existent.*

'Bastards,' said Jerry. 'Wish I could get my hands on them. Doesn't happen, though, does it? We never get the chance.'

'No,' I said.

I wrote up his notes and started packing my stuff away. When I was ready to go, I gave him a tap on the shoulder and said, 'Remember, Chelsea and Everton'.

'Aye, and bloody Rangers,' he said.

As they drove back to Cairnburgh, Carston was silent. At the wheel, Ross felt no need to make conversation. The two men had worked together for three years, complementing one another's strengths and helping to fill in any gaps left by their weaknesses. When Carston had first arrived in Scotland, some of his colleagues in Strathclyde had given him a hard time. There was the usual suspicion of outsiders. But an outsider who was not only a DCI but also English was particularly suspect. For some, the love-hate relationship with England was a source of harmless fun but for others, it went deep.

The move to the West Grampian force came about because he was good at his job and the then chief constable wanted to bring some respectability to his clear-up rates. The gentler, semi-rural social climate of the north east made no difference to colleagues' perceptions, however, and Carston's own occasional abrasiveness and quick temper did little to make his nationality more acceptable. Fortunately, Jim Ross was a well balanced individual whose shoulders were free of chips. His boss's tendency to indulge in speculations irritated him, but so many of those insights had proved accurate that Ross went along with most of them and was happy to supply the logic and the evidence they needed to ground them and make them acceptable to the procurator fiscal.

6

The views of open countryside with the distant Cairngorms as a backdrop eased some peace into Carston's mind. At the same time, though, the lushness of it all and the openness of the vast skies deepened his gloom at the scene they'd just left. The smell of death in that closed room stayed in his nostrils. It had been with him ever since his first experience of it in a student's bedsit down in England. The student, a nineteen-year-old from Leicester, had been bound, gagged, stabbed and left to die by her boy-friend. She hadn't been found for four days and, in the end, it was that smell which drew attention to her locked room. Carston was a member of the scene of crime team which had to work around her as she lay there and, ever since, the smell had been associated in his mind not with the physical horrors of death but with the pathos of wasted lives. She'd had years and years ahead of her. She'd walked into that room and bang – her future's just snatched away. And why? For a moment's insanity. How did people bring themselves to do such things?

With a sigh, Carston took out his mobile and called the practice where Tommy's brother was a GP. He was told that he was out on his calls but would be back at the surgery at two. Carston asked to see him before he started his afternoon appointments and slipped the phone back into his pocket.

They were passing a field full of Highland cattle.

'Sometimes I wish I was a cow,' he said.

Ross frowned, then said, 'So do I.'

Carston looked across at him.

'You wish you were a cow?' he said, surprised.

'No. I wish you were,' said Ross.

Back at the surgery, I soon got sick of the paperwork. What Jerry had said was niggling at me. I phoned Tony Murray. Asked him about the attack on his guy.

'The usual,' he said. 'Saturday lunchtime, couple of months ago. These lads had a skinful and they were on their way down Union Street singing, chanting – all the usual Alpha male stuff. Our guy was just in the wrong place. At the traffic lights outside the Virgin Megastore. Waved at his wife

across the road, called out her name or something. For some reason, this upset the lads and they started chasing him. Folk said it was like something out of Trainspotting – women shoved out of the way, complete mayhem.'

'And they caught him, obviously.'

'Yes. Too crowded for him to get away. He tripped over a pushchair. They dived in, four of them. Nine stab wounds and a fractured skull.'

'Bastards.'

'Yes.'

'What did they get?'

'What d'you mean?'

'Their sentences. With all those people around, they must have been caught.'

'Yes, they were. But Freddy got them off.'

Of course. Freddy. Well, you know as well as I do, in Cairnburgh, if you need legal help and your case is hopeless, that's who you call for. F. K. Reismann.

'There were plenty of witnesses,' Tony said. 'To the chase and the stabbing. And two of the gang had their knives out before they even caught him. Lots of shoppers saw the blades as they were running along. But the weapons disappeared, of course, and when it came to charging them, Freddy was called in by one of their fathers and he had a field day with all the crowds and confusion. Took the best proof there was and turned it round.'

'How?'

'There were two photos in the Evening Express. By an amateur, a guy out taking candids for his local club competition. It showed the gang charging along, knives out. They were in all the late editions. People saw them long before there was any thought of a trial so all Freddy had to do was say that everybody in Aberdeen had seen the photos, so it'd be impossible for the police to find an objective witness. It was crap, of course, but in the end, he got them off on technicalities about positive ID.'

'How does that guy sleep at nights?'

'His fees must help.'

8

'Will your man ever recover?'
'Not a chance.'
Yeah, that's where it started.

The atmosphere in the CID squad room was edgy. There were only two constables there, Spurle and Fraser, but neither of them liked record-keeping. They had no choice, though. Carston wanted everything up to date in case they had another quick inspection dropped on them.

'Punched her in the bloody mouth, didn't I?'

Spurle's voice was neutral, unapologetic, despite the things he was saying.

'I dinna ken how you can do that to a lassie,' said Fraser.

'After what she'd done?' protested Spurle, confident that it was he who was the injured party. 'Standin there in the pub, wrapped round the bastard?'

'Aye, well …' said Fraser, allowing his voice to tail off.

'What if it had been your Janice.'

'No chance,' said Fraser.

'Aye, that's what I thought till I saw Mandy.'

Fraser's head was shaking.

'I'm tellin ye, no chance o' my Janice fancyin nobody else. Not with what I've got between my legs.'

His idea was to lighten things up. But his words, implying as they did some sort of genital deficiency on Spurle's part, had the reverse effect. Spurle took refuge in dragging a file full of reports across his desk and slamming it open. Fraser turned away and re-read the words he'd been typing onto a charge sheet on his screen. Elsewhere in the building, they heard telephones, murmurings and shouted conversations but here the silence festered.

There was always something with Spurle. Fraser suspected that his problems came from the sort of things social workers were usually on about. They always tried to say that villains beat the shit out of folk because their own father had given them hidings when they were kids. Had all sorts of fancy words for it but that's what it came down to. Well, if they were right, Spurle's old man must have squeezed his balls with a vice every night. He was so bloody insecure. Always had to prove himself. Finding his fiancée with her arms round one of his pals in the pub was just what he didn't need. She'd said it was for a laugh. Said the guy had made her do it just to piss Spurle off. Looked like it had worked.

The door opened and Carston and Ross came in. Neither of the constables looked up. Carston sensed the tension but knew instinctively that there was probably nothing he could do about it. He put the files he was carrying on top of a cabinet in the corner and turned to go back to his office. The atmosphere was oppressive. He had to say something.

'Anything new on McPhee?'

Fraser looked across at Spurle. 'No, sir,' he said.

'How about you, Spurle?'

'Nothing,' muttered Spurle, his head still bent over the file in front of him.

Carston usually didn't care about the niceties of rank but Spurle's attitude always pissed him off. In the right circumstances, his brutishness sometimes made him a useful type of detective to have around but it needed to be kept in check.

'Where've you looked?' asked Carston.

Spurle looked up at him, tempted to make some wisecrack, but immediately saw the warning in his boss's expression.

'His case files, past associates, everything we've got on him,' he said, checking his anger and adding 'sir' after enough of a pause to make his point.

'Aye, sir,' said Fraser, coming to his rescue. 'It was him alright, but there's no way we can touch him.'

Carston nodded. His team had been working hard to collect evidence which proved that a local villain, Dougie McPhee, had been responsible for a robbery in an off-licence in George Street several weeks before. The shop's manager had been hit so hard that he'd suffered a stroke. He'd probably never talk again. It had McPhee written all over it but, as usual, proving it was very difficult. They had no witnesses, no clear prints, very few physical traces; just a tip from a source that had always been reliable that McPhee was their man. They'd interviewed him on several occasions and all the time, on the advice of his lawyer, he'd offered them nothing but silence.

'Well,' said Carston, 'don't give up yet. I want that bugger.'

'Aye, sir,' said Fraser.

Spurle nodded too and went back to his files.

Back in the other office, Ross was tapping data into his laptop. He looked up briefly as Carston came in then back at the screen again. Carston went to the window and looked out. A thin, middle-aged man jogged by, a brown pack bouncing up and down on his back and two small dumb-bells swinging high as his arms pumped with the rhythm of his running.

'Bloody hell. I couldn't run that fast even without all that weight,' said Carston.

Ross heaved himself up, looked out at the jogger and sat down again.

'Never mind,' he said. 'It may be good cardio-vascular exercise but his knees'll soon be shot with arthritis and all the diesel fumes he's breathing'll bugger up his lungs.'

'Ah well, that's alright then,' said Carston.

He sighed and sat once more at his desk, opened a folder, looked at it without enthusiasm and shut it again.

'Tell you what,' he said. 'Let's talk about McPhee.'

Ross stopped.

'OK. Talk,' he said.

'He's making us look like pricks.'

'We've got nothing, though.'

'Bit of police brutality might help.'

'Well, it's the sort of language he understands,' said Ross.

Carston looked at his watch and got up.

'How long is it since you had anything to do with him?' he asked.

Ross thought for a moment.

'Ages.'

'Why don't you give it a go, then?'

'How d'you mean?'

'Nip round. Have a chat. See if you can bend him a bit.'

'What, now?'

'No, no. See what Spurle and Fraser have tried. Think about it. See if you can get an angle.'

'OK,' said Ross.

'Right. I'm off to do a bit of bereavement counselling. I just hope the bugger doesn't cry.'

Carston had no need to worry. There were no tears from Davidson. The news obviously shocked him, but he reacted by closing into himself, taking a couple of deep breaths, then asking for the details.

'He left you a note,' said Carston. 'If you don't mind, we'll hang onto it until we've finished all the checks.'

Davidson just nodded.

'D'you know what it said?' he asked.

Carston handed him a piece of paper onto which he'd copied Tommy's note. Davidson took it, read it slowly and gave a single nod. There were still no tears. He was in control.

'You know what he's talking about, don't you?' he said.

'How d'you mean?'

'Saying I know why he did it.'

It was Carston's turn to nod.

'I think so.'

'He's been low ever since,' said Davidson. 'I've tried but … Not much you can say when something like that happens, is there?'

'Did he ever … well, talk about suicide?'

Davidson shook his head.

'No. But I should've seen it coming. I'm supposed to be a bloody doctor.'

'Don't start blaming yourself. No point,' said Carston.

'Aye, I know but …' He shook his head. 'Look, is there anything else? I've got patients to see.'

Carston was surprised that he was able to go on working.

'D'you think it's wise?'

Davidson looked at him, a question on his face.

'I mean, trying to concentrate on … Well, won't you feel …?'

He stopped. He'd broken this sort of news to people many times. They all had their own ways of handling it. Davidson seemed surprisingly cold, but it was up to him how he coped.

'You'll want me to identify him, I suppose?' he said.

'Unless there's anyone else.'

Davidson shook his head.

'When?'

'This evening, if it's convenient. Tomorrow …'

'This evening. Let's get it over with.'

As Carston drove back to the station, he thought hard about Davidson's manner. Maybe it was a family trait; keep the lid on everything, suppress it. That's what Tommy had been doing. He wondered idly whether Andrew was capable of going the same way.

TWO

Ross had made no more progress with McPhee than any of the others. He'd spoken with him, read through all the nastiness of his record but, for once, McPhee knew that they had nothing on him. Ross added just one bit of information to their picture of him: McPhee was a patient at Davidson's surgery. It was of no significance and it was only Tommy's suicide that had made him notice it, but it was the sort of coincidence that Carston enjoyed.

'If only we could place him in Ballater that weekend,' he said.

'Oh aye. Fit him up with a suicide,' said Ross.

'Wouldn't be the first neck he's sliced into.'

There was no lightness in his tone. Ross knew exactly what he meant and a silence fell between them.

'We're not going to get him for it, are we?' said Ross eventually.

Carston shook his head.

'Nope. He's got lucky again.'

'How did your session go with the doc?'

Carston shrugged. 'Hard to say. Took it like a professional, I suppose. He must see so much dying, it's just part of the routine.'

'Not when it's your own brother.'

'To tell you the truth, I don't think it surprised him.'

'Oh?'

'Aye, it was sort of like he was expecting it. I didn't even have to ask him to ID him. He offered to himself.'

Ross nodded.

'Like you say, a professional.'

Seeing Tommy was hard. I knew he'd been dead for a while before they found him, so I was expecting the bloodlessness, the waxy texture of his flesh. It wasn't that. It was the way your doctor kept the sheet tight up under his chin and ears. I suppose it made me imagine wounds and gashes which were

14

probably worse than what he was hiding. He looked so young. I wanted him to just sit up. Carry on where he'd left off last Friday. Poor Tommy. My little brother.

The verdict was fair enough. Suicide. No need to look any further. Obvious really. Sorting through his stuff was the worst bit. Kept the pain going, all the guilt, the loss. I gave most of the contents of his house to charity. Let Amnesty International and Oxfam fight over it all. I kept a few things. Private stuff. Lots of photos. Tommy'd kept shots of us as kids. I didn't have any. He even had some of me on my own – on top of Lochnagar, in a dinghy on Loch Skene, all sorts. I had no idea he'd kept them. Made me feel even worse. So did all the ones of Tara and the girls. All sunshine and smiling. They were beautiful wee kids. I could imagine Tommy sitting on his own looking at them.

He lived for them. You should've seen the bits and pieces in the drawers of his bedside table – poems, drawings they'd brought home from school, hair grips, pieces of ribbon. I just put them in a bag, took it home and put it in my attic. I couldn't throw them out. I didn't want to look at them again but I didn't want anybody else seeing them.

Christ, what a mess I was in by the time I'd finished with it all. Sad, yes. I did plenty of crying then. But angry, too. With me. Just thinking of Tommy out there on his own, with his photos of them. I should've seen him more often. I should've made him come back to Cairnburgh. And, of course, that set me thinking of all the other times I'd been a bastard to him. And it got worse and worse.

They must've noticed at the surgery. Nobody said anything, though. I tried to keep it all inside, but sometimes, well, I just lost it with folk. Not their fault, but any excuse to lose my temper. It was a bloody awful time. I'd lost the place, hadn't I?

The A90 dual carriageway climbs fairly steeply up from the bridge of Dee and out of Aberdeen. The forty mile limit ends just a few hundred yards up the hill and drivers are always keen to kick in their acceleration to start the long haul south.

That's why Rhona Kirk had decided to stand at the exit to the BP station a bit further on. She stood in the bright, late afternoon sun looking hopefully at each driver who stopped to fill up. She was twenty-six years old and had at last tired of the string of men who'd kept turning up to stay with her mum. Rhona had the upstairs flat and found it hard to avoid them and their paws because her mother was more or less dependent on them. In fact, Rhona had tired of them several months before, but didn't have enough money to risk setting out on her own. Now, with twelve thousand pounds tucked into a little yellow wallet in her suitcase, she knew she had the beginnings of her independence.

She was a good looking woman and, knowing that hitching was easier if she showed it, she had on a short denim skirt, high black boots and a white cotton blouse with two of its buttons unfastened at the top. At her throat was a black choker with a single blue stone at its centre, which sparkled in the sun and drew the eyes to the soft valley that led down between her breasts. She'd left her long black coat open to show drivers the goods they'd be transporting.

She hadn't had a car for ages, always preferring taxis and even buses, and, determined as she was to disappear from Cairnburgh and all her connections there, she knew that this wasn't the time to buy anything that was traceable. It was also the reason why she'd decided to hitch. Bus and railway stations had CCTV cameras everywhere. She'd taken one bus into Aberdeen, another to the bottom of Holburn Street, then walked over the bridge of Dee and up to the petrol station, trailing her suitcase and confident that she'd soon be chauffeured to where she wanted to go. In fact, her first stop would be Dundee. She'd already paid a deposit on a flat there and phoned the people she knew would be able to set her up with work. She'd told them her name was Laura McEwan.

When a black BMW pulled into pump number two and the driver got out to fill it up, she knew that she'd found her ride. He looked to be in his late forties and, from the moment he'd put the nozzle of the pump into his tank, his eyes never left her. She walked back into the petrol station and around to the passenger side of his car. He watched her all the way and smiled as she stood with her hand on the door handle.

When the tank was full, he replaced the petrol line, came round to her side, took her case and put it in the boot. She smiled back at him, took off her coat, threw it on the back seat and got in. As he walked back from paying, she looked carefully at him. The blue shirt would have been much better without the thin black and red stripes in the pattern and anyone of his age who wore a Bart Simpson tie had to be married with kids. He wasn't particularly attractive and, like most of his kind, carried too much weight. But he was going south. And he had a BMW.

They pulled out into the traffic and he hit the accelerator. In a very few seconds, they were up to seventy-eight miles an hour. Neither of them had yet said a word.

It was that night when I was drinking some Czech beer and listening to Eric Clapton playing the blues. That's when it really started. Well, not started, because it'd already been chewing away at me for a while. But I couldn't get Tommy out of my head, and I kept thinking of Tara and the girls, too. I looked around at all my ... stuff – all the chairs and side tables and lamps and pictures and carpets and I felt really, really ashamed. I'd made all the noises when they'd been killed, but I'd done nothing, bugger all. Just sat and been comfortable. I mean, there's supposed to be justice, penalties ... but there's not. There's no ... connection between ...

Anyway, I got up and looked out at the garden, and Tommy's words came back to me. 'I love you, though (although it's embarrassing to write it).' And I knew what he meant. We'd been close but you don't say soft things like that, do you? Only if you're American. But I'd been a terrible brother. I never showed him I cared. And I did. I still do.

I started crying again. And I suppose I decided to get pissed. But there were no more beers in the fridge so I went down to the cellar. That was it. I was taking a six pack off the shelf, and I stopped and looked around. You've seen the size of it, stretching under the whole house. No windows. Just the six pillars holding everything up, a roll of old carpet, half a dozen tea chests, nothing really. And I listened. Nothing. Eric Clapton was still playing upstairs but I couldn't hear a thing. I coughed. It just sounded dead. Lost. So I started walking around, touching the walls and the pillars, looking into corners. And it started coming to me. So I did some measuring, started working things out. I suppose I was thinking that, in the end, Tommy'd done something. He hadn't just sat about. He'd made his point. He had to die to do it, but he didn't wait for other people to do something. He'd done it himself. I wanted to do something, too.

Of course, it was stupid. I even remember laughing at the idea at one stage. But I didn't go back upstairs. I just stood there, working it out. It could be done. In the end, I put the six pack back, went upstairs, turned off the CD and came back down. I shut the door, turned off the light and groped my way across to one of the pillars. When I felt it, I just turned, sat down, and leaned back against it. It was freezing cold, and I'd never felt a darkness like it before.

Since the rape, Rhona had been with enough men to give her a pretty good idea of how they'd like their sex to be. She knew that, with this guy, it would probably be hard and rough. Their conversation had started harmlessly enough, but the speed with which he got it round to the dangers of 'such a sexy lady' hitchhiking and putting herself 'at the mercy of all sorts of weirdoes' left no doubts that he hadn't picked her up because he was a social worker. As he asked why she was prepared to take such risks, he slammed the car up and down through the gears, holding the steering wheel with just the finger and thumb of his right hand.

'You should have more faith in people,' she said.

'Huh, I've met too many of them,' he said. 'When it comes to sex, I don't trust anybody.'

'That's sad. You married?'

He lifted his left hand for her to see his ring, then gave a little shrug and said, 'Sort of.'

'Sort of?'

'We're both adults. Don't always share interests. She does what she wants. So do I.'

'Nice. Convenient.'

'Sometimes. How about you?'

'What?'

'You married?'

'What do you think?'

'I hope not. It'd be a waste.'

'How?'

'A guy having somebody like you all to himself.'

He gave a little laugh and, again, banged down into third to overtake a white van with ladders strapped to its roof.

Rhona looked out of her window at the North Sea stretching away to a horizon where the haar was gathering ready to roll in.

'Nobody'd ever have me all to himself,' she said, easing herself back into her seat so that her legs moved forwards and the short denim skirt lifted even higher on her thighs.

She'd made up her mind that she could handle this guy. He'd told her he was on his way to Edinburgh where he'd be spending a few days in a hotel while he tried to get access to some visiting Americans to persuade them to use his company to organize all their corporate communications in the UK.

'Tag along,' he said. 'I'll be free most evenings. We could do things.'

'I bet,' she said.

'I'm staying at the Caley.'

'Tempting. But I've got to get into my new flat. I'll be starting work this week and I need to get settled.'

'Not even one night?'

She looked across at him. He was even less attractive in profile than full face, his neck sagging down from his jaw, his gut pushing over his waistband.

'Not sure you can afford me,' she said.

He laughed, then looked across at her.

'You serious?'

She shrugged.

'Girl's got to make a living,' she said.

'Is that what you do then?'

'No, but if you're offering hotels and a good time, it's the same thing, isn't it?'

He laughed.

'I guess it is,' he said. 'OK. I'll go along with it. How much?'

'I don't know. What's the going rate?'

'How the hell should I know,' he said. 'I never have to pay for it.'

'Lucky you. But I'm no freebie.'

When he looked across at her again, she was facing him, a big, wide, sexy smile on her face.

'Christ,' he said. 'You're something else.'

'I think so,' she said.

I didn't sleep much. Just thought of Tommy and his misery. And the bastard who'd done it to him. And that darkness started to feel thicker somehow. I sort of lost any sense of how big or small I was, how much space there was around me. Strange, it was as if I was filling the cellar but, at the same time, sitting in some ... well, infinite space. I had no idea of time, either. I'd deliberately left my watch upstairs in the kitchen. I didn't feel tired. In the end, I did lie down. I think I dozed a bit. But even though I kept on waking up, I was never tempted to go up to bed.

I tried to guess when it was time to leave but my estimate was way out. I opened the door eventually and went back up the steps into the hall, but it was still dark. Went into the kitchen, turned on the light. Picked up my watch. It wasn't even half past three. I'd been down there less than six hours but it felt more like ten.

I made some coffee, still thinking about the things that'd been going through my head down there. I could've left at any time, but I started to sort of feel that I needed to stay there. I needed to have that blackness pushing against me. I'd tried to visualize lights, rooms, faces. I kept my eyes wide open, staring, but couldn't see a thing. I suppose it shows I was already in trouble. But it was all just ... nothing.

I still had to go to work. In a way, it did me good. The routines were ... reassuring, I suppose. Even all those bloody NHS forms and records. Often, between patients, I splashed my face with water to force away the fatigue but, underneath it all, I didn't really feel tired. There was a sort of energy that I'd got from the cellar. When I was driving home, I knew that I needed to do it again. But properly. Not like the previous night. Not on a whim like that. Properly. I'd measure it, think, look, feel. It had to be useful.

I had a quick meal and thought it out. There was no water down there, no lavatory, nothing. So, just before half past seven, I got a bottle of mineral water, a bucket and an alarm clock. I set it for 6.30 and went back down the steps, closed the cellar door, turned out the light and found my way back to the same pillar. I sat down, leaned against it, and let the darkness back in.

THREE

In terms of weather, the north east of Scotland gets a bad press. In fact, it doesn't rain too much and, instead of the quick switch from winter to summer that happens further south, Grampian enjoys lingering springs full of flowers. This year was a good one. Apart from a few days when the haar had crept along the coast, June had been all brightness and warmth. Carston was at the office window as usual, regretting that he couldn't be on the golf course or walking in the hills with his wife, Kath. His team's days were being taken up with petty offences. The flurry of activity around Davidson's suicide had quickly subsided after the verdict.

'No imagination nowadays,' he said.

Ross looked up from his computer.

'Shoplifting, credit card fraud – all so bloody predictable. What happened to all the Rippers?'

'They heard how good you are.'

'Yeah, maybe.'

Ross hit the print button.

'This is different,' he said.

Carston looked at the paper as it fed out into the tray. It was a missing person report. Rhona Kirk. Twenty-six years old. Last seen leaving her flat the week before. Reported missing by her mother.

'Name rings a bell,' said Carston.

Ross searched through a database until he found what he was looking for.

'That's what I mean,' he said. 'Here you are. Last August. Claimed she was raped but it never got to court. She dropped the charges.'

'The usual?'

'Don't know,' said Ross. 'Seems there was enough evidence for the fiscal but then she wouldn't testify.'

'Didn't fancy getting done over by the defence.'

'Probably.'

'Who was the guy?'

Ross read through the information on his screen.

'Robert Davies. Roustabout. Lived with her mother. Same address. The daughter's got the upstairs flat.'

'Twenty-six years old, living with her mum. No surprise she's left.'

'Maybe not, but she didn't say anything. It was only when her mother hadn't seen her for a couple of days that she thought to check.'

'Anything?'

Ross tapped the screen.

'Must've planned it. Packed a case, took clothes, credit cards and stuff. Nobody seems to be missing her.'

'What d'you mean?'

'Her mother reported it but wasn't all that upset. Said it was the sort of thing she'd do.'

'How about the folk at her work?'

'She didn't have a job.'

'So nobody has any idea of why she went? Or how?'

'Not yet. We'll check the airport and station. She's probably just shacked up somewhere, though.'

Carston nodded.

'Any boy friends?'

Ross shook his head.

'Well,' said Carston. 'Let's get it all checked out. Doesn't sound too drastic, though, does it?'

'I only mentioned her because you were moaning about being under-employed.'

'No, I was moaning because you buggers are under-employed.'

Five nights I stayed down there. On the trot. It was scary, but the fear was sort of fascinating. I mean, I knew there was nothing there but I thought I heard noises. In all the corners. Why was I doing it? Dunno. Trying to make it up to Tommy, maybe. Making myself suffer like him. Then I started thinking that maybe Tommy'd been wrong. He'd accepted things and that had pushed him down in the end. But you don't have to sit back and let it all happen. You don't have to accept stuff.

Maybe you can change it.

So the week after that, I didn't go back down. I got online instead. Engineering sites first, then newspaper archives, starting with those for the month Tommy's family had been killed. It only took a few days. I ended up with a few pages of notes and a list with five names on it.

It felt good to be doing something. At the surgery, they started saying I was 'like my old self' again. Esther, the new nurse, started fancying me. I could tell. And a lot of my patients went away cheerful. It works that way, if you're in a good mood, they think they're getting better. Jerry Donald picked up on it when I went to his house on call one Friday morning.

'You got a new woman?' he asked.

'No, why?'

'You're like a dog with two cocks nowadays.'

'Spending time with sophisticated people like you, that's what does it,' I said.

'You wouldn't like to tell my old woman that, would you?'

'You save your own marriage,' I said.

I pulled back the sheets to examine him and he watched the usual business of me pressing my fingers into his flesh and looking at the discolourations.

'Well?' he asked.

'Good news,' I said.

'Oh?'

'Yep. Brazil.'

'Eh?'

I pointed to his ankle.

'Blue and yellow,' I said. 'That bruise is fading nicely. Quicker than I thought. That's good.'

'So I'll be out and about soon, will I?'

'The sooner the better.'

'You serious, doc?'

I had to smile. I nodded and said, 'You just have to make sure you take it easy. No football, no clubbing ...'

'How about shagging?'

24

'D'you use your legs for that?'
'Can do. Don't need to, though.'
'Right then. Shagging without legs.'
'There's a good joke about that.'
'I don't want to hear it,' I said.
'I'll tell you next time.'
'There won't be a next time. No need for me to come again. You can come into the surgery if you need me.'
'That early?'
'Don't see why not.'
'Whoohooh, shagging without legs,' he said.

Despite feeling that Rhona Kirk's disappearance didn't necessarily imply that she'd come to any harm, Carston had briefed the team about her. He'd reopened the file on the rape incident and put it in the system, with her picture and all the latest details.

'This'll get you off your arses,' he said. 'Airport, bus depot, station – and go and see her mother.'

'She'll be off down south,' said Spurle.

'Who? Her mother?' said Fraser.

'No. The slag,' said Spurle.

'You know her then, do you?' said Fraser.

Spurle sneered a smile at him.

'It's always the same with these cows,' he said. 'She'll be shooting up in Leicester Square or getting shagged in Leith.'

Carston shook his head.

'How'd you get to be so bloody wise?' he said.

Spurle didn't look at him, didn't want to catch his eye.

'She'll be on something,' he said. 'They usually are.'

Carston clicked on a screen to enlarge the photo.

'Maybe, but she's Twenty-six. She looks pretty good still. Users don't usually look that good at that age.'

'Once a junkie …' said Spurle.

His black and white view of the world was depressing but statistics suggested that he might be right. They'd rake around, ask some questions, just in case there was some trace, but she'd probably be long gone. Even if she'd survived, she'd be way outside their patch. In the end, they'd keep her file open in the computer, ask other forces to keep an eye out for her but that would be that. True to form, though, Spurle wouldn't let it go. He was scrolling through the notes on his screen.

'She's just a prick teaser,' he said.

'I thought you'd finished, Sherlock,' said Carston. 'How d'you make that out?'

'This rape shite,' said Spurle. 'Says she's raped, then changes her mind. She knew she'd be found out.'

'No,' said Fraser. 'I don't think so. I think he did it alright. Why piss off if you're innocent?'

'Why not?' asked Spurle.

'No, he was guilty as fuck. That's why he took off.'

'Not surprised. Who wants to stay with a bitch screaming rape every time you look at her?'

Not for the first time, Carston wondered whether Spurle was a fit representative of the forces of law, order and morality. Some of his attitudes belonged with Genghis Khan.

'Well,' he said. 'As you're looking around, try not to prejudge things too hastily. There may be a woman out there somewhere who's not a slag, bitch, whore, or any of the other categories you seem to have come across so far.'

'Huh,' said Spurle, 'I'll try but …'

'We should check the guy out, too,' said Ross, seeing where the exchange was heading and knowing that Carston was capable of saying things he'd regret.

The others looked at him.

'The one who …' He stopped, leaned over a keyboard and clicked onto the Rhona file, looking for a name. 'Here he is. Robert Davies. Maybe she went looking for him. Victims do that sometimes.'

'Do what, sarge?' asked Fraser

'When they've been raped. Or knocked about. They go back to the guy who did it. It's hard to understand, but it happens.'

'They love it. Lap it up,' said Spurle.

Carston shook his head. Spurle was sick, no doubt about it. Ross continued to scroll down through the information on Davies. There wasn't much. A couple of months after the accusation was withdrawn, he was supposed to be on a flight out to his platform but just never turned up. His company looked for him but it seemed he'd left the area altogether. He was no real loss and they had no difficulty replacing him.

Ross closed the file and noticed a report just in from Aberdeen.

'Another one here,' he said. 'Ian Stride.'

The others listened as he read out the details. Stride had disappeared, but it certainly didn't seem to have been planned. He'd bought tickets for a show just before he left, his diary was full of appointments but he'd driven to Edinburgh in his BMW and vanished. There was CCTV footage showing him parking his car near the Caledonian Hotel, a day later than expected, then nothing. He hadn't actually checked in but no alarm bells had started because it was an open company booking, paid for in advance, and no-one had expected to hear from him during the time he was there. When he failed to show up for work the following week, his boss phoned his house. His wife, who'd thought he'd just extended his stay, phoned Grampian Police HQ.

'Looks more promising than our Rhona,' said Ross. 'They've got a witness who said he thought he'd seen him picking up a woman at the BP station on the Stonehaven Road. There's a blow-up shot of his car from another camera - a junction just north of Dundee. It's blurry, but there's definitely a passenger with him.'

'A woman?' asked Carston.

Ross shook his head.

'Hard to tell. Definition's too poor for an ID.'

Carston nodded. It was Aberdeen's case, not theirs, but it would probably be more interesting and more rewarding than trying to find a woman nobody cared much about who'd probably just left town for a change of scene.

'OK,' he said. 'Get on with it. And Spurle … just ease back a bit, eh? The psychos are supposed to be our targets, not our bloody role models.'

My first free weekend, I drove down to Edinburgh. Left my car in the Waverley Station car park and took a bus to the yard of a van hire company I'd found online. It was a small set-up, local to Edinburgh. They lease battered vehicles dirt cheap. They weren't too fussed about paperwork. I was wearing crappy old clothes, had a Boston Red Sox baseball cap pulled down over my forehead, put on a rough accent. I signed the papers, got the keys and drove straight over to Glasgow. Big builders' merchant's. Then another couple of specialist stores and, in a couple of hours, I was on my way home. In the back I had twelve bags of concrete mix, ten lengths of heavy duty chain, a pile of ex army blankets, two dozen packs of acoustic tiles, two chemical toilets and eight drums of disinfectant.

Back home, I reversed up to the front door, unloaded everything into the hallway, had a quick cup of coffee and set off back to Edinburgh. Returned the van, got a bus back to my car and came home. Twenty past eleven I got there. Totally shagged out.

It took me till the following Friday to finish it all. Every night I was down there. I'd stopped thinking about why. I was just doing it. Enjoying it, too. Working with new materials, doing heavy stuff, different from the daytime routines. I was starving most of the time, too. So I remember, on the Friday, making this huge leek risotto, opening a bottle of Chilean Merlot and sitting watching Channel Four news. Didn't take any of it in. When it was over, I went back down to have a look. I wanted to double-check everything.

I know it looked bad when you saw it but then ... well, it was new. I was sort of excited looking at it. I'd done a bloody good job. Acoustic panels everywhere, new concrete floor with the old carpet roll on it. The pairs of chains and cuffs on five of the pillars. And all the blankets, folded, tidy, waiting.

The only place the chains could meet was right in the centre of the cellar. I made sure of that before I put that chemical toilet there. Minimal, I know, but what else would they need? A bucket, wooden seat over it. Good enough for them. I even left them two rolls of lavatory paper.

And that was it. I'd done it. Trouble is, it meant I started thinking about it again. I didn't have time really when I was making it all. Well, I suppose I did, but if I'd started listening to common sense, I'd just have stopped and I'd be back at square one. But standing there looking at it, I began to see how ... crazy it was. It couldn't work. It wouldn't happen. But I suppose it was therapeutic. I told myself I was doing something for Tommy. There was a ... compulsion.

I turned off the light, closed the door and went back to the usual pillar. It was nice having a blanket for a change. I pulled it up around my shoulders and let the darkness back in again.

FOUR

Carston had heard a lot about displacement activities – things you did to avoid getting on with the job in hand. But he didn't reckon that a drink at lunchtime came under that heading. He spent too much time just plonked at his desk, sifting through bits of paper, scrolling down endless screens of words and figures. A stroll to the *Dolphin* with Ross woke him up and freed him to indulge in a bit of speculation. Facts were fine but sometimes they got in the way.

And anyway Spurle's brutalism had gnawed away at him through the morning. The problem was that, sometimes, some of his prejudices seemed natural and Carston found himself secretly agreeing with them, even though he'd never articulate them in the way Spurle did. Not the macho crap – all that contempt for women. He'd never subscribe to that and, if he did, Kath would soon be on his case. No, it was Spurle's knee-jerk reactions to the villains they came across that often mirrored his own.

He and Ross were sitting in their favourite spot in the bay window with two pints of lager on the table in front of them.

'I'm worried about me,' he said.

'I've been worried about you for years,' said Ross. 'Anything in particular bothering you?'

'You jumped in just in time this morning. Spurle gets right on my tits.'

'He's a surly bugger,' agreed Ross.

'Brings out the bad bits in me. Makes me just like he is. The way he can just dismiss women as if they're … well, things. I just wanted to put my boot in his crotch.'

'Aye, like you said, dead refined – just like him.'

'I know.'

He took a swig of his pint.

'There must be something wrong with us, though. To choose this job.'

'Speak for yourself,' said Ross.

'I am. I've always wondered how I could do this, why I

30

get pleasure out of it. And I do.'

'Pleasure?'

'Well, satisfaction maybe. We stand looking at blood all over the place, bodies crumpled in alleys, bloody mayhem. And we just chat about it. It's not normal.'

Ross drank deeply. This sounded ominous. More airy-fairy abstractions.

'I s'pose it's in all of us,' said Carston. 'Rubbernecking at accidents, reading the gory bits of trials and murders. Why're the papers full of it? Because the readers want it. It's as sick as Spurle.'

'Aye, but we're not just "chatting about it", we're doing something, stopping it, clearing it up.'

'I know but … well, what about Dougie McPhee?'

'What about him?'

'You know what he did. And he got away with it. Now there's another one – that off-licence manager. Even if we catch him and he doesn't manage to wriggle away again, what'll happen? Banged up for a few years, fed, looked after.'

'It's what civilised societies do,' said Ross.

'I know, but don't you have the gut reaction that you'd like to take him round the back, pull his intestines out of his arse and throttle him with them?'

Ross was about to take a bite of his sandwich. Pointedly, he put it back on the plate. Carston smiled.

'See what I mean? I'm just an upmarket version of Spurle.'

'Upmarket?' said Ross.

'I think that's maybe why I get so pissed off with him – he's saying things I think. Sometimes, anyway.'

'OK. But that's all he is – the aggro merchant, the hard man. No exceptions. That's not you, is it?'

Carston had to shrug a sort of agreement. The victims they had to deal with always triggered a real compassion in him, but that only led to more anger and a stronger desire to deal out some of his own justice to the people who'd done it to them.

The barmaid walked past their table carrying empty

glasses.

'Can I get you another one?' she said.

'No thanks,' said Ross. 'We've got to get back.'

She smiled and walked back to the bar, her hips rolling and her long blonde hair floating against her shoulders. Carston watched her and felt the pleasure her movements triggered in him.

'Christ,' he said.

'Aye, she could get a man in trouble,' said Ross.

'No,' said Carston. 'I meant Christ, I really am just like bloody Spurle. Same basic urges. Just a bloody animal.'

'Spurle with imagination. Now there's a nasty thought,' said Ross.

And that was it really. I'd done it, so I could settle back into my routines – diagnoses, counselling, house calls, prescriptions, letter writing, form-filling. None of it was a drag any more. It was even sort of comforting. The cellar was a fantasy. Making it, all the manual labour, it gave me a buzz for a while, but it was reassuring when I went down to look at it now and then to feel that that was enough. I wouldn't have to go the next step. I'd made the gesture.

But I was fooling myself. Seeing Tommy's body, looking through his things ... Know what brought it home? A bit of paper. Folded up. It was in a pile of books I'd brought from Tommy's and stuck on a shelf in my bedroom. It was a letter from the administrator of Scottish Ballet thanking Tommy for his kind remarks and inviting him and his two daughters backstage at the Edinburgh Festival Theatre after a performance of Carmen. Penny, the little one, was ballet mad. The date of the performance, May 13th, was her birthday. She was killed on the 4th.

It was a simple note but Tommy must've put lots of time and effort into asking for the favour. If Scottish Ballet let every dance-mad kid backstage, there'd be no room for the cast. Tommy must have used all his lawyer's skills to get them to say yes. I remembered Penny's own dancing, the times she'd actually managed to stay up on her points and the ones she hadn't. She'd tumble, stagger, giggle; she was a wee beauty. My favourite.

And that was the start of a very bad, very depressing day. There was the usual procession of time-wasters with their coughs, colds and sore throats, some apologetic, some who wouldn't leave without a prescription. There were two in particular ... I could smell the first one as soon as she opened the door. It was Jessie. You know, Jessie Givens. Sweat, pee, old booze, clothes that hadn't been off her back for days. She'd first come months before and it was already too late. Heart, lungs, liver, kidneys – all buggered up by booze and fags. Then I felt the lumps, referred her, and got the letter back from the hospital. Breast cancer, secondaries, all well advanced. I put her on Tamoxifen, but there was no way of knowing whether she took it or whether her liver was still capable of processing it. All I could give her were pain killers and she'd either take them by the handful or sell them to junkies to get money for more booze.

I gave her the full ten minutes. Not that there was anything new to say. As usual, the real fears only came up right at the end of the session.

'He's goin to murder me when I get home,' she said.

I knew who she was talking about. So do you. Her husband. Beat the shit out of her. Regularly.

'Why d'you say that?' I said.

'He said so. He's already had a go at Ella, and she's no even his wife.'

There was nothing I could do about it.

'Have you asked him to come in and see me, like I said?'

She shook her head.

'I tried but ...you know.'

'Tell you what,' I said. 'I'll come round. Pretend I've come to see you and maybe have a chat with him while I'm there.'

She just shook her head.

'When would be a good time?' I asked.

She shook her head again.

'I never know when he's there or not.'

Again, the loop closed. There were other people in the waiting room.

'OK, Jessie,' I said. 'Leave it with me. I'll call in. Maybe I'll get lucky, eh?'

She nodded and got up.

'He'll be waiting for me now,' she said.

'I can't come now. I've got surgery till lunchtime.'

She nodded again.

'OK, doctor. Thanks.'

When she'd gone, I opened the window and took a few deep breaths. It wasn't just to get rid of the smell but also to try to give myself a shake. Patients are sensitive to your moods, you know. They soon pick up any signs of depression. The trouble is, they tend to relate the signals to their own problems and start thinking they're more ill than you're saying.

I managed to keep up the pretence through the morning. Spent my lunchtime writing referral letters, signing prescriptions and looking through the post to check on what the hospital had to say about patients I'd sent for tests and x-rays. All automatic, sanity-preserving stuff. Then, late in my evening surgery, in came Donald Brewer. Donald's sixty-six. I've seen him a few times, not about himself but about his wife. He thought she was changing somehow. The more I talked to him, the more I could guess what was wrong with her. She was depressed a lot of the time, disorientated, asked the same questions over and over again, forgot things. And if Donald tried to talk to her about it, she just shouted at him.

I'd arranged for her to be assessed at the hospital's psychiatric unit. One of the letters I'd read at lunchtime confirmed what I'd suspected. Alzheimer's. This was the news I had for Donald. He didn't react at first. Looked around the room, his eyes avoiding mine. Then he said, 'Well, at least it's not cancer.'

I was surprised.

'Her sister died of that,' he went on. 'Brain tumour. Couple of years ago. I was afraid it was that.'

His voice caught half way through. He wasn't crying but

I could see the flush spreading up from his neck, the tightening of his muscles. We talked about what the illness meant, what he should expect, social services, all that. I noticed that he'd been calling her 'the wife' at first, but she'd become 'my Annie'.

He never did cry properly. Just stayed determined, dignified. Just said 'Thank you' as he left. I felt guilty to be sending him off to massive changes. They could crush him. And I could just close the door and get back to all my bloody comforts.

I packed up at about seven-thirty. I was in reception when the phone rang. Sally, the receptionist, said she was sorry but would I take the call. I did.

'Dr Davidson speaking. How can I help?' I said.

'Aye, that's what you call yourself, but ye're nae much fuckin use, are ye?'

The guy was angry, full of drink. Gave me no time to answer.

'I'm wantin somebody round here now. I rang you fuckin hours ago. Too fuckin busy, they said. And here's me in fuckin agony.'

I mimed a question at Sally asking who it was. He carried on cursing and swearing as she scribbled a name on her pad: Douglas McPhee. I should've known. He's never been one of my patients but I'd heard enough about him to know that he was one that the practice could do without. But that wasn't what I was reacting to. Somehow, the aggression of the guy, the threats, the knowledge of who he was – they clogged up my throat. I don't know, it was instinctive, feral even. It was one of the names on my list, of course. The one I'd made before I started on the cellar.

I covered the mouthpiece and asked Sally to bring through his notes. I had them open in front of me when he eventually said, 'Well, are ye comin or no?'

'No,' I said. I was surprised at how much control I had.

'What?'

'You should still have plenty of Co-Proxamol left from when Dr McIntosh saw you.'

'How the fuck do I know whether …?'

I didn't let him get started again.

'And, unless you've developed some other chronic condition in the five days since then, I can't think how I could do anything to improve things. It certainly doesn't seem like a house call's in order.'

'Ye lazy bastard.'

'Aye, maybe, but I suggest that, if you're still feeling the same in the morning, you come in and get Dr McIntosh to have another look. But I should tell you, I think she'll say the same thing.'

'Aye, ye're all the bloody same. Waste of fuckin space.'

'You'll have to excuse me now, Mr. McPhee. I've got work to do.'

'What about my fuckin chest here? Fuckin killin me, so it is.'

'Take the Co-Proxamol, just like Dr McIntosh said. Goodbye.'

I put the receiver back just as he was starting it all again.

As I drove home, I couldn't stop my mind flicking back and forth between McPhee and poor Donald Brewer. Normally, I force myself to blank out the day's events. You'd go mad if you didn't. But finding the letter to Tommy had started it, and Jessie and Donald had made me feel guilty and … well, so bloody impotent. And then McPhee's rants and all the things I knew about him … It was too much. I was angry. At him. And at me for being so bloody helpless. And so bloody compliant.

The Internet had made everything so much easier. Rhona had used it to make her Dundee contacts and, with their help, she soon had a website running. She knew that they'd charged her more than the commercial rate but she'd expected that. It had been the same in Aberdeen. But, within two days, she started getting the emails and the calls on her mobile from Dundee punters who were fed up with trekking to Aberdeen or Edinburgh. She kept her rates reasonable and made sure she met them in public places and that the sex they had was always in their hotel rooms.

She knew she was good. Since the rape, she'd given up on sex as a source of pleasure for herself. The first few times she'd forced herself to try it again, it was soon obvious that the fear and fury were as strong as ever. Not surprising, really; the trauma was deep. Her mum's boy-friend had jammed her face down on the carpet, forcing her arms up her back, and then sodomized her. It was hard to breathe and the tearing in her shoulders and the pain of penetration were almost unbearable. Afterwards, he'd just zipped himself up, fetched a beer from the fridge and sat down to watch snooker on television. When she'd called him names and sworn at him, threatening to tell her mother, he laughed and told her to fuck off.

The police had been understanding enough and she'd been treated very gently by a female officer, but it took ages for them to start collecting evidence and, by the end of the week, she decided that she had more to lose than he did and that, anyway, she could administer a more fitting and more effective form of justice.

Paradoxically, it was that experience that had honed her sexual techniques. Freed from the personal involvement she'd always felt with men before, the act had become mechanical for her; she was always in control. She made the noises they wanted to hear but, as she did so, she watched them, noticing what they preferred, subtly increasing the pressure she was applying with fingers, lips or tongue. While sitting astride them or lying beside and beneath them, the docile, compliant partner they wanted, she'd be calculating how to drive their hunger to its limits and make sure they not only paid what she asked, but often gave her extra and usually wanted to come back for more.

She'd quickly established a regular clientele, mainly in Aberdeen, where oilmen came and went and always needed sex when they visited from Norway, France, Holland or the States. They nearly all paid in cash and, before long, she was richer than she'd ever imagined she'd be. But something was still missing. When she lay in bed at night, she sometimes wanted to go back to when she'd been a receptionist in Anstey Oil in Cairnburgh, before the rape, before the guilt, when things like love and hope didn't make her laugh. Each coupling with a stranger was efficient, profitable, but ultimately left her with a small sadness that they were pleasures that she'd always be providing, but never sharing.

At the same time, it was obvious that her confident sexuality communicated itself to men whether she wanted it to or not. She got the usual whistles and Neanderthal remarks but, worst of all, she was always at risk from the predatory men her mother kept bringing home with her. It was their attentions, the money she'd saved and a tiny hope that things might be better elsewhere that had convinced her to leave. Dundee was the first stop; eventually she'd get to London. By then, she'd know where she really wanted to go.

She didn't think for a moment that her mother would bother looking for her but you never knew. It was important for her to disappear altogether. She'd been prepared to risk that the guy with the BMW could identify her, but then he'd turned really nasty and she'd found herself back at square one. It was as if bad luck was chasing her, whether she deserved it or not.

But tonight's punters were easy to please. She'd seen one of them the previous week and, after a relatively quick and very tame session, he'd taken her back down to the hotel bar and talked about what he'd really like to try. He'd always suspected that he was gay but didn't know how to set about getting it on with a man. Somehow, he felt that, if Rhona could arrange it and be part of a threesome, it would all be much easier. She didn't bother telling him that several of her customers had asked for more or less the same thing and, within a few days, she'd contacted one of them and set up dinner at an expensive restaurant in Edinburgh. Now, well fed and boozed up, they were up in the first punter's hotel room. She'd quickly helped them to get rid of their inhibitions, brought them together on the bed and let them get on with it. One of them was fatter than he should be; the other was covered in cheap, badly etched tattoos and, as she watched and encouraged them, she felt nothing.

FIVE

McPhee had been drinking since late morning and, as usual, it had turned him into a fighter. He'd been sucking back the whiskies partly to ease the real pain he felt in his chest but also because that was how he spent most days anyway. After the call to the surgery, he banged the receiver back down, punched the wall beside it and headed out to the pub again. There, they knew him well enough to leave him alone and let him get on with it. By ten o'clock, his money was gone and nobody else was buying. The pain in his chest was still there, though, and his resentment at the way Davidson had dismissed him had grown into a fury. He made one last try to get a drink on tick, swore at the barmaid when she refused him and staggered out the door.

July was easing towards August. The night was gentle and the sky was still light. McPhee started off down the street. He hitched up the collar of his jacket and walked with his shoulders hunched and bobbing in the manner of small men who would like to be big.

'Bastard,' he muttered. 'I could be fuckin dyin for all he cares.'

And, in the darkness, with no money for more drink and the nagging ache clenching still in his chest, all his venom turned towards Davidson. No bastard treated him like that. Fucking doctors thought they were God's gift to the world. Well, Dr fucking Davidson had another think coming.

I was listening to a Gerry Mulligan, Paul Desmond CD. I'd just looked through a list of patients I had to phone about blood tests and I was looking at the other list, the one I'd got out of the papers. The anger I'd felt about McPhee was burning all the way home. That's why I'd taken the list out. The names weren't in any particular order and I hadn't put down why they were there. But I knew that anyway.

You know them all, of course. David Campion, Douglas McPhee, Peter Dobie, George Waring, Christopher Bailey.

All guilty. But just a list. Nothing I could do about them.

The Body and Soul track came on, I remember. That's when the doorbell went. Made me jump. I thought about leaving it but then he started banging. Leaning on the bell and banging at the same time. The music had been calming me a bit but all of a sudden the anger was back. I went out and opened the door.

It was McPhee. When he saw me, he still leaned on the bell, but he pointed at me with the other hand.

'Ye bastard,' he said.

It was dark. The neighbours were too far away to hear anything but I looked past him, just in case he'd brought back-up.

'Aye, ye can fuckin look, pal. It's just me.'

'Listen …'

'No, you fuckin listen,' he said. 'Don't think you can fuckin brush me off easy. I'm no one of your fuckin wifies.'

'Why've you come here?'

'Why've I come? Why've I fuckin come? You don't know fuck all, do you? I told you. I got a fuckin pain in my chest. You're s'posed to be a fuckin doctor. S'posed to do somethin about it.'

'Ah. Right.'

'Never mind "ah fuckin right". I'm tellin you you're no gettin away with talkin to me like that.'

'Listen, it's late. You've had a lot to drink and …'

He leaned forward and spat in my face. I was too late to duck away. It hit me on the cheek. I felt it on my lip and in the corner of my mouth. Slippery. I wiped it away and shoved him back out of the doorway.

He shouted, 'Bastard,' grabbed my arm and took a swing at me. He was drunk. It was easy to lean away from it. But he fell forward into the hallway and knocked over a little table beside the door. He turned to look at me again. Spat on the carpet. Put up his fists ready to fight. It was pathetic.

'Come on, ye poncy fuckin bastard,' he said.

I'd wiped the spit away, but I could still feel it somehow. Like it was crawling on my skin and inside my lip. I was mad.

It would've been so bloody easy to give him the hiding he was after. He was still shouting, cursing, swearing, beckoning me onto him. He spat on the carpet again.

'Don't do that,' I said.

He hawked up some more phlegm. I jumped at him and grabbed him by the lapels.

'I said don't do it,' I said.

I was pulling his jacket tight around his throat. He was trying to pull my hands away.

'Listen, you low-life bastard,' I said, 'you don't come here messing up my place with your filth.'

'Fuck you.'

'No, fuck you, McPhee.'

'Ye're s'posed to be a fuckin doctor. All I'm wanting is fuckin pills. Fuckin pills, you useless twat.'

His voice was hoarse from the pressure I was putting on his throat. It was weird. The jazz was still playing. And, all of a sudden, I felt cold. A bit like when I heard his voice on the phone at the surgery. And then, everything was crystal clear. I know it's strange, but it was if someone had switched on a light. The front door, the overturned table, McPhee – they all sort of came into focus. Like I was standing further away from them. Like I wasn't angry any more. No need to think about it. Maybe that's when it started.

'OK,' I said. 'Wait there.'

I loosened my grip. He looked puzzled. He wasn't sure whether to take another swing at me. I just held my hand up and backed away, trying to calm him down.

'I'll get you your pills,' I said.

'No fuckin tricks,' he said.

'Just wait there. And don't touch anything.'

I left him in the hall. Went to my study, unlocked the drugs cupboard and shook a handful of aspirins from a bottle. I put two of them into an empty box, locked the cupboard again and went back out. He was just swaying slowly and looking around.

I gave him the tablets.

'These are stronger than the Co-Proxamol,' I said.

'There's two there. That'll be enough for tonight. Come and see me at the surgery tomorrow morning and I'll give you a prescription for more.'

I could hardly believe what I was hearing. I was playing at being a GP.

'Aye, well ye coulda saved yerself a lot of bother if ye'd give us these before,' he said.

'Just take them and go home,' I said.

He spat on the carpet again, then just left. Out into the night.

I was still ice cold. I closed the door and went out of the side door into the garage. There was an old canvas sail bag there somewhere. I used to have a dinghy. The bag was for the main and foresail. It was fairly big. I chucked stuff off the shelves till I found it. It had the sheets and halyards still in it so I took one of them, too. Knotted one end of it through an eye at the mouth of the sack and threw it all on the back seat of the car.

Opened the garage doors and drove out.

Carston was just at the bottom of the stairs of the Burns Road police headquarters when he saw Jessie stumble out through the front door onto the street as if someone had manhandled her and shoved her out. He knew that that was unlikely because to evict Jessie forcibly someone would have to actually touch her. The staff at Burns Road weren't fastidious, but they were aware of basic hygiene.

Jessie staggered to a stop, turned, lifted a grey hand and pointed at the closing door.

'You'll regret it,' she yelled at it. 'One of these days, I'll be dead and gone. Then you'll be sorry. All of you.'

Her finger was pointing at Sandy Dwyer, the desk sergeant, who'd followed her out. Carston pushed the door open and stepped out beside him. Jessie jumped back.

'Don't you touch me,' she yelled. 'Don't you try none of that police brutality with me. I get enough of that at home.'

Dwyer pushed a carrier bag at her.

'You left your suitcase, Jessie,' he said. 'I wouldn't want

you going home without it.'

'Huh, lot you care!' was Jessie's reply as she grabbed the bag, leaving him to wipe his hand hard against the side of his trousers. 'You couldn't care less if I lived or died.'

'That's right love,' said Dwyer, 'but I don't want our other customers suffocating, do I? Away you go now, before I start behaving like your old man.'

Jessie thought of prolonging the debate, but Dwyer had known her too long. His big arm lifted, his finger wagged a warning at her, then pointed away up the road.

'Now,' was all he said, and Jessie submitted and went off towards some more of her misery. Carston watched her go, smiled and turned to Dwyer.

'Masterly, Sandy,' he said. 'I must try that on Kath sometime.'

'Oh, I'd never risk that at home,' said Dwyer. 'My Mary'd have my arm up my back before I could blink.'

'Into Martial Arts, is she?' asked Carston.

'Only on me,' said Dwyer.

Carston laughed and started to walk away.

Further along the pavement, Jessie clutched her bag to her chest, pushing it hard against her to try to squeeze away her pain. She'd known before she went there that the police would offer no protection from her husband. But, in the back of her mind, she also knew that she had certain rights and wanted to make sure that, when they did eventually find her dead, they'd know where to look for her murderer. Despite the lateness of the hour and the chill in the air, she decided not to go home. Lennie, Dora and the others would probably be down by the canal or maybe up towards Castle Street. Somebody might have some sherry, or a couple of cans or something.

He was shuffling along the pavement towards the main road. That's where the bus stop was. I waited for him to get a little further down the empty street, then followed him. It was downhill. I switched off the engine and let the car coast. When I was near enough, I stopped, got out quietly, grabbed the bag and crept up behind him. He didn't hear me. He was still muttering stuff about 'fuckin doctors'. I jumped him and pulled the bag down over his head and shoulders. He fell forward onto his knees and I chopped the edge of my hand into the back of his neck. I knew it would make him nauseous. He tried to pull at the bag but I'd already looped the rope around him and pulled it tight. He was shouting, but you could hardly hear it. I used the rope to drag him to his feet, then looped it round him again and tied it off. I dragged him to the car, opened the back door, shoved him inside and tied the loose end of the rope to the bottom of the passenger seat. It held him down behind it.

Then I went for a drive. Fast, hard. Down to the main road, back out into the country. I flung it about. Childish, I know, but I wanted to make it as uncomfortable and confusing as I could for McPhee. I did that for ten, fifteen minutes then drove home.

He had no idea where he was. I pulled him out, dragged him inside then down the steps to the cellar. He tried to resist, but it was no good. The rabbit punch, the bag, the drive, the fact that he was drunk to begin with – what chance did he have? He fell into the cellar. I pulled him up and pushed him towards the pillar I'd sat against all those nights. My pillar. He banged against it and twisted onto his side as he fell. It was easy to snap the bottom pair of cuffs around his ankles. He still had the bag over his head and I got the other two bracelets onto his wrists just as easily. It was all over in seconds.

Then ... well, I just stood there. He was whimpering and swearing, but ... I was more aware of me somehow. That was it, you see. I'd done it. McPhee wasn't a person any more. He was ... well, part of a scheme. That strange coldness of mine was still there. I could still see sharp, clear outlines to everything. And I was doing something. I'd made my point. I didn't think past that. Didn't know what I was going to do next. I suppose the idea was that I'd keep him there for a day or two, frighten him a bit, and take it from there. Just teach him a lesson, I suppose.

I didn't say anything. He didn't know it was me. In the end, I just switched off the light, closed the door and went back up the steps to think. I left him in the darkness, with the bag still over his head.

It should've been Waring, of course. Not McPhee. Not any of the others. If it'd been Waring, it would've made some sense. Maybe not much, but some. But after the day I'd had ...Oh God, I don't know.

SIX

Carston was a handsome enough man in his forties. He still had all his hair, his brown eyes were clear and altogether his appearance was pleasant, attractive but unremarkable. That evening, though, his get-up was unconventional. He was standing on a coffee table in a long cotton dress with a ruched floral-patterned bodice and a waist that was gathered high into ruffled pleats. His shoulders were too wide to allow the back of the dress to be fastened so it gaped provocatively down his spine, past his waist and on into the furrow of his buttocks. If he looked to his left, he could see most of himself in the oval mirror hanging in the alcove. In his right hand he held a box of pins, in his left the telephone.

'Look, Sandy,' he was saying, 'you've caught me at a very bad time. Can't one of the others deal with it?'

He listened.

'Alright. I'll see if I can get in touch with Jim. He'll look after it for you. Anyway, it's not exactly urgent. Not by the sound of it, is it?'

He listened again.

'No, it's alright. I'm only working through more bloody reports next week. It'll keep. Yes, OK Sandy. See you Monday. Bye.'

He handed the phone to his wife, Kath, who was standing beside him, waiting patiently for him to finish and looking critically at the hem of the dress which she was adjusting.

'Don't tell me,' she said, putting the phone back on the table beside the sofa, 'you've got to go.'

'Wrong,' said Carston. 'Just more bloody paperwork. He was wondering if I'd be in at the weekend, that's all.'

'That's usually the signal for you to drop everything and disappear,' said Kath, taking some more pins from the box in his hand and bending to continue working her way round the dress.

'I can just imagine what Sandy'd say if I walked in wearing this thing.'

His wife stood back appraisingly.

'You're right,' she said, 'the blue taffeta's more you.'

In fact, the wearing of dresses and other women's garments was not altogether an unusual occurrence for Carston. He was around six feet tall, of medium build and only just beginning to accumulate a bit of flab. He wasn't an ideal shape, but whenever Kath, who was only a few inches shorter than her husband, needed to make any adjustments to the length of skirts or dresses which she'd bought, he was better than the hallstand. She bent once more.

'If you'd only agree to that course of hormone treatment,' she went on, 'that bodice wouldn't be so much of a problem.'

'No but Sandy would,' he said. 'Have you nearly finished?'

'Just a couple more at the back.'

Carston waited quietly while she finished the pinning, stood back and studied the effect, asked him to turn round so that she could check that it was all level. At last she said, 'That's it. Thanks, love'.

With her help, Carston eased carefully out of the dress and started putting his own clothes back on. Kath was folding the dress into a carrier bag.

'I shouldn't speak too soon, I suppose, but in fact, you haven't been too bad recently.'

'What d'you mean?' he asked.

'Work. You've been here quite a lot. Not so many early morning or weekend sessions. No villains about, I suppose.'

Carston gave a gentle shake of the head.

'I wish,' he said. 'No, they're just not getting caught, that's all. Getting better at it. It's only the silly sods who get nicked, and you don't need detectives to find them.'

'I'll make some coffee,' said Kath.

She went out and Carston went across to the window. He felt tired. It was always the same when he wasn't busy; his mind seemed to slow down, become cloudy.

The ringing of the phone on the sill beside him made him jump. He picked it up. It was Ross.

'Hullo Jim. What's up?'

'Sorry to bother you at home, but I thought you'd be interested. It's McPhee. He's done a runner.'

'Surprise, surprise,' said Carston. 'How'd you find out?'

'I've just come from his place. There's no sign of him. Neighbours say they haven't seen him for a day or two.'

'Maybe that bloody lawyer of his'll listen next time.'

'Want to bet?'

'No thanks. Have you put out a call for him?'

'Aye. What else?'

'Nothing we can do, is there? He'll turn up. But not until we've wasted more bloody time and energy chasing him around.'

'OK then. See you later.'

'Aye.'

As Carston replaced the receiver, he felt a dull spread of weariness. Ross's visit to McPhee's home was another sign of how slack business was. They'd been desperate to nail him for the off-licence guy, and now he'd disappeared. They knew he'd done it but arrest and conviction were even further away.

'Shit, shit, shit,' said Carston to himself.

Five young boys rode down the pavement on skateboards. Given Carston's mood, it was just as well that he didn't know that they'd spent their afternoon in the park where there were mothers too busy looking after their children to attend to their handbags and old women who were easily scared by the sight of a Stanley knife.

At first, I thought I'd keep him for a couple of days, make my point, then drive him somewhere and let him go. He'd never know who it was. But making his meals mornings and evenings changed it somehow. I'd worked out what it would need to keep him alive. I'd bought dehydrated and canned things. Paid cash. And I'd chosen stuff to make sure there was enough variety to keep it interesting – not for them, but for me. I was the one who had to prepare it.

I thought about it all through the day after I'd caught

him. The drive was supposed to make him think he was a long way from my place. I wanted to keep it that way. It would be a bit bloody stupid, wouldn't it, for him to find out who I was so that, when I let him go, he could go straight to you lot and get me put away. So I had to stay anonymous. I put on old black jeans, black sweater and a ski mask. Just slits for my eyes and mouth. That was embarrassing. Felt like I was in some crappy telly play. But … no choice.

I made him some porridge in the microwave, put it on a plastic plate and took it down to the cellar with a bottle of tap water and a plastic mug. As soon as I turned on the light, I was glad I was wearing that mask. During the night, he'd worked the rope loose. The sail bag was off. Just lying beside him.

He was breathing quickly. The sight of me in the mask must have scared him.

'What the fuck's goin on?' he said.

I didn't say anything. Carried the food and drink across, put it on the floor beside him. I could smell his fear as well as the fumes of last night's booze and cigarettes. It reminded me that I hadn't thought much about letting him wash. It could wait.

'I'm no eatin that fuckin shite,' said McPhee.

He was still aggressive, but I could hear the catch in his voice. He knew he was in trouble. I didn't answer. I picked up the bag and rope, went back to the door, stood for a while watching him, then turned out the light and went back upstairs again.

Then – this is something I don't understand – I went to work. Completely normal. And that's how it went on, right from that first time. I saw patients, filled in forms, had meetings and phone calls and, all the time, I was asking myself why nobody noticed anything different. I mean … I had a guy chained up like a dog in my cellar, but it was all smiles and chats and business as usual.

Like the night I was called to a flat in King Street. It was a woman. Her baby was crying. She said she'd tried everything but it wouldn't stop. I checked it all over. There was nothing wrong. As far as I could tell, it was crying because that's what babies do. So I tried to tell her not to worry, but it was obvious that there was something else going on. I talked with her and, eventually, out it came. The real problem was her boy friend. The baby's noise made him get angry. If she couldn't shut it up, he'd lose his temper and beat her up. There was nothing I could offer her to solve that. In the end, I suggested various things she might try to keep the baby happy but I knew that, before too long, she'd be at the surgery or in A & E. There it was again: injustice, evil, and me unable to do a thing about it.

Luckily, the next call was at Jerry Donald's place. His legs were playing up again. I was almost looking forward to seeing him. There are things I can do to help him, so chatting with him usually cheers me up.

He had a varicose ulcer on his left leg.

'Maggots,' I said.

'Is that you being rude about my legs?' he asked.

'No. That's one of the treatments they use nowadays for this sort of thing.'

'What?'

'Live maggots. They're the best thing for cleaning up ulcers. They only eat dead flesh. Never touch living tissue.'

'What d'you do with them?'

'Just put them on the wound and let them get on with it.'

'You mean you want to turn my leg into a bloody Pizza Hut for flies?'

'Why not? You're not using it.'

He shook his head.

'I'll just have the normal stuff if it's alright with you,' he said.

'Honey, that's another thing. Works better than ointments and creams.'

'I'm not a bloody lab rat. The normal stuff if you don't mind.'

'Boring old sod,' I said.

I got out a tube of powder and started tapping some onto the ulcer.

'This'll have to do,' I said. 'It'll dry it and keep infections out. You'll have to be careful with it, though.'

'More shagging without legs, you mean?'

'Is that your only hobby nowadays?'

'Not hobby, vocation.'

I smiled.

'Never did tell you the shagging without legs joke, did I?' he said.

'No, thank God.'

'Right. RAF guy in a bar sees this bird. She's got no legs and she's in a wheelchair.'

My expression must've told him what I thought about that.

'No listen,' he said. 'So he's chatting her up and she's nice and, come ten o'clock, he offers to take her home.'

I was stripping the backing from a dressing pad and putting it over the ulcer.

'Well, on the way through the park, she says, "You can shag me if you like, you know".'

'The way women do,' I said.

'Right. But the RAF guy looks at her and says "I can't. I mean, your legs ..." But the woman says, "No, look, just lift me out and hang me on the railings there."'

The disgusted sounds I made made no difference. He was launched, living the shag vicariously.

'So he hitches her on the railings and gives her a right seeing to. And it's good. He enjoys it. And, when he's finished, he takes her down, puts her back in the chair and starts pushing it again. And she says, "You're not stationed at Leuchars, are you?" "No," he says. "Thought so," she says. "Lossiemouth, eh?" The guy's amazed. "Yes," he says. "How d'you know that?" And the woman says, "Those bastards from Leuchars always leave me hanging there."'

I groaned. But it didn't matter. Jerry was laughing enough for the two of us.

Jerry's feelgood effect lasted until I got home. My life had obviously split into two. Away from home (and the cellar), I was the guy everyone had always known. Inside my front door, though, I was ... the other one. A different me. The nutter, as Jerry would have put it. Because that's what I was – am. I know it. And I still don't understand it. I was fascinated just by the idea that McPhee was there. He'd become part of my routines. Meals twice a day, his questions all the time, silence from me. He seemed less afraid of me but I think the darkness was getting to him. I mean, he was there all night, then all day, with just two quick blasts of light when I took the meals down. He'd started gabbling strange things, making no sense, talking about working in submarines, engine rooms, mines. Just trying to make me say something, I suppose.

I'd been looking in all the local papers but there was no sign that anyone had noticed he was missing. In a way, it was too easy. OK, he'd more or less got himself into the cellar – calling the surgery, turning up at the door like that. But, in spite of the weirdness of it all, nothing had changed. It seems you can just take somebody off the street and that's that. No repercussions. In a way, it puzzled me. And it made me start thinking of the next step. I'd more or less decided that I wouldn't let him go, not for a while, anyway. But I started getting twitchy. Needed to move it on somehow. So I got out the list again. Just to see how far I was willing to go.

The door to Carston's office opened just as the water in the coffee machine began dripping through the filter.

'Good timing,' he said, nodding his head towards the machine as Ross closed the door.

Ross said nothing. It was a point in his favour. Carston liked peace and quiet, and the working relationship he'd developed with his sergeant was ideal. Not that Ross was devoid of conversation. Just a couple of pints on their occasional visit to the pub were enough to loosen a tongue that was surprisingly ready. At work, however, he seemed to welcome the silence in which they normally operated. He hung his coat on the back of the door, and went back to pour the coffee into two mugs. As usual, Carston had made it too strong; it was thick and sludgy. Ross handed a mug to his chief and took the other to the window. He blew on his coffee and looked out at the grey day.

'Any news?' asked Carston, as he took time off from his papers to drink.

'What d'you mean? McPhee?' said Ross. 'Nah. He's away. Have you talked to his brief yet?'

'No, I've just got in myself. Give him a ring, will you? See what he says.'

Ross moved round to his own desk, looked up a number, picked up the phone and dialled. He sipped some coffee, swore because it was too hot and was caught in mid oath as the person he'd called answered.

'Aye, sorry,' he said, making a face at a grinning Carston. 'This is Detective Sergeant Ross. Is Mr. Reismann available please? … Aye, I'll wait.'

He leaned back in his chair. Carston, without looking up from the file he was reading, held up a hand and started unfolding fingers one by one to indicate seconds passing. Ross smiled as he dabbed at his still stinging lips. They usually bet on how long the statutory wait would last. Like all lawyers, Reismann needed to convince you of how busy he was and so you never got straight through to him.

'Good morning, sir,' said Ross into the phone. 'Sorry to disturb you. I was wondering if you've been in touch with your client Mr. McPhee recently.'

Reismann's reply was obviously fairly curt. Ross listened and answered in a tone full of unconcealed irony.

'Not at all, sir. In fact, we're rather concerned about him. You see, he seems to have … well, vanished … That's right.'

Reismann spoke at greater length. Ross waited, not looking at Carston but concentrating on what he was hearing. At last he flicked a glance across at his chief and spoke.

'If you'll just hold on a second, sir, I think it'd be as well if you had a word with DCI Carston.'

Carston heard, shook his head violently, then his fist as Ross shrugged at him and said, 'I'll just put you through then'.

He pushed a button on his phone, spread his hands in

apology and said, 'Line two'.

Carston put down the file, made his seconds-counting gesture again and at last picked up his own phone.

'Mr. Reismann. What can I do for you?'

'Cut out the crap for a start,' said the lawyer.

'Of course, sir, consider it cut,' said Carston sweetly. 'Anything else?'

'You rang me, remember? What's it all about?'

'You tell me. He's gone, innocence and all.'

'Look, you had nothing on him. We both know it. It doesn't matter what sort of a … person he is or what either of us thinks of him, the evidence wasn't there.'

'So why's he gone then?' asked Carston.

'That's exactly the question I'm asking,' said Reismann. 'The only sort of pressure he's been under recently, the only thing that might make him do something stupid, has come from you and your colleagues. You haven't let up, have you?'

'So you think we may have upset him? Is that it?'

'I'm suggesting that your hounding of him bordered on harassment.'

'OK then,' said Carston, 'get in touch with him and advise him to sue us. I'd love to hear from him.'

There was silence on the line for a moment. When Reismann spoke again, there was a strange quietness in his tone.

'You will,' he said. 'Always assuming, of course, that your attentions haven't set him up as a target for some of his less salubrious acquaintances.'

'Meaning what?' asked Carston.

'I'll be in touch,' said Reismann and the line went dead.

Carston replaced the receiver and sat back, tipping his chair onto two legs.

'He's a funny bugger,' he said, half to himself, half to Ross. 'Takes on all these villains as clients. Can't stand them really but he still gets them off the bloody hook. Something seriously wrong with him, I reckon.'

'Aye, he's got strange priorities, right enough,' said Ross. 'What did he think?'

56

'What about?'

'McPhee.'

'Oh. Police harassment, what else?'

Ross just nodded and the two men went back to shuffling through pieces of paper.

SEVEN

I chose Peter Dobie. Because of his connection with Jenny Gallacher. You know, Jill McIntosh's patient. Her name came up after one of the practice meetings. Jill and I were in the coffee room. She seemed to be down. It wasn't like her. I asked why.

'*The usual,*' *she said.*

'*Any particular usual?*' *I asked.*

'*Jenny Gallacher. Student at Robert Gordon's in Aberdeen. Nineteen years old. Pretty wee thing. Bright, too, by all accounts.*'

'*And?*'

'*She won't be finishing her degree. I got her results through this morning. Aids.*'

I just nodded.

'*So unnecessary,*' *she said.* '*She had everything going for her.*'

'*What happened?*'

'*Och, the usual. Man's inhumanity to woman.*'

'*Eh?*'

'*Her boyfriend. Been going out with him for five months. He's AC/DC. Never told her.*'

'*Carrier, is he?*'

She nodded.

'*HIV positive. Hasn't affected him yet, of course. The worst thing is, he got her pregnant too. That's what made her more susceptible. Lowered her resistance. Well, you know.*'

'*Aye.*'

'*She had no idea, poor thing.*'

'*Who is he?*'

'*Dobie, Peter Dobie.*'

'*Didn't I read about him in the papers? Didn't they try to charge him with harming her or something?*'

'*Aye. They got nowhere. One of Freddy's cases. He got him off. No case to answer, he said. Came up with all sorts of insinuations about her sleeping around. Made her look like a prostitute.'*

'That sounds like Freddy.'

'Destroyed her.'

'What did Dobie have to say for himself?'

She gave a sort of snort.

'What d'you think? Doesn't want to know – about her, about the baby, anything. Dropped her. None of his business. I doubt she'll last the year out.'

I read the newspaper reports of the trial with all the 'love-rat' headlines. Dobie's a callous bastard. Never accepted responsibility. In the photos of him leaving the court after being acquitted, he's got a smirk all over his face, he's in his flash Paul Smith suit, revelling in the fame, caring bugger-all about the story behind it. It was depressing. I've never understood how people can do such things to each other.

As soon as he answered the phone, I could tell that he was stoned. I did my rough accent again. Held a bit of my scarf over the mouthpiece as well.

'Who's that?' he said.

I didn't mess about.

'How would you like a half of Lebanese Gold?' I said. 'Donnie told me you might be interested. Donnie Bryant.'

'Donnie?' he said.

'Aye. Where d'you think I got your number? Look, d'you want the stuff or not? I can't hang around like this. I can easy shift it somewhere else you know. It was just that I was talking to Donnie and he mentioned you might like a sniff.'

Jill had told me all about him. I knew Donnie was his regular supplier. I was hoping his name would make it all sound legit. It seemed to be working. We arranged to meet in Macaulay Park, not far from his place. On the way there, I only saw one old couple walking their dog and a group of three kids sharing a cigarette. I parked, climbed up the slope into the bushes and waited.

I saw him after about five minutes. He was singing to himself. He looked around. I whistled and called him over. He came up to the bushes and bent to look into them. I'd filled a little atomizer with fentanyl. I gave him a faceful of the spray. He shouted once, jumped back and started rubbing at his eyes. I waited. He was swearing, trying to see where I was. He lunged towards me but managed only three or four steps before the fentanyl kicked in. He fell to his knees, then slumped forward and blacked out.

I injected 0.2 milligrams of naloxone into a vein above his elbow. I knew I had to be quick. I'd no idea what drugs or booze he'd already taken. The fentanyl could easily boost their effects, make his blood pressure drop and his breathing shallow. It could be dangerous. On top of that, I couldn't be sure of how the actual dose would affect him. Naloxone's a recognized narcotic antagonist. Blocks the brain's opioid receptors pretty quickly. The standard dose is 0.4 milligrams. I reckoned the lower dose would be effective but it would slow down his recovery from the fentanyl. See what I mean, though? Weird, isn't it? I wasn't being a nutter – it was all cold, calculated. Who the hell was I being?

Anyway, there was blood dribbling from the corner of his mouth. He must have bitten his tongue as he fell. I kept pressure on the puncture mark on his arm. Waited for the naloxone to take effect. His breathing was fluttering a bit, his pulse was slow but, after a couple of minutes, he started coming round. I tapped at his cheeks to speed up the recovery. Spatters of blood splashed across the leaves beside his face.

I looped his arm over my shoulder and heaved him to his feet. There was no-one around to see us as we staggered along - just a couple of drunks. When we got to the car, he still didn't know what was going on. He fell into the back and I used some handcuffs – the Glasgow trip again. Fastened him to the bottom of the passenger seat. It was McPhee all over again. I pulled the sail bag over his head and looped it round him. I was taking a chance there, too. If he vomited with the bag over his face, he might aspirate it. Even if he didn't, it could asphyxiate him. Maybe that shows how far I'd slipped already. It was a chance I was prepared to take.

I'd taken off the ski mask, of course, and I was surprised

at how steady my breathing was. I felt sort of detached from everything. It was crazy. Here's me, a pillar of the community, driving through Cairnburgh with a hooded, handcuffed man in the back. I bet Jerry would know a joke about it. But, for me, it was unreal; a challenge. A bit frightening, too. There still was a bit of normality there, though. I did stop every so often to lift a corner of the bag and check his colour. I was lucky; he was surviving.

Back home, I pulled him out of the car, helped him along the path, into the hall and down the stairs. He didn't struggle much. I put on the ski mask, untied the rope and took the bag off his head. Then I opened the cellar door and pushed him inside. I switched on the light, guided him over to the nearest pillar and shackled him up. He panicked, tried to resist, but he was too feeble from the drugs. McPhee had his arm up over his eyes because of the brightness. I turned the light out again and left them together. The darkness would take care of him. Same as it did with me. your eyes are wide open but you don't see a thing. You lift up your hand in front of your face and you feel the air shifting as you move it, but still nothing. Just that blackness. your breathing's right up close to you. It's claustrophobic. Your body feels huge but all that night around it feels even bigger. Full of things you can't even guess at.

EIGHT

They found what remained of Ian Stride at the bottom of a gully which ran alongside a minor road near the A90 six miles south of Dundee. A retired teacher, out walking his dog early one morning, couldn't get the dog to come back when he called him and had to struggle down through thick bushes to find out what all the barking was about. When he saw the grossly disfigured and liquefied body, he couldn't stop himself being sick. He dragged the dog away and called the Tayside police on his mobile. They were there in less than fifteen minutes.

The body was face down, the arms and legs twisted into unlikely contortions. The bones of one hand had been dragged away, presumably by some predator. Lying amongst the putrefaction were the rags of a blue shirt, with thin black and red stripes, a pair of underpants and a single sock. One shoe was lying less than a meter away, the other was in a small tree growing out of the slope. The broken branches to one side of the body suggested that it had probably been dumped at the top of the slope and rolled down into the gully. There were three deep depressions in the skull and around the neck vertebrae was a tightly-knotted Bart Simpson tie.

'Jammy bastards,' said Spurle, when the report came through.

'Who?' asked Fraser.

'Bloody Tayside. That Aberdeen guy's turned up.'

'What, the one in Edinburgh?'

'Aye. Murdered. Knocked on the head then strangled. Been lying in a ditch since he went missing, they reckon.'

'Christ, that's a while. Bet he was ripe.'

'Teacher who found him threw up all over the place. The scene of crime boys were well chuffed.'

'Who's on the case?'

'I told you, bloody Tayside. They'll get Aberdeen involved but we won't get a sniff.'

Fraser called the report up onto his own monitor and read

quickly through it.

'Pity it wasn't McPhee,' he said.

It was as if I was somebody different. Had a new self, a new way of taking control. And, all the time, the shadows of Tommy, Tara and the girls were there. Folk didn't see that, though. They had me round for dinner, said it was good to see me getting back some of my old enthusiasm. They knew all about Tommy dying and his family getting killed. I could tell that some of them wondered whether it had been too much for me. But now I was getting involved again and they all seemed keen to help me. Folk were desperate to matchmake me so I kept finding myself at dinners with the same two divorcees. I think the secret I was keeping must have given me an edge. Made me interesting maybe. They were all over me. Especially Gayla Campbell.

She's a history teacher. Her husband left her for a French woman in the marketing department of TotalFinaElf in Aberdeen. The woman must've been good. He agreed to almost all Gayla's demands in the divorce settlement. She ended up with a big house in Cairnburgh, new car, big bucks in the bank. He went to Aberdeen to live in his girl-friend's flat. It was too small for two people and they'd started to piss each other off pretty quickly. Then the Frog's transferred back to France and Gayla's ex is left looking for a place of his own. Meanwhile, Gayla's cut her teaching down to three days a week and spends the rest of the time gardening, painting and enjoying herself.

I mention her because she's the one who brought up another of the names on my list. She was sitting beside me in Anne and Bill Sturrock's dining room. Nice house – one of the Victorian ones overlooking Macaulay Park. There were six of us there. We were on the cheese course. We'd already got through one and a half bottles of Chenin Blanc, two Buzets and we were well into a Fronsac. Mind you, that was on top of the margaritas they'd given us when we arrived. They were one of Bill's specialties. According to him.

'It was such a cliché,' Gayla was saying. 'I mean, an

office party, for God's sake.'

We'd been talking of an affair a friend was having with a much younger woman.

'And how old is she? Nineteen? Twenty? She could be his grand-daughter, never mind his daughter,' said Anne.

Bill had had his own fling with a seventeen year old secretary not so long ago. I knew it, but nobody else there did. It was funny watching him covering his tracks.

'I don't know what the hell they see in older guys,' he said. 'Or what the guys get out of it. I mean, they must know that women that age don't fancy them.'

'Blow jobs,' said Anne.

Everyone except Stu spluttered into their wine or looked at her. Stu blushed and dabbed at his lips with his napkin. He's an American. And a Christian.

'What d'you mean?' said Bill.

'Keeps everybody happy,' said Anne. 'He can't believe his luck and she's down there, working away. She doesn't have to see his face, so it doesn't matter how old he is.'

'That's disgusting,' said Bill. 'What about all that curly grey hair?'

'Old men may be bald down there,' said Anne. 'What d'you think, Gayla?'

'Why ask me?'

'You're a woman of experience.'

'Cheeky bitch.'

'What about it, Andrew,' said Bill. 'You must have seen a few in your line. D'you get many bald genitals?'

'I'll tell you what,' I said. 'If you'd all like to help yourself to more cheese, I'll give you a quick lecture on geriatric scrotal alopecia. And there's a very interesting impetigo which ...'

'OK, OK, we'll pass on that,' said Bill.

'Gosh, you people,' said Stu. His smile was pretty forced.

'Anyway, what they should do is make prostitution legal,' said Gayla.

'What the hell are you talking about?' said Anne.

'Sex. If it was legal, people like Jimmy Wilson wouldn't

need to have it off with Glynis from accounts or whoever.'

'That's right,' said Anne. 'Legalize it. You could tax it, make the girls have regular medical check-ups. It would give us all a break.'

'I can't believe you're saying that,' said Stu.

'It's true,' Anne insisted. 'I mean, it's happening. With all the money slopping around up here and people coming and going with the oil, it's all over the place. We might as well make a profit out of it.'

'I don't know that there's as much of it as you think,' said Bill.

'Of course there is,' said Gayla. 'God, they even advertise in the papers.'

'And on the web,' said Anne. 'Chatlines, Working Girls, Escorts ...'

'But they're just whores,' said Stu.

'No, no, no,' said Gayla. 'Haven't you seen Belle de Jour?'

Stu looked at her and shook his head.

'Respectable woman, just like us ...'

She and Anne laughed.

'... Works as a prostitute. For kicks.'

'Yeah, in the movies maybe, but ...' said Stu.

Gayla raised a finger, wagged it at him and stopped him.

'Not just in movies,' she said. 'Here, too. Weren't you here when Marion Bailey was killed?'

It was like a punch in the stomach for me. Marion Bailey was a patient of mine. The others went on laughing and arguing, but I started thinking about her and her husband. Well, you know. I was called to give evidence at the trial. All the abuse in her marriage. She'd told me all about it. He was beating her up on a regular basis. You knew that. I knew it, too. She wouldn't let me do anything about it, though. Just wanted medication for her cuts and bruises and pain. The fact that her name had been mentioned was another coincidence.

I realized they were all looking at me.

'... haven't you, Andrew?' said Gayla.

'Sorry?' I said.

'See?' said Gayla. 'He was miles away. I told you. It's all men think of.'

'Gayla, darling,' I said. 'You know I think only of you.'

'What's she got to do with prostheses?' asked Anne, with a laugh.

I paused for a minute, then had a flash of insight. The new me. Edgy.

'She's beloved,' I said.

'What? What's that got to do with it?'

'Prosthesis.'

'What?'

'When you add a letter or syllable at the beginning of a word; that's a prosthesis. Like the 'be' added to 'loved'. She's beloved.'

'Bloody hell,' said Bill. 'We were talking about artificial willies. I'm glad you're not my doctor.'

Stu wasn't enjoying himself but the rest of us laughed and the drink dragged us on through more childish gags and associations. I laughed along with them, but the reference to Marion Bailey stayed with me. It was as if I was being reminded to carry on. I'd already decided that Christopher Bailey would be next. He was on my list,. McPhee and Dobie were nothings; Bailey had influence. He'd be missed. It was a real challenge. And it was like McPhee; I hadn't gone looking for the name, it had presented itself. That was good enough for me.

I shared a taxi home with Gayla and spent the night with her. Since her divorce, she's had sex less frequently than she'd have liked so she's greedy for everything we do. When she eventually fell asleep, I just lay there, listening to her breathing. I was thinking about Christopher Bailey and wondering how to approach him. He knew me. He wouldn't be turning up on the doorstep like McPhee, and he wouldn't be doped up and malleable like Dobie.

Rhona was right; Dundee was easier to work than Aberdeen. There was less competition but still plenty of punters. She was in one of the rooms on the first floor of a Travelodge, kneeling on the bed astride a man who'd introduced himself as Matt. He wasn't bad-looking, young enough (for a change), although a bit on the thin side. They'd been there for over half an hour and so far, he hadn't managed to get an erection. His hands were tied behind his head with the belt of his dressing gown. The ends of the belt were around his neck and Rhona was pulling at them, increasing the pressure as he tried to force his head up from the pillow. His face had been red before they'd started but the colour had deepened and the veins in his forehead and temples were bulging.

She was anxious. They'd found the body of the man who'd given her the lift from Aberdeen. Even her bitch of a mother would've noticed that she hadn't been around for a while and probably reported it, so the police up there would know she was missing. She wondered if they'd somehow make the connection between herself and the man. If they did, it surely wouldn't take them long to realize that he was the second one to disappear after being with her. The newspaper report said there was a CCTV shot of a female passenger in his car. Perhaps, after all, it would be better to go back, tell them he'd given her a lift and set the record straight. If she didn't and they then found her, it might look bad.

The trouble was that she was minting it in Dundee. She had punters coming from Perth, Stirling and even down from Aberdeen to see her. That had started within a day of her new website being up and running. The fact that she'd changed her name made little difference. She'd had messages from three different men who'd recognized her from her photos (despite the unsubtle but effective blurring of her face in every one) and who remembered what a good time she'd given them when she was working in Aberdeen. One of them, who called himself Billy, had been a regular up there and it was sort of reassuring that he could be bothered to start up again, despite the hour's drive each way.

No, going back would interfere with the good business she was doing. She'd opened an account with the twelve thousand she'd brought with her in the little yellow wallet and, despite the expenses of setting up and buying new outfits and equipment, it had grown.

At last the oxygen deprivation was beginning to work. She felt the man's erection beginning to grow in her hand and began working it hard, looking straight into his eyes and telling him what a stud he was. He was gasping for breath still, his fingers pulling at the dressing gown belt. She opened her lips and made little gasping sounds to tell him the pleasure it was all giving her then slid herself down to finish him off.

As they lay together afterwards, the purple weal around his neck was very obvious. She traced her fingers along it, kissed it and told him that he'd better be careful to keep his shirt collar buttoned or everyone would see it. She knew that most men appreciated not being hurried away when it was over and that, even just getting ten extra minutes convinced them that they'd somehow got special treatment.

So they talked a while. She was always first with the questions, asking about them, keeping the conversation away from herself. Sometimes they were interesting and most of them were different enough from one another to make the conversation easy, but before long, she wanted to leave, let her shoulders relax and just be herself. It was never something she articulated, even to herself, but she felt the distance between herself and Laura McEwan. Laura had a different wardrobe from her, lived a different life, had different friends. In fact Rhona had no friends in Dundee yet. It was Laura that was taken to restaurants, stayed in fancy hotels. And it was Laura who had sex with strangers.

When Dobie didn't report for work for a week and no-one could make contact with him, the manager of the bookshop phoned the police. Two uniformed constables were sent round to his flat and, when they got no answer, found it easy enough to open his door. There were no signs that Dobie had gone away voluntarily; his cheque book and credit cards were on top of a chest of drawers in his bedroom, there were coats hanging in the hallway and no obvious gaps in the rails of shirts and jackets in his bedroom cupboards. He was put on the list and the usual procedures were started. There was no great urgency about them since no-one was pushing to find him and the notoriety which remained from his court case was enough to suppress any anxiety that anyone might have felt on his behalf.

Once again, it was Ross who spotted the name on the list of missing persons. He and Carston were in the office as usual.

'Well, well,' he said. 'Another of our friends has slipped away.'

'What are you on about?' said Carston.

'Peter Dobie. Remember him?'

Carston recognized the name immediately.

'Yes. Is he missing, too?'

Ross nodded.

'Christ. D'you think somebody's doing us favours?'

'How d'you mean?'

'Mopping up the nasty buggers for us. Taking them off the streets.'

Ross shook his head and held up a long list of names.

'If they are, they're catching a lot of others in their trawls.'

'I know. Still, McPhee, Dobie, Rhona Kirk. You know what I think of coincidences.'

Ross did. Carston loved them; he himself preferred facts and evidence. He also enjoyed winding his chief up.

'Don't forget the guy who was supposed to have raped her,' he said. 'He went missing, too.'

Carston grinned. It was tempting to select the names that suited him and start inventing conspiracies. And it was a bit strange that McPhee and Dobie should vanish within a few days of each other. Both of them had got away with crimes. But there was no point following it up; the people upstairs, especially Superintendent Ridley, would soon start asking why he was wasting time and resources. All they wanted was statistics. Good, positive statistics that convinced Holyrood that crime in Scotland was on the wane. Pillocks.

'What we need is a bloated corpse with fingerprints and

bits of DNA all over it,' he said.

'Move to Tayside,' said Ross.

Carston grinned.

'Aye, weird, that,' he said.

'What?'

'He parks his car in Edinburgh, then he's found up near Dundee.'

'So what?'

'I looked at the report. The place they found him, the only access to it is from the southbound carriageway, so he was on his way back to Edinburgh when it happened.'

Ross shrugged.

'Had something to hide. Didn't want his own car seen in Dundee.'

'Maybe,' said Carston. 'Not our problem, anyway. Unless he turns out to be one of Freddy's clients.'

'Which immediately makes him a villain, right?'

'Naturally.'

'So he had it coming?'

'Cynical bugger. Get on with some work.'

NINE

It took me a while to work out what sort of thing might hook Bailey. I was pretty sure he wouldn't remember my voice, but I decided to stick with the accent I was using in the cellar.

I tried it out first. Rang my own home number on my mobile. Wrapped a piece of cloth over the mouthpiece and spoke as low as I could. I left a message on my answering machine. Pretended to be a patient, just in case anybody else heard it. Christ knows who. Made up a few symptoms. I was amazed when I played it back. Sounded weird. I don't even think folk who knew me would've recognized it. I gave it a try, though. Tucked the cloth tighter around the mouthpiece, tapped in the code to withhold my number and phoned Gayla. She must have been near the phone. She answered right away.

'Is that Mrs Campbell?' I said.

'Yes.'

'Good morning, I'm phoning on behalf of a national audit organization and your postcode's been chosen for a special offer. Would you mind answering one or two questions?'

'What are you selling?' she said, polite but wary.

'I'm not,' I said. 'I just need to ask you a few questions to help us to establish the preferences of people in north east Scotland in the area of replacement windows.'

'I don't need any.'

'I know but your co-operation will help us to target consumers and bring them a more competitive service than they've enjoyed for a long time. You see ...'

'Look,' she said, 'I don't want to be rude. I know you're doing an awful job and I'm sorry that you have to but I don't want anything, so I'm going to ring off.'

'I understand perfectly,' I said. 'Thank you for your time.'

'Goodbye,' she said, and the line went dead.

So that was it. I looked up Bailey's number.

Bailey stretched out his right arm and pulled aside the curtain of his sitting room's large bay window to look out at the weeping birches at the end of his lawn. His left hand held the telephone which he'd just picked up.

'Yes,' he said.

'Mr. Bailey?' said Davidson.

'Yes, who's that?'

'That's not important for the moment,' Davidson went on. 'Let's just say that I think you'll find it's in your interest to listen.'

'Oh, is it?' said Bailey, letting the curtain fall back into place. 'Well I'm not used to holding conversations with …'

Davidson didn't let him finish.

'JJ Construction Group,' he said. 'Their ordinary shares are opening today at 134. By midday they'll be around 178. The chart breakthrough level's 185 and Talbot Milne's interest is due to be renewed.'

The words had the desired effect. Bailey's readiness to dabble in volatile stocks was well known to all his acquaintances. Curiosity prevented him putting the phone down.

'Very interesting,' he said, 'but it doesn't alter the fact that I want to know who I'm talking to.'

His voice was still sharp with irritation.

'Later,' said Davidson. 'What I want to know is if you're interested.'

'Interested? What the hell are you talking about? I don't deal with anonymous callers.'

He made the last two words sound like things you stepped in on the pavement.

Davidson's voice was unchanged.

'So you don't want to do business, talk percentages?'

'Percentages? Doing business?' Bailey's scorn was undisguised. 'Anonymous tips, dubious access to privileged information? Whoever you are, "doing business" obviously isn't your day job.'

Again, the words were stressed and sarcastic. Davidson

showed no sign that they'd got to him.

'You're right, I'm not on kissing terms with many brokers. That's why I'm calling you. I got hold of this information, right out of the blue. I knew that several groups have expressed an interest in JJC, and thought I might make a little profit from it for myself. Nothing extravagant, just ten, twelve grand. So, are you interested?'

Bailey looked at his watch. He was tempted, but trusted no-one.

'No,' he said.

'Ah well, never mind, I'll give Welgrave Finance a ring. They've got an eighteen per cent stake already.'

Bailey was intrigued. The caller seemed to know all the right names. It might only be guesswork but it sounded impressive.

'Look, where exactly did you get all this information?' he asked.

'Sorry, we don't have a deal. It's Welgrave Finance's turn. Maybe …'

'Stop pissing about,' said Bailey. 'This isn't Monopoly.'

'I know. That's why I got in touch before you left for work. You'll need to know the score for the production meeting this morning, won't you? You never know what might come up.'

'All right. Very impressive.'

'Thanks. How about a meeting?'

'I can't just slip away for meetings without …'

'Now who's pissing about?' said Davidson. 'Look, if you're interested, I can meet you on your way to work this morning. I've got two names for you. As soon as you hear them, you'll know it's legitimate. Do we have a meeting?'

The temptation was still strong but Bailey wasn't ready to take the chance. He had too many enemies.

'Not unless you tell me who you are and …'

'This could be another Belway Engineering,' the voice cut in. 'You wouldn't want that, would you?'

Bailey stopped, surprised, certain now that the caller was no friend. He had too much information altogether. This wasn't about share dealing, this was something else.

'What do you know about Belway? Who the hell are you?' he hissed into the phone, quietly, angrily.

'Just another missing person,' said Davidson, 'like you're going to be, along with some of your friends.'

'Yes, that's more like it,' said Bailey, growing angrier. 'It's not about business at all, is it? It's just threatening phone calls. Kid's stuff.'

'Oh no, it's not kid's stuff, Mr. Bailey,' said Davidson. 'Definitely not. Goodbye.'

Bailey heard a click and put the phone back on its rest. He felt a trickle of sweat between his shoulder blades. This was no joke call. At first, the information being offered had seemed impressive, but everybody knew that JJC was up for grabs and the rest of the things the man had said could all be inventions. The mention of Belway made it all a bit more sinister, though. This was personal. It was a name that had brought him a lot of trouble when he was already under investigation by the police. He wasn't sure but he thought the only record of his connection with the Belway affair was in a file at police headquarters. There'd been reports in the papers, of course, but he couldn't remember whether they'd mentioned Belway.

His hand was still resting on the phone. He hated the idea of leaving a potentially serious matter unresolved. He wanted to know who the man was and the real reason for his call. With a shake of his head he lifted the phone and dialled 1471, only to hear the usual 'The caller withheld his number'.

He dialled again. A woman's voice answered, asking if she could help him.

'Yes' he said. 'Christopher Bailey here. I need to speak to Mr. Reismann.'

Carston didn't like outside interference in police work. F. K. Reismann didn't much like Carston. Phone calls between them were rarely friendly affairs; the one Reismann made to Carston after hearing from Bailey was no exception.

'I hear that another ex-client of mine is missing,' said the lawyer. 'Peter Dobie.'

'Yes.'

'Any comments?'

'No.'

'You are actively pursuing enquiries, I take it.'

'We always do.'

'I'd appreciate it if you told me of any progress.'

'I report to the chief constable.'

'Yes. A good friend of mine.'

'Is this a social call, Mr. Reismann?'

'No. First it's Mr. McPhee, then Mr. Dobie, now it seems another of my clients is being pressured by things emanating from you and/or your colleagues.'

Carston said nothing.

'I've just had a phone call. An old acquaintance of yours. Mr. Bailey. Christopher Bailey.'

He paused again, knowing that Carston would recognize the name instantly.

'He's not missing I hope,' said Carston.

'Very funny. No, but he does have a complaint.'

'That's unusual. Still, perhaps the chief constable would be your best bet. He seems to be more responsive to Mr. Bailey's needs than simple policemen like me.'

'Well, well,' said Reismann, his tone lightening with what could have been a smile. 'I'll let that one go for now.'

'Good. Is that all, then?'

'No, it's not. Look, whatever your opinion of my client, he was cleared. There was no case and he has the same legal right to a private life as the rest of us. And that means that whatever information you've got stacked in his files should stay there.'

'Who says it doesn't?'

'He does. He had an anonymous phone call this morning. The man threatened him and used information that Mr. Bailey thinks could only have come from your offices.'

'I find that hard to believe.'

'That's what he claims.'

'Has he got any proofs?'

'No, but he's concerned enough by the threats to have got in touch with me.'

'What sort of threats are we talking about?'

'Non-specific, but real enough for him to call me.'

'Mr. Reismann, this isn't like you. A 'non-specific' threat? Leaked information? You usually come straight at us, case already made. What's the exact nature of the complaint?'

'You know very well that the action you tried to take against him cost him a seat on the board of Belway Engineering, don't you?'

'I'm not au fait with boardroom shuffles,' said Carston.

'Don't give me that. You knew what was going on. He told you about it himself.'

'So?'

'So where did his anonymous caller get to hear about that?'

'You tell me.'

'I can't. That's the problem.'

'Well, I don't really see how I can help you then.'

There was a silence on the line. When Reismann spoke again, his voice was calm, official.

'Something clearly seems to be amiss with your procedures. It would be most regrettable if that should lead to charges of negligence.'

'Oh, I see,' said Carston. 'A warning, is it?'

'Oh, don't be tiresome. A client has contacted me; he's a private citizen and expects protection from the law. I shall, of course, write formally to you informing you of the details and circumstances of his complaint but I thought a courtesy call such as this would help you to expedite matters. Clearly, I was wrong.'

Carston's patience snapped. He broke into the smooth flow.

'When you tell me what there is to be 'expedited', I'll 'expedite' it. But don't bother me with the sort of veiled suggestions that're always around where Bailey and his lot are concerned. I had a bellyful of them when we had to deal with him before. If you've got something to say, say it. Don't worry, if there's a case to answer, I'll answer it.'

His bluster stopped as he tried to control his anger again. Reismann's voice came back at him oily with satisfaction.

'I'm delighted to hear it. Meantime, I'll collate the details of Mr. Bailey's complaint and …'

'Yes. Do that. And I tell you what, just to show good faith, I'll call round and see you so that we can 'expedite' it together, eh? And maybe you can help us to start looking for your missing clients.'

It was the lawyer's turn to fall silent. Carston let the offer hang.

'Very well,' said Reismann eventually, 'if you think that'll help. My secretary will fix an appointment.'

'Very kind of her,' said Carston.

'I look forward to seeing you then,' said Reismann in a tone which belied utterly the words he used.

He hung up before Carston could reply. Carston slammed his own receiver down and said 'Bastard' to the window just as Ross opened the door.

'What've I done now?'

'Not you. Bloody Freddy Reismann.'

'Ah.'

'Bloody Christopher Bailey's at it again.'

Ross's glance showed that his reaction was the same as that of Carston. They'd both heard far too much of the name Bailey a couple of years previously.

'Who's he working for nowadays?' asked Carston.

'Pullins, the engineers, I think,' said Ross.

'So he even got a job out of it?'

Ross's shrug was as expressive as a whole sentence. Carston shook his head in disbelief at yet another instance of how immersion in sewage unaccountably coats some people with the sweetest of perfumes.

'Well, well, well,' he said. 'And now somebody's threatening the sod. Maybe the world's not such a bad place after all.'

'Tell them that,' said Ross, pointing at the ceiling. 'Don't forget he's got pals on the fourth floor.'

78

Carston made the appropriately disgusted gestures and sat back. When allegations of police corruption were periodically made, he always reckoned they started their investigations too low down the chain of command. The real corruption went on at the Rotary Club dinners, or up and down the fairways of the Golf and Country Club. The strings that had already been pulled on Christopher Bailey's behalf were like hawsers.

'What's it all about?' asked Ross.

'He reckons somebody here's threatening him.'

'What?'

'Aye. Something about Belway Engineering. We're the only ones who knew he'd been refused a seat on their board, apparently.'

'That's bollocks,' said Ross, frowning and punching some keys on his PC. He clicked quickly through some pages then scrolled down through the one he'd been looking for.

'I thought so,' he said. 'He's talking crap. I mean, I know we spent a lot of time on it, but other folk knew about it, too. Look at this.'

Carston leaned forward. On the screen he saw the headings identifying it as Bailey's file. Below them was an article from the *Press and Journal*. Ross pointed at the bottom paragraph. The report was one of the many that had told the story of the prominent local figure and the accusations that had surrounded him. As he read it, Carston saw at once what Ross was getting at. The paragraph ended: 'It seems unlikely that Mr. Bailey's proposed move to Belway Engineering will now go ahead. Belway's, a family firm well-known for its traditional attitudes to trading practices, would not welcome the unsavoury attention this matter has attracted, whatever the case's final outcome.'

'So much for it being classified information,' said Carston. 'Thanks, Jim. I'll take a print-out when I go to see him. Not like him to miss something like that, though. He must be slipping.'

'Freddy never slips,' said Ross.

'No, you're right,' said Carston. 'So what's going on

then? McPhee and Dobie vanish, Bailey's threatened. What is it? The Get-Freddy season?'

'I hope so,' said Ross.

TEN

The tedium of sorting through pieces of paper was throbbing in Carston's skull like a hangover. He found himself more and more frequently taking little walks to the window to look out at the boring normality of things, or to the front desk on the off chance that some major (or even minor) piece of villainy had just been reported. Even Fraser and Spurle seemed too subdued by administrative chores to irritate him with their usual crassness. In fact, Spurle had been acting almost like a normal human being. Carston knew nothing of the dispute he'd had with his fiancée and therefore wasn't aware that they'd now made up their differences and that Spurle was experiencing a rare period of security and shared affection. McNeil, the only woman in the team, was away taking her sergeant's exams and life seemed to be dominated by the paper chase. The occasional meetings with Superintendent Ridley about procedures or proposed rescheduling of resources were as dull as they had always been but at least they broke the monotony of his desk. He sat before it now, his pen tapping on a blank pad.

Ross slurped a mouthful of coffee from his cup (a habit which Carston hadn't noticed before), and continued his reluctant riffling through notes. Carston imagined what it would be like to have a woman sergeant to replace him, preferably one with ash blonde hair, hazel eyes, a 36C bra and a French accent. Shit – another impulse that linked him with Spurle. The office air stirred lazily.

When the phone went, they both reached for it. Carston got there first. It was Sandy, the desk sergeant.

'You play a bit of golf, don't you?' he said.

'Yes,' said Carston.

'You'll love this one, then.'

Carston waited.

'Twitcher, bird spotter. He's phoned in. Thinks he's seen something unusual in the rough beside the eighteenth fairway of the Royal.'

The Royal Cairnburgh was Carston's club.

'I spend a lot of time in the rough there myself. What's he seen?'

'Well, he's a bit of a crime book reader and he reckons it may be a grave.'

'What?'

'That's what he said. He was up in a tree near the green, looking for blackbirds, redcaps, blue tits, greenfinches, whitethroats – I don't know, something with a colour in it anyway, and he noticed this dark patch in the rough.'

'You always get dark patches. Turf gets re-laid, they try out new pesticides ...' said Carston.

'Aye, he said that. But this was different. He saw it from the tree and went to have a look. It was already pretty thick there but this was even thicker and longer. Lusher than the stuff around it. He's sure there's something.'

'So what's he want us to do about it?'

'I don't know. He's reported it. That's that.'

'OK, Sandy. Leave it with me.'

He put the phone back.

'OK, you're the intellectual,' he said to Ross. 'What are the chances that an extra-lush bit of vegetation on a golf course marks a burial spot?'

'You serious?'

Carston nodded.

'Whereabouts? Fairway? Rough?' asked Ross.

'Rough.'

'This'd be the right time of year for it to show up,' said Ross. 'Flowering period. You don't get much soil disturbance in the rough. It just gets cut back. If you dig it up and put it back, you loosen the soil. It holds water better, helps growth. Then you've got the nutrients from the decomposition ...'

'OK, OK, you've convinced me. Somebody's found something at the Royal. Get the GPR boys onto it. You never know.'

GPR was ground penetrating radar. It was a quick way of deciding whether the find was interesting or not.

'Wow,' said Ross, pushing away the files in front of him.

'A body. We can start being investigators again.'

'Or gardeners.'

The interior betrayed the fact that whoever owned the house preferred to live in a sort of velvet comfort. All the furnishings were soft, period pieces. Smoked glass vases carried feathers and wispy dried plants, the carpets were supplemented by deep rugs, and the rounded lines of the chairs and sofa were further modulated by the scatter cushions heaped on and in them. Low, pink-shaded lights on squat tables spilled patches of warmth into corners and even the sound of a concert on Radio Three seemed to be filtered through chocolate into the room.

A middle-aged man sat at a computer, incongruous amongst all the opulence. Beside him stood a glass of Madeira. His lips glistened with the sip he'd just taken from it. On the screen before him was a picture of three children. They were naked. Two of them were simulating, or having, sex; the third was watching, her hand cupped around her pubis. The man made a small growling noise of pleasure at the back of his throat and picked up the glass once again. The warble of his telephone cut through the music and into his mood. He swore, but, sighing heavily, forced himself to get up and go out into the hall to answer it. His tone was brusque as he spoke into the receiver.

'David Campion speaking.'

'Yeah. Payback time.'

A wariness came over Campion. Despite the fact that he was alone, he turned to face the wall, as if to keep the conversation secret.

'Who is that?' he asked.

'Could be any one of a number of people, couldn't it? Take your pick.'

'Look, who is it? You've got no right to ...'

'Now, now. Don't talk about rights. I mean, if you thought people had rights, you wouldn't do the things you do, would you?'

'Oh, come on. It's all over, that. You know it is. I ...'

'Don't make me angry. I'm phoning to help. Sally Brookes, remember?'

Campion's expression shifted from wariness to fear. His hand came up to cup the earpiece, trying to contain the words that were being said, restrict the secret information even more severely.

'Oh, so it's blackmail, is it? What do you want?'

Briefly, there was anger in the voice.

'No, it's not bloody blackmail. I'm not interested in making profits out of the things you get up to. I'm a policeman, based in Burns Road HQ. I've seen your file. That guy Ross is reworking the case. Don't be surprised if you get another visit from us.'

'But it's over. The police …'

'I know all that, but Ross hasn't given up. Some new stuff's come up.'

'What new stuff?'

'DNA stuff. I don't want to talk on the phone.'

'Oh no. You can forget that. I'm not meeting you. God knows what sort of …'

'My name's Spurle. I'm a detective constable. You can check me out. Just don't say why you're asking. We can meet anywhere you like. You choose.'

'Why should I? Even if you're legit, why would you want to help me?'

'I don't. It's not a question of helping you. Ross is my sergeant. He's been on my case too fucking often. It would suit me if … well, never mind. Are we going to meet? Or d'you just want Ross to go ahead with it?'

'What guarantees have I got that …'

He was interrupted this time by a short laugh.

'Listen to yourself. Guarantees? Be sensible.'

Campion shifted the handset to his other ear. It seemed that he was caught. If he ignored the caller, the police might well be back onto him; and, if that was going to happen, he'd prefer to know why. On the other hand, as the man had said at the start, there were plenty of people who imagined they had scores to settle with him. He couldn't take chances.

'I won't come out to meet you. You'd have to come here.'

'You know, pal, you're bloody tiresome. I've seen enough in your file to get the papers camping on your doorstep again. You're in no position to bargain.'

'You can't just expect me …'

'OK. I'm sick of this. I'll come to you. It'll have to be an evening. Some of us work. Tomorrow?'

'Look, I need to think about this. You could be anybody.'

'I've told you who I am. Check it out. Ring me at Burns Road. Just don't say who you are. Make up a name.'

'Ah, I thought so.'

'No, you're wrong. Think a minute. If they know you're in touch with me, they'll know who passed the leak on. I can do without that sort of hassle.'

Campion hesitated. Everything the man said sounded reasonable. And he wasn't even pretending to be a friend; he obviously had his own agenda.

'Tomorrow,' he said at last.

'I'll be free by eight. I'll come straight round then.'

The phone clicked dead. No goodbyes, no second thoughts. Campion went back to stand by his fireplace. The demons were back. In truth, they'd never gone away but he could usually ignore them. Now, it looked as if they were on the move again.

ELEVEN

It was risky giving Campion a name. I'd seen Spurle during the Bailey case. The name had just come to me when I was working out what to do. I was pretty sure Campion wouldn't try to ring the police station. He was guilty as hell. He'd do anything to keep clear of the law.

Know what I did, though? After I'd put the phone down? Wrote some referral letters to the hospital. Just switched back to being a GP. It was that easy. Most people have daydreams and fantasies; Walter Mitty stuff. Trouble was, this was more like Patrick Bateman.

I finished the letters and went down to the cellar. As usual, they opened their eyes to the dazzle as soon as they could. It was as if I was switching the sun on and off. Maybe it wasn't just revenge; maybe it was the power that was getting into me. It was a question from Dobie that started me thinking about it. He reckoned he was allergic to what he called 'the bracelet thing' around his leg.

'So what?' I said.

'Well, I'm getting a rash underneath it. I wonder if you could ...'

'What d'you think I am, a fucking doctor?' I said.

His voice cracked. He was only just managing not to cry.

'I've had these skin things before. They can turn very nasty.'

'Tough,' I said.

'You never know with allergies,' he said, a bit desperate. 'They can be fatal, can't they. I wouldn't be much good to you dead, would I?'

What a thing to ask! I couldn't resist it.

'It wouldn't bother me at all,' I said. 'I'll tell you what does bother me, though. That's too easy, a quick exit like that. I mean, when it comes to dying, we're talking about special methods, aren't we? For Bailey I'd want a claw hammer. The new lodger, the next one? ... I'd've thought shoving a cattle probe up his rectum or something might do it. And then for

you it'd have to be some sort of needle, wouldn't it?'

The blood drained out of his face. McPhee's head was bent, but he was listening.

'And McPhee? Well, the cheese wire, isn't it?'

McPhee lifted his head and looked straight at me. At last he knew why he was there. I reckon he realized I was mad enough to go through with it, too.

One of Carston's little fantasies was that he'd one day find himself on the eighteenth fairway with a short pitch to the green and a chance of at last breaking eighty. Today, though, the screens and the fluttering blue and white tape in the rough just short of the two bunkers gave him a completely different feeling. The GPR had been positive and the forensic archaeologist had begun her careful scratching away at the surface. It gave Carston no pleasure that there was some unfortunate victim underneath the grass, but his recent desk-bound existence was becoming frustrating.

The archaeologist, Patricia Begg, nodded at him as he ducked under the tapes.

'What d'you think?' he said.

'Not sure. Looks to me as if whoever did it was careful to cut these top turfs so that he could put them back.'

'Makes sense.'

'Apart from that, not much I can say yet. I think we should be OK; it's not too acidic or wet round here. Might not be totally skeletonised. Depends how long it's been here.'

'Any guesses?'

'No. I doubt whether it's more than a year, though. Somebody would've noticed it last summer. You get plenty of hackers through here.'

Carston didn't volunteer the fact that he was one of them.

'But I'm saying nothing till we get there,' added Begg.

Carston watched as she moved the last of the covering turfs away onto a plastic sheet and took another set of photos. He'd seen her at work before and admired the meticulous way she set about it. With her, there'd never be any problems about procedures or evidence. Archaeology is always a destructive process, so keeping a record of every stage is essential. When she'd finished, they'd have a three-dimensional model of the site to which she'd add information on temperature variations over the months, the type of soil, evidence of insect and rodent activity, humidity and rainfall levels, together with the estimated size and weight of the body and details of any clothing that was on it. They'd be able to feed it all into the computer and examine everything from every angle. In some ways, it took away the excitement of discovery, in others, it added to it precisely because it gave him so much on which to speculate.

'Reckon you'll be finished by this evening?' he asked.

Begg looked around the site.

'Maybe,' she said. 'Depends what we come across. I hope so anyway. I want my weekend clear. We've got tickets for the Usher Hall tomorrow night.'

'I'll use them if you can't make it,' said Carston.

Begg paused just long enough in her photo-taking to give him the finger.

'God, I love it when you do dirty things,' he said.

Friday afternoon surgery was the usual mixture. Straightforward stuff but also the oblique calls for help. Lisa Bennett, for instance, woman in her late thirties, told me about some localized stomach pains she'd been having. Look, bear with me. It's important. You need to know just how bloody weird and normal my life was all the way through this. And how things kept cropping up. Sort of reminding me of the shit all around.

I examined her, couldn't feel anything and I knew it was about something else. She'd dressed up to come to the surgery – a lot of them do – and she looked neat, correct. But nervous.

'I think it's probably just a little gastric upset,' I said. 'I could prescribe something to settle your stomach but you're just as well taking some Bisodol. What d'you think?'

She nodded. I waited.

'Is there anything else that's troubling you?' I asked

after a while. 'Anything that's making you worry?'

She kept her head down, looking at her hands folded on her lap.

'You know you can tell me if you want to,' I said. I tried to be gentle.

There was a moment's silence, then she sighed and looked up at me.

'It's none of my business,' she began. 'I don't like interfering.'

I let her take her time to get round to it.

'It's my Mary, really,' she said.

Mary's her daughter. About six years old.

'She used to go and play with Lizzie Ramsay. Every afternoon she was round there after school. Then, last Wednesday, you remember? It was raining.'

I nodded.

'I thought she was round there again but I looked out the kitchen window and there she was, playing on her own outside. In the rain.'

She took out a tissue and dabbed at her nose. There was no need for me to say anything; now that she'd started, she wanted to tell me exactly what was troubling her.

'I called her in and asked her why she wasn't at Lizzie's. She wouldn't tell me at first, then she just said she didn't like it round there. Didn't want to play with Lizzie any more. Not at her house anyway. I asked her if they'd had an argument but she said no. Said Lizzie was still her best friend but ...'

She suddenly leaned forward in her chair, her face squeezed with worry.

'I think something's going on there, doctor. I think maybe wee Lizzie's being ... abused or something. Mary's afraid to go to her place. She said ... she said Lizzie cuts herself with a knife.'

I just nodded. The only surprising thing about her story was that she'd let her daughter go round to the Ramsays' house at all. They're a violent bunch. History of abuse at several levels. Nothing ever blatant enough to bring your lot in but the Social Services are always there and I'd treated

Mrs Ramsay for the things her husband's bad moods had done to her – physical and mental.

'How old's Lizzie again?' I asked.

'Six, same as Mary.'

'Aye, we'll have to see what's going on, won't we?'

'You won't say it was me that ...'

I shook my head and patted her on the arm.

'I'll get Dr McIntosh to drop in, just for a check-up. She's their doctor. And don't worry; nobody'll say anything about you. You were right to tell us, though. It was the right thing to do.'

She was reassured. She smiled but the nervousness was still there.

'You never know, do you?' she said. 'I mean, when it's kiddies, you've got to say something, haven't you?'

'Absolutely,' I said.

I scribbled a note on my pad. She stood up. She'd got what she'd come for. I stood up too and led her to the door.

'Don't worry,' I said. 'We'll do what we can. Thanks for taking the trouble to come in.'

I closed the door and phoned through to Jill McIntosh.

'It's no surprise,' she said, when I told her about it. 'Usual story. It's like a bloody virus; once it gets in, everybody catches it. Lizzie'll be on the receiving end now but she'll hand it out herself when she has kids of her own. OK, Andrew, I'll check it out. Don't hold your breath, though.'

I rang off. The weariness in Jill's voice made my own mood even worse. Another spin down the spiral.

I checked my weekend commitments on my laptop and set aside the letters I had to write. All the time, though, I was thinking about abuse. And, of course, Bailey. You know how he treated his wife. His name was one of the first I'd jotted down. He'd avoided the cellar, but he wasn't going to get away with it. I switched on my mobile and dialled his number.

TWELVE

Bailey was in his office at Pullins Engineering. It was all tubular chrome furniture, glass table tops and stripped pine walls. He sat leafing through a set of engineering drawings and making notes on his computer. The phone warbled beside him. He picked up the receiver.

'Call for you, Mr. Bailey. Line three.'

'Thank you.'

Bailey finished typing a note, saved the file onto a disc, pressed a button and said, 'Bailey here, what is it?'.

'Just called to say you're a bastard,' said the voice at the other end.

Bailey was immediately attentive. It was the same cold, muffled voice which had made the JJ Construction offer. The stranger again.

'Who is that?' he asked.

'Never mind that,' Davidson went on, 'I gave you your chance the other day. I tried to do you a favour but, well, you weren't interested. So we'll have to do it another way.'

'Do what?'

'Business.'

Bailey's anger boiled up.

'Listen, friend. If you've got anything to say to me, come in and say it to my face, instead of skulking at the end of …'

He was given no chance to finish his sentence.

'Stop giving me your bloody orders, shitbag. I've got nothing to say to you anyway. When it happens I just wanted you to know why. You've been getting away with it long enough. Soon, it'll be all over. Think about it.'

'What the hell are you on about? Why do you …?'

'Dying, that's what I'm on about. You. Dying. I'll be in touch.'

The line went dead. Bailey put the phone slowly back on its rest. He'd received such calls before; insulting, vindictive crap. From a variety of ill-wishers. Especially during the murder enquiry. Nothing had ever come of them. But this time there was an edge of venom. It was more than just a nuisance call. It was a direct promise of death. That was a first.

I tell you what, making a death threat – that was a huge surprise. I don't know where the hell it came from. The idea was to try to fix a meeting, use a different tactic. But ... I don't know ... as soon as I heard his self-important, self-satisfied bloody voice, I lost it. Just lost the place. I didn't mean to speak about dying. It certainly wasn't part of my plan. Maybe I just wanted to frighten him too much. Unsettle him. So I pushed too hard. Could be the power thing again. Whatever it was, it was bloody stupid. I mean, what chance was there of him agreeing to meet me after that? I was angry with myself, so I used the anger. I went to Campion's place.

With the data on the golf course burial still being collated, Carston made the promised visit to F. K. Reismann's office. The place was designed to be reassuring, to tell clients who were shown into it that they were in good hands and that, in a changing world, lawyers were the same as they always had been, as respectable as maiden aunts.

Reismann himself sat at a vast mahogany desk. On it were an inkstand made of brass and crystal, a pile of signed letters, a black and gold fountain pen, a tray containing more letters waiting for his signature, an open diary and two coffee cups on coasters. Two large bookcases held rows of reference books and on the walls between them hung dark paintings of dead birds and eighteenth century gentlemen on horseback. Carpets and wallpaper seemed equally thick so that the whole room had a dull soft feel and absorbed the voices of clients and lawyer alike. Carston had noticed the muting effect of all this from the start of their conversation. His guess was that it made it more difficult for tempers to be lost or harsh words to be uttered in the course of what must sometimes be trying consultations.

Reismann didn't seem as sharp as Carston had expected. He was somehow distracted and had been very surprised when presented with the computer print-out showing that the information about Bailey had been published in the newspaper. He even had the grace to apologize. His client's assumption that no-one else knew of the Belway connection had been false and the whole basis of the complaint was therefore destroyed. After such a concession, the only topic for consideration was the nature of the threat that remained and whether Bailey merited any special protection.

'Hard to justify really,' Carston was saying. 'I mean, all we've got is this offer of some dodgy share dealing, isn't it?'

'It's not about that, though, is it? The share information was all invented. None of what the caller said happened. It was only at the end, when he talked about Belway and missing persons that the real reason for the call started coming through. The whole idea seems to have been just to lure my client into some sort of trap.'

'And he was smart enough not to go, so that's that.'

'But it's not. There's been another call. A death threat.'

Carston held his gaze for a moment.

'From the same person?'

'Yes.'

'And what did he say?'

'That the call was about him dying.'

'Just that?'

'It's enough, isn't it?'

Reluctantly, Carston nodded.

'So where do we go from here?' asked Reismann.

'Burns Road,' said Carston, drinking the last of the coffee in his cup.

'I beg your pardon?'

'Back to the station. We'll put together the information you've given us, make a few enquiries …'

Reismann looked at him.

'I hope you're not going to be flippant about this. I mean, your dealings with him in the past haven't been exactly impartial, have they? There was a lot of adverse publicity over that unfortunate business.'

Carston sat back in his chair.

96

'Murder's more than an "unfortunate business". And anyway, it's because we managed to stay impartial that Bailey's still free to carry on wheeling and dealing when everybody with any sense knows that he should be doing a minimum of thirty years. With the sort of things he gets up to, it's hardly surprising that he's getting threats, is it?'

Reismann wagged a finger at him.

'That's slander, you know.'

'It's also the truth,' Carston went on, 'and you know it too, don't you?'

The lawyer leaned back and half turned in his chair to look at one of the paintings. His silence confirmed Carston's suggestion.

'How can you do that sort of thing?' Carston asked.

'What sort of thing?'

'Protect people like Bailey, Dobie, all the others that you've helped to wriggle out of convictions.'

Reismann's gaze stayed on the painting.

'I resent the "wriggle out",' he said, without showing any particular signs of resentment. 'You forget, "innocent till proved guilty". What I believe, what I know, that's irrelevant. My job is just to make sure that the law's properly applied.'

'Like letting Bailey get away with murder?'

'There you go again,' said Reismann, in the same thoughtful, even tone. 'There wasn't enough evidence. You can't play around with justice. The law says there's got to be evidence. If there isn't any, there's no argument.'

Carston knew the lawyer was right, but his sense of injustice was still strong in Bailey's case. He said nothing. Reismann turned to look straight into his eyes.

'You agree with me really,' he said. 'I know you do. We can't afford to rely on hunches, suspicions. You don't arrest people just because you know they're … nasty.'

'No, but some cases are so bloody obvious. It's not …'

'No exceptions,' said Reismann, still holding his stare. 'It doesn't matter whether I share your thinking about Bailey or Dobie. It doesn't matter what my personal opinion of them is, whatever sort of trash I think they are. If there's not enough evidence to convict them, it's my job to see that they're freed.'

His eyes dropped to the desk and his voice became softer.

'I'm not the monster you think. You think I get some sort of perverted pleasure out of cheating you and your colleagues out of convictions. It isn't like that. Between you and me, I loathe some of my clients as much as you do, but I can't let that get in the way, can I? Nothing makes any sense if I do.'

It was a sincere and surprising little speech which left a silence between them. Carston broke it at last by standing up.

'Something wrong with the system if you ask me,' he said.

'Maybe,' said Reismann as he too pushed himself out of his chair, 'but it's all we've got.'

The two men walked to the door of the office. Before leaving, Carston paused.

'So there's nothing wrong at work or at home for Bailey?'

'Nothing,' said Reismann.

'And he had no idea who this caller was?'

'None. Disguised his voice apparently.'

'So all we've got is a man on the phone who could be a real threat or a practical joker?'

'Yes.'

There was nothing left to say. The two men shook hands and Carston left the building and walked quickly to his car. As he drove back, he thought about what Reismann had said and the strange sincerity of what had been a sort of confession. The lawyer was right; Carston knew that there was sometimes a large gap between law and justice but he, too, respected the rules and knew they were essential. And now that the phone call had turned into an apparently real death threat. It was worth looking into, if only out of curiosity.

When Campion heard the doorbell, his pulse began racing. He had to let the man in but he'd prepared little surprises all around the house in case things turned ugly. Knives and scissors were tucked behind cushions and, everywhere they were likely to go, he'd made sure there was something he could grab and swing at the man's head. He used his left hand to open the door. The right held a small bronze statuette.

The minute the door started to open, I banged into it. He was right behind it, so he fell back on the floor. I kicked the door shut and sat on his chest. I had the atomizer full of fentanyl again. I held my breath and sprayed in his face. He squeezed his eyes closed and shook his head. I stood up quickly and stepped back through the door, not taking a breath until I was outside. I braced myself against the door to keep it open. No need to. Campion managed to struggle to his feet but then fell down again. Fifteen seconds later, when I went back in, he was lying full length, his trousers stained with urine and a bronze statuette beside his head.

I did the same as I'd done with Dobie. Injected naloxone into a vein and waited. For a while, it looked as if he wasn't going to respond. I watched him. I didn't care. Eventually, he started moving feebly and I dragged him up and out to the car. Put the sail bag over his head and trussed him up. We were away in less than two minutes.

Nobody'd heard anything. I stopped now and then to check his colour. One time, I got this strange feeling. As I was lifting the bag, I realized I was enjoying myself. His distress ... pleased me.

When we got to my place, he was still helpless. In the hallway, he found it difficult to walk and had to lean against the wall. At the top of the cellar steps, I put the mask back on and took the sail bag off. I guided him down the steps, opened the cellar door and turned the light on. It needed another tap to get him moving again. He kept his eyes down and shuffled forward, sniffing and sobbing. The others squinted at him.

'New boy,' I said. 'I'll introduce you later.'

As I shackled him to his pillar, I felt strange, excited. I was treating them the same they'd treated their victims. There was more evil in me than I'd imagined.

THIRTEEN

Rhona usually kept her private and business worlds separate. It could never be foolproof; she'd seen the occasional punter in town, shopping with his wife or dragging a couple of kids behind him but, naturally enough, they never acknowledged her and she gave no sign that she knew them. As far as possible, she stayed anonymous while Laura did the work.

One man in particular could turn out to be a problem. She wasn't sure whether he'd been a punter, didn't know his name, what he looked like, anything. Their contact consisted of phone calls. They'd started a couple of weeks after she'd arrived in Dundee. At first, the man seemed to be just using her for phone sex. Again, it went with the territory and she put up with it, just to see whether he'd follow through. But they'd gradually been getting more personal and she soon realized that he'd been digging around and finding out things about her. It made her curious, but when he started mentioning Bob Davies and the rape, little alarm bells started. The temptation had been to put the phone down each time she heard his voice, but she needed to know what he wanted, how much he knew, so she listened and shivered at some of the things he said.

She'd told Billy about him. Billy was different. He was the only one she felt she knew well enough to let him come up to her flat. She'd known him in Cairnburgh. He was one of her regulars. He'd been down to Dundee several times already and each time, he'd booked a hotel room but never stayed overnight. It was only for sex with her during the day. He was always the perfect gentleman and kept saying that what he liked most, apart from the wonderful sex, was that, when he was with her, it was just like having a girl friend. This was no surprise to her; lots of her punters said the same thing. It was crazy. If that's what they wanted, why didn't they just go out and find a real one?

Billy was young enough. A bit quiet, maybe, but not unattractive, and he certainly knew how to treat her. He asked too many questions, but she didn't mind too much. Maybe the girl friend ploy was a way of trying to get what she was offering for free. No chance. He was different, though. Sometimes, he didn't even want sex and often, when he did, it was quickly over and he was embarrassed and apologized for not being able to control himself better. She'd laugh it off and claim that she was so good that it was the same with all her clients. So it was more relaxing when they went out for a meal and just talked and he took her back to her flat, paid her, kissed her goodnight and drove back to Cairnburgh.

Tonight, though, was a sex night. And, as usual, it was over almost as soon as they'd got on the bed and she'd used her mouth to put on his condom (a trick she'd learned very early and which had earned her plenty of bonuses and repeat calls). She lay in the crook of his arm, her head against his shoulder, feeling safe and ready to be the girl friend for a few more minutes.

Billy looked at his watch.

'Don't suppose you'd marry me, would you?' he asked. It wasn't the first time.

'You know I won't. Anyway, I'm a total bitch if I'm not getting paid for it.'

'Don't believe you.'

'Besides, you're too young to be married. You should be out shagging everything that moves,' said Rhona.

'I only want to shag you.'

'Well, you just did, so shut up.'

She kissed him on the chest. They lay quietly for a while, his fingers trailing slowly up and down her left arm.

'D'you think you'll stop this one day?' he said. Again, it was a question he'd asked before in one form or another.

'Nope,' she replied.

'You don't see yourself married with kids and stuff.'

'What d'you mean, stuff?'

'The usual – house, car, telly …'

'… mortgage, saggy tits, fat gut.'

'That's up to you,' said Billy. 'You could join a gym.'

'Bloody hell,' she said. 'I'd have to call myself Barbie or

something.'

'You can't do this for ever, though.'

'Why not?' she said, lifting her head to look at him before settling back again. 'Science is amazing. By the time I'm middle aged, they'll have open-crotched zimmers, so I'll never have to retire.'

'That's gross,' said Billy, laughing.

'Thank you,' said Rhona. 'All part of the service.'

They were quiet again. The fingers still slid up and down her skin. After a while, Billy checked his watch again, heaved a huge sigh and turned to kiss her. It was a long kiss, his tongue deep in her mouth and his hand softly moving over her shoulder.

'OK, if you're not going to marry me, I gotta go,' he said at last, pushing himself off the bed.

She watched him dress, making him laugh with her comments about the various bits of his body as he covered them up. When he was ready to leave, he came back to the bed, leaned over and kissed her again. As he straightened up, the phone beside the bed began to ring. He shook his head and wiggled his fingers at her in a little wave. She blew him a kiss and picked up the phone.

'Hello,' she said, her tone neutral, guarded until she knew what sort of call it was likely to be.

'Laura,' said the voice. 'It's been too long since we had a wee chat. Are you on your own?'

'No,' she said, her voice sharper than she intended, a slight edge of panic because of Billy's presence.

'There's a few things I'd like to talk about,' said the man. 'I think you'll be interested. Nothing bad. Well, not really. You see, I was wondering about the guy who gave you a lift to Dundee. Remember? He stayed the night with you? Ended up in a ditch. Now ...'

Billy, who'd been turning away, had stopped when he heard her tone and leaned over the bed again.

'Is that him?' he whispered.

Rhona shook her head.

'I bet it is,' hissed Billy and he grabbed the phone away

from her.

'Listen shitface,' he said into it, 'fuck off, right? Leave her alone.'

There was a silence and Rhona heard the man start to speak again, but Billy cut into him.

'I'm telling you, pal, you fuck off and leave her alone or I'll find where you are and cut your fucking heart out.'

He banged the phone back down, sat down hard on the bed and grabbed Rhona to him. He was rough, angry.

'Bastard, bastard,' he said, sounding close to tears. He kissed her hair again and again, then held her away from him and looked hard into her eyes.

'Listen,' he said. 'If he rings back, tell me, right?'

After a pause, she nodded.

'Promise?'

'Promise.'

It was a promise she had no intention of keeping but she wanted to calm him down.

'I meant it, you know. I'll cut his fucking heart out if he bothers you.'

'He won't. Not now,' she said, pulling Billy to her and hugging him hard.

What Billy couldn't know was that Rhona found his protection as offensive as the caller's intrusions. It was another proof, as if she needed any more, that men were a bloody nuisance.

I think that was the first time it really came home to me – what I was doing, I mean. I was watching Campion and it struck me how ... ugly it all was. I mean, I know it was all premeditated, and I'd had plenty of time to realize what a total dickhead I was being – a dangerous one too. Let's face it, it's not the sort of thing that's done by anybody in a normal state of mind. So who the hell was doing it? Certainly not the me who laughed with Jerry, who really cared about my patients. I was used to that me. When I'm in the courtroom, my defence'll say 'Hey, look. The guy's obviously insane.' But the prosecution will just prove that the planning was cold-blooded and spread over a long period. They'll remind the jury how I've been working and acting normally. All the time. My colleagues'll confirm it. Indisputable. No, I've been sane all along, still am. And I know why I did it. For Tommy. But then, when I was looking at Campion, I knew it was chewing its way deeper inside me. And ... yes, it's true ... it was affecting my mind. I'd been cool, calculating when I worked it all out. In a way, it wasn't real then. But the contact with them was beginning to change me. I should've quit while I was ahead.

Christ, what a weird set-up it was. Like some bloody club – only they couldn't leave it. They were scared stiff – even McPhee. He tried to hide it, but I could tell.

'You're wondering why you're here, aren't you?' I said. 'Well, let's start with Campion here. He's got a thing about children – boys, girls, he doesn't care, just so long as they're young and available. Well, not even available. He's not fussy about that. He was at it again this year, weren't you?'

His eyes were tight shut. So were his lips. I bet he'd have shut his ears, too, if he could.

'Gave a little girl a lift in his car. Sally Brookes. Took her to the Forestry Commission place, up towards Elgin. All pine needles and silence. At least, there was silence, until he started pawing away at her. Seven, she was. Had no idea what was going on. Thought he was playing. Then it started hurting. You can imagine, can't you? Seven year old girl, and a bloke Campion's size lying on her, pinning her down, forcing her legs open, ripping her apart.'

I felt tears on my face. I remember pushing the mask against the wetness on my cheeks. That was a surprise.

'Seventeen stitches, she had. And, on top of that, Christ knows how many stitches she's going to need in her mind as she grows up. Splinters, that's all her life is. Just so that Campion here could have a fuck. Just to keep him going till the next one. Back among his antiques – oh yes, he's got a nice little set-up at home. Beautiful place. Not like his little girl-friend. She lives in a caravan. A mobile home, but it's got no wheels, so it's not really mobile. Neither is she, yet. I

104

suppose she's lucky to be alive still, although that's debatable. She screamed, see. He was having such a good time that he let go of her mouth for a second, and she screamed. There was a bloke out for a walk. He heard her and shouted. Campion must have had enough. He just up and left her.'

The others were looking at Campion.

'Somebody'd seen his car on its way to the forest tracks. Reported him. He's well known, him and his habits. On the register. He's been at it before, you see, lots of times. Not as serious as this, but bad enough. Here's the problem though; everybody knew he'd done it, but he got away with it. "Insufficient evidence" was what the papers said. One witness reckoned the car was red, another one said it might have been brown. The fibres they got out of the little girl's hair and from under her nails matched his jacket. But he buys some of his clothes in M & S, so his brief showed that at least two members of the jury could have been convicted on the same evidence. Thanks to that, and some other bits of legal dodging about, he can go where he likes, fuck more wee kids in a forest or a lay-by somewhere.'

The cellar was quiet. Really quiet, even sort of heavy with quiet. There was evil there alright – in McPhee and Dobie too – but it was all focused on Campion now. It was easy for the others to feel that he was responsible for all the bad things that were happening to them. I let them think about it for a moment, then started again.

'Hang on a minute, though. Before you condemn him, just think why you're here with him. You're not some sort of jury here to try his case. You're here for the same reason; you got away with it. Our managing director, the one who's not so keen to join us, I'd like to ask him about Mrs Bailey. What happened to her, eh? And you, Dobie. Your old girl-friend Jenny. How long's she got left to live? Six months? Nine? And what sort of thoughts went through your head, McPhee, when you sat behind that taxi-driver that Christmas?'

I went back to the door.

'Know what you are really?' I said. 'Things. Just like your victims were to you. I'm telling you now so that you know what to expect.'

I turned off the light, shut the door and paused a minute to listen. Nothing. Not a breath. Not a whisper. Deep, deep silence.

FOURTEEN

They were still waiting for an analysis of the findings at the golf course dig. The archaeologist had promised to send her report in by the end of the day, though, so Carston was having to find things to fill in the time. He was looking at the most recent set of charge sheets. What he read didn't help to improve his mood. There was the usual rash of drunks and associated assaults, the equally predictable vandals, one group of them caught this time in a churchyard overturning concrete tubs full of flowers and throwing benches through a stained glass window. And then, in the middle of the pile, he came across a sheet detailing the havoc wreaked in a council flat by its drunken tenant in the early hours of Tuesday. In addition to a list of broken mirrors, splintered chairs, smashed crockery, and battered doors, the prime article of the charge, the one that had at last prompted the accused's wife to get the police, stated simply that the couple's ten month old baby had been admitted to hospital suffering from a broken arm, severe bruising of head and body, and cigarette burns on the soles of its feet.

He pushed the pile aside and reached for one on Christopher Bailey that he'd asked Ross to fetch for him. Not so very long before, he'd known the contents of the file only too well and, as he flicked through it now, the mood created by reading the charge sheets became even more sombre. Officially, the file was closed. Bailey still had too many friends upstairs for it to be openly available so there was a tacit agreement between the station staff to 'hide' the information about him. A cross-reference pinned inside the cover ironically noted, 'See also: Bailey, Marion. Victims.'

He took one of the sheets of paper from the file and read it as he poured himself a mug of coffee.

'It was decided, after due consideration of the available facts, and with proper regard for the informed opinions of the investigating officers, that there was insufficient evidence to justify proceeding with the case. On the recommendation of the chief constable, therefore, the investigation was suspended and, given the severe stresses which the subject had been under since his wife's death and the publicity it had provoked, it was further suggested that the case should not be re-opened unless new information of genuine significance became available.'

He carried his coffee and the piece of paper back to his desk, still baffled by what 'genuine significance' was supposed to mean and how the hell any new information could materialize if no-one was allowed to look for it. He replaced the sheet of paper and looked through the rest. There were full transcripts of every interview they'd had with Bailey, and they all told the same story: masses of circumstantial evidence proving that he was guilty but none of it substantial enough to shake his continued refusal to admit it. Under Reismann's prompting, he'd played the bereaved husband, then the outraged innocent, aware all the time that he was going to get away with it. The papers had first of all hunted him as a prime suspect, then, just at the wrong moment, they found out that, in her spare time, Marion Bailey had been on the books of an escort agency. The agency was as legitimate as such enterprises ever are and suggestions that she was simply an upmarket whore were strenuously denied by its manager. But, of course, the public preferred its own, fleshier version of affairs and poor dead Marion, whom Carston had last seen as a collapsed bundle in their plushly appointed kitchen with a textured stain where her head should have been, became a filthy prostitute who'd been dispatched by a frenzied client. Simultaneously, her husband was transformed into a respectable and terribly wronged local businessman earning a living while his wife snaked her way through the swamps of the city's night.

When Ross came in, Carston was standing at the window.

'Coffee's ready,' he said.

Ross noticed his tone.

'Something up?' he asked.

'Not really. Just the usual,' said Carston, nodding his

head towards the file on his desk.

'Don't know why you need to read it,' said Ross. 'The bugger's engraved on my mind.'

'Yes.'

'Anything from Pat Begg?' said Ross.

Carston shook his head, turned and came away from the window.

'You got anything?' he asked.

'No. I've checked again with missing persons, all the latest computer listings, the patrol boys are keeping their ears and eyes open, just in case. Not a whisper about anything.'

'So nothing about Bailey, and McPhee and Dobie've just vanished.'

'And Rhona Kirk.'

'They on the computer list?'

'Yes. Along with some missing wives and sons, several teenage girls and a merchant seaman some of the lads wanted to question about drug-pushing.'

'The usual, in fact.'

'Yes.'

'So, we're back to wits and guesswork.'

Ross said nothing. Carston carried on, half to himself.

'Why are we bothering with this bloody Bailey nonsense? A couple of phone calls. That's all we've got. Not even a bloody crime.'

'One of them was a death threat.'

'Hoo-bloody-ray.'

'And Freddy's on his case.'

'Yes, he won't let up,' said Carston. 'But if we don't come up with something else, I don't know how the hell we're going to get any further with it.'

'Well, let's just hope whoever's having a go at him doesn't give up,' said Ross.

Carston looked up at him and caught the remnant of a smile.

'Aye. I know what you mean,' he said.

The two of them continued to turn round the unpleasant thoughts that the story had provoked. Carston went back to the window, opened it and let some cooler air in to scour away some of his gloom. Then, as he watched the shoppers, pushchairs, cars and buses, he began to see an obscure, even fanciful connection beginning to form. Gratefully, he moved away from the window.

'There could be something there, I suppose,' he said. 'A link.'

Ross looked up, uncertain of what his boss was referring to.

'The guy on the phone to Bailey talked about missing persons.'

'And?'

'Rhona Kirk was raped by a guy who went missing. Dobie and Bailey both got rid of their woman.'

'I don't get you.'

'I don't know, it's folk being ... unfair to women,' said Carston. 'Let's just assume that they are connected. I don't s'pose there's anybody who knows Dobie and Bailey personally, so maybe it's a general sort of vengeance that's going on. Maybe there's a female vigilante operating. There's plenty of them around and they can be as bestial as men when it comes to GBH.'

'Maybe, but if Dobie's AC/DC, it's more likely he's off with one of his gay pals. Found himself a daddy and gone to Tangiers for the operation. I mean, there's almost as many queers on that missing list as there are young girls. It's no real surprise to find Dobie there.'

'No, I suppose not. I still think I'll have a little scratch round this Dobie guy, though. Just in case, eh?'

'Anything to help out Mr. Bailey,' said Ross.

Then there was the day Jill McIntosh came to my surgery – to talk about wee Lizzie Ramsay. She'd been to see the family and, from what they said as well as plenty of reading between the lines, she'd got a fair idea of what was going on there.

'The usual call for attention,' she said. 'The poor wee thing doesn't know where she is. That's why she's cutting herself.'

'And there is abuse, is there?'

'Aye.'

'Who from?'

'Her brother Ewan, I think.'

'How old's he?'

'Nearly twelve. But I'm not surprised. He's been on the receiving end himself. That stepfather of his. For ages. He's just passing it on.'

'Aye. It's the only currency they know, isn't it? Poor little sods.'

'It's what passes for love in their family.'

'Not just theirs either.'

'No.'

She was right. Sometimes the only sort of attention kids like Lizzie get comes from their abusers. They learn to tolerate the violence, expect it. Helps to explain why they become abusers themselves as they grow older. Lot of the time, anyway.

'What're you going to do?' I asked.

She shook her head.

'What can I do? Nobody's complaining, there's no evidence. I've told the social worker about it. We'll just keep an eye on it all and hope it doesn't lead to anything critical.'

'Aye. Sorry, Jill. I dropped you into this.'

She smiled.

'Somebody had to do something. No doubt I'll return the favour before long.'

She went out. My mobile began to ring. It was Gayla.

'Nice surprise,' I said.

'Was I that bad?' she said.

'Bad?'

'Sex, Dr Davidson. Remember?'

'Oh, was that you?'

'Depends how much you remember.'

'Not much. How are you, Gayla?'

'Fine. Wondering whether you were going to phone again. You said you would.'

'I know. I meant it, too. Just ... busy. You know.'

'So it wasn't bad then?'

'Not at all. It was only slightly less than mediocre.'

'Want to try again?'

'Could do.'

'Maybe make mediocre this time.'

'We can try.'

'Your place or mine?'

I loved the directness of it all. None of the pretending or sidling up to the idea of sex via small talk. Very refreshing. On top of that, there was the idea of having sex at my place, knowing the guys were in the ... Anyway, I jumped at the chance.

'We tried your place,' I said. 'Maybe we'd have more luck at mine.'

'It's not the geography that concerns me, it's the biology.'

'Has anyone ever complimented you on your chatting up technique?'

'With my other men, I rarely have to talk.'

'Count yourself lucky that you've found an intellectual, then.'

'I'm not so sure. When are you free?'

'Can't make it tonight or tomorrow,' I said. 'How about Friday?'

'Bloody hell, I can't have been all that bad, then.'

'Eight o'clock?'

'Sure.'

'I'll make dinner.'

'I'll eat it.'

And she rang off.

Amongst everything else, the thought of uncomplicated sex with Gayla was great. That last time, it was good and, when I said I'd phone her, I meant it. I knew that, for the time anyway, she wouldn't expect anything more than sex. Being considered an item with her would protect me from other complications.

I had my reasons for putting her off until Friday. It was a Wednesday night, see? Changeover time for lots of crews on *the rigs. Earlier, I'd phoned the heliport. Said I was a researcher from Aberdeen Royal Infirmary. I'd checked the passenger manifests. Struck lucky on the third one. George Waring. He was due back from the Falcon Alpha platform at six. I knew that, by nine o-clock, he'd be in his usual pub and already pissed out of his mind.*

Patricia Begg was pleased with herself. She'd called Carston and suggested he could pick up her report in person so that she could take him through some of its implications. He'd jumped at the chance and gone straight to her office. The two of them stood beside her desk on which she'd opened the report with all its accompanying illustrations.

'We don't know who he is yet,' she was saying, 'but I think we'll be able to give you a pretty tight window for the date.'

'Excellent,' said Carston, bending over the various photographs she'd spread about. 'So, what've we got, then?'

Begg shuffled through the pictures and picked one out. It was a close-up of soil and pieces of wood.

'Plenty of roots there, lots of them severed at the same time. See the rings?'

Carston peered closely.

'I've checked them against the undamaged roots,' said Begg. 'There's been some growth since they were cut, but not a lot.'

'So sometime last year, then?'

Begg smiled and shuffled through the pictures again.

'We can do better than that,' she said, slipping out another close-up for him to see. 'Look what we found in the back-filling.'

The shot showed a torn wrapper from a chocolate bar. Carston noticed that the bar code on it was intact. He pointed to it.

'This what you mean?'

Begg nodded.

'Get the batch number dated by the manufacturers and your job's easy,' she said. 'The roots give you the year and

114

the wrapper gives you the month, or at least, the earliest possible time for the burial. But judging from the root growth, I'd say that, whatever month you get for the chocolate, that's when it happened.'

'Nice to have the certainty of youth,' said Carston.

'What would you know about youth?' said Begg, searching once again through the pile. She took out two more photos.

'Two things about the skeleton,' she said. 'See the break in the forearm? A parry fracture.'

'Right, so there was a bit of a fight.'

'Well, he tried to defend himself anyway. And this is probably what finished him off.'

She pointed to the other photo, a close-up of the skull. Running along its centre was a darker patch with breaks at its edges.

'Depressed fracture,' she said. 'Pretty severe one, too.'

'And no ID yet,' said Carston, still looking at the photos.

Begg started gathering them together again to put back in the file.

'No. There's plenty to go on, though,' she said. 'The jaw's intact, plenty of DNA, few bits of clothing. Once you get the date, it'll be a doddle.'

'A 'doddle'? Funny word for a young woman to use.'

'That's me trying to talk old.'

'For my benefit?'

'Yes.'

She closed the folder and handed it over.

'I'll send my report over as an email attachment, too,' she said. 'In case you need to work it into your stuff.'

Carston took the folder and held out his hand. She shook it.

'Thanks, Pat,' he said. 'You're right. You do make my job easier.'

She smiled.

'No problem, Jack,' she said. 'Now mind how you go on the stairs.'

FIFTEEN

Waring didn't care that the pub was full. He leaned forward against the bar as the barmaid filled yet another glass with the cloudy ale he preferred. He put his arm around the woman sitting beside him, a gesture of ownership even though this was the first evening that they'd ever spoken to one another. The Dubonnets she'd drunk had anaesthetized her sufficiently not only to put up with his coarse, malodorous attentions but also to convince her that she was back in the prime of her youth when the application of make-up hadn't been the major reconstruction job it was nowadays.

This evening was shaping just as evenings always had since nearly thirty years ago when she'd first started going out with men. Waring had been flattering, cajoling, polite as he'd asked to sit with her and talked about her job, her interests. Then, as more alcohol had gently eased their pretences aside, the small talk was replaced by innuendo, the beginnings of seemingly accidental contact, and finally the full-blown indulgence in sexual gropings. She was under no illusions; this was no fairy prince. She could feel Waring's weight pressed against her right side and the clutch of his arm crooked around the back of her neck. Suddenly, the arm moved, and her left breast was grabbed in a grip devoid of all sexuality.

'What about this one then, Karen?' shouted Waring, hanging on mercilessly. 'Makes even yours look small, eh?'

The barmaid smiled at him, her eyes betraying the fact that her nightly experience of such events had done nothing to diminish the contempt they made her feel.

'Aye, but are you man enough to handle it, George?' she asked.

By way of answer, Waring dug his fingers harder into the woman's flesh, turned his face towards her and snarled his masculinity into the side of her head, nipping her ear-lobe and pushing his tongue roughly into the ear itself.

The woman yelled her pain and pulled herself away from

him. Deprived of her support, he almost fell.

'That hurt, you pig!' she said.

'Aye, you love it, don't you?' said Waring, reaching for her once again.

She half shrugged his hand away, intent on making her point but keeping her man. The hand grabbed the sleeve of her jacket and pulled her towards him. Her token resistance was unconvincing; Waring's arm was once more draped around her shoulder and the hand was back over her breast.

'Bastard,' said the woman affectionately.

The full pint was put down beside the Dubonnet that had already been served.

'That's what all his friends call him,' said Karen as she took a tenner from the money Waring had put on the counter.

'Surprised he's got any,' said the woman, being careful to accompany her words with a movement that slid her hand out of sight between Waring's legs.

Waring, obscurely aware that he was being got at by the two of them, but more directly sensitive to the position of the sliding hand, picked up the pint and bought time by sucking two big mouthfuls from it. He liked the feel of the breast in his left hand. He was right; it was big and full. Twenty years older than Karen's maybe, but still substantial. He put down his glass. The squeeze of her hand inside his thigh brought a grin to the side of his mouth and he looked at the faces of the other men around him. None of them was receiving that sort of attention from a woman; it made him feel confident, powerful.

Karen put his change with the rest of the money on the counter and turned to serve another customer. Waring's hand left the woman's breast as his forearm lifted her head towards him. There was no longer any resistance. Her face turned up and his mouth opened over hers to suck at her slack lips. He felt no sexual excitement, only an increase in the power he enjoyed. His mouth pressed harder, forcing her head back against his arm which he held firm so that there was no escape for her. She wanted to pull free. He held on, making his point, enjoying her weakness. Only when he was ready did he bite into her lower lip, pull his head back and let his arm fall away from her.

There were tears in her eyes. She swung her hand at him and caught the back of his head with her clenched fist before pushing away from him through the crowd towards the Ladies. He laughed and picked up his pint again.

'Bloody women. Never satisfied, are they?' he said to his immediate neighbours. She'd be back, and in any case, he didn't give a shit if she flushed herself away. He could take them or leave them. Karen was in front of him, leaning forward, the top of her breasts tempting as they fell into the shadows of her blouse.

'Any more of that and you're out, George. You hear?' she threatened, hard and low.

'Jealous?' said Waring.

'I'm warning you,' said Karen.

Waring was saved from the need to find a reply by the ringing of his mobile. He fumbled in his breast pocket for it, flipped back the top and hit a button.

'Yeah?' he shouted into it, clamping his right hand over his other ear.

'It's Doug,' said his caller.

'Doug? Doug who?' yelled Waring.

'The Doug who saw you kill the woman and her wee girls.'

Waring shook his head slowly.

'I don't know any fucking Doug,' he said.

'You will, you bastard,' said the voice.

And the line went dead. Waring shouted 'fuck you' into the phone and shoved it back into his pocket.

In the darkness of the driveway outside his house, Davidson put away his mobile, got into his car and drove off into the town centre. The call had confirmed that Waring was there and that he was full of booze.

'What d'you do that for, you bloody sadist?'

The voice made Waring jump. The woman was back for more. He looked at her. She'd retouched her make-up although her lip was still seeping blood and around her mouth

118

the marks of his violence were still evident.

'Piss off, you old bag,' he said.

Her face reddened as she turned to him to match his insult. He was ready.

'One word. Just one word and I'll pull that tit right off. You heard me. Piss off!'

One final look convinced her. She moved away without any attempt to answer him, only muttering a tight 'Bastard!' to herself as she pushed through the hard wall of men, trying to hold on to her tears until she was clear of them.

Two pints later, Waring had had enough. He staggered out and waved down a taxi. The driver saw the state of him and knew the sort of incoherent ramblings to expect. Tonight, though (and he remembered it when the police asked him about it later), it was different. It concentrated on the name Doug, threatening impossible torments and throwing out what sounded like brash challenges. At one point, (and this he remembered very clearly), Waring said 'Crushed her, the bitch! That'll teach 'em', but otherwise, there was nothing but threats to the mysterious Doug and the ranting of a night's booze.

Rhona was taking a night off. She'd turned down two regulars. One of them was Billy, who always understood when she said she wasn't available. The other wanted her to come to his house to 'christen' a new garage he'd built onto it. She'd been there a few times already and didn't like the set-up. He always preferred to arrange a meeting when his wife was in the vicinity, visiting a neighbour, shopping, or doing some other activity which meant that she could come home at any time. Rhona had little doubt that, if or when she did get to the garage, his wife would be in the house.

Tonight, she just wanted to enjoy her own space. She was drinking vodka and orange and watching a quiz show which seemed to rely on people being impossibly stupid, especially the presenters. The mobile was switched off, so none of her clients could bother her, but the phone beside the bed had been ringing for ages. She hadn't left it off the rest because she'd heard that that caused all sorts of problems. Only a few of her friends knew the number but, somehow, the nuisance caller had got hold of it, too, and she felt too fragile to cope with him. Laura could handle him better.

She didn't understand why the person ringing didn't give up. Surely by now it was obvious that she was out, or that she wasn't going to answer it. But, as it kept beating out its insistent double trill, she began to wonder whether it was someone who knew she was in and who had important news for her. Maybe something had happened to her mother. Maybe the police had been asking about that guy who'd given her a lift. No, nobody else knew about that. In the end, once it was obvious that it wouldn't stop, she got up, went through, grabbed the phone and almost shouted into it.

'What? Who is it?'

Immediately, she shivered as she heard the answer.

'If you ever make me wait like that again, I'll get very angry.'

It was the man. She felt the adrenaline surge. Said nothing. Waited.

'I hope your friend with the bad temper's not there again. Told him about me, did you? What is he, a minder?'

'He's a friend.'

'Ah. Bit of a mouthy one, though. Anyway, I was wanting to talk about your man. You know, the one they found in the ditch. They'll be looking for people who saw him, spent any time with him. Have you been in touch with the bizzies yet?'

Rhona shook her head, then realized what she was doing.

'No,' she said, her voice surprisingly clear.

'Don't you think you should? I mean, with him being killed, with a photo of you sitting in his car with him. I bet there's bits of his DNA stuff in your flat. He shagged you there, didn't he? Played a bit rough, too. You could probably say it was self-defence.'

Rhona felt her helplessness with him. He knew so much, but why was he playing with her? She was too scared to risk protesting.

120

'What d'you want?' she said.

'Oh, I'm just a bit of a tease really. I'm not sure what I want. Don't worry, though. I won't be saying anything to anybody. Well, not yet, not for a while. I know, let's talk about sex. How about telling me some of the things you get up to with your friends?'

Rhona was puzzled. Surely this wasn't it. Phone sex? There was more to it.

'What d'you mean?' she said.

'Your ears going, are they? Is that what too much fucking does to you? You heard me, I want to know what you do. Start with the boy friend. The mouthy one. What's he like?'

'I'm not talking about people,' Rhona began. He didn't let her get far.

'I don't think you understood me. Now listen. I'm telling you I want to hear what you get up to with your punters. I want details, size of pricks, where they put them, everything. Got it?'

OK, if that's really all he wanted, she could handle that. Or rather, Laura could. She took a deep breath and started talking.

SIXTEEN

When the report of Campion's disappearance came in, Carston grabbed at the chance to get out of the office. Ross was in a meeting so he took Spurle and Fraser with him.

'What the fuck's happening?' said Spurle. 'One minute we're shoving bits of paper about, the next we're up to our balls in missing persons.'

'You're never satisfied,' said Fraser.

Spurle drove and Carston wasn't surprised to hear that quite a few of the other drivers on the road were wankers.

'Ever thought of anger management?' he asked at one point.

'Canna help it, sir,' said Spurle, the 'sir' being drawn out a little as always, just to show that he didn't mean it. 'If folks piss you off, it's natural. No point managing it, the bastards'd win every time.'

Carston sighed. Spurle's relentlessly brutish consistency was depressing enough in itself, but each time he heard an example of it, Carston was uncomfortably aware that it reflected some of his own reactions. Either he'd spent too long with villains and their excesses or there was a blackness inside himself which he'd rather not think about. He felt it again when they stepped through Campion's door into the plush interior and looked round at the chairs and paintings and ornaments. Spurle whistled and said, 'Tell you what, if this wasna a crime scene already, I'd bloody well like to make it one.'

'I know what you mean,' said Fraser. 'When you think of the bastard living here with all this lot, and then the wee lassies he's …'

He stopped, unwilling to think about the damage that Campion did to his victims, and Carston had to push back the thoughts of what he'd do to Campion if only society would let him.

'Same as that fucking Gary Glitter. I'd castrate the bastards,' said Spurle.

122

'OK,' said Carston, 'We all agree the guy's a worthless shit, but let's do what we're paid for. Fraser, take a look upstairs, Spurle – the rooms at the back.'

As they went through the various rooms downstairs, it was obvious right away that this wasn't just about a missing person. Something nasty had gone on here. There were all sorts of knives in strange places, shoved down behind cushions and sellotaped under side tables. But the main focus was the hall. A small bronze statuette lay on the pale carpet near a yellowish stain, and some marks on the front door suggested it had been kicked open. Upstairs, everything was in order.

'Somebody came for him,' said Fraser.

'Doesn't look as if they took anything, though,' said Carston.

'There may be a safe somewhere,' said Fraser.

'Yeah, but look at all this stuff lying about,' said Carston. 'Dead easy to nick. It'd fetch a few bob, too.'

Fraser nodded.

'No,' said Carston. 'Whatever went on, it all happened out here by the door.'

'What about all the knives?' asked Spurle.

'Maybe they're always there,' said Carston. 'A prick like him – he'd always be scared of somebody wanting to have a go at him. Maybe he just wants to be prepared.'

Suddenly, a tiny female voice said, 'Two-twelve p.m.'.

Fraser held up his arm and pulled back his sleeve. He was wearing a brand new wrist watch.

'Talkin watch, sir. Present from Janice. Want to hear it again?'

Before Carston could reply, he pushed a button and the woman's voice repeated 'Two-twelve p.m.' He kept his finger on the button and Carston heard a cock begin to crow.

'Magic, eh, sir?' said Fraser, very pleased with himself.

'Shite,' muttered Spurle.

'Wonderful,' said Carston. 'Now switch the bloody thing off and let's get back and start things moving.'

As they got back into the car, Carston had a smile on his

face. Spurle might be a constant reminder of the beast that lurked within, but Fraser was the perfect foil for him. It was utterly predictable that he'd have a new gadget almost every month and take a childlike pleasure in sharing it with the world.

Back in the office, Ross was at his computer.

'Another one, Jim,' said Carston, as he came in and sat down to start organising the scene of crimes team.

Ross looked up.

'Campion. He hasn't done a runner; somebody came for him.'

Ross nodded slowly.

'Beginning to look like a pattern, isn't it?' he said.

'All Freddy's clients, you mean.'

'Aye. I mean, every time we get a new missing person recently, it's seemed like good news.'

Carston smiled.

'You're right. We need a bit more than that, though. What else connects them?'

Ross shuffled through some notes he'd been making, shaking his head as he did so.

'Nothing.'

Carston sat down and leaned back in his chair.

'You know, them being missing's one thing, ' he said, 'but I hope we're not going to get their bodies turning up all over the place.'

'Aye,' said Ross.

He knew what his boss was thinking and had had the same fears himself. While they simply had this puzzling series of disappearances, it was a challenge. The real concern, though, was that they might be some variation of the standard pattern of serial killings. Every police force knew the difficulties that that brought. One by one, victims disappear. Sometimes, but not always, the motive's sexual. If it isn't, it's not obvious that there's any connection between the murders unless you get some freak repetition of a pattern. Or else the sheer accumulation of unexplained disappearances starts you thinking that way. That's the nightmare.

When there's no motive, no bloodbath or orgy of killing, just this strange, relentless series of unexplained homicides, none of the normal methods of detection applies. There's no family or other relationship between murderer and victim, and according to the case histories, the guilty person's a perfectly ordinary human being, living an unremarkable life. The usual enquiries amongst informers produce nothing because serial killers don't belong to the criminal classes and so the other villains don't know them. However much they wanted these people to get their come-uppance, neither Ross nor Carston wanted to uncover that sort of menace in the town's granite streets or the empty glens around it.

At his front gate, Waring counted out the exact fare, handed it over with no attempt to add any tip, and turned to stagger away up the path. The driver offered a brief V-sign to the tottering back, got back into his cab and drove away. The house was one of a terrace. The previous owner, or maybe his predecessor, had planted a few Cypressus along its front to screen it from passers-by. On nights such as this, when he came home alone, Waring's habit was to turn aside as he got to his front door and lean back against the wall of the house to relieve himself at the base of the trees. He had an indistinct idea that urine was probably good for plants. It was the only type of gardening he ever bothered with. He fumbled with his zip, almost damaged himself as he eventually pulled it down, and began to snigger as he imagined, not for the first time, the scenario at the casualty department if he were to walk in brandishing an organ of which he was inordinately proud and demanding that it be set free by the sexiest nurse in the place. The relief as the stream of urine hit the tree trunk combined with the burst of amusement to drive Doug and the evening's disasters from his mind.

'Here you are, nursey,' he said out loud. 'Grab hold of this one.'

He saw nothing in the darkness, no shape, no movement. But, suddenly, his words were choked in his throat. Davidson had been waiting. One step was all it took to be beside

Waring and pull the sail bag down over his head. It was too late to react. He was in no state to resist anyway. His words were cut off. Hard, abrasive material was pressing against his face, his arms were pinned to his sides. He tried shouting but his cries were muffled. He felt rope being tightened around him. He threw himself to the side to try to get away but fell over. Breathing was hard and he felt the gorge rising in his throat. Strong fingers dug into his arms as he was gripped and pulled to his feet. He was hit, pushed, and bundled along, not knowing the direction he was taking, unable to cry out, hardly able to breathe, and quickly being sobered up by the terror of this unknown and unknowable attacker. He tripped and was immediately hauled up and shoved forward. He fell and struck his shins on some metal and the side of his head banged against something else. He knew he was in a car, on the floor. His hands were grabbed and clicked together by what felt like handcuffs, his legs were doubled up against his stomach, the car door was slammed and, very quickly, they were on their way.

He was in deep shit. The guy who'd chucked him into the car obviously didn't care whether he'd broken any bones and had left him tangled behind the seats. The bag or whatever it was over his head was still choking him and the soreness in his heaving throat was as acute as the pain jabbing through his shins and head. At this time of night, no-one could have seen anything, and the car was now banging along at speed, shaking him against the floor and the seats. The driver obviously didn't care whether he survived the journey or not. Yes, he was in deep shit.

With Waring, it wasn't like the others. He's what it's all about, of course. Tommy, Tara, Penny, Sally. So I tried to make myself think about them. I couldn't make the connection, though. There was something else going on. Things were changing. There was ... I don't know ... another reason, a thing I couldn't get into focus. It was more to do with me than with Tommy now. I was supposed to be ... well, redressing the balance but, instead, I was just ... feeling good.

Waring's unbelievable, though. When he was chained up and I took off the sail bag, he looked round the cellar and started right away.

'What the fuck's this?' he screamed. 'Fuck this, fuck this. Get these fucking things off, you bastard.'

'Shut up,' I said.

'Fuck you,' he shouted. 'Stop fucking me about.'

I picked up the sail bag and dragged it back over his head again. It didn't stop the screaming but it muffled it. I went up to fix myself a whisky and make a call. I was high.

Bailey's house stood amongst trees, shrubs, and herbaceous borders. The land behind it levelled off into woods that marked the beginnings of what the local farmers were forced to recognize as an environmentally sensitive area. Despite the pressure to develop it, and even the EU subsidies that had been offered for specific planting schemes, Bailey and his powerful neighbours had always managed to ensure that the vista from the back of their properties remained uncluttered.

Bailey had left the office early for a meeting in town, then, drawn by the sun, decided to spend the rest of the day in his garden. His particular pleasure lay in his roses. Over the trellis which had been staked at the bottom of the west wall, the clean clusters of 'White Cockade' mingled, thanks to his informed pruning and training, with the crushed creams and pinks of 'Compassion'. Beneath them, arching out from its base, was an unusual, buff-coloured musk-rose, whose name he'd never discovered because it had been given to him by a colleague. The combination of the three scents was overwhelming, and particularly pleasing to Bailey because it was his care which had ensured that they all kept flowering so late into the edges of winter. As well as enjoying their fragrance, he was working to prolong their display even further. His secateurs snipped, his ties were checked and repositioned, and the whole arrangement was carefully shaped and coaxed into a form that would continue to produce blooms well into November.

The high warble of a telephone needled into his mood. It came from the summer house in the south east corner. It was an extension line which he'd had installed because he'd already lost two mobiles, which had fallen out of his pocket as he was gardening, and spent ages looking for others which had dropped into shrubs or the compost heap. The house was too far away for him to hear the phone ringing there and get to it quickly, and he hated the idea of missing out on any deals that might be going. With a little flick of annoyance, he disentangled himself from the branches whose thorns plucked at his shirt, and walked the half dozen steps to the little white pavilion. He sat in its shelter, looking back towards the trellis, picked up the telephone and spoke, a little more brusquely than usual.

'Christopher Bailey.'

'It's me again, bastard,' was the immediate reply.

Bailey recognized the voice at once and his irritation turned instantly to anger.

'What the hell is this?' he said. 'Are you retarded or something? Stop playing stupid bloody games. You're …'

He broke off as a hissing sound came from the phone.

'Ssssh. No orders. No insults.'

'What's the game, then?'

'No game.'

'What the hell d'you want, then?' asked Bailey, chilled by the calm, quiet insistence of the caller.

'I've already told you,' said Davidson. 'It's death we're talking about. Yours.'

Bailey swallowed hard, desperate to stay in control.

'Yeah, well, I've talked to the police, pal. They know how to deal with sick phone calls,' he said. 'Easy to be brave and threatening, but they'll soon sort you out. They'll …'

Again the voice cut him off.

'Just listen, prick. Just sit there in your fancy garden shed and listen.'

Bailey felt another little chill of alarm. How did the caller know about his summer house? How did he know that's where he was taking the call rather than in the house? The voice ground on, clearly aware of the effect it was having.

'I'm thinking that it's maybe time to practise what I've been preaching. I think you can assume that it's over for you. I'll maybe call you again, maybe just once more. But that'll be it. There won't be any more. Won't be any need for them. You won't be around to answer them.'

The line clicked dead. Bailey was sweating. The man meant it. This was no crank call. He really was in danger. He sat staring at the roses, their perfume cold and sour in the air.

I wasn't surprised when I made the death threats that time. It was madness, posturing, but I couldn't resist it. I wanted to unhinge him, slap aside his smug bloody self-satisfaction. And it was satisfying too.

I was still OK at the surgery. Normal there. It was the usual. Relatively trivial stuff – counselling, prescriptions. One girl – I'd seen her twice before – she's probably got a crush on me. She reckoned she was having non-specific discomforts in her breasts and groin. I sent her through to Jill. Then, towards the end of the afternoon, Jimmy Roxburgh was a bit of a surprise. He'd been coming for about a year and a half. Ever since he'd lost his only daughter, Anne. Her mother died when she was seven and he'd brought her up on his own. Anne was a teacher. She'd taken some kids from her school off to Austria on a skiing trip. Near the end of the first week, on her way up the mountain in a chair-lift with two of the kids, their chair just fell off its cables. The retaining clips snapped, the safety back-up was too badly corroded to do its job and the three of them were flung out onto the rocks. Anne and one of the kids died in the hospital, the other kid's in a wheelchair. Always will be.

Jimmy was shattered. He could cope with bereavement. He'd had practice with his wife dying. But it was what the other people involved did that really upset him. The children's parents, the education authority, the headmaster, the travel agents, the ski-lift company; all of them started ducking and diving. The buck was flashing about like a bloody Frisbee. The two bodies and the mangled kid in the wheelchair didn't seem to matter. Everybody was trying to minimize damage to reputations or maintain cash-flow – sick stuff like that. Between them, they managed to spread the responsibility so thin that nobody could pinpoint who was really guilty. The maintenance firm had short-changed on the servicing, the operating company hadn't supervised them properly, the tour organizers had just assumed the people on the Austrian side knew what they were about, the school had never had any problems like this in the past ... And Anne was dead.

I'd talked a lot about it with Jimmy. Tried to help him through the worst times, gave him anti-depressants but mostly just listened and talked away some of the stresses. That afternoon, though, it was as if he was seeing all the ghosts again.

'What's up, Jimmy?' I said.

'The case is over.'

I knew that he meant the case for compensation brought by the parents of the two children involved. They didn't have their daughters any more, so they thought they'd like some money instead. They'd brought the case in Austria.

'What happened?'

'Judge said they shouldn't've let their children be looked after by unqualified adults.'

'So he's saying it was the parents' fault?' I said.

'That's the way it looked at first. Of course, all the rest of them – the education authority, travel agent, ski company – they were dead chuffed. They were off the hook.'

I waited. I could guess his news.

'So it's all down to the unqualified adult. That's what they called her. It's all Anne's fault.'

'The bastards,' I said.

'Aye,' he said. 'As well as being a teacher, she should have been a social worker, a ski-lift mechanic, and a bloody clairvoyant.'

'Can you appeal?'

'What's the point? I want to be rid of it all, Doc. I'm sick of it.'

130

I let him talk. It was a question of giving him the chance to unload some of the pressure. After about a quarter of an hour, I was beginning to get anxious about falling behind with my appointments. He asked if I could prescribe some more sleeping pills for him. I looked at him. Wondered what he was thinking.

'You wouldn't be planning anything ... desperate, would you, Jimmy?'

He looked at me.

'What? Suicide, you mean?' Then he smiled. 'No. Don't worry. Anne would never forgive me.'

'Neither would I.'

I wrote the prescription, fixed another double appointment to give us more time to talk and shook his hand.

'You'll get through it. Don't let the bastards win,' I said.

'They probably already have,' said Jimmy. 'But they won't win the second leg.'

Davidson's last patient was Jessie. She told the usual tale of threats from her husband and wanted more pain killers. Davidson checked her records and realized that it was far too early for a repeat prescription. He talked with her, sympathized but, eventually, sent her home with instructions to take her pills properly and regularly, and rest as much as possible.

It wasn't yet five when she got home but, just after she'd arrived, her old man had been brought home from the pub by his pals. She heard them coming and hurried out into the passageway to hide under the stairs. Squinting out at them, she saw from her husband's state that at least he wouldn't be causing any trouble that evening. The men carried him through the door into the flat. Jessie stayed put, waiting there until she heard them leave. Then, when she was sure that everyone had gone, she crept quietly back, closing the door without a sound.

Looking at the two of them now and the state of their flat, it was difficult to believe that Harry Givens had once held down a good job and lived a comfortable suburban life.

He was a maintenance engineer who'd specialized in turbines. He'd worked at Pullins Engineering for eighteen years and it was a shock when he saw his name on a list of redundancies one December. His union had tried to fight for him but Christopher Bailey had brushed their protests aside with spurious statistics about streamlining the operation and rationalizing resources. Harry was fifty-eight and found it impossible to get another engineering job. He'd worked for a while as an assistant in B & Q, but relied more and more on booze to ease his troubles. Eventually, it cost him that job, too, and, from then on, the downhill rush just got faster.

Jessie's care as she crept up to him was wasted. He was laid out on the sofa, head lolling back, saliva dribbling down across his cheeks, breathing the coarse breaths of the heavily sedated.

'Pig,' said Jessie, in a whisper. The rasping breaths continued.

'Filthy, fat pig,' she said, in a normal voice. Still there was no response.

'Filthy, fat, bastard pig of a bastard,' she said, quite loudly, making V-signs right under his nose. The man slept on.

It was a long time before she began to tire of this private vengeance. Only when Harry snorted and half-turned on the sofa did she suddenly fall into a terrified silence and leap back against the wall. Luckily for her, his coma was unbroken. The action of turning had, however, uncovered the side pocket of his jacket, and Jessie's eyes were caught by the corners of some pieces of paper sticking out of it. Her heart thumped inside her scrawny ribs as she bent forward to look more closely. It was money. She looked hard at his face. The snoring was deep. Her head tight with panic, she moved beside him and reached for the notes. They caught on the flap of the pocket and she had to pull to ease them free. Still there was no sign from the sleeper. One more gentle pull and they were in her hand. A tenner and a fiver. There was a lot of change in the bottom of the pocket, but she didn't intend to risk getting at that; the fortune she held was enough. She took it to the bedroom and jammed it into the gap under the skirting board behind the wardrobe. She knew that, when he woke up the following day and realized how little money he had in his pockets, he'd curse himself for having spent so much in the pub. His temper would be taken out on her, but at least he'd never suspect that she'd taken the money. His opinion of her was too low to allow that she might dare to do such a thing.

SEVENTEEN

DC Bellman had been detailed to follow up the findings on the golf course grave and collate them as they came in. They'd already established that the body had been buried last October at the earliest. By checking their lists, they'd quickly given the forensic guys some possible IDs of people who'd gone missing around then.

Bellman knocked at Carston's door and came in.

'We've got a name for you, sir. The golf course guy.'

'Great. Who was he,' said Carston.

'Robert Davies. Lived in Aberdeen. Stayed in Cairnburgh now and again. Worked for an offshore drilling contractor.'

'Name rings a bell,' said Carston, looking at Ross.

Ross clicked keys on his computer.

'Yes, Rhona Kirk, remember? She said he raped her. He disappeared a couple of months later.'

'Bloody hell. And she's gone AWOL, too.'

Ross nodded. Bellman was hovering, waiting.

'OK,' Carston said to him. 'Great stuff. What else is there?'

'Well, we knew he had a fight, but it must've been a real ding-dong.'

'How come?'

'Stuff between his teeth. They reckon it's not his. He was biting at something or somebody. Probably scratching, too, but there wasn't a lot of flesh left on his hands, so they couldn't really say.'

'Any DNA in it?' asked Ross.

'Aye,' said Bellman. 'They're sending the profile with the rest of the stuff.'

'Good. OK, stick with it. Let me have anything that comes in.' said Carston.

Bellman went out.

'Well, what d'you think?' said Carston.

Ross pondered for a moment.

'I don't see that it connects with the others at all,' he said.

'Maybe not,' said Carston. 'But it's another man who had a go at a woman and got away with it. Same as Bailey and Dobie, and Campion, too, except that his was a wee girl.'

'We'll have a job bringing them together, though,' said Ross.

'How about what's-her-name? – Rhona Kirk? Anything turned up?'

Ross shook his head. He was scrolling through names on his screen.

'No,' he said, 'but there is one thing.'

He highlighted some text and turned the screen for Carston to see. It was a name, Ian Stride, and a date, June 30th.

'The guy they found near Dundee?' said Carston.

'Yes, but look at the date. He went missing more or less the same time as she did.'

'So?'

Ross swung his screen back and clicked it clear.

'Nothing really. Just that the only two missing guys who've turned up so far were sort of connected with her. Both dead.'

Carston laughed.

'Christ, Jim. I think I'm contaminating you. Not like you to play guessing.'

'What else have we got?' said Ross.

Carston nodded.

'OK. Let's try looking a bit harder for her, Get her photograph sent round again. Try Dundee, Perth, the places near where that guy's body turned up.'

Ross made a note.

'Now, this Davies guy. Let's see if we can find out what he was doing on the golf course back in … October, wasn't it?'

Ross nodded.

'Check him against the stuff we've collected.'

When the archaeologist had finished her work, they'd

made a thorough search of the whole area and asked around to find out who had access to the golf course back in October, and whether anything special was going on there. Apart from a new development of luxury homes on the land behind the clubhouse and a pro-am tournament sponsored by an oil company, no-one remembered anything out of the ordinary.

'One thing,' said Ross.

'What?'

'With all this going on, I think we should maybe pay a bit more attention to Bailey's phone calls.'

'You should be running a charity,' said Carston, but he knew that Ross was right.

When I started thinking about Gayla's visit, I was too busy to worry about the cellar. I called in at Sainsbury's on my way home. Got some duck breasts and salad. She came just after eight. The table was laid, Modern Jazz Quartet playing, smell of roasting duck. I wanted her to know I'd gone to some trouble. We went through to the living room – bottle of Chablis, bucket of ice. No expense spared.

'Go easy with mine,' she said, as I started pouring. 'I have to drive home.'

'Not necessarily.'

'Oh? You going to keep me here?'

'Maybe.'

'You have plans?'

'Only one.'

We clinked glasses, drank and sat on the sofa. She was wearing a long, loose skirt and a blouse made of some synthetic material. Looked like satin. Felt like it, too. She didn't need make-up, but she'd brushed on a touch of eye shadow. Her eyes looked darker than usual.

'You look good,' I said.

'So do you.'

It was a while since I'd entertained a woman on her own. Gayla was easy to be with, though. No pressure.

'Busy day?' she said.

'The usual.'

'Any gynaecology?'

'Not yet.'

We talked a bit more. I felt myself relaxing. Before she came, I was busy preparing the meal, getting ready. Now, with the wine, her perfume and the idea of what we'd soon be doing, the tensions just went. Never occurred to me to think of the guys in the room below us.

The food was good. We took our time over it.

'You're in a good mood,' she said, as I was clearing the plates away.

'It's you. You're so relaxing.'

'I don't want you falling asleep, though.'

I topped up the wine.

'I won't. Tell me about your secrets.'

'What?'

'You know, things that might surprise me if I knew them.'

'I haven't got any. Mind you, even if I had, I wouldn't tell you, would I?'

'How about fantasies?'

'Oh Andrew, that's a bit blatant, isn't it? I thought you were more subtle.'

'No, I don't mean sexual ones. Well, not necessarily.'

'What other sorts are there?'

'I don't know,' I said. 'Power, changing the world, making it better.'

'God, no. That's not fantasy, that's politics.'

'Same thing.'

'What's this all about? Terrorism? Yob culture?'

'No. Just ... people. Closer to home. Ordinary stuff.'

'Is that what you were thinking of, then?'

'Sort of.'

'Tell me.'

'Oh nothing. It's just ... there's a patient up at Foresterhill. In a coma. Kicked in the head by hooligans. And nobody got charged for it.'

'Ah,' she said. 'Justice fantasies, is it?'

'Don't you ever feel you want to do something about it when you read about that sort of thing?'

'Yes, I suppose so. Most people do, don't they? Can't, though.'

'Can't what?'

'Do anything.'

'Why not?'

'Look what happened when the News of the World got the paedophile hunters on the streets,' she said. 'Drove that paediatrician out of her home. And those poor bloody immigrants: everybody taking turns to beat the shit out of them.'

'That's different. But if you know somebody's guilty ... definitely know ...'

'According to the Daily Mail, that's just about everybody.'

'You know what I mean.'

'Yes, I do. But there's nothing we can do. It's OK for Charles Bronson but I don't see me acting as a vigilante. Or you.'

I nearly laughed. I wondered what she'd think and say if I took her downstairs, showed her the men in their chains. She'd be ... shocked, speechless. Then, all of a sudden, I found myself thinking of chaining her to one of the other pillars.

'Bloody hell,' I said.

'What?' she said.

I just shook my head. I had to smile. Where the hell had that come from?

'Ever been into bondage?' I asked.

She put down her glass.

'I'm getting a bit worried about you,' she said. 'your mind's jumping about like a ... well, like a thing that jumps about. Power? Changing the world? Vigilantes? Bondage? What are you on?'

Good question. For a moment, I toyed with the idea of answering it, telling her the real motives that were driving me then, telling her about the cellar. Stupid bugger. I'd never be able to do that. With anybody.

'Nothing really,' I said. 'Just ... you get patients stuck in *situations that've got nothing to do with them. Things they didn't ask for. It'd be nice to be able to make things better.'*

'According to whom?'

'What?'

'What do you mean by 'better'? Maybe their idea of better wouldn't be the same as yours.'

I looked at her.

'Christ,' I said. 'Sex and wisdom.'

'Yes, about sex ...' she said.

'What about it?'

'That's what I mean, what about it?'

There was a smile in her eyes but the question was genuine. We kissed. Long, gentle. I knew sex wouldn't be all screaming, scratching and biting. It'd be slow. We lay back on the sofa. Neither of us was in a hurry. By the way, I'm telling you all this because it's important. It was all slow, stroking, easy. Then she starts sighing and I can sense how much she wants it. But it was different. I was enjoying it alright. All the usual stuff. But nothing was happening. With me, I mean. All the enjoyment was sort of in my head. Not where I needed it.

She soon knew something was wrong. Well, bound to wasn't she? She didn't say anything. Just smiled, kissed. But nothing.

'Sorry,' I said.

'What is it?'

'No idea.'

'Is it me?'

I kissed her again.

'Definitely not. You're beautiful, gorgeous, sexy ... It's me. I don't know.'

'Let me try again,' she said, but I wouldn't let her.

'No. Let's leave it a minute.'

We were quiet then. Still kissing, stroking, but it felt wrong. I think she thought it was her fault. It wasn't, though. Christ knows what it was. It had happened before but usually when I was too drunk to perform. I wanted her, I was enjoying everything we'd been doing, so what the hell was going on?

We talked about it. She said it'd be a one-off problem and that it wouldn't stop her trying again in the future. She said it didn't matter and she was great about it. After she'd gone, though, I couldn't stop thinking about it. Why? What was different? I had no idea.

EIGHTEEN

Rhona was having to turn down business. She now had so many regulars that she was booked over two weeks in advance. It varied, but most days she saw four or five men and she wanted to make sure she kept some place for a social life. She'd met some female students who shared one of the flats in her building and enjoyed going to pubs and clubs with them. None of them knew what she did, and her lack of flirtatiousness made them all think she was a shy wee thing from the country somewhere. But she loved listening to their comments about the men they saw and was sometimes surprised by their naivety. They all seemed to think that they'd have their flings, then settle into a relationship with someone and do interesting things. Rhona had heard too many women complaining about the terrible sex they had in a marriage and knew that even the most compliant men played away.

As she drove home from an appointment in a private house just outside Perth, where she'd spent three hours basically helping a man of sixty to fuck a bowl of fruit, item by item, she loved the feel of the warm air blowing in the car window. It was the first day of September and the beginning of what promised to be a long, soft Autumn. On her right, the Tay was sparkling, and she was glad that the evening's visitor would be Billy. He was never demanding and talking to him was usually fun.

Back home she ate a salad of rocket and feta cheese with black olives as she watched the news. She had a quick shower and was brushing her hair when the phone went. The caller's voice immediately cut into her feeling of well-being. It was the man she thought of as the stalker.

'Busy?' he asked.

When she answered, Rhona's voice was quiet, meek even. It was astonishing how her toughness dropped away when she heard him.

'I've got an appointment later,' she said.

'Not that wanky boy-friend again?'

'Just … an appointment.'

'Only, I was wondering, what did you think of that baby elephant thing in your mother's front room? What d'you think she uses it for?'

Rhona was no longer surprised by how much the man knew about her. He'd already proved that he'd been watching her for weeks, maybe months, and that he'd even been inside her house in Cairnburgh.

'I don't know what you mean,' she said.

'Course you do. That thing with the oversized trunk. I reckon it might be a vibrator, don't you?'

'I don't know.'

'Surprised she needs it, really. With the procession of dads she brought home, eh? Or were they for you?'

'No,' she said.

'That vibrator of yours is much better. More … you know … more … discreet. Handy where you keep it, too. Underneath that doll in the drawer.'

Rhona couldn't hold back a little gasp. Her flat was too high up for anyone to see through the window. Somehow, he'd got in. She looked around, trying to see evidence of the intrusion.

'What d'you want?' she said.

There was a pause before he answered.

'We'll get round to that one day. No rush, is there?'

'If you want me to talk about sex, we'll have to …'

'No, no. I've had enough of that,' he said, interrupting her. 'All gets to sound the same after a while, doesn't it? Don't get me wrong, you're very good at it. But it's not the real thing, is it?'

Rhona tried to put the sexiness back in her voice.

'Is that what you want? The real thing? Because I'm good. I could …'

Suddenly, there was anger in his voice.

'Shut up,' he said. 'Stop talking like a slag. Listen, you'll know soon enough what I want. For now, just remember, I know everything about you. Try me. Go on.'

'What?'

'Ask me something.'

Rhona shook her head but said nothing.

'Any time,' he went on. 'Any time you want to check how much I know, just ask.'

Rhona could think of nothing to say. She didn't want to make him more angry. When he spoke again, his voice was under control, metallic in its coldness.

'Scary, isn't it? Not knowing who I am, when I'm watching you. Not knowing when I'll introduce myself. Because I'm going to. One day I'm going to. Not when you've got a customer. I wouldn't do that to a guy. Well, maybe to that mouthy prick of a boy friend. No, not even with him. When you're on your own. That'd be the thing.'

'Is this about Bob Davies?' she asked suddenly.

Again there was a pause.

'No, but I'll tell you all about you and him if you like,' he said. 'About the rape, about how he disappeared, just like that.'

The doorbell made her jump. The man obviously heard it, too.

'Ah, pity. Time's up,' he said. 'Never mind, another time.'

She went to the intercom, lifted the handset and heard Billy's voice.

'It's only me.'

'OK, come up,' she said, pressing the release button for the front door.

'Look, I've got to go,' she said.

'I know. Don't worry. Just one thing, remember I always know when you're in. So if I phone and you don't answer, I'll get angry. You got that?'

'Yes,' said Rhona.

'Good. Now have a nice evening.'

And he rang off.

Rhona took several deep breaths before she opened the door. Billy was just turning onto her landing. She smiled at him, put her arms round his neck, kissed him and hugged him hard. It surprised her how good it was to see him.

'Wow,' he said. 'I haven't even paid yet.'

She kissed him again and they went into the kitchen. She poured a glass of wine for herself, opened a beer for him and they took them through to the bedroom.

'Can we just lie down for a bit?' she asked.

'I thought that was the idea,' said Billy.

She smiled, folding herself into him on the bed.

'I'd just like a bit of a cuddle first.'

He held her, kissed her hair.

'What's this all about, then?' he said.

'Ssssh,' she said, and they lay there, each making gentle, stroking movements over the other's skin.

So close did they feel that, when their strokings evolved into progressively more eager foreplay, for both of them it felt like making love. It also helped Billy to last longer than usual and, when they'd finished, he gave a huge sigh and said, 'Christ, I bet that's going to cost me a fortune'.

She laughed, filled their glasses again and came back to prop herself beside him on the bed. The mood was still good and they talked and joked and Billy probed away to try to find out what was so different this evening. In the end, she felt so good with him that she told him that she was still getting the calls. He made angry noises again, but settled down when she said she needed him to be as calm and good as he'd been before.

'He called just before you came,' she said. 'It upset me. I was glad to see you.'

'Well, if that's the effect,' said Billy, 'I wish he'd call more often.'

'I don't.'

'No, sorry. Stupid thing to say.'

They talked some more then, in a silence that neither of them felt the need to fill, Billy said, 'You know the answer, don't you?'

'To what?'

'Him. The guy on the phone.'

'No, what?'

'Come and live with me. He won't try anything there.'

It was another of his recurrent themes. Rhona knew that he meant it and, if she'd been a normal woman with a normal job, the idea might have had some appeal. But they both knew why it wouldn't work. She put her glass on the bedside table and rolled over so that she was lying on top of him.

'And you'd let me take calls from punters on your phone?' she said.

'Yes.'

'And you'd sit at home while I went out to hotels and restaurants with other guys.'

There was a hesitation before the answer.

'Yes,' said Billy.

'You're a big great bloody liar,' she said, punctuating each adjective with a kiss on a different part of his face. 'But thanks for asking me. You're one of the gentlemen, Billy.'

She felt him responding to her but, just as she slid her tongue down across his stomach, the phone rang again.

'Shit,' said Billy.

Rhona didn't want to stop what she was doing but she remembered the man's threat. She looked up at Billy, who raised his eyebrows and gestured his permission for her to answer it. She picked up the receiver and had no time to say anything. The voice started immediately.

'I know your customer's probably still in the shop, but I thought I'd let you know they've dug up Bob Davies. I should've mentioned it earlier but I forgot.'

And the line went dead. She put the phone back and Billy noticed little beads of sweat on her forehead right up at the hairline.

'Him again?' he asked.

She nodded.

'I should've answered it,' said Billy.

'No,' she said. 'Just cuddle me again. That's what I want most.'

The impotence was good for some people though. I thought the guys in the cellar would probably be going without food that night – what with Gayla staying and so on. But when she'd gone, I heated up the usual rehydrated stuff and dumped it onto their plastic plates. I had to change into my black jeans and sweater and put on the mask. I was still confused about Gayla. It made me more irritated that I had to prepare food for them and couldn't just sit down and work it all out. I thought about them, one by one. What they'd done. So I picked up the salt cellar, took its top off, poured a pile of salt in the middle of each plate, mixed it all up. Bloody childish. Made me feel good. Calmed me down. Brought the other me back, I suppose. I was in charge again.

For a change, I stayed with them while they ate. Obsessive, see? About all of it. I suppose I was making myself see the reality of what I was doing. The noises they made, the ridiculous scene, the smell – it was all down to me. I was as chained down there as they were. I had to feed them, empty their bucket. My planning was good, the timing, the effort, it had all worked, against all the odds. And I was stuck with it. Nobody knew they were there. I'd done it. Except for Bailey, of course, but I'd deal with him in time.

'What's going on then?' said Waring.

I just looked at him.

'What's the idea? Going to top us, are you?'

Silly bugger. He didn't realize what terrible timing it was. They all wanted to know, of course, but they were afraid to ask. It was a question I'd asked myself, too. But not for a while up till then. Suddenly faced with it like that, especially that evening, after the fiasco with Gayla, I felt I ought to make up my mind. Up till then, I'd been more or less toying with alternatives. The problem was, I didn't know the answer. So what I said ... well, it came as a surprise to me as well as them.

'Probably.'

I was never going to kill them. That wasn't the idea. Just teach them a lesson. But, with all of them there, and me thinking back on what they'd done, and, worst of all, feeling that there was little difference between them and me, I started to think that maybe death was the only logical outcome. I

147

didn't know what was right any more. It was all so bloody awful. So many victims, so much contempt for other people, and there was I, in amongst it, adding to it. There was no way out. They all had to go. Including me. And, of course, Bailey.

NINETEEN

Ross was keeping an eye on the list of missing persons and so he quickly picked up the fact that Waring had disappeared too. One of his pals from the rig had gone round to see him and found a couple of days' papers sticking out of the letter box and no sign of him. It was easy to trace his movements. He'd only come ashore the previous Wednesday and no-one had seen him after the taxi had dropped him at home. A word with the barmaid and the taxi driver helped to paint a very clear picture of the hours before he vanished.

Carston had looked out Waring's file to refresh his memory. It wasn't really necessary but he forced himself to read all the notes anyway. It had happened just over two years before. Waring had spent a long Saturday lunchtime at his usual pub. He'd drunk five pints of lager before driving to a bookmaker's to put on a fifty pound win Yankee. He drove back to the pub, watched the first race on the pub's television, swilling down more beer, and some extra whisky chasers for luck. His horse lost and, to make things worse, the commentator announced that the one he'd chosen in the next race was a non-runner. His own form was more reliable than that of his horses. His predictable response to what he saw as his bad luck was to become more aggressive, insult everyone within shouting range, and eventually throw a half full glass of beer into the fireplace. That's when the landlord chucked him out onto the pavement.

As he always did, whatever his condition, Waring got into his car and drove off. Less than two hundred yards away, where the street joined the main road, shoppers screamed and jumped aside as he failed to make the bend, drove onto the pavement, and smashed Tara Davidson and her two children up against the wall of the Post Office.

He was arrested, found guilty, sentenced to a year in prison and banned from driving for ten years. The six months remission he was given for good behaviour completed a neat equation; two months in jail for each life he'd taken.

150

'What a bastard,' said Carston, as he closed the file and pushed it away.

'Aye,' said Ross. 'He's not learned from it either. The taxi driver said he was talking a lot about some woman on his way home. It must have been the one he ran over. 'Crushed the bitch. That'll teach her.' Stuff like that. No remorse. No guilt about it. Even seemed to be boasting, according to the driver.'

'Well, if somebody's topped him, there's plenty with bloody good motives,' said Carston.

Ross nodded. At the time of the trial, lots of folk in Cairnburgh had had their say about the gap between the deed and the punishment. There'd been plenty of threats of the kind that began 'Just give me a few minutes on my own with him and ...'

'It's too bloody weird altogether though,' said Ross.

'What?'

'Well, the guy whose family he killed committing suicide in June and now he disappears. Got to be linked, hasn't it?'

'You'd think so,' said Carston. 'And Rhona Kirk and her guys, and McPhee and the others.'

'If they're all part of the same thing, we're in trouble.'

Carston's expression was serious.

'Yes. But there's too many for it to be just one guy, surely.' He reached for his note book and flicked back through the pages. 'Two at the end of June, nothing in July, then 3rd, 17th, 20th, 27th August, and now Waring.'

'Speeding up, isn't it?'

Carston nodded. 'Looks like it. We'd better start getting serious.'

As they talked on, their conversation simply confirmed what they'd already more or less admitted; that the only connection between the missing persons was the fact that, apart from Rhona Kirk and Ian Stride, they'd got away with some pretty serious crimes. The victims of Waring, Bailey, Dobie, Campion and Davies had been female but those were the only potential links. The men and the woman belonged to very different age and social groups, their habits, their haunts, their preferred pastimes – none of them overlapped. They had absolutely nothing in common.

'That's maybe a link in itself,' said Carston.

'How?'

'Well, there's no accidental connections they might have had through business or leisure activities, no mutual acquaintances, no obvious avenues of contact. It's connection by default.'

'Don't get it.'

'It's a bit iffy but they're so far apart that whatever links we do find are more likely to be worth following up.'

Ross's reply was cut by the phone ringing. Irritated by the interruption, Carston picked it up and said, 'What is it?'

'Detective-Inspector Carston?'

'Yes. Who are you?' said Carston, aware that he was being ruder than he should since the caller was obviously a member of the public rather than one of the men on the front desk.

'Christopher Bailey. I take it you remember me?'

Carston resisted the temptation to say 'only too well'.

'I'm not sure I do,' he said.

'This is no time for the stuff you call wit. This is serious.'

'Very well, Mr. Bailey,' said Carston, resigned to an unpleasant few moments. 'How can I help you?'

'I'm being subjected to some very unpleasant abuse.'

'That's hard to believe, sir.'

There was a silence on the line.

'Look, I'm talking about a threat to my life. You may be used to violence but I'm not.'

Carston thought plenty but said nothing.

'I've already had three calls, all from the same individual and …'

'I know, your friend Mr. Reismann has been on to me already.'

'Good.'

'I take it you've no idea who this caller might be?'

'No.'

'Well, we do have one or two other things that are occupying us at the moment, but we're already looking into Mr. Reismann's earlier report and I'll send someone up to see you first thing in the morning. If you'd like to give me one or two details now, I'll be able …'

'Not good enough,' Bailey interrupted. 'Death threats don't just happen during office hours.'

'Look, where are you phoning from?' asked Carston.

'Home, of course.'

'Good. Are the doors and windows locked?'

'Why?'

'Because if they are, there's no immediate danger. Why don't you give me the details now so that I can brief someone and send them over tomorrow morning?'

'Listen Carston, to my direct knowledge, you've already had four separate interviews with your chief constable. You wouldn't want there to be a fifth, would you?'

'Rather an epidemic of threatening telephone calls, isn't there?' said Carston. 'Save your breath, Mr. Bailey. There's nothing I can do tonight. Don't worry, though. I'll make sure you get the best treatment available. I'll come round myself in the morning.'

Although she still had her own council flat, Jessie had taken to spending time with some of the homeless men and women at various spots in the city. She'd attached herself to two particular individuals, Lennie and Dora. They were sitting on a bench beside the canal. On the days when one of them had got hold of some booze, they became philosophers and forgot about the acrid little quarrels that erupted into every other day of their contact. Instead, Lennie always reminisced about the social heights he'd scaled, while Dora deplored the pollution of the water that flowed by them and remembered a time when trout with silver skins had leapt onto the hooks of school friends who'd stopped briefly on golden afternoons on their way to jam scones and loving homes. Jessie could never match the quality of their experiences, her mind having been preoccupied for too long with a husband and his fists and the pains in her chest and stomach.

It was late afternoon, and the gods had obviously decided that it would be a good one. The healing grazes under Jessie's lower lip and a spread of invisible bruises on her chest, stomach and back betrayed the fact that her husband hadn't been too pleased to wake up skint and had punished her for it ever since. But she'd hung on to the money, keeping it hidden, afraid to spend it unless he found out and made the connection. Bit by bit, though, she'd used it up and today, she'd spent the last of it on a bottle of sweet sherry (Lennie's favourite). Down by the canal, it had bought her some instant friends.

Across the water, two lads in black leather jackets were sharing a spliff. They'd been watching the antics of Jessie and the rest for almost forty minutes, laughing at their exchanges, fascinated by the slow ballet of their movements. Jessie was dancing, some of her new friends stood up and gesticulated at her, others shouted, others began their own versions of the dance. Music and arguments threaded across the water to the two young men. One of them spat.

'Dirty old bastards!' he said.

'Look at that one,' said his pal, pointing. They looked as Jessie stood preening herself beside Lennie. Her movements continued as she carried her bottle to a bald man in an army greatcoat and a grey scarf. She offered him a drink, then held it behind her as he reached for it. She obviously wanted payment. The two youths were disgusted as they saw the man lean forward, put his hand on Jessie's chest and his mouth against hers. They heard her laugh as she broke away from this grotesque embrace to hand the bottle to him. As he tilted his head back to drink, Jessie's hand went between his legs and stayed there. The man showed no sign of noticing. The leather jackets creaked as their wearers sat up.

'That's fucking gross,' said one.

'Aye,' said the other. 'Shouldn't be allowed.'

His pal looked at him knew what he meant. He smiled and nodded. They looked back at the group over the river, their attention fixed on Jessie as she danced on.

154

TWENTY

Carston and Ross arrived at Bailey's just after nine o'clock. They rang the bell and had to wait for two minutes before the door was finally opened and Bailey motioned them in. He pointed at a door leading off the wide entrance hallway. They waded through the carpet and into the room he'd indicated. It was some sort of study, and, for a room that was supposedly a working area, its opulence was certainly not understated. Georgian furniture, velvet curtains, walls crammed with oil paintings, vases, glasses, antique crystal decanters, and a bookcase carrying rows of volumes whose appearance suggested that if they weren't first editions, they certainly deserved to be. Carston wasn't surprised to see Freddy Reismann standing at one of the windows.

'Can we get on with it?' said Bailey, sitting at the chair behind the desk. Reismann moved across and sat beside him.

'Right then,' said Carston, choosing a chair beside the window, 'tell us everything you can about this business.'

Reismann nodded approval to his client and Bailey began describing the phone calls he'd received, giving only snorted answers to the questions Carston interposed on the way.

'And you say you've no idea who it might be?'

'Of course not.'

'Nothing special about the voice? It was definitely male?'

'Yes.'

'Any accent? Peculiarities? Old? Young?'

'It was difficult to say. It was muffled.'

'And you've no particular enemies? No more than the rest of us, I mean. No-one who might wish you harm?'

'Not that I'm aware of.'

Carston resisted the temptation to provide a ready-made list for him.

'Did this caller give any idea of how he might be planning ... whatever it is he's planning?' he went on.

'Is that likely?' sneered Bailey.

156

'I mean indirectly. He didn't perhaps let something slip, some expression that didn't belong, a word, anything?'

'Nothing. He was … well, cold.'

Reismann sat forward on his chair.

'It must be obvious that my client is under considerable stress,' he said.

Carston wondered whether Reismann realized how much that cheered him up.

'Yes, I know, Mr. Reismann,' he said. 'I don't really know what to suggest, though.'

'He seems to know an awful lot about Mr. Bailey – his gardening, his summer house …' said Reismann.

'Not difficult really. A pair of binoculars up in the woods would surely give that away.'

'So he's been watching me,' said Bailey.

'I suppose he may have. But studying you from a distance and actually getting to you are very different exercises.'

'Is that what you call death threats, exercises?' said Bailey.

Carston saw how uncomfortable he was. He had no time for the man, but he'd do his job.

'I'll do everything possible to get to him,' he said. 'So, with your permission, I'll arrange for a crime prevention officer to come over later this morning to check over your precautions, your alarm systems, locks and so on. Is that convenient?'

Bailey sighed.

'Yes. I can ring Joan and get my calls transferred here. Fridays are usually relatively quiet.'

'Good. Once they've finished here, I'll get them to look over the office as well. That'll be this afternoon, I expect.'

'Very well,' said Bailey, resigned now to being in Carston's care.

'I don't suppose you'd consider taking some time off work, would you?'

Carston's question was serious. Bailey looked at him.

'Why?'

'Just makes things easier if you stay in the one place, that's all. I mean, if we check over everything here, you'll probably feel happier and we'll know exactly what we're dealing with, won't we?'

Bailey sighed.

'I'll arrange to bring things home this afternoon and get on with them here next week,' he said.

'That's fine. Let's hope it's been sorted by then.'

His dislike of Bailey was gradually being supplanted by his fascination with the caller's approach and technique. He still felt the guilty pleasure at the man's pain, but he was searching about for a way of anticipating the next phone call, trying to get inside the mind of the person who was making them. He must have known, or at least suspected, that Bailey would bring in the police and get their protection. Maybe it wasn't the same man. Maybe there was no connection with McPhee and the rest. Carston looked at the edgy Bailey. His tormentor knew what he was doing. He'd wanted him to suffer, and he'd succeeded. It would have been enough to make him pity Bailey if he didn't know just what a bastard he was.

OK. I knew from the start that it'd be unpleasant. Couldn't be sure in what ways, but I thought ... well, insofar as I thought at all ... I thought I'd be able to handle it. I tried an experiment one night, though. It showed how much I'd changed.

I make pretty regular visits to the hospital pharmacist and, one time, I managed to grab a sample of Rohypnol. Hid it in amongst the legitimate drugs I was collecting. I was sort of getting an idea of what I might do with them, but I needed to test exactly how well the Rohynpol worked on each of them. Has different effects in different individuals. Shivering, mild nausea – they'd all have that. Their skin would tingle and gradually they'd lose all feeling in their arms and legs, then the rest of their body. Their heart rate would slow down, breathing would be shallow and then they'd move into the phase which intrigued me – the one the textbooks call stupor.

They'd just lie there then. Catatonic, muscles paralyzed, but still conscious. All Edgar Allen Poe. Scary, eh? They'd be lying there helpless, knowing what was going on, but not being able to do a thing about it. If the Rohypnol didn't do the business, I had a supply of Midazolam. That could be fatal, of course. But it gets eliminated from the body very quickly. See, I was thinking like a criminal. Easy.

I put the Rohypnol in their coffee. As I was measuring the doses, I knew that too much would kill them. Too bad. I mean, I didn't want them to die. Not yet. But, you know, it wouldn't bother me if they did.

I handed out the cups and watched them. I should've told you that, by then, they were used to it. We almost had a sort of relationship. They'd learned what they could and couldn't get away with. They knew if they behaved themselves, I'd stay a bit longer and they'd get a bit more light.

When the drug kicked in, it was obvious. Four of them just lying there with no noise, no movement. I checked their pulses. They were all slow, but regular. All but Campion were running a slight fever too. Nothing drastic though.

I used Waring for the trial. I'd brought a long sterile syringe with me. I squatted beside him and felt the back of his left hand. It was limp and soft as I lifted it, like a cut of meat. I felt down the groove between the bones of the middle and fourth fingers. Just below the knuckle I dug a bit harder to leave a white mark on his skin. Then I pushed the syringe through the mark until it came out through the palm on the other side.

It was strange. Waring had seen the syringe, so he knew that something was going on, and whatever it was, he guessed that it wasn't going to be good for him. Trouble is, he couldn't turn his head to look down, so he didn't know exactly what I was doing. As the needle was being pushed through, his face showed no sign of any pain, nothing. His muscles were slack, so his expression gave nothing away of what he was thinking. But you should've seen his eyes. Drilling into me, full of all sorts of pleading and begging and promises. And yet he didn't know what he was pleading for or what he should be afraid of. It was strange for both of us.

Maybe that was my eureka moment. I could do what I liked with them. Go as far as I liked. Mutilate them if I wanted to. It was like being God.

I did a few more things. Must've scared the shit out of Campion when he saw I was holding a scalpel. I took it down out of his eye line. Towards his groin. I just nicked him in the end. He didn't know that, though. Of course, sticking things into them, or even slicing bits off them was no good if they couldn't feel it. There was no point in dishing out physical punishment if I anaesthetized them first, but I'd got what I wanted out of the experiment and I knew I could knock them out if I wanted to. So then, I just ... messed about a bit. Childish really. Self-indulgent. I unlocked their wrists – held the chains up for them to see they were free. Made a few incisions, did a few procedures that'd make them feel uncomfortable when the effects of the Rohypnol wore off.

And I enjoyed it. As soon as Bailey was out of the way, I could finish it all.

The air outside looked crisp and sharp. With September came the first touches of Autumn. Before too long, Grampian would shrug its way into winter and the number of days Bailey could spend with his shrubs and roses would be severely curtailed by the winds and rain of November. He looked out at the tumble of grey and green foliage along the side wall of his patio, the lush spread of the lawn and the patches of muted colour where late-flowering shrubs showed how they'd been coaxed into a longer display than usual by the summer's surprising gentleness. He hadn't done any serious work in the garden since the previous week. The decision to put off reading the pile of papers that his secretary had parcelled up for him was easy. His attention was needed down at the bottom of the garden. Some of the rose-bushes had grown tall and leafy, and even though they still carried some blossoms, they'd have to be pruned back before the winds began to get at them and rock them about in the soil. And anyway, out there with his flowers, he could at least allow himself to feel that he could still choose how to spend his time. The house might be his temporary prison, but the garden offered its usual liberty. There was no debate. Just after two o'clock, he set aside the calculations and columns of figures and, in brown corduroy trousers and a grey sweater, he made his way down towards his summer house.

TWENTY-ONE

Rhona made sure that, when she went shopping, she dressed in simple, plain skirts and jackets and wore very little make-up. She was determined to keep Laura well out of sight. It was a quiet release for her to walk among people, unknown and unremarked. But her sex appeal was powerful and, although she didn't know it, she moved with a confidence that was at odds with her anonymous appearance. Despite the drabness she tried to cultivate, men still looked at her.

The stalker knew her habits, of course, and frightened her more and more by revealing just how often he'd seen her, what she'd been wearing, what she'd bought. She was beginning to feel that he was there all the time, one of the pale faces in the streets around her, always watching, maybe sometimes brushing against her. He'd begun to sprinkle his calls with sharp little threats. There was never anything specific, but little by little, his tone was changing. He lost his temper more often and, twice recently, had shouted that he was getting impatient and very angry with her before banging the phone down.

It was after one such outburst that she'd decided to get out among the crowds and try to feed off their normality. As she walked, she wondered how soon she'd be able to get away from Scotland altogether. Her bank account was healthier than ever and, even if she got no punters when she went south, she'd be able to live comfortably on it for several months. She'd have to set up a different website and make sure that the photos on it were as unlike Laura as they could be because she knew that he'd still come looking for her. And if she ran away, and he found her …

She shook the thought away and began flicking through a rack of CDs. None of them attracted her; lately, they all seemed to sound the same. The local evening news was just beginning on rows of television screens away to her right. She looked at her watch. She was due in Edinburgh for dinner and an overnight stay. It was a new punter and he couldn't make up his mind what he wanted so she'd decided to take the usual outfits – schoolgirl, nurse, policewoman and so on – and give him a little parade. They were packed and ready and she had plenty of time. She began to stroll back out towards the car park but suddenly stopped as a face flicked onto the television screens. It wasn't there for long but it sent a shock through her. It was a fuzzy snapshot of herself. She recognized it as one her mother had kept in a wooden frame on the mantelpiece. It had been taken at the wedding of a cousin and showed a Rhona who hadn't existed for a couple of years. The hair was dark, the face open, smiling, pretty, and she wore a large-brimmed blue hat. A telephone number ran across the front of her dress at the bottom of the screen. Rhona was too far away to hear what was being said and, as she started to move towards the sets, the picture changed and the newsreader moved to an item on whether cats or dogs made better pets.

She stood there, looking around. No-one else seemed to be taking any interest in the TVs. Even if they had been, they wouldn't have made any connection between the smiling, dark-haired wedding guest and the redhead in the drab coat gaping at the screens. But Rhona needed to know why, suddenly, she was being featured. She'd been away from Cairnburgh for over two months; what had happened to make her newsworthy?

She found a newspaper seller and bought the latest evening edition, turning the pages as she walked away from him. The photo was on page four. Beneath it was the unimaginative headline, 'Missing Cairnburgh Woman'. There was a single paragraph saying that she'd been missing from home since June and asking anyone who might have seen her to contact Tayside police.

Rhona folded the paper and dropped it into a waste bin. Why the sudden interest? And why the Tayside police? If it was about her mother, it would be West Grampian. The news item made no suggestion that the photo had appeared before or that this was a reminder of any sort. So how come they'd decided to start looking for her after all these weeks? She'd been expecting something since they found the body of the guy who'd given her a lift but that was nearly a month ago. As she drove back to her flat, she went through every possibility, but none of them made much sense. There must be something new, something she hadn't thought about, something the police had found, maybe.

And she was faced with a dilemma. She could go back and see what it was all about, or she could pack up everything now and head south, disappear properly, for good. But that would make her completely vulnerable. Here, she had her regular punters, Billy, even her mum if she got really desperate. Down there, wherever it was, she'd be on her own. And if the stalker traced her, there'd be no protection.

As she put her small suitcase in the boot and set off for Edinburgh, she still hadn't made the choice. Whatever it was, though, she needed to get as much money as she could. So, for this evening, she'd be a traffic warden or headmistress or whatever he wanted. She'd make up her mind in the morning.

Jerry had been overdoing it and, inevitably, another clot had developed in his leg. When he limped into the surgery, I gave him an earful.

'You know bloody well you shouldn't be walking about with a DVT,' I said as I was feeling his swollen leg and the tightness of the skin.

'Don't be silly. People fly to Australia with them.'

'Wrong. They pick them up on the way. It's no joke, though, Jerry. If this throws off an embolism and it gets into your lung ...'

'I know, I know,' he said.

'Well, be sensible, then. I'll get a taxi for you. You go home, you wear the support stocking, you keep it elevated ...'

'... and I stop shagging.'

'Definitely.'

He sighed and, briefly, his face clouded.

'It's a bastard, you know. I don't feel like a bloody invalid.'

'You're not. You've just got to be sensible.'

I eased the elastic stocking back up over his calf.

'Heard about the blind man in a shop swinging his dog around on the end of its lead?' I said.

'No.'

'Shop assistant says, "Can I help you?" The man says, "No thanks, I'm just looking".'

It did the trick. Made him laugh.

'Sick,' he said.

'I'm a doctor,' I said.

He got off the couch, slipped on his shoes, stood up and hobbled to the door.

'Just sit in the waiting room. I'll get a taxi.'

'OK. Thanks Doc.'

I opened the door for him.

'Just one more question,' said Jerry.

'What?'

'About food.'

'Go on.'

'If I eat pasta and antipasta, will I still be hungry?'

'Piss off,' I said.

Seven patients later, surgery was over. My mobile rang as I was sorting out the notes for the afternoon session. It was Gayla.

'Just phoned to touch base,' she said.

'Sure you want to?'

'Of course. Why?'

'In a word? Detumescence.'

'Never heard of it. Anyway, I wanted to tell you about King Cnut.'

'What?'

'Guy with the waves' she said. 'Much maligned. He didn't try to stop them, he was proving just the opposite.'

'Have you been drinking?'

'No, listen. I made a note of this for you. He brought in this criminal statute, eleventh century. This is how to treat criminals. "Let his hands be cut off, or his feet or both, according as the deed may be, and if then he hath wrought greater wrong, then let his eyes be put out or his nose and his

ears, and the upper lip be cut off, or let him be scalped so that punishment be inflicted.". Now that's justice. Cool, eh?'

'Wonderful.'

'Or you could call up a 1530 Act which authorized poisoners to be boiled alive.'

'Gayla, stop. What are you on about?'

'You wanted to be a vigilante. I'm just contributing some ideas.'

I took a deep breath before I answered. It was hard to joke about it.

'I'm sincerely worried about you,' I said.

'Help me then,' she said.

'How?'

'Come to dinner.'

Her tone was softer. This wasn't a joke.

'After last time?' I said.

'Come to dinner.'

'OK. Thanks. When?'

'You tell me.'

I checked my desk diary.

'Next week?'

'OK.'

'Thursday?'

'Perfect. See you then.'

'Yes. Thanks, Gayla.'

'Bye.'

I was surprised she'd remembered what I'd said about changing things. I must've been more passionate about it than I realized. I was looking through the notes for my afternoon patients again and saw that one of them was a Marion Duguid. It made me stop. The name made me think of Marion Bailey. Her notes were full of visits when she'd come asking for pain killers or sleeping tablets and insisting that there was nothing else wrong with her. But I'd seen the bruises, old and new, dealt with the sprains, twists and fractures. And yet Bailey had always stayed secure in amongst his tight social circle. Marion's murder was brutal and it wasn't only physical abuse she'd had to suffer. The fact that she'd had time and leisure to enrol with an escort agency and spend evenings entertaining strangers implied that he didn't take much notice of her comings and goings. What sort of husband was that? The marriage was a nonsense. Marion Bailey was a very lonely woman.

As I drove home that evening, I couldn't get Bailey out of my mind. I knew he'd probably already told you about the phone calls, so the chances of getting him were even slimmer. I didn't bother with a meal. Just had some tomatoes and cheese as I was preparing their plates.

After the coffee episode, they'd become a bit wary. But they had no option. They were only just getting enough to keep them alive. All of them were losing weight, especially Campion. They had to eat and risk being drugged or just starve. No contest.

As they were eating, I asked them whether any of them would complain if I decided to cure Campion's funny tendencies by cutting his balls off.

Waring sniggered. McPhee looked briefly at Campion. Only Dobie tried to pretend to be reasonable.

'If we were sure he was guilty, well ... that might be different. First of all, though, there'd have to be proof, wouldn't there?' he asked.

'So you need to stand by and see his hand in the little girl's knickers first?' I said. 'Hear her screaming for a while, eh?'

Dobie was uncomfortable.

'No. But there ought to be evidence.'

'OK. How about this one then? You can be the jury. Christmas Eve, right? Taxi-driver, fifty-eight years old.'

It got a reaction from McPhee. Just a turn of the head, nothing else, but his eyes were staring at me.

'He's volunteered to do Christmas Eve because he's a widower, lives on his own. And he wants to get in a bit of overtime and make sure he's free for when he goes to see his grandchildren for Christmas dinner. He's got about seventy quid in his pouch in takings. It's eight o'clock in the evening and he picks up a fare outside a club. Two guys see the man

who gets in the cab, but they're a bit pissed, and they don't take much notice of it anyway. Well, who would? Anyway, the next thing is, the taxi's four miles away, out on the Aberdeen road.'

They were listening carefully, hunched against their pillars, looking at me. The place was reeking of sweat and urine, but just for that instant, it felt ... good.

'The bloke in the back doesn't fancy doing overtime. He's never fancied anything in the way of work. Always made his money by nicking things off other people. And everybody needs a bit extra at Christmas. Trouble is, he can't just nick the driver's takings, because he'd be identified and, with his record, that'd be that for a long time. So while the driver's sitting waiting to be paid, his passenger takes out this cheese wire he's brought along with him. Just happens to have it in his pocket, see? A cheese wire. Funny that. I mean, it's not as if he worked in a cheese shop.'

Only McPhee and Waring were looking at me now.

'Anyway, he whips it round the driver's neck and pulls. Hard. I don't suppose you need telling what happens when you do that, do you? Thin wire like that. Just one thing though. If you're thinking of trying it, wear the right gear. It makes a helluva mess. And that's interesting too, because about an hour after that, a bloke walks into a chip shop with stains all over the sleeves of his jacket, buys a fish supper and pays for it with money out of "a sort of satchel thing". That's what the woman behind the counter called it when she got round to telling the police about it. They picked up a guy. He had no alibi and his form made him a dead cert for the job.'

I stopped. McPhee looked away. Waring was still hooked.

'What happened?' he said, like a kid listening to a bedtime story.

'Nothing. Instead of the suspect getting put away for it, the two guys who'd seen him getting into the cab were made to look like piss-artists who couldn't recognize their own granny after six o'clock at night, and the woman in the chip shop finished up convinced that she was colour-blind and

168

couldn't tell blood from diesel oil.'

'So he got away with it, then?' said Waring, as if he was pleased with the result. I looked at McPhee.

'Oh no', I said. 'He didn't get away with it. He thought he did, but it all caught up with him in the end. Eh, McPhee?'

'How?' asked Waring, too thick to give it up.

McPhee jumped up and tried to get at him.

'Shut it!' he said. 'Stupid bastard. Just shut it.'

He stood there, shaking, his chains stretched hard out from his pillar. He was desperate to get at somebody. It terrified Waring. He suddenly realized what I'd been on about. He looked at McPhee with a sort of respect.

'Christ,' he said.

'So,' I said, 'what about him? What do you suppose he deserves? Buggered up that family's Christmas, didn't he? Surely somebody ought to take a piece of wire to him. Or a razor maybe. Sometime when he's sitting there helpless. What d'you reckon?'

No answer. I wasn't really expecting one.

'Then there's Mr. Bailey, of course,' I said. 'The one who didn't want to join us. Beat up his wife, he did. With a claw hammer. Then swore blind he was playing bridge with somebody from the Chamber of Commerce that night. Nasty bugger, he is.'

I suppose they wondered why I was talking about Bailey again. I don't know really. I was talking as much to myself as to them.

'Looks like he did get away with it,' I said.

'Good luck to him,' said Waring.

'He killed his wife,' I said. 'Used to beat her up, too.'

'So what's new? They ask for it half the time.'

'You really are the most unpleasant bastard I've ever come across,' I said.

'It's true,' said Waring. 'They all need a slap now and then. It's a well-known fact. Don't do them no harm. Makes 'em respect you.'

What an idiot. He knew what I could do to him. He'd drunk the coffee, been terrified by me wandering around

169

them, doing what I liked. And yet he still challenged me. This guy who'd killed my brother's family. I felt like going across and beating the shit out of him. I didn't, though. That would be too easy. Might even have been what he wanted. I'd decide when to do it, not him. I was in control.

I stood up, collected their plates and carried them over to the door. Then I turned back.

'He hasn't got away with it,' I said. 'In fact, he'd probably have been better off here with us.'

And I turned off the light.

TWENTY-TWO

'Bailey still surviving, is he?' said Carston, after his first swig of lager.

He and Ross were sitting at their usual table in the pub.

'Aye. I was up there this morning. It's like Fort Knox. Infra-red lights outside, motion sensors in all the downstairs rooms ...'

'Good. Anything else?'

'Like what?'

'Well, the taxi driver. The one who drove Waring home.'

'Not really. Waring spent most of the time talking about somebody called Doug. Seems he wanted to cut his balls off.'

'If anybody needs his balls cutting off, it's Waring,' said Carston.

'You knew Freddy Reismann was his brief, too, did you?' said Ross.

'Was he?'

'Aye. He didn't actually follow the case right through or anything, but he was the first brief Waring went to. It was Reismann who passed him on to the one who dealt with his case in the end.'

'Brilliant,' said Carston, with a smile on his face. 'When did you find that out?'

'Can't remember,' said Ross. 'Some time when I was looking through my notes.'

'You secretive sod,' said Carston. 'Right, then. Now we know where to go, don't we?'

Ross drank deep again and wiped his lips.

'It'll be on your desk tomorrow, with any luck.'

'What?'

'A list of Reismann's clients over the past couple of years.'

Carston shook his head in slow surprise, then, with careful deference, added, 'Nice of you to keep me informed of the course of your investigation.'

Ross smiled.

'Still no sign of Rhona Kirk,' he said.

Carston shook his head.

'No, but I had a chat with Don Kingdom in Dundee. He's sending up copies of all the stuff they've got on Ian Stride.'

'What d'you think?'

'Dunno. We'll check it against our Davies stuff. You never know.'

Ross nodded.

'One thing,' Carston went on. 'The guy on the CCTV tape in Edinburgh, it's not him.'

'How do they know?'

'Can't see his face. He wore a hat. Everybody they've talked to says it couldn't be Stride. Not tall enough, and he never wore hats.'

Ross whistled.

'So it could be the guy who did it?'

Carston shrugged.

'Bit risky, but I guess so. Gets rid of his man, parks his car where it's supposed to be. Nobody notices he's missing. Not for a while anyway.'

'Have they enhanced the shot?' asked Ross.

Carston nodded.

'Doesn't tell them much, though,' he said. 'They reckon it was Stride's clothes but that maybe the guy wearing them was a bit thinner. There's not enough to get an ID, though.'

He stopped and took another mouthful.

'Tell you what would be nice,' he said.

'What?'

'If Stride's name was on that list of Freddy's clients.'

'No,' said Ross. 'Too easy.'

'Easy's good. I like easy,' said Carston.

I'm used to death. Seen plenty of corpses in my time. Some patients have even asked me for a lethal injection. But this was different. Deciding consciously, cold-bloodedly to get rid of someone – that's something else. I thought long and hard about Bailey, went back over all his flaws, his ill-treatment of his wife, his exploitation of everyone and everything. There were no saving graces. He was an inhuman bastard, full stop. That's why he was on my original list. He'd shown as little concern for other people as McPhee, Dobie, Campion and Waring. If I'd managed to get him into the cellar, I could never have let him go. The others were thick or guilty enough to be freed without fear of any come-backs. None of them would go to the police. But Bailey had a position; he ranked in society. He'd never let go. Not after being treated like that. He'd find out who'd done it and make them pay. So, logically, it meant that, right from the start, I must've been prepared to take him out of society altogether.

It kept me awake. And gradually, I realized I'd stopped wondering whether I was capable of murder and I'd started planning how to do it. It was another challenge. What was the next step? Face to face was impossible. I knew all about contact traces. I knew that, however careful I was, something would contaminate either me or the scene and create the link that you'd need. So, no blood, no violence, no beatings. Only one way: poison. But what? And what dosage? And how could I get him to take it?

The answer was easy. Ricin. Everybody knows about it now. Star status, it's got. Markov, the Bulgarian killed by it in London, had had just 0.2 milligrams injected via the end of an umbrella. Agonizing death. They had samples of it in the toxicology lab. It was three-thirty but I was still wide awake. I got up and went through to the study. I've kept most of my medical text books. I add notes on new symptoms and complaints when they crop up. One of them's got a big database of toxins. I checked out the Ricin entry. Twice as powerful as a cobra's venom. Just one speck, ingested, inhaled or absorbed, induces vomiting, haemorrhaging, a total destruction of the red blood cells and, effectively a melt-down of the entire physiological system. It took Markov four days to die, but experiments on pigs showed that it could take as little as twenty-five hours. That was the stuff for Bailey.

Strange thing – as soon as I'd made up my mind, I went back to bed and dropped off right away.

It was the same next morning. I felt good. In the car on

the way to work, I started to work out how to deliver the dose. I knew the layout of his place. I'd been there to see Marion often enough. I knew it was burglar-proof. Well, all those antiques and paintings ... But I knew Bailey's habits pretty well, too. I'd seen him in his garden and summer house. That's where he'd be vulnerable. I decided to go that evening.

Patients, letter signings, a practice meeting – they all flew by. I've never been more efficient. I was the last to leave as usual. By the time I'd parked the car well away from Bailey's and walked through the lanes and fields to the bottom of his garden, it was already getting dark. I had on an old pair of jeans and a sweatshirt. The idea was to keep them until the job was done and then burn them.

Climbing in was easy. There were lights in several of the rooms but I knew he wouldn't be coming outside this late. The bushes at the base of the wall were pyracantha and berberis. Big sharp buggers. The spines caught my sweatshirt and jeans. A few even scratched my skin. But the summer house was just there. You've seen it – ordinary Yale lock. Enough to keep me out, though. I looked through the window. Hardly anything there. Two faded old rugs on the floor, wickerwork table inside the door, with a phone on it. Curved receiver but with a flat back. I noticed the smudges on it from Bailey's hands. And that was it, really. The rest was a chair, gardening tools, books and magazines.

I checked the window. It opened. That was a surprise. I levered it up, reached inside and held my hand near the phone. It's a good, simple design. Fits nicely in the palm if you pick it up. That would do nicely. I shut the window, went back through the bushes and over the wall. The whole visit took just four minutes. Easy. So, I could get the Ricin and deliver the dose. Just had to work out the details.

It was Billy's birthday but, to Rhona, it felt more like hers. To celebrate it, he'd checked that she was free, then booked them into an old manse which had been converted into a small hotel down in the Borders. They'd driven down at lunchtime and spent the afternoon wandering around Melrose Abbey, lingering over the spot where the heart of Robert the Bruce was buried. Neither of them was political, but the magic of the name and the myths that swirled around it held them as they stood in silence looking down at the simple stone with its inscription.

They walked around, held hands, enjoyed the afternoon sun and behaved like any other young couple. Back at the hotel, at Billy's request, the manager had left a bottle of champagne on ice in their room.

'You'll make somebody a good husband,' said Rhona.

'Just say the word,' said Billy.

'Pour,' said Rhona.

They laughed and lay back among soft pillows on the huge bed. Slowly and with great care to make it last as long as possible, Rhona kissed and touched him and whispered sweet things as she nuzzled into his neck. Dundee, the stalker and all her troubles were miles away and she felt happy at the pleasure she was giving him. He lay there, his hands occasionally straying over her breasts and shoulders but mainly moaning at the intensity of the feelings she was creating in him. She used all her skills to take him to the edge, stilling her lips and fingers just in time to stop him and then starting the slow exploration all over again. At last, with the champagne bottle almost empty and Billy further into lust than he'd ever been before, she sat across his hips, took him inside her and, with a gentle rocking, eased him to the most intense orgasm he'd ever had.

When the last sighs had died away and he was lying, his right arm across his eyes, his left moving slowly over her thigh, she kissed him on the neck and whispered, 'Happy birthday'.

At dinner, they laughed and acted like lovers, drinking lots of wine and enjoying the excellent food. It was when they were in the lounge, sitting in front of an unnecessary but romantic log fire, that Billy got serious again.

'It could be like this all the time,' he said.

'Have you won the lottery then?' she said.

'Doesn't have to be here. We don't need hotels.'

'Speak for yourself.'

'I'm serious, Rhona.'

She looked at him and smiled. She didn't want to say anything to spoil the mood. He'd been a real gentleman all the time she'd known him and this trip had obviously taken some planning.

'I know, Billy, and if I was ready for anything like that, I wouldn't look further than you.'

'Well, then,' he said.

'I don't think I'm ready,' she said. 'Anyway, what do you really know about me? I'm a good fuck, I …'

'Don't say that.'

'You mean I'm not?' she said.

He smiled.

'You're more than that,' he said.

'If only you knew.'

'Anyway, I don't care. You haven't seen my flat. It's plenty big enough for two. You could give it a try, see whether it'd work.'

She turned to him and poked a finger into his chest.

'Easy, there,' she said. 'We've been here before. You know what I think about it.'

'Times change. You could change. How d'you know until you've tried it?'

His face was open, serious. He really meant it and Rhona began to wonder whether it might be a way of coping with the pressures of the stalker, and the new complication of her picture being posted all over the place.

'It's a lovely offer,' she said, 'but you really don't know anything about me, Billy.'

'But I …'

'For a start, the police are looking for me,' she interrupted. 'My photo's been in the papers.'

'I know. I've seen it. It's 'cause you ran away, that's all.'

'How do you know?'

'That's what it said. What else could it be?'

She shrugged.

'You never know with them. Now be quiet and buy me a

drink.'

She drank more Cointreau while he had whisky and they let their talk wander off into speculations about what it would be like to live in a house like the manse and have everything done for them by the folk below stairs. At one point, Billy couldn't resist saying, 'That's how you could have it.'

'What?'

'You could be the lady and I'd be your slave.'

'Here?'

'No, in my flat.'

She smiled and giggled.

'Ahah, that's what you've been after all this time, is it? A dominatrix.'

Billy didn't laugh.

'I've been after you, Rhona. I love you.'

It was the first time he'd said such a thing. The booze must have had something to do with it, but it was also the fact that they'd relaxed so completely with one another, had such a marvellous day, and were about, he supposed, to have an equally marvellous night. The words shocked Rhona. Punters had said them before but never with the intensity and conviction that Billy had used. She reached across and stroked his cheek.

'You're sweet,' she said.

He saw the tenderness in her eyes.

'Come and stay with me,' he said. 'Just for a few days, just to see whether it could work.'

She knew that she should never make promises when she'd been drinking but the shock of seeing her face on the television had limited her options. She'd more or less decided to risk going back to Cairnburgh and showing up at the police station. She'd even got as far as ringing her mother but had hung up before she got a reply. Maybe Billy was the answer. She didn't want his love, and the prospect of marriage was deadly, but she could maybe take a wee break from her punters, stay with him for a week or so, then set off again, somewhere where the stalker couldn't find her. She sat forward in her chair, almost falling as she leaned to take her weight on her right hand and missed the arm of the chair.

'That just shows you how pissed I am,' she said. 'And how much I'm going to regret this in the morning, but …'

'But what?'

'Here's the deal,' she said. 'I stay with you for a week.'

She paused, waiting for a response.

'Magic,' said Billy.

'I won't see any punters.'

'Even better.'

'I'll pay rent in kind.'

'Christ, I've died and gone to heaven.'

'And you won't tell me you love me ever again.'

Billy's wide smile faded.

'I meant it,' he said.

'I know, love,' she replied. 'But I can't handle it. I'll let you down. I'm bound to.'

'What if you don't? What if it's great and … ?'

She put her finger on his lips, missing at first and jabbing it into his cheek.

'Sssssh,' she said. 'We'll give it a try and take it from there.'

After a pause, he held out his hand and said, 'It's a deal.'

She took his hand and shook it.

TWENTY-THREE

What I needed was a fine, hollow alloy spine. It would have to be very small so that Bailey wouldn't notice it. Trouble is, I know bugger all about metals or how to work them. It would've been easy for a watchmaker or a surgical instrument manufacturer, but I couldn't ask anybody for help. I knew you'd find out how it had been done in the end, so I didn't want to leave any traces. That's why I didn't want to use the Internet either. You'd check my machine, find out exactly where I'd been. So I spent a couple of evenings at the library, reading about stress fractures, expansion, extrusion profiles and all the ways you can mould and work metal. I became a bit of an expert in things like aluminium and duralumin. All very interesting, but it didn't help.

It was when I was reading about something called Hooke's Law that I got the idea. It's about the deformation of a body, applied stress, elastic limits – wonderful stuff like that. Basically, it was about the difference between elastic and plastic. When metal's elastic, it goes back into shape when you take the strain off it, when it's plastic, it doesn't. I'd been hung up on the idea of using metal but I suddenly realized that I could get hold of plastic much more easily and it'd be easier to work.

So, the day after that, in my lunch hour, I went to a marine services shop and bought tins of resin and hardener and a packet of fibreglass. I wasn't bothered about them identifying me later, because there are dinghy and boat folk buying little thermoset kits of that sort all the time.

I got quite excited about it all. Rushed through my paperwork that night, fed the animals, and got going. I took five different-sized needles and pins from the sewing basket, stuck the tip of each into a pat of butter, then pushed them into the washing-up sponge, leaving their points sticking upwards. Mixed up the resin, added spoonfuls of black and red paint, and put a thin layer on each point. When the resin was dry, I took the pins and needles from the sponge and slid the little black and red plastic sheaths off them. So I had sort of minute cones of resin. I got a magnifier and an ordinary nail file, and worked them down to the size and shape I was after. I sharpened the tips, made a little mark just below them and filed around them there to weaken the resin. I broke a few of them, of course. Had to learn just how much pressure I could put on the file and how thin I could afford to make the material. And so on and so on. Made up more cones, experimented some more and gradually got better at it. By eleven o'clock, I had a matchbox filled with cotton wool, with five tiny, hollow thorns lying on it.

I was on automatic really. It was so absorbing. Never thought about what I was doing, or why. I took the thorns through to the study, put on a mask, eye-shield and surgical gloves and filled each one with a drop of Ricin infusion. I tell you what, I've never been more careful with anything in my life. I sealed the bottom of each thorn with a dab of fibreglass and put it back in the matchbox.

I was on the road out towards Bailey's just after midnight. Same clothes as before, matchbox on the passenger seat.

There was a half moon. Just enough light to see into the summer house. I opened the window, propped it up with a piece of wood, took out the matchbox and , picked up the first thorn with a pair of forceps. I squeezed a single drop of instant glue onto its base, reached through the window and held the thorn above the centre of the phone. It was at the wrong angle so I had to take my arm out, adjust my grip and try again. It took me four tries, but then I managed to lower the thorn onto the phone and hold it right in the centre of the handset. I made myself wait for well over a minute. My hand was still and I was incredibly calm. When I lifted the forceps away, the thorn stayed in place.

Just to make sure, though, I took out a small torch and shone it through the window. I had to look hard, but I could see a tiny smear of glue and just make out the tiny spine. The smear would soon dry and, unless you were looking for it, the thorn would be invisible.

Now this is the weird bit. I went back to the car, got in, reached to turn the ignition on, and, all of a sudden, I was crying. Yep, crying. I just sat with my arms on the steering wheel, my head bent forward, and sobbed. Couldn't stop.

The morning's briefing was frustrating. Fraser, Spurle and the rest had been collating everything on the missing persons which Carston had put onto his special list. They'd found nothing which wasn't already known and, until the dossier on Reismann's clients arrived, there were no new directions to send them in. As ever, there was a backlog of petty incidents which required no detection but did need to be tidied and prepared for the courts. That simply meant yet more paperwork. Carston and Ross were glad to get away from the heavy silence which greeted this news and the edginess which filled it. Unusually, the irritation stayed with them as they went through to their office. A sort of intolerance prickled in the air between them.

As lunchtime approached, Carston's calls to Dwyer on the desk to check whether Reismann's client list had arrived multiplied. It was only when Dwyer's reply had been, 'How nice to hear from you again' that he admitted the stupidity of what he was doing. It was twelve-thirty. He heaved himself up and took his coat. Normally, he didn't bother too much with food in the middle of the day, his brief hunger being quickly satisfied by a cup of soup and the salad roll or tomato sandwiches he brought with him. That morning, though, he'd already eaten the sandwiches with one of his cups of coffee. It had passed some time.

'I'm off to the *Dolphin* for a snack,' he said. 'Give me a shout if anything crops up.'

Without looking at him, Ross nodded.

'You never know, do you?' said Carston, a little embarrassed at the way he'd let his impatience colour the morning. Ross looked up and gave a little twitch of the head in reply. His eyes showed that he, too, was feeling uncomfortable and Carston felt even guiltier.

'See you later,' he said, trying a smile.

182

'Aye, OK,' said Ross, turning back to his file.

Once in the street, Carston immediately began regretting his decision to leave the office. He quickened his pace as he headed for the pub, his mind imagining the file being dropped on his desk at that very moment. He was annoyed with himself for wasting time, for being obsessive. He'd always thought he'd grow out of this sort of thing. Not for the first time, he resolved to get the impatience under proper adult control. The Reismann file would arrive when it got there. That was all.

He was back at the station before one and annoyed to learn that there was still nothing for him. Ross was eating a sandwich and drinking coffee.

'This'll keep you occupied,' he said, as Carston flopped into his chair. 'Phone calls.'

'What about them?'

'Well, there's Bailey's death threats. And Waring got that call at the pub just before he left. Dobie told his neighbour he'd be in all evening, but she heard his phone go just before he went out. We don't know when Rhona Kirk, Campion or Stride actually went missing so we've got nothing on them and the only thing about McPhee and the phone is that he called his doctor around the time he must have vanished. He was on some sort of medication. Wanted more. I've talked to the receptionist there. She said he talked to one of the doctors and got the brush-off. Guess which one.'

'Davidson,' said Carston, after a pause.

'Exactly. And Waring happens to be the guy who killed his brother's wife and kids.'

Carston nodded. The coincidence had already struck him.

'D'you want me to talk to him?' asked Ross.

'No, it's OK. I'll do it. See if you can get a list of his patients. Be discreet.'

'My middle name.'

'According to the squad, your middle name's wanker.'

Before Ross could answer, the phone rang. He picked it up, listened and said, 'OK, Sandy, put her in three.'

Carston waited.

'Well, well, well,' said Ross. 'Guess who just got lucky.'

'We did,' said Carston.

'Yep. We've got a lady caller. Room three. Rhona Kirk.'

Carston whistled in surprise.

'Excellent,' he said. 'Come on, we'll both see her.'

Rhona was sitting at the interview table, her hands in her lap, her red hair pulled back from her face. She wore hardly any make-up. When Carston and Ross came in, she looked straight at them, meeting their eyes. Without knowing why, Carston felt that, on the surface at least, she was no victim. She sat still, composed and ready for them. She'd deliberately made herself look unattractive but she couldn't hide the power of her sexuality. It brought an involuntary smile to Carston's lips.

'Rhona Kirk?' he said.

'Yes.'

'What brings you in?'

'I saw the photo. Saw you were looking for me. Thought I'd better let you know I'm OK.'

'Good, glad to hear it,' said Carston. 'Been away?'

She nodded.

'Where?'

'Why d'you want to know?'

'Curiosity. Working, were you?'

She stared at him for a moment, then shook her head.

'I'm here, that's all. You can take me off your list.'

'Good,' said Carston.

'Why did you bother to come in?' asked Ross. 'You could've phoned us. We'd've sent someone round. Staying at your mum's are you?'

'No. I'm staying with a friend.'

'Who?'

'That's my business.'

Carston noticed the defiance in her tone and look. It was the stance of someone who didn't really trust them but also of someone who was used to being in control. He smiled and turned the conversation to more general things, like her health and the problems that had caused her to leave home. He asked whether the rape had left any scars and if there was anything they could do to help. She was defensive at first but, with Ross's backing, he managed to disarm her antagonism sufficiently to move back to her disappearance.

'It took you a while to send out my photo, didn't it?' she said at one point.

'Well, that's it, you see,' said Carston. 'We did put it out locally, when you were first reported, but something else came up, so we put it out again.'

'That's a bit caring, isn't it?' she said.

'That's what we're like,' said Carston, matching her tone. 'Anyway, there was something else.'

She waited.

'Robert Davies,' said Carston. 'He turned up … sort of unexpectedly, you might say.'

They saw no reaction in her face at all. She said nothing.

'Looks like he had a fight. Somebody killed him.'

'Good,' she said.

'Last October. You were here then, weren't you?'

'Why? D'you think I did it?'

'You were here, weren't you?'

'Yes, but he wasn't living at our place any more. Mum kicked him out after …'

She stopped. Carston nodded.

'Don't suppose you've any idea who might have killed him. Friend of yours maybe? Getting their own back for you.'

Rhona laughed.

'If I did know, I'd hardly tell you, would I?'

'When did you last see him?' asked Ross.

'He stayed at our place for a week or so after he raped me, then she kicked him out. Didn't see him after that.'

Ross took out his notebook and flicked it open.

'I wonder whether you could help us with some other names,' he said.

'What other names?'

'Just some people we want to get in touch with.'

'People I know?'

Ross smiled and looked at his book.

'That's what we're wondering,' he said. 'How about Peter Dobie?'

Rhona looked at him, a frown on her face.

'Douglas McPhee? … David Campion?'

'Never heard of them. What's it about?'

'Ian Stride, then?'

She couldn't hide her reaction and she knew it.

'I … I think … He was in the paper, wasn't he?' she said. 'Didn't they find him in a ditch or something?'

'That's right,' said Carston.

Rhona's head was shaking. They knew more than they were telling her. She suspected that they'd invented the other names just to set her up for Stride.

'That's all you know about him, then?' insisted Carston. 'Never came across him personally. At work maybe?'

'I don't work,' said Rhona.

'Oh, don't worry. We're not after you for that,' said Carston, with a big smile.

'What d'you mean, "that"?' said Rhona.

Carston's smile didn't change.

'It's not working girls we're interested in,' he said. 'It's these men.'

Ross looked at him. It was the first time the suggestion that she was on the game had come up but her reaction suggested that Carston had hit the spot.

'You see, we've got a photo of Mr. Stride's car,' Carston went on, 'with him driving and a female passenger.'

The reference to her working as an escort had unsettled her. They obviously knew an awful lot. She decided that her best tactic was to tell them as much of the truth as she dared. Since she'd been staying with Billy, there'd been no calls from the stalker and life had begun to be more relaxed. She didn't want the police on at her every day.

'I wondered whether it was him when I saw the report,' she said. 'You don't like to think it, do you?'

'Think what?' said Ross.

'Well, that somebody you've been with's been … murdered.'

186

'You did meet him then?'

After a pause, Rhona looked down at her hands and nodded. She told them that Stride had given her a lift, then stayed the night in her new flat in Dundee.

'So that'll be you in the photograph, then?' said Ross.

She nodded.

'Bit generous of you, letting him stay the night, just for a lift, wasn't it?' said Carston.

She looked at him for quite a long time before answering.

'You said you're not interested in working girls,' she said.

'That's right,' he said.

'He stayed the night and left the next morning. And that was it.'

'What date would that be?'

'June 20th, maybe 21st, 22nd. You'll have it on the photo, won't you?'

Carston smiled.

'Yes,' he said.

'What was he like?' asked Ross.

Rhona shrugged.

'Normal,' she said. 'Typical sales rep. Full of himself. Still thought he was a stud.'

'Wasn't he?'

A rare smile came from her.

'How would I know?'

'Did he give you any reason to think he might be in trouble? That somebody was after him, maybe?'

She shook her head.

'No. He talked about the deals he'd be doing in Edinburgh. Made it sound high level. I didn't believe much of it.'

'Why not?'

'You get to know people. It's the quiet ones that get things done. He was all mouth.'

'No reason to murder him, though.'

'No, you're right, it's sad,' she said.

'Bit more than sad,' said Ross.

'No, I mean, the way he was, the boasting, his clothes. He was a sad man. A loser.'

'What about his clothes?'

'What d'you mean?'

'He wasn't wearing them when he was found,' said Carston.

'No, that was in the paper. Just that silly bloody tie,' said Rhona.

Carston and Ross both hid their reaction.

'His tie?' said Carston.

'Yes. Bart Simpson. Fancy being strangled with that.'

'Whatever you use, it has the same effect,' said Carston.

They talked for another ten minutes, Ross taking notes as she described everything she could recall about Stride, the clothes, what he said, the names he mentioned. She felt more and more comfortable with them and gave them as much as she could. It was when they asked where they could contact her that she became defensive once more.

'Couldn't I just give you my mobile number?' she asked.

'That'd be good, yes,' said Ross. 'But mobiles get stolen, you know. We need to know where you are.'

'Why?' she asked.

'Well, you never know what might come up,' said Carston. 'You could confirm things for us, save us lots of time.'

'I'm staying with a friend. I don't want him to be involved.'

'There's no need for him to know.'

'There is if you come banging on the door.'

'We won't. We'll call you on your mobile if you'd prefer it. And we'll be discreet. But we do need to know where you are.'

Reluctantly, dragging as many promises as she could from them that Billy would get to know nothing about it, she gave them his address. Ross noted it and the three of them stood up.

'One last thing,' said Carston. 'Who's your doctor?'

'Why?'

'Just curiosity.'

'Dr Milne, Porlock Road.'

'Ah. Right.'

They walked to the front door with her and, again, Carston saw the looks that she drew from the constables in the front office. If that was the effect she had when she hadn't bothered to try, the full impact must be pretty dynamic. He was also irritated with himself again that he'd felt her attraction too. More of his Spurle syndrome. When they'd thanked her for coming and shaken her hand, she walked out into the crowds on Burns Road. Carston and Ross went back to their office and, as the door closed behind them, they looked at one another.

'Bingo,' said Carston.

'The tie,' said Ross.

Carston nodded.

'It wasn't in any of the reports we released,' he said. 'Has to be her. I want somebody watching her as of now. But don't let her know it.'

Ross nodded.

'What was the idea of asking about her doctor?' he said.

Carston smiled and shook his head.

'If she'd said Davidson, it would've been nice.'

Ross grinned.

'OK Jim,' said Carston. 'Get that surveillance organized then bugger off home. You've put up with enough from me for one day. When that Reismann file gets here, I'm just going to switch off the phone and work my way through it … I've got bags of time … Kath's out tonight, so I'll probably stay on for a while … There's no need for you to hang around.'

The speech had been longer than he wanted, awkward, faltering. Ross had listened with something like politeness, knowing that it was Carston's way of apologizing for breaking his balls all morning.

'Well, it's always a pleasure to spend time with you, sir,' he said, 'but Jean did want me to fix a cupboard in the kids' room, so maybe I'll drag myself away.'

The conversation with Rhona had turned the day round. The frustration of waiting for a file which might contain nothing was forgotten. She'd placed herself firmly in the frame for Stride's murder and, if she was capable of that, there was a chance that she had a hand in the Davies killing, too. Carston knew from experience that people found the second time easier.

TWENTY-FOUR

It was a fine evening and Bailey was working his way through his roses, his concentration firmly focused on the bushes as he cut them back to within eighteen inches or so of the ground. Occasionally he stood and dragged himself free of the thorns which caught at his jumper and trousers to carry a small bundle of prunings to a wire basket in which they'd lie until they were dry enough to be burned. Sometimes he actually spoke to one of the bushes. He was no believer in theories about the linguistic sensitivity of vegetation, but his concentration was such that he spoke his thoughts out loud without realizing that he was doing so.

It was the perpetual struggle with the thorns that produced most of the remarks.

'Don't be stupid,' he'd say to a floribunda as it took him by the sleeve, 'it's for your own good. You'll be stronger next summer for it.'

The bushes were always unimpressed, and he was silenced until the next encounter.

It was in one of the frequent pauses he had to make in order to remove some of the thorns that had broken off in his hand and on his sleeves that he heard the phone in his summer house. He picked absent-mindedly at his jumper as he walked into the little house and sat down. Uncharacteristically, he continued to sit there, flicking at his sleeve. Whoever was calling wasn't going to hang up. He was surprised to feel the sweat prickling on his back. He took off his glove, reached out and grabbed the receiver, feeling the jab of another thorn as he did so but too angry to care about it.

'Bailey,' he snapped.

'Ah, good,' the voice replied, immediately confirming all his fears. 'Flowers OK, are they?'

'Yes,' said Bailey, thrown by the question.

'Tucked up all cosy in your little summer house?'

'What d'you want?'

Bailey's voice was shaking and much quieter.

'Oh, don't worry. Nothing. I've got it now,' said Davidson.

'But … why me?'

'Why you? Stop being stupid. Why you? Why somebody who can treat his wife like shit, mince her head up, then play the innocent and walk away untouched?'

'Look, I'm just an engineer. I … I didn't kill my wife. That was all a mistake. I was never even charged with it. Ask my lawyer, he'll …'

'No, no, no. Forget about law. I'm talking about justice.'

Davidson stopped. Bailey heard the slow breathing.

'OK, you bastard,' he said. 'So what's the story? What's the great plan?'

The breathing turned to a barely audible chuckle. There was still no answer.

'Look, you've got the wrong idea,' said Bailey.

'I don't think so,' said Davidson, adding, after a long pause, 'Too late anyway.'

'We could meet. Talk. I … I could pay you. I've got …'

Briefly, Davidson lost control.

'You bastard. You slimy, evil bastard. Don't fucking insult me. We're not all like you. You can't buy all of us. Keep your money. All of it. It's no bloody good to you any more, I'll tell you that.' His voice calmed a little. 'You know, I even thought at one stage that you might get a reprieve. Why should I make myself a murderer, I thought. Just because you're so fucking wicked. Reprieve? You should die hundreds of times. Hundreds. Well, once'll be enough, and it's on its way, and it's going to hurt. Believe me.'

And that was all.

Bailey felt a warmth on his thigh and looked down at the stain spreading under the corduroy. His hands fell into his lap, the receiver still held loosely, and his head jerked forward as he felt the sharp tears push into the corners of his eyes.

'Bastard,' he said.

He banged the receiver back on its rest and slapped his open hand onto the table. He threw down his secateurs, pushed out through the door and stumbled up to the house. His feet slipped on the paths and on the grass, his chest burned with anger and effort and his hands lashed out at the tall grasses and stems that hung in his way. Once inside, he dropped his wet trousers onto the floor, locked the French windows, closed their shutters, drew the blinds and stared around at the useless elegance. When his breathing eased, he went to his desk, sat down, picked up the phone and dialled the police station.

When Bailey got through, Carston was the last person in the world who should have answered. Acting on the DCI's instructions, the desk sergeant had tried very hard to deflect the incoming call to someone else, but Bailey had been almost hysterically insistent, and uttered threats of a degree of retribution far beyond anything Dwyer had ever heard of before.

As Carston lifted the phone, he was ready to bawl the hottest of obscenities at whoever was daring to interrupt his studies. Dwyer knew that.

'Mr. Bailey, sir,' he said quickly, to redirect Carston's bile.

'What about him?'

'On the line. Insists that he's got to speak to you. I tried to divert him, but nobody else'll do. Life and death, he reckons.'

'Always does, the stupid bugger. Wouldn't he tell you what it was about?'

'No sir. Categorical, he was. Sounded a bit … distraught, too.'

'Categorical? Distraught? What the bloody hell have you been reading, Sandy?'

'*The Psychology of Deviance in the Criminally Insane,*' replied Dwyer, unexpectedly.

'You'll go blind,' said Carston. 'Alright. Put him through.'

As Bailey began to protest and splutter, he couldn't possibly guess how ill-disposed to him the policeman was.

Carston had been flipping through the various reports of his lawyer's activities over the past few years. Bailey was, to Carston's mind, a particularly fortunate and undeserving beneficiary of Reismann's skills so there was no pretence at sympathy as he listened to the whining on the line.

'Look, get over here,' said Bailey. 'Look at the state I'm in.'

'Can't be done, sir, I'm afraid. Not right away, anyway. There's a security alert. I've had to deploy men all over the place tonight.'

'What do you mean, security alert? What about my security?'

'You do remember that Balmoral's just up the road, don't you? And I'm sure even you recognize that there are still a few individuals that rank above you in terms of national status.'

'Fuck you, Carston. You don't care, do you? You're enjoying this. Getting some sort of dull-witted pleasure out of my discomfort.'

'There you are, sir. If it's only discomfort we're talking about, it can wait, can't it?'

He didn't allow the explosive interruption that greeted his words to get beyond its own detonator. His voice insisted as he continued.

'Now then. Where are you?'

'At home.'

'Inside? Not in the garden?'

'No. Inside.'

'And all the doors are shut and the alarm systems on?'

'Of course.'

'Right. Keep it that way. Don't open up for anyone. I'll get round as soon as I can. It may be tonight, but I wouldn't count on it. Don't worry though. I'll be there tomorrow morning.'

The spluttering started again.

'And, Mr. Bailey, if you ring me here again tonight without good reason, that'll set my work back so far that I won't possibly be able to get round to you until late tomorrow. You do see that, don't you?'

'Callous bastard,' said Bailey.

'Just get some rest,' said Carston before pressing the button to disconnect the call.

He lifted his finger again and dialled the front desk.

'Sandy,' he said when Dwyer answered, 'if he rings back, I'm busy. Whatever he says, whatever he threatens. As far as he's concerned, Balmoral's teeming with Royals and we're looking after them.'

'Even the Countess of Wessex, sir?'

'I said Royals.'

'Right sir,' said Dwyer.

Carston sat back, fingering the folder on his desk once again. His dislike of Bailey seeped into his thinking about Reismann, distorting it. He still didn't understand the lawyer but he had a sneaking regard for him nevertheless. He stretched the law to its limits, but he wasn't a crook. Most of the material in the folder could be categorized as simply background information, but Carston had noted names, dates and little personal asides as he had read through it, taking out the relevant individual files and stacking them on a chair which he'd placed beside him specifically for that purpose. He hadn't yet completed his reading, but the list was filling out. One thing that disappointed him slightly was that there was no mention anywhere of Rhona Kirk. That was a pity; he liked neatness.

Carston and Ross arrived at Bailey's just after nine the following morning. It was Reismann who greeted them at the door, warning them that all was not well with his client. As Carston made to ask a question, he put his fingers to his lips and ushered them into the study. Bailey was just inside the door, using it as a sort of shield. It was clear at once that he had slept very badly or not at all and that Reismann's warning was well-founded. Bailey's features were unremarkable, average in every way except where his money could make a difference. The clothes he was wearing, brown slacks and cream shirt under a silk dressing gown, were neatly tailored and hung well on him; the haircut, even in its now relatively dishevelled state, was exact. But Bailey himself was in distress. Red eyes burned in dark hollows scooped in the face, tremors ran through the hands that jutted from the sleeves of the dressing gown, and his whole body seemed to be arched protectively around itself, twitching reactions at everything near him. A quick look passed between the two policemen; clearly, they had noted and reacted to his condition in the same way.

'Satisfied?' said Bailey. 'Believe me now, do you?'

'What happened?' asked Ross.

'How the fuck do I know,' snapped Bailey. 'He phoned again. Like I told you last night. How often does it have to happen?'

'You've been at home all night? No-one else has been here?'

Bailey snorted in exasperation. It made him begin to cough. The coughs were dry but wrenched out from deep in his chest. Without another word, he went out of the room to go to the kitchen for a drink of water.

'I told you,' said Reismann.

'How long's he been like this?' asked Carston.

'No idea. He called me last night, then again at six this morning. It came on overnight apparently.'

'Yes. He called us, too.'

'And you ignored him.'

Carston said nothing.

'Is it just nerves getting to him?' asked Ross.

'Does it look like that to you?'

Ross shook his head. Either Bailey was highly suggestible, which he doubted, or he'd somehow picked up some sort of virus. Whatever the truth of it, Bailey himself was convinced that it was connected with the phone calls.

'Why did he call you?' asked Ross.

It was a question that had been on Carston's mind.

'I'm his lawyer.'

'I'd've thought a doctor would be more use.'

Reismann smiled.

'Mr. Bailey's not convinced that you've been taking this as seriously as it obviously should be taken.'

'He's getting ready to sue us, is that it?' said Carston.

Reismann said nothing, holding his smile and reawakening all Carston's dislike of him. His connections with the missing persons as well as many other examples of his manipulation of the law had come into clear focus as Carston had read through his dossier. His skill at interpreting obscure sub-clauses and recalling forgotten precedents had earned him lots of money but some very dubious associations.

'D'you know anyone who might have a score to settle with you?' said Carston.

The smile was replaced by an expression of surprise.

'With me? Why d'you ask that?'

'Just a line of enquiry we're following. Well, do you?'

The smile returned.

'You know my reputation. Take your pick.'

Carston managed a smile. When he had only McPhee, Dobie, Waring and the threats to Bailey to go on, he was groping for something to bring them together, but when he'd realized that his own response to each new disappearance was one of satisfaction, a more logical connection emerged. The evidence that they were all tied in with Reismann was reassuring. Unless the doctor, Davidson, gave him something new to go on, he was guessing that, somehow, Reismann was the link.

'I think we should go and see how he is,' said Reismann.

All three of them left the study and turned towards the back of the house. From his previous dealings with Bailey, Carston knew the layout very well. The carpet sucked at his shoes and as he padded through it he looked again, impressed in spite of himself, at the spare lines and the gorgeous colours of the Japanese prints which were gathered in groups on the walls. In the kitchen, cream tiles and chrome and copper containers shone brightly at them. Light streamed in through huge picture windows looking onto the garden and the woods beyond. In the distance, the blue of the Cairngorms lifted against the sky. Carston couldn't help looking at the spot on the floor where Marion Bailey's brains had been spread. No sign, of course. The evidence had disappeared as totally as she had.

Bailey was bending over the double stainless steel sink, retching violently but almost noiselessly. Carston and Ross looked at one another. It was going to be even less pleasant than they'd anticipated.

TWENTY-FIVE

It was predictable. Rhona had been staying with Billy for just three days and, already, they'd had their first row. It came as no surprise to her; she'd even warned Billy when she first arrived that they were no different from other people so it was inevitable that they'd fight. What did upset her was the rage it had aroused in him.

She'd felt bad about having to give the police his address and, that evening, she'd told him all about her visit. He was at his computer, surfing the geek websites he enjoyed, and his attention was only partly on what she was saying.

'It was just so that they'd stop looking for me,' she said.

He shook his head.

'Wrong move,' he said.

'Why? I'm not missing. They can forget about me now.'

He picked another address from a drop down menu, hit the return key and turned to her.

'Why d'you think they put your photo out again?' he said.

'They told me that. They found Bob Davies' body.'

'Is that it?'

Rhona saw no need to mention Stride. She nodded.

'So do they think you had something to do with it?'

'Of course not. He's been missing for ages. Why should I have anything to do with that?'

Again he shook his head. The new home page was patching itself onto his screen.

'So why send out your photo?'

She was silent.

'Christ, Rhona,' he said. 'For somebody as savvy as you are, you've got some weird ideas about how the police work. Guilty till proved innocent, according to them.'

'I don't think so,' she said. 'They were OK.'

'Never. They're never OK.'

He turned back to the monitor and started scrolling through menus. She watched the flashes of the graphics and wanted to be back in a space of her own.

'I had to give them my address,' she said quietly.

He stopped keying and looked at her again.

'What address?'

She pointed at the floor.

'Here? You gave them my address?' he said.

'I had to. I'm sorry.'

He was on his feet, shouting.

'Sorry? What the fuck use is that? So that's me on file down there, is it?'

'Of course not,' she said, taken aback by the suddenness of his anger.

He threw open the top drawer of his computer desk.

'Know what I've got in there? A dozen Es and enough dope to keep us going for a month. And now I'll have to get rid of it all.'

'Why?'

He grabbed her by the arm.

'Because your fucking friends in blue might drop by and want a look round.'

She tried to pull her arm away.

'Let go, Billy. Don't do this,' she said.

'Why the fuck did I let myself in for this?' he said, shoving her away so that she fell against the sofa. 'Should've fucking known. You stupid bloody cow.'

She watched him as he raged, not looking at her now, furious with himself. She rubbed at her sore arm.

'Your love didn't last long, did it?' she said.

'Oh fuck, Rhona,' he shouted. 'First you set yourself up, then you dump me in the shit. What the fuck are you on?'

Suddenly, he started scrabbling in the drawer. He took out some small white packets and a black lump wrapped in cling film.

'Shit, shit,' he kept saying as he searched.

He made a final check of the drawer and slammed it shut.

'Listen,' he said, pointing a finger at her. 'When they come back for you, you say nothing to them, right?'

She held his glare, back in control, refusing to accept his

dominance. She'd been genuinely sorry that she'd had to give them his address, but she wasn't prepared to be submissive. It was a mistake coming here. She'd known it would be. Men couldn't resist it. They had to be top dog.

'I'll handle it,' she said.

'Say nothing,' he said again.

Still she held his angry, threatening gaze.

'I'll leave,' she said. 'That'd be best. I'll tell them I've gone.'

Billy turned away and punched the back of his chair hard.

'Fuck,' he said.

'I'll get my things,' said Rhona.

She'd just lifted her suitcase down from the shelf in the bedroom when she felt his arms come round her from behind. They held her tight and Billy's mouth was against her ear.

'Stop,' he said, his voice harsh.

'I've messed things up for you,' she said, tolerating his grip.

She felt his head shake violently against hers.

'It's me, it's me,' he said. 'Forget it. I was just worried about the Es and the dope. Don't go.'

Slowly, she turned to face him. There were tears of anger still in his eyes, but the bully had vanished. Her threat of leaving had shocked him.

'I need you here,' he said.

It was a dependence that she resented and rejected; a pressure that she knew would drive her away sooner rather than later. A week with him would be plenty.

'We said a week,' she said. 'Let's see how it goes.'

He nodded, his arms still tight around her. They sat on the sofa and, soon, she was giving him sex. It was a one way process, Rhona making sure she stayed in control. She'd dropped her guard too often with him. There'd be no more of that.

I couldn't believe what I'd done. I kept looking at myself in the mirror, searching for signs, but it was the same face.

Couldn't see any mark of Cain or anything. But I felt as if I was ... a stranger. Felt sort of huge distances inside me, unfamiliar pictures in my head.

I told them about it.

'I've got some news about Bailey,' I said. 'He's dead. All but. I've killed him.'

If there'd been silence before, God knows what name to give the stillness that came after that.

'So. I'm confessing. I'm a murderer. Just like all of you. No better than any of you.'

I stopped. There was a little snort from Waring but the others were still. I walked round them all.

'Depends, though, doesn't it?' I said. 'I mean, motive has got to be part of it. I mean, I didn't kill him for ... money, or to make my life easier, or to prove what a big man I am. I killed him because he was a bastard.'

I looked at each of them in turn.

'So what do you think? Guilty? Not guilty?'

I stopped again. Not for them to say anything. More to think about it for myself. Then I said, 'No. Doesn't make it any better – the motive, I mean. It's still murder.'

The kitchen of Jessie's council flat in Orchard Street was tiny. It was crammed with everything that had anything to do with cooking as well as everything that Jessie and her husband didn't want in the other two rooms. The small space beside the sink on which food was prepared was a bacteria farm. Each day fresh spillages added to the nutrients available to the microbes and their colonies prospered to such an extent that they were starting to make their way up the net curtains that hung across the window behind the taps.

Harry belonged in such a room. His lank hair spiked down over a patchwork face, his grey shirt and its matching cardigan had obviously spent some time in a garage inspection pit, and the paunch that wallowed out over his belt spoke volumes about his self-image. His mood was darker than its usual sombre grey. He was hungry and Jessie had vanished. That was a direct, personal affront. In the fridge there were three eggs, a carrot, an empty milk bottle, and a carton of soft margarine. In the wall cupboard, as well as some mugs and plates there were tea-bags, a bottle of coffee essence, a packet of Bicarbonate of Soda, four tins of peas, one of baked beans and two others with Chinese writing on them. He didn't want any of that, mainly because it would have meant that he actually had to open a can. For him the expression 'instant food' had to be a literal, exact truth.

Having already given up hope, he tried one last despairing look in what was supposed to be the airing cupboard. He knew that it only ever contained saucepans and empty biscuit tins, but his hunger drove him to wrench the door open and slam it back against the wall. Yes. Saucepans. Biscuit tins. Just as he'd known there would be. He took the nearest tin and opened it, in case a miracle had left some forgotten biscuits there. He saw no biscuits, but his breath rattled in his chest and he swore hard when he saw what was in it. It was a bottle. It had contained sweet sherry, but only a drop remained, an indication that whoever had emptied it had held it to their lips for ages to make sure that nothing was wasted.

'Crafty fuckin bitch,' he wheezed. 'Where'd she get the money for that? And how come I didn't get none?'

He threw the tin to the floor. The bottle bounced without breaking. He kicked it against the waste-bucket that was overflowing under the table. This time it shattered. He went out onto the landing and began to shuffle his arms into his overcoat. He had to go out and get her. She couldn't get away with this sort of thing. He knew that she'd been with the scum down by the canal. His pals in the pub had told him about it, and their perverse notions of hierarchy made them – drunken layabouts with council flats – the social superiors of homeless alcoholics. His empty belly and the empty bottle provoked in him a double fury against her that he knew would be upheld by any court in the land. A wife was supposed to look after her husband, and if she came across a bottle of booze, she was certainly supposed to share it with him. He went out, slamming the door, intent on finding her and making sure she didn't do it again.

To keep Reismann quiet, Carston had asked the station sergeant to get a constable to call at Bailey's house at regular intervals during the day. Constable McHarg had drawn the short straw, missed out on what had been a quiet shift on the first day, and been back and forth to Bailey's place since nine that morning. Bailey's mood had worsened since Carston and Ross's visit and, as he swore at McHarg and insisted that he do something, the young policeman had wavered more and more, anxious to oblige, but not knowing what to offer. On his fourth call, in the early afternoon, he found Bailey in his bedroom. It was a huge relief. He looked in, established his presence, then decided to have a rest from it all and sit outside on the landing. He'd brought a motoring magazine with him and, after looking at his watch and noting that in just a couple of hours he'd be off-duty, he opened it, flicked past the adverts for unaffordable cars and began reading an article about fuel injection and carburettor maintenance.

Inside fifteen minutes he'd given up. The noises coming from the bedroom had progressed from moans to harsh cries of intense pain. Bailey wasn't doing this for effect; the suffering was genuine. McHarg couldn't pretend that he was concentrating on the words and pictures before him. Every sound lanced into him and when he heard them spill over into a prolonged fit of coughing and retching, he got up, opened the door and went in.

Right away, it was obvious that action was overdue. Bailey was twisted on his bed, his head hanging down over the side of it, the blankets and sheets tangled around his limbs. Pain was spiking through his bowels and stomach and he was in the spasms of a retching fit. He'd been violently sick on the bedclothes and the carpet. His breath was fast and the flesh on the side of his face that McHarg could see was flushed and shining with sweat. The heaving of his diaphragm prevented him from articulating any comprehensible sounds, but the distortion of his features left no doubt that he was in agony.

McHarg knew that there was little he could do to relieve his distress. He went round the bed to the table beside it, picked up the telephone and dialled 999. When he'd ordered the ambulance, he dialled again and explained what was going on to his sergeant. Dwyer said that he'd tell Carston. McHarg put back the phone and set about trying to make the sick man comfortable. He fetched a towel and a bowl of water from the bathroom, sat on the bed, avoiding the mess that Bailey had made, and began to sponge at his brow. The man was running a high fever. The sweat was pouring off him and his eyes stared pathetically at McHarg. They wanted relief, forgiveness, comfort, reassurance, life. There was no doubt that Bailey suspected that he was at the edge of the terrible darkness which had been threatening since the telephone calls began. His fingers wrapped hard around the constable's wrist, trying to grab some of the younger man's vitality. The expression on his face came from the other side of a gulf which frightened McHarg as he recognized it.

'I'm sorry,' said Bailey, his voice now scraping from his throat.

'Don't you worry, sir. The ambulance'll be here soon. They'll sort you out.'

'It's not your fault. It's that inspector. Carston. I told him. So many times.'

'Don't worry about that now. Just try to relax.'

'I'm so sorry,' Bailey said again, and the tears in his eyes were as much from self-pity as from pain. 'If only …'

Another retching fit took over from the words. McHarg held his burning forehead as his body arched and heaved on the bed. The throes were so violent that it was difficult to believe that they were simply being produced by the muscle spasms of such a small body. It would have made much more sense to imagine a huge hand gripping Bailey and shaking him like a bundle of twigs. Nothing so fanciful crossed McHarg's mind. He was concentrating hard on easing the distress as much as possible and trying to still the flailing limbs. It seemed like days before he eventually heard the buzzer that told him that someone was at the gate. He activated the lock release, and went out gratefully to meet the ambulance men.

TWENTY-SIX

Carston left home as soon as he got the desk sergeant's call. The time he'd spent with Bailey and Reismann when he and Ross had visited them had made him realize how far he'd been allowing his dislike of the man to interfere with his professional judgment. He wasn't proud of himself.

Constable McHarg saluted as Carston came in.

'Well done, lad,' was all the acknowledgement he got as Carston went past him. 'In the bedroom, was it?'

'Yes sir,' said McHarg, hurrying after him.

Their noses told them the direction to follow. The sharp edge of bile was in the air as the smell of the drying vomit met them. Carston looked briefly at it, uncertain as to what he was looking for, but vaguely wondering whether he would see blood or something other than the substance that was deposited so frequently on the floor of the holding cells, especially at weekends.

'What's he been eating?' he asked as he went on into the room, wrinkling his nostrils against the assault.

'Nothing much that I know of, sir. He said he had an egg and some toast this morning, that's all.'

'How about yesterday?'

'Same then, apparently. Only stuff from the fridge and freezer, like you ordered.'

Carston had taken the obvious precautions against food that might have been tampered with, and yet the signs were looking ominous.

'There was a phone call while you were on your way here sir. From the doctor who came with the ambulance men.'

'Spit it out then,' said Carston, still looking at the vomit and regretting his choice of words as soon as they were uttered.

'He said his temperature and his blood pressure both came down again on the way to the hospital.'

'Is that good or bad?'

'He thought it might be …' McHarg studied his notebook

very carefully before trying the final word, '... septicaemia.'

'Blood poisoning?' said Carston. 'Well, I suppose that fits. But how the hell did he get that? Did the doctor say anything else?'

'No sir. They're just making Mr. Bailey comfortable, settling him in. They've given him some sort of sedative apparently. To counteract the muscle spasms, they said. The doctor said he'd write a report and let us have it as soon as he could.'

'So at least it's not the food. I don't suppose he gave you any idea if he's in danger?'

'He couldn't say. I did ask. I thought you'd want to know.'

'Good lad. Well done. Is there somebody on duty down there?'

'Where?'

'At the hospital. It'd be just our luck to send him off because of a bit of blood-poisoning and have some visitor slope in and cut his throat.'

McHarg looked quickly at him.

'Sergeant Dwyer sent somebody down before the ambulance got there, sir.'

Carston nodded approval, then looked around the peach-coloured room. It was all so secure, so protected, and yet someone had managed to introduce a venom not only into the house, but into its owner's body. Still, if that was the case, it meant that there was something specific to look for. There was no point in going over to the hospital yet. Experience told him that medical staff were unwavering in their priorities; only when they were sure the patient was comfortable would they let non-medical considerations take over. He decided to ferret about the house, with the help of McHarg, and save the hospital trip till later.

They were both in the study, McHarg looking at the leather spines of the books on the shelves and Carston trying to be systematic in an examination of every inch of the surface of the desk, when the call came that fundamentally changed all the his intentions. It was the same doctor who'd spoken to McHarg. He was sorry to have to tell them that Mr. Bailey had become progressively more violent, despite their attentions. His state was confused, wild, hysterical, and he'd died at five-seventeen.

I only realized what I must have been like to work with when Jill came in after work one evening after the practice meeting. I was stuffing papers into my briefcase.
  'Sorry, Jill,' I said. 'Busy evening. Have to rush.'
  'It's a professional call,' she said.
  'Problem?' I said.
  'Don't know. Is there?'
  'What d'you mean?'
  'Something bothering you?' she asked.
  'Not really. Just ... got a lot on.'
  'So what's new?'
  I shrugged.
  'We've always got a lot on,' she said. 'This is different.'
  I stopped messing about with the papers. It wasn't fair to try to fob Jill off. She was clearly concerned about me.
  'Yep, you're right. Can't fool you, can I?'
  She smiled.
  'So what is it? Anything I can help with?'
  'No,' I said. 'It's ... it's to do with Tommy. I've been sorting his things out. Not easy to get over it.'
  'D'you want to talk about it?'
  'Not really. I appreciate your asking, though, Jill. It's ... it's classic bereavement stuff really. I know it. I'm sorry if it's affecting things here. I don't want it to get in the way of my work.'
  'Oh no, it's not that. On the contrary – you're making the rest of us look like three-toed sloths. I just don't want you wearing yourself out.'
  I managed a smile.
  'Don't worry. I won't. I can see the signs.'
  'Well, just slow down. Take it easy now and again.'
  I went across to her.
  'Tonight, I'm having a romantic dinner, tête-à-tête, with

a sexy lady. Is that easy enough for you?'

She tapped me on the cheek.

'If you put as much energy into her as you've been putting in here, she'll be exhausted before the coffee's served.'

'Not sure we'll bother with coffee. Or even food,' I said.

She smiled again and opened the door.

'Remember, though,' she said. 'If there's anything I can do ...'

'Thanks, Jill. I appreciate it. Really. And if I keep on getting on people's tits, remind me.'

'Have a nice evening.'

'You too.'

It wasn't a surprise – what she said, I mean. I was aware that I'd needed to keep on moving, to stop my mind straying back to Bailey and what it meant. The shifting in and out of identities was getting harder, too. That's when the receptionist called through to tell me you wanted to see me and you came through to my room.

Carston sat in the chair beside the desk. Davidson sat facing him.

'Who is it, then?' asked Davidson. 'What have they been up to this time?'

The puzzled look on Carston's face told him that he'd misread the purpose of the visit.

'Sorry,' he said. 'Usually, it's one of the patients who's been misbehaving.'

Carston smiled.

'Well, it's a patient alright. And he's misbehaved right enough. But this time, he's disappeared.'

Davidson waited and listened as Carston told him about McPhee and asked him about the phone call he'd made. He was surprised to feel a cool quiet come into his mind. He hoped that nothing showed but his previous helter-skelter rushing about to clear his desk had vanished. He was focused entirely on the moment and on Carston's words.

'Ah yes,' he said. 'He's not my patient in fact, but I

know plenty about him. I shouldn't say so, but he's a very unpleasant individual.'

'It seems you didn't exactly try to … humour him when he called.'

Davidson shook his head.

'I know. Very unprofessional. It was late and he was being unreasonable… But that's no excuse.'

Briefly, Carston felt the return of the embarrassment of his own recent lack of professionalism. He shook his head to get rid of it.

'Do you remember anything he said? Anything that might have suggested he was … I don't know … planning anything?'

Davidson shook his head again.

'We get so many calls. I just remember him swearing, insisting I should give him some more medication, something stronger … As I say, I don't really remember.'

'This medication he was on, would it be serious if he couldn't take it?'

'No, no. They were tablets, simple pain-killers. Why?'

'We found them by his bed.'

'Ah. Well, if he'd been planning to … disappear, as you said, he'd probably have taken them with him.'

'Yes, that's what we thought. How about his condition? Is it serious? Could he have … I don't know … collapsed somewhere.'

'Anyone could collapse at any time,' said Davidson. 'You'd have to check with Dr McIntosh. He's her patient. But I wouldn't have thought he was in any particular danger of that.'

'What d'you normally do when you get a patient calling like that? You know, it's late, you're tired, had a long day, you want to get home …'

Davidson smiled.

'It happens more than you might think.'

'So what do you do?'

'Depends on the patient. Nine times out of ten, it can wait 'til the morning. Sometimes you go and see them.

There's no set rule.'

'But it didn't occur to you that Mr. McPhee might have been desperate.'

Davidson looked at him.

'Can I be honest with you?'

'Of course.'

'I wouldn't have cared if he was. Jill McIntosh has been run around by him for ages. He treats her like dirt. The practice owes him nothing.'

'I take it you know of his history with us?'

'You mean the murder charge? The taxi driver? Yes, we all know about that. It doesn't make it any easier to treat him.'

Carston stood up.

'No, I suppose not. Still, I'd be grateful if you'd have a think about that phone call, see if you remember anything that might be useful.'

'Of course. But I wouldn't count on it.'

Carston smiled.

'Memory does strange things.'

Davidson was standing up as Carston turned back to him again.

'There's another piece of news that might interest you.'

'Oh?'

'Aye. Strange coincidence. Another missing person.'

There was the tiniest pause before Davidson asked, 'Who?'

'George Waring.'

Davidson held his gaze, various possible responses galloping through his mind. He rejected each as artificial.

'Good,' he said.

'Yes. It must still be very painful,' said Carston.

'It's fading, but the leniency of the sentence … Well, it didn't help. Any ideas what's happened to him?'

'Not yet. We're on the case.'

He held Davidson's gaze for a beat before going to the door. Davidson went with him and opened it. The two of them shook hands.

'I hope you don't find him,' said Davidson.

Carston simply nodded and left.

I don't know whether you noticed it, but I was in helluva state when you left. Blood pounding, cheeks flushed. I tried to think straight. Perhaps it was just a coincidence. I'd taken McPhee's call. And it was natural that you'd tell me that the guy who'd killed Tommy's girls was missing. I was linked directly to both men so there was no need to get upset. Then, when the panic died down, I felt good again, excited. It was different. Life wasn't predictable any more. There were complications in it that I hadn't felt since ... well, being a teenager with sex, drugs and all the rest of it. So I decided your visit was logical. And welcome. It did me good.

I had a call to make on the way home. A patient to check on. It didn't take long. She was responding well to the regime I'd put her on and feeling good. When I left, I drove back up Macaulay Road towards the park. That's where I saw Jessie. She was sitting on the bench outside the main gate with two men. I didn't really want to get involved with her but I turned into a side street, parked the car and went back to see her. She greeted me like I was her closest friend. She'd obviously had plenty to drink.

'You shouldn't be out here, Jessie,' I said. 'It's getting too cold.'

'I'm fine, doctor, fine. Better off here than back home with him.'

'Aye, but ...'

She turned to the two men with her.

'This is my doctor. Great doctor. Nice man.'

One of the men reached out a hand. I shook it. It was greasy.

'Looks after me,' said Jessie.

'Aye, that's why I stopped, Jessie. I think you should be indoors.'

Her head was already shaking.

'I've told you before, doctor. It's dangerous for me there. Dan-ger-ous.'

'Aye, what she's needing is a wee dram,' said the greasy man. 'Just one, like. Just to keep out the cold.'

I looked closely at Jessie's eyes. They were dead, unfocused, the lids blinking slowly.

'You're doing yourself no good staying outside,' I said.

She looked at me and, for a moment, I saw the light come back into her eyes.

'Doctor, there's all sorts of things you know and, like I said, you're a good man, a kind man, a nice man... But you don't know what I go home to if I go home. Honest, I'm better off here.' And she nodded several times to underline the sincerity of what she was saying.

I knew she was right, and I felt helpless again. Her take on things was simple. She had few choices and she hid nothing. I gave her a tenner. It was the wrong thing to do. She'd buy more booze, which would keep her on the streets and do more damage to her liver. But what were her alternatives? The booze would give her a few hours of forgetfulness. It was more than I could offer. She thanked me. There were tears in her eyes. I didn't stay.

A couple of hours later, I was standing at the door of Gayla's house, holding a bunch of white chrysanthemums, a box of Belgian chocolates and a bottle of Burgundy. She opened the door, a warm rush of garlic-scented air came out and I handed over the presents.

'Is this all?' she said, looking out as if to see where I'd left the delivery van with the rest of it.

'There'll be more later,' I said.

'Yes, they all say that.'

We went in, she put the gifts on the hall table and we kissed. A real kiss. One that said we'd be having sex before too long. She went back to her stirring and mixing. I took some wine out of the fridge, topped up Gayla's glass and poured one for myself. It was all so ordinary, soothing. I went over and put my arms round her.

'What's that for?' she asked.

'You look nice.'

'Thank you.'

She put down the wooden spoon, turned and we kissed again. It was long, gentle and, to my surprise, and probably hers as well, I got an almost instant erection. Sorry. That's probably more information than you wanted to have, but it's important.

'Well, well,' she said.

The meal was good but, all the time, some of my mind was elsewhere. Gayla obviously noticed it. When we'd finished eating and cleared everything away, she poured us a couple of glasses of Islay malt and said, 'You've got something on your mind, haven't you?'

'Lots of things.'

'Problems?'

'Not really.'

'Want to share them?'

'Not really.'

She didn't insist.

'I've done some very foolish things,' I said after a while. 'For all the right reasons, but stupid bloody things, all the same.'

'Like what?'

'Oh, nothing. Not stuff that ...'

I stopped. She was lying with her head in my lap. I had my fingers in her hair.

'Are you a jealous person?' I said.

'Depends.'

'Do you bear a grudge?'

'Not usually, no. Do you?'

'Oh yes,' I said. 'In bloody spades.'

'And who are you thinking of?'

'Lots of people.'

'Like who?'

'Ian Paisley, Margaret Thatcher, George Bush, Hitler. People like that.'

She turned her head to look at me and see if I was joking.

'Is that all?' she said.

'Anybody who doesn't give a toss about other people,' I said.

She turned so that she was facing fully towards me.

'Is this you wanting to change the world again?' she asked.

I thought about it and the cellar came into my mind.

'How d'you fancy a holiday?' I said.

'What?'

'I haven't had one this year. Where shall we go?'

She sat up, resting her hand on my thigh to keep herself upright.

'Andrew, are you feeling normal?'

'Completely.'

'Holiday? Us? Together?'

'Why not? I'll teach you how to form sentences.'

She laughed and lay down again. Her head was at the top of my thighs.

'Where would you like to go?' I said.

She thought about it.

'This time of year?' she said. 'New England.'

'OK. Want me to book flights?'

'You mean it, don't you?'

'Yes.'

'When?'

'Whenever you like. Next week?'

'Alright.'

I nodded. We clinked glasses. It was a deal. She took a sip and thought for a while.

'Will we be travelling as Dr and Mrs. Davidson?' she asked.

'No. Batman and Robin,' I said.

'That's OK then.'

And then we had sex. There on the carpet. And it was fabulous. Whatever it was that had got in the way before, there was no sign of it. She loved it. So did I.

TWENTY-SEVEN

Carston's reliance on Ross was greater than he'd like to admit. While he, Carston, let his imagination ride over possibilities, Ross collated materials, highlighted anomalies, inconsistencies and parallels. Bailey's death had pushed their work rates through the roof. Briefings every morning and evening, liaising with Grampian and Tayside, and still keeping on top of the day to day things meant that they were biting deep into their overtime allocation. Carston remembered their recent, relatively inactive phase with a little regret and felt that he was more than compensating for it now. It meant that Kath caught only glimpses of him as he passed through the house to grab meals, showers and changes of clothing. That very morning as she'd been stumbling across the landing to the bathroom, she'd seen him at the bottom of the stairs, pulling on his coat, and shouted, 'Excuse me. Haven't we met somewhere before?'

He'd looked up at her, blown a kiss and replied, 'Don't think so. I'd've remembered.'

It was still before eight and he was in his office, coffee steaming beside him, the papers in front of him gradually being sorted and discarded. Ross was showing signs of the hours he'd been putting in, too. It didn't help that, at home, he had two small but demanding daughters who needed to be read to, played with and spoiled. He was sitting opposite Carston, looking through a chunk of fan-folded paper which had been delivered from the remote computer print-out station in the basement. Put simply, it was a list of cases that tabloids had highlighted as miscarriages of justice in the past two years.

Not surprisingly, the name of Reismann occurred fairly frequently. Ross skipped over the details of these cases because Carston had already noted them as he'd read through the lawyer's file. The rest of the examples listed were all too vague in the end. It came as no surprise to Ross, who knew that, to use computers properly, you had to play the game with their rules. Their terms of reference had been too wide. Nevertheless, his careful examination had produced twenty-three more names, ranging from wife-beaters to a con-man.

'Nice,' he said as he read the details of the last case.

Carston looked up. 'What?'

'This guy. Spent ninety-seven thousand pounds of his firm's money setting up export deals with a series of Paris restaurants.'

'And?'

'The firm's got bugger all to do with food. Manufactures seismic equipment for surveying the sea-bed.'

'And he was done for it?'

'Aye.'

'Should've been promoted. Shows lots of initiative.'

'He was released on a technicality connected with foreign exchange controls.'

'That's not a miscarriage of justice; he deserved to get away.'

Ross didn't agree but he knew what Carston meant. He put the list with its twenty-three names in the green box. They'd already checked on most of them and found that none of them was missing. In that respect, it hadn't added much to their knowledge, but the fact that it contained the names Dobie, McPhee, Waring, Bailey and Campion confirmed that there was a discernible link between them.

Amongst his mail, Carston found a large envelope from Tayside. It was the data on Ian Stride that he'd been waiting for. He scanned quickly through it, looking particularly hard at two of the photos. The first was the blurred, distant shot of him driving with a female passenger. Reluctantly, Carston had to admit that it could have been Rhona, but equally that it could have been several hundred other women. The fact that she'd admitted it was her helped a bit, but it needed corroboration. The other photo showed a figure in a hat locking a car door. Its only value was that they could estimate the person's height as he stood beside the car. Another sheet carried eye witness reports from some drivers who'd seen what could have been Stride's car in a lay-by on the main

Dundee-Edinburgh road. Some of them said the car was empty and there was no sign of anyone near it, others reported another car, a black VW Golf, parked near it. No-one had seen the drivers of either vehicle. A loop of CCTV footage at one of the roundabouts to the south of Dundee had caught Stride's car with two black Golfs close behind it. Apart from that, the envelope just contained more detail on what Carston already knew. He pushed it across the desk to Ross.

'Wonder what Stride was doing meeting somebody in a place like that,' he said.

Ross skimmed through the reports, nodding as he did so.

'Aye, I see what you mean. Might be no connection, though.'

'What the hell was he doing stopping in a lay-by then?'

'People do. That's what they're for.'

'But he'd just left Dundee. He was only eight, nine miles down the road.'

'Breakdown.'

'How did the car get to Edinburgh?' asked Carston.

'Pass,' said Ross.

Carston sat back, tapping his pen against his lip.

'OK,' said Carston. 'Things happen. So, for whatever reason, he stops there. The other guy pulls up. The two of them go off in the VW. The guy kills him, comes back and drives his car to Edinburgh.'

'Whoah, that's a lot of assumptions you're making there,' said Ross.

'They all fit.'

'So Stride goes meekly off with this guy to be strangled?'

Carston shrugged.

'Nobody saw any fighting or anything. It's a busy road. Somebody would've noticed,' he said.

'OK, so he went with him willingly. Why?'

'Maybe he knew him. That's why they stopped.'

They fell silent, each mulling over the different scenarios, looking for the most plausible one.

220

'Has Rhona got a car?' asked Carston.

'Dunno.'

'Why hitch a lift with Stride if she has?' He pointed at the envelope. 'Have a look at the rest of the stuff in there. See if you can't match it up with anything on Davies.'

Ross tapped some commands into his computer and began looking from the papers before him to the screen and back again.

Carston checked his watch. It was just past nine. He picked up the phone and dialled his home number. Kath answered almost immediately.

'Hullo, love,' said Carston. 'You can probably guess why I'm phoning.'

'To say sorry?'

'Eh? What for? What have I done?'

'I don't know, but there's usually something.'

'OK,' said Carston. 'Sorry.'

'Right,' said Kath. 'Anything else?'

'Yes. I'll be late.'

'Oh, is that all?'

'Sorry love. We'll go away somewhere. Next week maybe. Edinburgh, Glasgow.'

'Promise?'

'Promise. Start planning it. Anywhere you like. We'll stay away the night. Yes?'

'Who's paying?' asked Kath.

'You are.'

'OK. Bye love.'

'Bye.'

Carston put the receiver back and sighed. He loved spending time with Kath. Of all the people he knew, she was not only the one he loved, she was also a very good friend, the only one he allowed inside himself. He was always sorry when he had to spend too much time away from her and his determination to make up for it was genuine.

'Bloody hell. We got lucky again.'

It was Ross's voice, eager, excited.

'What?' said Carston.

Ross turned his screen and held a piece of paper up beside it. Both showed the familiar bars of a DNA profile and it was fairly obvious, even to their untrained eyes, that they were at least similar and probably identical. Ross tapped the screen.

'This was from the stuff they found between Davies' teeth,' he said.

He flicked the piece of paper and added, 'And this is one of the traces they found on Stride.'

Carston's smile was as broad as Ross's.

'Christ, we did get lucky,' he said. 'It's got to be Rhona, surely.'

Ross made a little face. 'We can't be sure, but it's a start,' he said.

'Did we get a sample from her when she was raped?'

Ross was scrolling through menus again.

'It never came to court remember, so technically she wasn't.'

'Even better,' said Carston. 'If we did get one, it may still be lurking around. The case may still be open so the evidence'll still be there.'

He knew as he said it that it was probably wishful thinking, but, once again, his luck was in.

'Yep. Here it is,' said Ross.

He hit the print button and two DNA trace charts fed out of the machine, one was Rhona's, the other from the Davies material. They put them beside the third sheet, from Stride's file and were immediately disappointed. The two from the murder victims were identical; Rhona's was nothing like them.

'Shit,' said Carston.

Ross was looking through the Stride file again. He slid another sheet free, looked at it, nodded and silently handed it to Carston. Carston put it with the others and saw at once why Ross had chosen it. Tayside had found two DNA traces on Stride's body apart from his own; one matched the traces on Davies, the other was Rhona's.

'OK, good. So it confirms that she was with him,' said

Carston. 'She's told us that already but it's good to have the evidence. But who the hell's this other stuff from? Who else knew both of them?'

'No idea,' said Ross.

'Well, she's the only thing we've got. Let's get her in again for a chat.'

'How are you going to play it?' he asked.

'By ear.'

'Hard to think we'll get lucky again,' said Ross.

'The Lord looks after his own,' said Carston.

Jessie had decided not to bother going back to her flat and Harry's fists. Despite the cold, the piece of canal bank she'd commandeered was for her exclusive use, and the blankets and cardboard boxes she'd managed to gather became a surprisingly cosy cocoon once she'd lodged herself inside them and drawn the lids and flaps around her. At first, she didn't know what to do with them, but she watched as a youngish man folded his cardboard into a sort of tube. When he was satisfied, he began pushing newspapers down inside it and arranging them carefully along the bottom and up the sides. Jessie copied him as closely as she could. At last, he eased himself down into his nest and, with one hand, pulled at a piece of cardboard which folded miraculously down to enclose him completely. One minute there was a man there, the next there was just this enormous cardboard cigar.

Jessie's construction had none of the professionalism of her model, but once she'd crawled down into it and shuffled for ages with the pieces of newspaper that had bunched up beneath her, the energy she'd expended had generated enough heat to insulate her from the night's mists. No-one else existed; her husband and his demands had gone. There was only this warmth and the last of the wine she'd bought with Davidson's tenner.

TWENTY-EIGHT

Booking the tickets for the flight to America was easy. We'd leave Aberdeen on a Tuesday at a quarter to twelve, change planes in London and be in Boston at six-twenty. I used the Internet to hire a car and book hotels in Vermont and New Hampshire. It was only when I'd given them my credit card details and confirmed all the bookings that I stopped to think about it all. I mean, there were obvious problems.

I'd be away for about ten days. I could leave enough fruit and food in the cellar for them to survive until we got back. If I wanted to. Or I could release them. – No, I couldn't do that. I'd confessed to them, told them about Bailey. At least one of them would want to get some sort of revenge for what I'd put them through.

I suppose what I was doing was deliberately forcing my own hand, pushing myself into making a final decision about them. The flight to the States was a new beginning, a way of leaving behind the mess I'd made. All I had to do now was work out how to come back to a mess-less life, with my debt to Tommy paid, and the darkness I'd found inside me satisfied and back under control.

At Bailey's the crime scene posed a few problems. To begin with, there was nothing for the photographer to do. He flashed off a few shots of the bedroom, then, for the sake of form, covered the other rooms in the house, but it seemed more like an assignment for *Homes and Gardens* than a murder record. Nor was there any point in the doctor or the pathologist being there at the moment because the body was absent. And the officer in charge, Ron Duveen, was sceptical.

'What do you reckon the chances of finding any contact traces are?' he asked Carston.

'If you get any, it'll be a bloody miracle,' replied the CID man. 'No-one's been here for a week or more. Except me, Jim Ross and Reismann.'

'Aye. Christ knows what I'm looking for. I mean,

nobody could've got in, could they? Not with all his security systems.'

'Just see what you can find, Ron. You never know.'

'The cause of death was some sort of poisoning, you reckon?'

'Don't know for certain yet, but they said septicaemia to begin with, so it's more than likely. That's what you want to be looking for, though, the way he did it. That's your best bet. I might even be able to narrow it down a bit for you, too.'

'Oh?'

'Yes. The guy who was threatening him, on the phone. Apparently, he asked him about his flowers. And the summer house.'

'So what?'

'I reckon he was just making sure where Bailey was. Out in the garden, sitting in his summer house. It always struck me that that was where he'd be vulnerable. Worth a special look, eh? What d'you reckon?'

'He spent ages out there,' said Ross. 'But it's just a garden.'

'Aye,' said Duveen. 'And crawling with tetanus germs and Christ knows what else in the way of lethal microbes. I suppose you thought of that?'

'Yes,' said Carston. 'Can't take it any further 'til we've heard from Dr Taylor, though.'

Taylor was the pathologist who'd been assigned to the job. Duveen nodded and moved away to organize the setting up of floodlights in the garden.

'I've been poking around a bit,' said Ross.

Carston looked at him. Waited.

'How did you get on with Dr Davidson?'

Carston shrugged.

'He doesn't like McPhee any more than we do.'

'Did you tell him about Waring?'

'Aye. Same again. He hopes we won't find him. I got the impression he'd like somebody to be slicing his balls off with a blunt bread knife. Why? What's this all about?'

'Remember Jenny Gallacher?'

Carston thought for a moment. Shook his head.

'Dobie's girl friend. The one he infected.'

'Oh aye, right. What about her?'

'She was a patient at his practice, too.'

Carston raised his eyebrows, nodded his head.

'One of Davidson's?'

'No, one of the women doctors there. But …'

He paused.

'Stop pissing about, Jim. But what?'

'You've forgotten, haven't you? Davidson was Marion Bailey's GP.'

'Of course. He gave evidence at the trial, didn't he? Bloody hell. Bailey, Waring, McPhee, Dobie. It can't be that easy, can it?'

'Harold Shipman got away with it long enough.'

'Oh Christ, don't say that. I don't want anything like that on our patch.'

'Bit of a coincidence, though, isn't it?'

Carston nodded. Where crime was concerned, he didn't believe in coincidence. He thought back to his meeting with Davidson. The man had seemed open enough. He hadn't concealed his obvious dislike of McPhee and Waring. The memory flashed a little warning at him. For all their apparent respectability, there was no reason why doctors shouldn't play the vigilante. Dying was part of their everyday experience. So was power. And you didn't have to be a freak to want people like Bailey and the rest to suffer; he himself had felt a guilty satisfaction at the thought. So had Ross. It was normal.

'The more you think about it, though, the better it gets,' he said.

'How?'

'The phone calls – they had to be from somebody who had some sort of hold over these buggers, somebody they'd take notice of. And none of them knew each other as far as we know, so it's not going to be one of their pals phoning them. In fact, the only thing they had in common was their dealings with us and the fact that they're all connected with

Davidson's practice.'

'Lets Reismann off the hook, doesn't it?' said Ross.

'Unless Davidson's connected with him somehow.'

'D'you want me to check it out?'

Carston just nodded. Suddenly, light seemed to be flooding into the puzzle. Davies and Stride seemed to be separate from all this. He hadn't yet had time to talk to Rhona but she was still firmly in the frame for Stride at least. It was hard to imagine that Davidson was involved with the others, but he did draw them all together. Of course, it was still possible that there was no connection between any of the disappearances and Bailey's murder, but they'd come hard on top of one another and the new revelations helped to freshen Carston's mind.

'Has your mate finished with the French windows yet?' he asked.

Ross looked up to see the fingerprint man sticking lengths of sellotape on a piece of card which he'd already labelled.

'Looks like it,' he said.

'Right. I'm going to have a stroll outside. Tell Ron, will you?'

'Right,' said Ross.

The fingerprint man confirmed that he'd finished, so Carston went past him out into the cold, clinging air. He walked well away from the house and began stitching together the persuasive threads that led to Davidson. He hummed to himself as he strolled along and was surprised to hear a telephone ringing nearby. Immediately he remembered the summer house and Bailey's last call. He made no attempt to find and answer the phone. It probably was for him, but Duveen's men hadn't yet been to the summer house and he knew better than to smear yet another layer of contact over Bailey's things. He turned back towards the house and soon heard Ross's voice calling him.

'Here Jim,' he called back. 'I'm on my way.'

'Telephone,' said Ross. 'Dr Taylor.'

'Oh good,' said Carston with a sigh.

The receiver in the study was off its rest. Carston picked it up.

'Dr Taylor?' he said.

'Jack, how are you?'

'Curious.'

'I can imagine. Anyway, I've got a probable cause of death for you.'

'Good. What's the story?'

'Acute toxaemia, I'd say.'

'Yes, the hospital doc thought it was septicaemia at first,' said Carston.

'That's right. He was certainly poisoned.'

'Any idea of the type of thing involved?'

'No, not yet. You've dealt with all the food, have you?'

'It's all here. Still in the fridge or freezer. Nothing's been touched. The trouble is …' Carston hesitated.

'Well?'

'I had it all checked. When we first started looking in on him. I warned him then to stick to stuff he already had in the house.'

'I see. Fascinating. Alright. Might be a day or two before you get my full report. They're stacked up like fish fingers down here. I'll let you know once I've had a bit of a delve, eh?'

'I'd appreciate it if you could make it sooner rather than later.'

'Your man's viscera must take their place in the queue. Bye.'

He made viscera sound even worse than they were.

228

TWENTY-NINE

The normal focal point for the evening's gatherings down by the canal was a small fire in an old oil drum. It was just enough to hold away the cold and get the people there ready for the hours of darkness they had to get through. Jessie had been given six fifty pees and some ten pees as she'd walked around the shops that afternoon, her hands held out to the passers-by. One young couple had even given her a pound coin and laughed as they'd said to her, 'There you go, darlin. Penny for the guy.'

She'd bought some sherry, but had become wary of drinking it in front of the others. The half bottle of it that remained was clutched inside her coat as she pulled her pieces of cardboard together. She was warm with the amount she'd already had and was singing a cracked song to herself as she prepared her bed some way apart from the rest.

Across the canal, the two young men who'd watched the drunken activities of Jessie and her friends not so many afternoons ago were taking a handful of fireworks from the carrier on the back of one of their motor-bikes. There were no rockets or sparklers. The names on the tubes made it obvious that the function of these varieties was to make the maximum of noise. Thunderclaps, Bazookas, Atomic Flashes, and the astonishing Cosmic Holocaust were laid on the ground at their feet. They shared them out, stuffed them into the pockets of their jackets and sat down to decide on their strategy.

Jessie was almost into her tube. She shuffled the last couple of feet very carefully, learning fast that speed of entry was the thing that caused the newspapers to bunch up into uncomfortable and thermally useless bundles. The two youths watched her head slide down and disappear into the cardboard. One of them nudged the other with his elbow and they stood up.

On Jessie's side of the water, some eighty yards away, her husband was stumbling along with two of his pals. They were drunk, but trying to make as little noise as possible as they made their way towards the figures around the fire. Jessie hadn't been there on the other occasions that Harry had come looking for her, so he reasoned that the only safe time would be at night when there was nowhere else for them to go.

Jessie had pulled the flap of the box inwards and was settling herself down inside its soft darkness, her hand already reaching for the sherry bottle. There were very few noises from outside, only the crackling of the fire. Her voice began to fumble with her comfortable little song again.

Superintendent Ridley had been on to Carston to ask whether the Bailey and Davies cases were connected and to suggest that, if they weren't, he should hand one of them over to someone else. It made sense, but Carston was reluctant to let go of either. He'd given non-committal replies but knew that, before long, the question would arise again. He was still waiting for the full report on Bailey, so it gave him the chance to switch his attention to Rhona.

He and Ross were sitting with her in the same interview room they'd used on her previous visit. Billy was at work, so she'd had no need to make any special excuses for going out. They'd talked a lot about Stride and she'd repeated what she'd said before. It was when she got to the tie again that Carston put on a little pressure.

'Yes,' he said. 'Bart Simpson. You weren't impressed.'

'Great program, but a crappy idea for a tie,' she said. 'What message do they think it gives?'

'Don't know, but it makes a good ligature.'

She said nothing.

'How did you know that, by the way?' asked Carston.

'What?'

'You said he was strangled with his tie. How did you know? It wasn't in the reports.'

Rhona looked at him. He saw surprise rather than guilt.

'You sure?' she said.

'Positive.'

They waited. Rhona was thinking. At last, she shrugged.

'No idea,' she said.

'There's only one way you could've known, isn't there?' said Carston.

She shook her head.

'If I did it, you mean? Well, I didn't.'

She was cool, self-assured.

'So the tie was a lucky guess,' said Carston.

'I don't know,' she said, the first tick of anger coming into her voice.

Carston picked up her tone.

'Well you'd better start remembering, because you could be in trouble here.'

'Charge me then,' she said.

'If we do, it's murder,' said Ross.

'Do it,' she said.

'We found your DNA on him,' said Carston.

She was silent for a moment, surprised by the words.

'Is that legal?' she asked. 'Without my permission?'

'Would you have given it?' said Carston. He stood up, not waiting for a reply. 'We're trying to do this easily,' he went on. 'No tape recording, no charge … yet. But you're making it hard.'

'I didn't do it,' she repeated.

'We've got your photo with him in his car, another photo of you parking it …'

'Impossible,' she said.

'… we've got your DNA on the body.'

'Surprise, surprise,' she said. 'He shagged me. Stayed the night.'

'And?'

'And what?'

'After "the night".'

'He left. Went to Edinburgh. Well, that's what he was supposed to do, but he didn't get there, did he?'

'No, he was strangled with his tie. We know that, and you know that. And the killer knew that, and I'm bloody sure I didn't kill him. Which only leaves you,' said Carston, pushing harder than before.

He stopped when she gave a little gasp.

'What?' he said.

'Christ,' she said. 'Oh, Jesus Christ.'

'What?'

'He must've done it.'

Carston and Ross looked at one another. Carston gave a little shake of his head to stop Ross saying anything. They waited as Rhona confronted the thought she'd had. Slowly, Carston sat down again. Eventually, in the silence, she looked at them. There was bewilderment on her face. And fear.

'He told me,' she said.

'Who?' asked Carston, his voice gentler.

'This guy. That's when I heard about the tie. It must be him. He's been phoning me, messing me about. Sort of stalking me really.'

'What's he look like?' asked Ross.

She shook her head.

'I've never seen him. He just phones. All the time. Knows things about me. All sorts of things. He was the one who talked about that rep. He knew he'd spent the night at my flat. Knew what time he left. Knew about his car. He told me about the guy being strangled with the tie.'

She sounded sincere, but Carston had been here before and needed more convincing. Gradually, he drew out more and more information about this man that she'd introduced. If she was lying, she was very good at it. They used all sorts of techniques to try to trip her but her story was totally consistent. Then came the clincher. She was talking about how he knew what her mother's home was like inside when she suddenly stopped and took in a sharp breath.

'Christ,' she said. 'Bob Davies. That was him, too.'

Neither Carston nor Ross had mentioned Davies at all.

'What d'you mean?' asked Ross.

'He knew all about him. About him being dug up. Told me there was a fight. Said somebody hit him over the head. That's what killed him.'

She stopped and looked from one to the other of them.

'Is that true?' she asked.

'We'll maybe come to that later,' said Carston.

'He killed both of them,' she said, her voice very quiet and the fear in her eyes even greater.

'OK, let's think about this guy,' said Carston. 'You say he knows all about you and, if he knows about your mum's house and about Bob Davies, it means he's known you for a while.'

Rhona nodded.

'And he's still phoning you?'

'Not since I've been back, no.'

'But when you were in Dundee?'

'Yes. He knew all about my flat there, too.'

'He's been inside it?'

'Must've been.'

'So who've you had in there?' asked Ross.

'Nobody. Me, the rep who was killed, a boy friend, a couple of neighbours, that's all.'

'Who's the boy friend?'

Rhona shook her head.

'I don't want him involved in this.'

'Were there any break-ins while you were in Dundee?'

'I don't know. There must've been, though. He knew where things were, what it looked like.'

'Well,' said Carston. 'If he didn't see for himself, he must've been told by you, or one of your neighbours.'

'No, they're students. Just folks I met. All they've done is look in the door, really. They don't know the sort of details he talked about.'

'Your boy friend, then.'

'Or the rep,' she said. 'Before he killed him.'

'Maybe,' said Carston. 'But we really need to check out your boy friend.'

Rhona shook her head violently.

'No. He'd go spare. He'd ...'

She stopped. Suddenly, something like a smile came briefly into her face.

'It couldn't be him,' she said.

'Who?'

'My boy friend. He knew I was getting the calls. He was there a couple of times when the guy phoned. He answered him once. Shouted at him.'

'It could've been a show. To impress you. They could be working together.'

'I don't think so,' said Rhona. 'He was furious. He'd've … done something nasty to him if he could've got hold of him.'

'Has he ever been to your mum's house? The boy friend, I mean,' asked Carston.

'I don't think so. I've never met him there.'

'When the … stalker called and your boy friend was there, what sort of things did he say?' asked Ross.

Rhona shrugged.

'The usual,' she said.

'What, asking you questions, just talking to you?'

'I s'pose so,' she said. 'Once, Billy just …'

She stopped, realizing she'd made a mistake.

'Don't worry, there's too many folk called Billy for us to check them all,' said Carston with a smile.

'You were saying?' said Ross.

Rhona sighed.

'Billy knew it was him. My voice, my face, I don't know, something made him think it was him.'

'What did he do?'

'Grabbed the phone and told the guy to leave me alone.'

'Did he get an answer?'

'I don't know. I think so. Billy didn't want to let him talk, though. He was threatening to do all sorts of things to him.'

'Protective, is he?' asked Carston.

Rhona nodded.

'More than I want him to be,' she said.

'What does Billy do?' asked Ross.

'Computer stuff. Not sure what.'

Carston leaned forward across the table.

'Rhona, you're mixed up in something pretty mucky. I'll be honest with you, you're still in the frame, at least for Ian

Stride.'

He lifted a finger as she made to protest.

'But we'll need you to help us if we're going to get anywhere. We really do need to talk to … Billy.'

Again she shook her head. Carston persisted.

'We'll try to find a way of making it seem like a routine enquiry if you like.'

'He'll know,' she said. For the first time, there was a shimmer in her eyes that suggested that tears weren't far away.

'If this stalker guy knows as much about the murders as you say he does,' Carston went on, 'he's potentially a very dangerous individual. Dangerous for you. So we need to get onto him. Now.'

Rhona's head was lowered, her eyes on her fingers, which were scratching little patterns on the table.

'It was Billy's address you gave us, wasn't it? You're staying with him.'

Still she said nothing.

'We'll check, you know,' said Carston.

Rhona just nodded.

'OK,' said Carston, 'what we'll do is come round to talk to you and just happen to find him there and see what happens.'

It took a little longer to convince her that they could make their visit look like a routine event, but at last she agreed. When they eventually let her go, neither Carston nor Ross had decided whether she was off the hook, but both were encouraged by the fresh information she'd come up with.

'What was the stuff about Billy talking to the stalker all about?' asked Carston as they walked back up to the office.

'Just an idea I had,' said Ross. 'Easiest thing in the world to rig a computer so that it dials a number at a set time and passes a message to the person on the other end.'

Carston stopped.

'So what? You're saying the stalker's the boy friend?'

Ross stopped too and turned to face him.

'Could be,' he said. 'He knows when he's going to be with her, programs the call for then, so it puts him in the clear.'

They started up the stairs again.

'Devious bugger,' said Carston.

'Who, Billy?'

'No, you.'

At lunch time, Carston was back in the pub. This time, he was buying a drink for the police pathologist. He'd left Ross to sort through their Davies file to see whether the information they'd got from Rhona changed anything. His own attention was firmly back on Bailey.

He carried two whiskies back to their table on which sat a fat envelope that Taylor had brought along with him. They raised their glasses, took a sip and said 'Cheers.'

'Bet you're dying to know about this, eh?' said Taylor, tapping the report.

Carston was surprised that he was being so direct. Usually he took stupid little pleasures in making people wait for the things he knew they most wanted.

'I wouldn't mind a quick run-down, certainly,' he said.

'Fascinating,' said Taylor as he picked up the folder. 'Know what his blood count was? Thirty-three thousand per cubic millimetre!'

He stopped for an appropriate response. Carston duly played the dumb layman.

'Is that bad?'

'You could say that. Especially when the normal white blood cell count ranges from five to ten thousand.'

Carston was genuinely impressed.

'What the hell caused that?'

'Interesting question. You see, there's no trace of anything dodgy there at all.'

'He was poisoned though, wasn't he?'

'Unquestionably. And I think we're talking about castor beans.'

He stopped and sipped at his whisky.

'Castor beans?' said Carston, dutifully.

'The infamous Ricin. The military love it. Makes Anthrax look like a mild cold.'

His voice was deliberately loud, attracting the attention of other customers, preparing no doubt to repay their curiosity by putting them off their drinks.

'Causes utter bloody chaos. Blood, pain, vomit, everything more or less liquefies inside you.'

The eavesdroppers were regretting their curiosity already. Carston wanted to interrupt the flow to pinpoint the sort of information he needed to have.

'How d'you know it was that?' he asked.

'What? Ricin? Can't be absolutely certain of course, but I'd bet a lot on it. It's a protein, generates antibodies. That's where the high blood count came from. It's broken down by the body though, naturally. Does all the damage, then disappears from your system. Wonderful stuff.'

Carston persisted.

'I still don't see how you pinned it down to that, though.'

Taylor assumed a patient expression.

'Pinned might well be the word,' he said, loving the enigma. 'You see, if he had the stuff in him, how did it get there? It's not the sort of thing you find just floating about the place. Have a look at this.'

He took one of the photographs that accompanied the printed report and passed it across to Carston. It showed a hand, which lay, palm upwards, fingers slightly curved.

'See the marks on it?' said Taylor, pointing at the centre of the photograph.

Carston leaned forward to look. There were lots of small dark points on the skin.

'What are they?'

'Just little punctures. Rose thorns, most of them. Not that one though.'

Here he pointed to a smudge almost exactly in the middle of the palm.

'That's no rose-thorn. There's a circular area of inflammation there with a central puncture mark barely more than a millimetre across. At first, it looked like all the others, but something made me have a second look. And guess what I dug out of it? A thorn which wasn't.'

Carston was willing to forgive all of Taylor's foibles. He was certainly coming up with the goods for him.

'What d'you mean?'

'Special piece of work. More or less the size of your average rose thorn but a fabricated job. Just the end of a fine spine made of GRP. Snapped off. Beautifully made. Tiny little thing. Small enough for subcutaneous penetration but big enough to carry a lethal dose.'

Carston sat back, shaking his head in unreserved admiration.

'Great job,' he said.

'So,' said Taylor. 'Narrows it down a bit.'

'In what way?'

'Not many people can get hold of stuff that toxic. Your lot could, medics, pharmacists. That's about it really.'

Carston didn't like to disillusion him by pointing out that the Internet had made every substance ever discovered available to anyone who knew where to look. But, even if that's where it had come from, it was a clear focus for their enquiries. And, of course, the ease of access medics seemed to have to such lethal substances added another link to Davidson. Taylor was right; at least they now had something more than an unknown phone caller to start investigating.

'The position of it, too …' Taylor was saying, '… helps you to narrow your search.'

Carston waited.

'Right in the middle of the palm like that. I think he's put his hand on something, grabbed it, picked it up. Somebody knew he'd do it. Just put the wee spike there.'

'Something in his garden, I'll bet. That's where he got the phone calls; it's about the only place somebody could get at. We'll have a closer look at the tools, the door handle on that summer house, the stuff inside it.'

Taylor was nodding his agreement. He picked up his glass and drained it.

'I think you've earned yourself another of those,' said Carston. 'In fact, a double.'

Taylor beamed. He agreed.

THIRTY

Cairnburgh was in one of its Indian summer phases. Big, pastel skies and a warm autumn evening brought out the Sunday drivers and slowed Carston and Ross's car as it headed for Billy's flat. Ross was driving, Carston was tapping his fingers on the arm rest.

'Maybe we ought to forget about McPhee and the others,' he said. 'There's no time to follow them up as well as all the rest of it.'

'Campion's different,' said Ross. 'He was abducted, remember – lights on, marks of a struggle, all that.'

'Yes, but Bailey and Davies are taking all our time. If we can bring them all together, we will. We've got to keep focused, though. We'll worry about the others when their bodies start turning up.'

Despite his words, he sensed that all of these people were connected. The pattern was persuasive. He'd looked back over his Bailey notes and remembered that the first threatening call had tried to arrange a meeting. If Bailey had gone to that, maybe he'd have just disappeared, too. If that was the case, where were the others? His throwaway line about the bodies turning up had been more than half serious.

They'd been lucky in the garden. Ron Duveen's team had found fibres caught in thorns on bushes at the base of the wall near the summer house and there was even dried blood on some of them. They'd already checked it against Bailey's; it wasn't his. If they did round up any suspects, they'd soon be able to eliminate or charge them. But they had to get them first.

They pulled up outside the tenement block where Billy lived. Carston had toyed with the idea of bringing Spurle with him, in case there was trouble, but the approach had to be kept subtle. Subtle wasn't in Spurle's vocabulary. Instead, he'd given them the Sunday off. First thing tomorrow, they'd be checking the phone accounts of all the names on his list and visiting the hospital to look through the register of

242

visitors who'd logged in to the pharmacy in the days leading up to Bailey's death. There were other places where a resourceful person might get Ricin but they had to cover every angle, no matter how obvious.

They knew that Rhona would be out but, when Billy opened the door, she was the one they asked for.

'She's not here,' said Billy.

'Ah, pity. We really needed to talk to her. Get a few things cleared up. Who are you?'

Billy paused before he answered.

'Billy Marshall. Why?'

'She didn't mention that anybody lived with her.'

'Other way round,' said Billy. 'It's my flat.'

'Really?' Carston managed to sound surprised. 'She your girl friend, is she?'

'Yes.'

'D'you mind if we come in and have a chat?'

'What about? She's not here.'

'No, but you might be able to help us.'

Billy tried some more stalling tactics but, to Ross's surprise, Carston's relentless charm offensive prevailed. The flat was small but tidy, with an impressive computer array taking up most of one side of the main room and two laptops on the coffee table. Beside them was a printer, a box of paper and a small pile of stamped envelopes, all ready to be posted.

'Wow, really into computing, aren't you?' said Ross.

'It's my job.'

'Programmer?' said Ross.

Billy nodded. Carston let Ross make the running with questions about broadband, ISPs, resource allocation and all sorts of other things which sounded to him like a Star Trek script. Billy, though, was quietly impressed with Ross's knowledge and seemed to relax more as the tech-talk got deeper. Eventually, Carston interrupted, apologizing for doing so, and brought the chat round to Rhona again.

'The problem is,' he said, 'she's getting these nuisance calls.'

Billy said nothing.

'Did she tell you about them?'

'No,' said Billy.

'When she lived in Dundee,' said Carston.

Billy held out his hands, palms upwards.

'Sorry, can't help you,' he said.

Carston smiled, then sighed.

'Pity,' he said. 'You see, she may be in danger.'

'Not here with me, she's not,' said Billy.

'Well, that's good to hear, but I wouldn't count on it. I called them nuisance calls; they're more than that.'

Billy was shaking his head, apparently unconcerned at the threat to Rhona.

'Nothing'll happen to her. Trust me.'

Carston nodded.

'Fond of her, are you?'

Billy looked at him, a challenge in his stare.

'Yes.'

'Good. Nice,' said Carston. 'Known her long?'

'What's that got to do with anything?'

'Just curious.'

'Well, have you? Known her long?' asked Ross.

'Long enough.'

'Nice looking girl,' said Carston. 'You're a lucky man. There's plenty of guys who'd like to be in your shoes.'

A flush came into Billy's cheeks.

'This guy, the one who's been calling her. He's probably seen her, fancied her …'

'Hey, fuck off,' said Billy, unable to suppress his quick anger.

Carston spread his hands.

'Happens all the time. Good looking women, they attract all sorts of weirdoes.'

'She's my girl, right? I can look after her.'

'Yes, but he might be mixed up in a murder enquiry,' said Carston. 'If he is … well.'

'I told you. She's OK here with me.'

'I hope you're right,' said Carston with a smile. 'Well, no point in wasting your time. We'll be off.'

244

Ross was surprised at the sudden decision. He looked a question at Carston, who just smiled at Billy.

'Sorry to have disturbed your Sunday. Although it doesn't look like it's a day of rest for you.' His hand indicated the computer equipment spread about the place. Billy said nothing.

'Right. Thanks for your help,' said Carston.

At the door, he paused.

'Have you got a car?' he asked.

'Yes,' said Billy.

'What sort?'

'Why?'

'I'm a cop. I'm nosy.'

'Ford Focus.'

Carston nodded.

'What colour?'

'Blue. It's parked outside. Why? What's it about?'

'Nothing,' said Carston. 'If anything does come up, though, would you mind if we came back for another chat?'

'I don't know anything about it,' said Billy.

'No, but you never know,' said Carston.

Billy shrugged.

'OK.'

As he walked to the car, Carston took out his mobile and rang the squad room. It was Spurle who answered.

'Busy?' said Carston.

'Yes,' said Spurle.

Carston covered the mouthpiece.

'Remind me to kick Spurle in the balls,' he said to Ross.

Ross nodded. Carston spoke to Spurle again.

'I want to run a check on car rentals in and around Dundee for the date Ian Stride disappeared. We're looking for a black Golf.'

'It'll take a while,' said Spurle.

'Better get started then,' said Carston.

As he hit the button to disconnect, he shook his head.

'How did that bugger ever pass the exams?' he said.

Ross said nothing. They got in the car and drove off.

'That lad was lying,' said Carston.

'Maybe she's the one who's lying,' said Ross.

'What do you think?'

'He was uncomfortable. Didn't like the idea of somebody else fancying her,' said Ross.

'Bit hard when she's a working girl,' said Carston.

'We don't know she is for sure.'

'Want to bet?'

Ross shook his head.

'That computer gear,' said Carston. 'Anything?'

'He knows his stuff,' said Ross. 'The screen, totally customized. Plenty of specialized software. The phone rigging I was talking about, that'd be no bother for him.'

Carston thought for a moment.

'If he did phone Rhona using that computer, he'd have to record the message into it, right?'

'Aye.'

'He'd dump it afterwards, though, wouldn't he?'

'Aye, but there's always ways of getting it back. He'd have to reformat his hard drive to get rid of it completely.'

'So, if we could get a search warrant, we might get lucky.'

'On what grounds? We've got absolutely nothing on him.'

'Not yet,' said Carston.

From his inside pocket, he took an envelope. Ross looked at it.

'What's that,' he asked.

'Billy's outgoing mail. I thought I'd post it for him.'

'You nicked it?'

'No, no. I'm going to post it for him. After we've checked it for DNA traces. It's the good, old-fashioned sort, the ones you have to lick.'

'You can't use …'

'Before you start trying to teach me the rules of evidence, I know. But I need to kick start this properly. I'll get this done unofficially and if anything shows up, I'll get a warrant. Then we can play by the rules.'

'Dundee United, Holland,' said Jerry as soon as he came into my room. 'Know what that means, don't you?'

'Surprise me,' I said.

'Phlebitis.'

'I don't remember that from medical school.'

'Well, take it from me. Sure sign.'

'OK, let's have a look.'

He began rolling up his trouser leg. I knew he was probably right. I leaned over and touched the skin at the back of his calf. It was tight and had an orangey tint.

'Want a second opinion?' I said.

'No need, but you can tell me if you like.'

'You're right, it's phlebitis' I said. 'So what treatment d'you recommend?'

'Keep it elevated, work the muscles. Wait for it to go away.'

'Spot on.'

'Wish they hadn't banned Butazolidin. That used to crack it right away.'

'Aye, did all sorts of other damage, too. D'you want some pain killers?'

He shook his head.

'I'll just pray.'

I looked up at him. He had his usual grin.

'Didn't know you were religious,' I said.

'You've heard what I think of Rangers, haven't you?'

'Aye but I thought that was just bigotry.'

'It is. I gave up praying when I was still a wee boy. Got fed up with throwing up.'

'Eh?'

'Aye. Used to have to rush out of church before Father Farrington had finished.'

'Why?'

His face was serious for a moment.

'Why don't they think about what they're saying?' he said. 'The effect it could have? I mean, I must've been about nine, ten. And there he is saying, "this is my blood of the New Testament", and they make you drink it. I thought it was all *true. Felt like I had a mouthful of blood. I just gagged. Had to go out and throw up over the tombstones.'*

'You're too sensitive.'

'I know.'

As he got up and started for the door, it was obvious that his calf was hurting.

'You sure you don't want something for the pain?' I said.

He stopped at the door and shook his head.

'If you change your mind, talk to Dr McIntosh.'

'Why? She the practice's pusher, is she?'

'No, but I'm off to the US of A, and I'm not prescribing stuff for you from there.'

'Who with?'

'What d'you mean?'

'You're not going on your own, are you? So who's it with?'

'None of your business.'

'Ah, a woman, then.'

'Maybe I'm gay,' I said.

'Don't think so. I'd've noticed.'

'I'm discreet.'

'So you're off for a bit of foreign pornography, eh?'

'It won't be pornographic. Faintly erotic maybe.'

'Know the difference between eroticism and pornography?'

I sighed, shook my head and waited for the punch line.

'Eroticism is when you pleasure a woman with a feather. With pornography, you use the whole chicken.'

I laughed.

'So be careful,' he said. 'And have a good trip.'

'Thanks. I will,' I said.

He cocked his finger at me and made the gun-shooting gesture then went out and closed the door.

Rhona had had enough of Cairnburgh. Not because of the police; she'd found them easy to handle and thought that they were both quite attractive, especially the older one. The fact that she'd had no calls from the stalker had made his threat recede and she was finding that living with Billy was becoming demanding. Billy was all care and concern but he was smothering her and he'd settled into a mode that seemed to be treating their arrangement as permanent.

On top of that, to her surprise, she found that she was missing working. It wasn't just the fine restaurants, plush hotels and expensive wines. It wasn't even the money. It was the punters themselves. Even though she'd started out with a loathing of men as her motivation, the ones she'd met had been so varied that they'd kept life interesting and made every day different. Some used her as if she were a psychiatrist or a Samaritan, some rushed to her for a quick shag while the wife was away, but others had been genuinely friendly and treated her with real respect. She remembered one in particular who was in his sixties and had cried when she'd caressed him. Afterwards, he said it was because he'd been widowed several years before and had come to believe that no-one would ever touch him again. He'd become a regular after that and she could see the difference that meeting her had made. It was obvious that she was selling more than sex; it was always part of the deal, but it came wrapped in a surprisingly wide range of packages.

The problem was that Billy was even crazier about her than before. Maybe the fact that he wasn't paying her for sex made a difference, but she thought it was more than that. He was acting as if they were engaged or something. Men always looked at her and, when she was out with him, he'd glare at them and sometimes say, 'What the fuck d'you think you're looking at?' He'd even squared up to a couple of guys in a pub who'd started chatting to her when he was away getting drinks at the bar. She'd warned him about it and he'd apologized but there was no doubt that it was getting worse.

When he told her about Carston and Ross's visit, she couldn't believe that he'd lied to them.

'Why'd you tell them you didn't know he was phoning me?' she said.

'Why should I? They didn't even know it was my flat, didn't know you had a boy friend. So how could you have told me?'

'I did, though. They're going to think I'm lying now.'

'No they're not. It's nothing. They'll soon have other things to do.'

'What?'

'I don't know. Police stuff.'

'You don't get it, Billy, do you? The stalker knew all about Bob Davies and that rep. He must've killed them.'

'Why?'

'He knew about it. Stuff that wasn't in the papers.'

Billy waved a hand.

'So what? He could've heard about it somewhere. Some cops shooting off their mouths.'

She looked at him.

'Doesn't it bother you that this guy's phoning me?'

'He's not. He's stopped.'

'But when I go back …'

'No need. Stay here.'

There was no insistence in his tone; it was matter-of-fact.

'No, Billy. I came for a break, remember. It was never going to be for ever.'

'It could be, though.'

He reached across and pulled her to him, kissing her on the cheek and leaving his arm around her shoulders. She shook her head against him.

'No,' she said, softly. 'I can't stay. I need to get back. I've got to make a living.'

'No need. I'll pay for you. You can stay here. We'll …'

'No.'

'Why not?'

'Because I need to. I don't want us to be like a married couple.'

'We won't be.'

'Oh Christ, Billy, we are already.'

She felt his arm stiffen but he said nothing.

'We'd still see each other,' she said. 'Like before. It was good, wasn't it?'

'And what about when he starts phoning you again?' said

Billy, his voice hard.

'He won't,' said Rhona. 'I'll move. He won't know where I am.'

'He'll find you.'

She sat forward, away from his arm, and gave him a playful punch in the shoulder.

'Hey, whose side are you on?' she said. 'Trying to scare me, are you?'

'He'll find you,' he said again.

She saw the anger in his eyes. It made her even more determined to get away. If he moved any further along this track, he wouldn't be her boy friend, he'd be her jailer. She settled slowly back into his arm again. It was still taut and he didn't let his hand fall around her shoulder. His silence wasn't the sad resignation that he'd shown on other occasions; this time it was resentful, an angry brooding, ready to block her freedom. For the first time, she realized that Billy could be dangerous.

Carston was driving home. His mobile bleeped at him. He pulled over and answered it. It was Ross.

'What is it? Billy's DNA through?' said Carston.

'Not yet. They're having to do it on the sly remember, thanks to you.'

'If you've phoned to nag me, forget it. Kath's way ahead of you.'

'Got something that might be convenient if you want to have another word with Davidson.'

'Oh?'

'Aye. We got a call. From down by the canal. Fraser and Thom went to check it. Bit nasty. One of the winos. Burned to death.'

'How?'

'Not sure. The lads are still talking to them. Trying to get some sense. Could've been a spark from the fire. Looks more like somebody set fire to her, though.'

'Bloody hell. So how's Davidson involved?'

'It's one of his patients.'

'Christ. He should come with a health warning.'

'Aye. Suspicious death, though. The police surgeon's reported it to the procurator fiscal. He'll want the patient's notes. I was thinking maybe we could go and get them, have a chat with him.'

'Good idea, Jim. Leave it with me. I'll tell him.'

'I phoned the surgery. It's closed.'

'Got his address?'

Ross ruffled through some papers and eventually found Davidson's home address. Carston copied it down.

'Right,' he said. 'I'll go there now. Catch him off guard maybe.'

'He's not going to have her notes at home, is he?'

'I don't know that, do I? I'm just a policeman.'

THIRTY-ONE

They'd just finished their meal. I was watching them again. It would probably be all right to let them go. I was pretty sure none of them knew who I was or where they were. If I released them, they'd talk about it with their pals, especially Waring, but would they report it? Don't think so. They'd had too many run-ins with the police to go to them voluntarily. But they knew I'd killed Bailey. That made me an easy target for blackmail, so maybe one of them would start digging around.

I did have an alternative. I could just leave. Shut the cellar door and take off. By the time I came back, the problem would have solved itself. If I let them go, the chance was I'd be exchanging their liberty for my own. If I just left them there to die in their chains ... well, it'd be just like the justice I'd already handed out to Bailey. I could see the logic in that.

They were sitting, waiting, knowing that something was going on. And I'd sort of made up my mind.

'I'm going to let you go. Maybe soon,' I said.

There were movements, shufflings. They all looked at me. At first, no-one spoke but, after a while, Campion said, 'Thank you very much.'

'If only I could be sure you'd learned something,' I said. 'It'd make it all that much more ... worthwhile.'

'We have,' said Campion.

Curiously, I realized that I believed him.

'You see, I'm going away, so I need to bring some sort of closure to this. And the only ...'

That's when you arrived. I stopped. The sound of the doorbell upstairs was a surprise. Normally, I wouldn't have heard it but the cellar door was open. I rarely have visitors in the evenings. I didn't panic, though. I was just annoyed. I bet they were, too. Just when I'd started to tell them ...

'Don't go away,' I said.

I left the light on but shut the door. Just as well, wasn't it?

Davidson climbed the steps, went straight along the hall and opened the front door. It was Carston.

'Oh, hullo,' said Davidson.

'Evening, doctor. Hope I'm not disturbing you.'

'Well, I'm just cooking dinner. Will it take long?'

'I hope not,' said Carston.

He was surprised at the tatty black clothes Davidson was wearing. Davidson noticed his glance.

'I was clearing stuff out,' he said.

'Always a messy business,' said Carston. 'Can I come in?'

Davidson stood aside. Carston came into the hall and turned, waiting to be shown which room to go to. The clearing out obviously didn't involve the hall; it was spotless, although Carston was surprised that it didn't smell as fresh as it looked. The air had a slight dampness to it, an unwashed staleness. He looked around. There was a hat stand with just two coats hanging from it and a golf umbrella propped up in its base. At the foot of the stairs was a telephone table but it had none of the usual spread of notelets. The pad on it was squared off in line with the phone and a pen lay neatly beside it. There was a closed door at the end of the hall and two others nearer to him. Through the first, which led to the kitchen, he saw three large wine bottles and two cardboard boxes on the table, but, again, they were neatly stacked ready for disposal. The other door led to the sitting room and Davidson gestured for him to go through it. Here, too, the clearing up had already been done. It was a dark, comfortable room, expensively furnished and with what looked like top of the range audio equipment in a cabinet against the wall opposite the window.

'I won't keep you,' said Carston, as Davidson invited him to sit.

'No problem. What's it about?' said Davidson.

'I'm afraid I'm bringing some bad news,' said Carston.

Davidson waited.

'One of your patients, Jessie McIver. I'm afraid she died

last night.'

Davidson frowned. Why was Carston telling him this?

'No surprise,' he said. 'She's been very ill.'

'It wasn't that.'

Davidson nodded.

'No, I didn't think so. You don't deal in natural causes much, do you? What was the problem?'

'She was burned to death,' said Carston. 'We think it was deliberate.'

Suddenly, unaccountably, Davidson felt tears in his eyes. He didn't trust himself to speak and waited for Carston to go on.

'Our lads are talking to the folk there. Can't get much sense out of some of them, but we'll get there.'

'Poor Jessie,' said Davidson.

'Aye. Anyway, the procurator fiscal's involved so he'll want her notes.'

'Of course. They're at the surgery.'

'Yes, I thought they would be.'

'When d'you need them?' said Davidson.

'Well, soon as possible.'

'I'll organize it tomorrow if that's OK.'

'That'll be fine.'

'If anything comes of it, though, you'd better contact Dr McIntosh.'

'Why?'

'I won't be there, I'm afraid.'

'Oh?' said Carston.

'Two weeks holiday. I'm off to Boston.'

Carston couldn't entirely hide the little alarm that this news caused in him. The strategy he'd been working on as he drove over fell away. Davidson was doing a runner.

'Why now?' he asked.

'I'm sorry?'

'The holiday – why now?'

'I booked it a while ago. New England in the fall. Ever been there?'

Carston shook his head.

'Unbeatable,' said Davidson.

Carston's mind was racing.

It's … it's a bit … your timing's a bit unfortunate,' he said.

'If you want to see New England in the fall, you've got to go in the fall.'

'Yes, but I was hoping you'd be around. I need some help from you with a couple of things I'm working on.'

'Like what?'

'Well, you know about George Waring and McPhee …'

Davidson waited.

'There are a couple of others… Folk missing.'

Carston was hoping for Davidson to react but there was nothing.

'You see, the thing is … these people have all got … well, they're all connected with your practice.'

'Who are the others?'

'Jenny Gallagher?'

The name didn't seem to register with Davidson.

'Her boy-friend, Peter Dobie,' said Carston. 'He's gone missing.'

'Ah, yes. I remember her now.'

'And, of course, there was Marion Bailey.'

'I'm sorry,' said Davidson, 'but I don't seem to be making the connection here. These people, they're all patients of ours and they're all criminals, or what?'

'They're either missing or dead.'

'And?'

Carston frowned. Davidson was too cool, too unconcerned. He'd moved from an apparently genuine regret at the death of the burned woman to a watchful control.

'Well, it's a bit of a coincidence, don't you think?'

Davidson thought, then nodded.

'I suppose it is, yes. But what's it got to do with my holiday?'

The obvious answer was 'nothing', but Carston just shrugged.

'I mean, my partners will give you all the help you need.'

Carston nodded, then looked up and held Davidson's gaze.

'The thing is,' he said, 'they don't have the same connection with George Waring.'

Davidson continued to hold his look. Carston found it slightly unnerving, as if he were the one under suspicion. A little smile came to Davidson's lips.

'I'm sorry, are you saying I'm a suspect or something?'

Carston returned his smile.

'Of course not.'

He had nowhere to go. There was nothing linking Davidson to these people but coincidence, and yet his instincts told him that there was more to be learned.

'It's a tricky one,' he said.

'Why?'

'Remember what you said about Waring?'

Davidson shook his head.

'You said you hoped we wouldn't find him.'

Davidson nodded.

'I meant it.'

'Yes, and you weren't all that concerned by the news about McPhee.'

Again the nod.

'You see, all the people I'm talking about are the same.'

'The same?'

'Yes, they all deserve whatever it is they're getting.'

'Is that what you think?'

'Off the record, yes. But you can see the way it's bound to set my suspicious policeman's mind working, can't you?'

'Not really, no.'

A silence fell between them. At last, Carston looked up at Davidson.

'I really wish you weren't going to America,' he said.

'You could always extradite me.'

'How long you there for?'

'Couple of weeks.'

'You'd be home before they'd filled in all the forms.'

They smiled at one another again. Each sensed that there

was some sort of truce or understanding between them, and each knew that they'd be following this conversation up at some stage.

'OK, I'll let you get on,' said Carston. 'You must have lots to do.'

'A bit,' said Davidson. 'Loose ends.'

They walked out through the hall and Davidson opened the front door.

'Have you got any idea at all who burned Jessie?' he asked.

Carston shook his head.

'Could be an accident, could be one of the crazies she was with, her husband, who knows?'

Davidson nodded.

'Well, this time,' he said. 'I hope you do get him.'

'We will,' said Carston, pausing at the door to add, 'we usually do. Have a nice holiday.'

'Thanks,' said Davidson. And he shut the door.

Carston drove away, certain in his own mind that he'd be back. Davidson's reactions had been unnatural. Apart from the emotion triggered by the news of the burning, it was as if there'd been no-one home the rest of the time. The tone of his voice had been flat, he'd not been disturbed or outraged at Carston's suggestion of a greater involvement. Perhaps doctors were so often faced with extremes, they had to learn to control themselves, but this was more than that. The trip abroad was a nuisance and Carston was forced to console himself with the thought that it at least gave him some time to find some more compelling evidence. It wasn't much of a consolation.

That changed things completely, of course. You suspecting me. Freedom for the bastards in the cellar and incarceration for me. I didn't fancy that. It was a travesty. They were going to get away with it again. I went down, collected their dirty plates. I didn't say anything to them. Turned the light out and closed the door. I washed the plates, left them to drain and phoned Gayla. She was surprised to hear from me but she was just out of the shower and pleased that I wanted to come and see her.

It took me eighteen minutes to drive to her place. She looked and smelled fresh when she opened the door. Just for a flash, it made me sorry I'd started the whole cellar business. It would've been so much easier just to do my job, have fun and sex with her, and forget everything else. Too late.

I kissed her hard. Poured two glasses of the chilled champagne I'd brought and we went through to sit in the lounge. On the drive over, I'd been trying to work out how to tell her. Couldn't see any way of wrapping it up, though. She solved the problem for me.

'OK, Andrew, what's wrong?' she said, after we'd taken a couple of sips.

'Nothing.'

'Liar.'

I smiled at her.

'OK,' I said. 'You tell me why you think something's wrong and I'll tell you if you're right.'

'Easy,' she said. 'You never ring and come over at the last minute. You just kissed me as if I was Jennifer Lopez on heat. And I know you, and I can see that something's not right.'

'That transparent, am I?'

'Sometimes... Well?'

I put down my glass and turned to face her.

'The States. I'm sorry, I can't go. Something's come up.'

Her disappointment was clear, but she quickly flashed a smile to hide it.

'Oh, that's a shame.'

'Yes. I was looking forward to it.'

'What's the problem? Work?'

'No, it's ... sort of personal, really. Bad timing.'

'Sod's Law.'

'It doesn't mean you can't go,' I said.

'What?'

'The tickets are paid for, the hotels are booked.'

'Cancel them. I don't want to go on my own.'

'Sure?' I said. 'Think about it, beans and ham for lunch in a Shaker village, a hotel in the middle of the White Mountains Forest Park, New Hampshire, a two hundred year old inn in Grafton, Vermont....'

'What are you, a travel agent now?' she said. 'I'm not going as a sad single, however nice it all is. Anyway, isn't New Hampshire the place where they have "Better dead than red" on their number plates?'

'Yes, but the foliage ...'

'Next year maybe.'

She got up and put a different CD into the player. Weird, she'd had a piano sonata on and, suddenly, it was the Seventies' Greatest Hits. She sat down again, reached across and drew her finger across my cheek. I put my arms around her and shoved my face in her hair. It was a different embrace. It wasn't sex, or the prelude to it. I needed her but I don't suppose she knew how much. And certainly not why. Nor did I, for that matter.

'Anyway, it's bloody scary in the States,' she said.

'Scary?'

'Yes. Even worse than it used to be. All the flags outside the houses, the car stickers, God bless America, Intelligent Design, all that stuff.'

She was right. That was scary.

'I mean, they're very welcoming, but they're so convinced that they're right. I feel like a bloody communist when I'm there.'

'Maybe it's good to have that sort of certainty,' I said. 'Just go with the flow.'

'Not me, thanks. That's the first step towards the Stepford Wives.'

'They mean well.'

'That's not enough. They're so sure that they're the good guys.'

'Christ,' I said. 'Sex and moral philosophy, too.'

'Which d'you prefer?' she asked.

'Well, I'm no good at moral philosophy,' I said.

'Well then.'

But I didn't take up her offer. Instead, I snuggled more deeply into her. On the CD, Marvin Gaye sang 'I heard it through the grapevine'.

'I've been trying to be a good guy,' I said.

'You are.'

'No. Not the way I've done it. I've done some really bad things.'

'D'you want to tell me?'

'Yes, but I can't. Believe me, they really are bad. You said the Yanks are scary. Not compared with me, they're not.'

'We've all got things we've done,' she said.

I nodded.

'I thought I was doing it for the right reasons, trying to make a difference.'

'And?'

'Self-delusion,' I said. 'There are times when I don't like me at all.'

'Lucky I'm here then,' she said.

Obviously, she couldn't know what I was on about but she stroked me, held me. We drank the champagne with the stupid bloody music in the background.

I say stupid, but it was one of the tracks which unlocked the silence. The Hollies. 'He Ain't Heavy.' As soon as I heard it, I gave a little laugh. Nothing was funny, though.

'What?' said Gayla.

'This,' I said, waving my hand towards the CD player. 'I used to love it. Used to feel sorry for people who didn't have a brother.'

Gayla had no siblings. She was quiet.

'You're still grieving, aren't you?' she said, very gently.

I nodded.

'I don't think you ever stop,' I said. 'Pointless, I know, but you can't help it.'

'Is that why you can't go to Boston?'

I had to think about that.

'In a way,' I said. 'Tommy was a much better brother than I was.'

'What d'you mean?'

'He cared about me, kept in touch. I was always wrapped up in ... oh, I don't even know. There was always something, though. I wasn't even much good to him when Tara and the girls were killed.'

'Of course you were.'

'No,' I said. 'I should've realized how bad he felt, should've known that sort of thing never stops hurting. I was no bloody use at all.'

Gayla wanted to argue with me but she didn't know how. She brushed her hand softly over my arm and shoulder. The same gentle strokes.

'He knew it,' I said. 'If I'd been any use to him, he'd've called me instead of ... He just sits there, he can't get away from it, can't escape into anything. It's for life, so he just ... I wish he'd called.'

'He wasn't thinking straight, Andrew. In a way, it was love that made him do it, wasn't it?'

'Yes. And he knew he couldn't get any from me.'

'Nonsense. You're being too hard on ...'

'No, I'm not.'

I broke away from her stroking hand and sat forward.

'Our Granny used to live near us when we lived in Aboyne,' I said. 'A big house. We used to go there, Tommy and I. She'd always give us stuff. Sweets, money ... One time, she was away and Mum gave me the key to her place to go and fetch some recipes or something from the kitchen. Tommy came with me. I opened the door, we both went in, then I closed the door again. It was pitch black. I heard Tommy start doing little breaths, sort of panting or gasping. So I crept up beside him and suddenly grabbed him. For a laugh. Scared the wits out of him. You know what he said? 'Mummy.' Just that. One word. And I felt the biggest bastard of all time. I turned the light on and calmed him down but he was still breathing fast and shivering.'

'What happened after that?'

'Nothing. I never said anything about it. Nor did he. But I've remembered it lots of times. He must've been about five or six. And big brother Andrew dumps on him in the dark. Great, eh?'

'Kids do it all the time.'

'I know, but it doesn't help when I think of him now, think how fragile he was at the end.'

She reached out her hand and pulled me back until I was tucked beside her again. Her fingers began stroking my hair.

'What are you going to do?' she asked.

'In what way?'

'You can't go on beating yourself for ever. Tommy would never have wanted that.'

'No, you're right. I'm going away.'

'Where?'

'Don't know. Just to sort things out.'

It was no good. I'd tried to tell her something but it was ... well, unsayable. We drank some more champagne. We both needed it.

'Andrew,' she said. 'If there's any way I can help, you'll ask me, won't you?'

I kissed her on the side of the neck.

'Yes. There's nothing, though.'

'And will you call me when you get back?'

I didn't say anything right away. Then I just nodded. But I was on my own, out of her reach.

THIRTY-TWO

Throughout the investigation, the briefings had been short. None of the missing persons excited much interest in the public, so there were no reconstructions or broadcast appeals and, consequently, relatively small mounds of information to process. On the last Monday in September, though, the slow, careful collecting of material brought its rewards. Carston came into the office humming to himself. Ross looked at him.

'What?' said Carston.

'Pleased with yourself?' said Ross.

'Smug bastard's more like it,' said Carston. 'Come on, let's get going.'

They went through to where the others were waiting.

'Bonjour, patron,' said Fraser, in an accent that, after months of night school and practice, was beginning to sound slightly French.

Carston ignored him and went straight to the white board which Ross had kept meticulously up to date. He'd organized it so that it was easy to see at a glance where any real evidence had accumulated and, by the time he'd added Fraser's reports from the hospital and Spurle's phone lists, the busy little arrows linking individuals were beginning to point persuasively at two conclusions.

No-one believed any more that there was just one perpetrator. Davies and Stride were linked by the DNA trace and by their contact with Rhona, but there was nothing to connect them with the others. McPhee and the rest, however, showed enough overlapping connections for it to be reasonable to treat them as part of a single investigation. But it was the Stride case that produced what they were looking for when Spurle gave them the results from the car hire firms. His job had been made easier by the fact that very few of them offered VW Golfs. On the days either side of Stride's disappearance, only seven black models had been rented, one of them to a William Marshall from Cairnburgh.

'Good one, Spurle,' said Carston, in a rare moment of

warmth towards the man.

'Tricky though,' said Ross. 'It's Tayside's case.'

'Yes, but we've got that DNA link with Davies. That's our investigation,' said Carston.

'We've got nothing to link him with that, though,' said Spurle.

Carston took a sheet of paper from his inside pocket.

'We have now,' he said. 'It's a match. The DNA on Stride and Davies. It's Billy's.'

'Christ,' said Ross.

'Yes,' said Carston. 'Now all we've got to do is make it official. Spurle's rental car evidence is enough to put to the fiscal for a warrant. We'll only mention the DNA I got from that envelope if he thinks it's a bit iffy.'

Carston handed the piece of paper to Ross.

'So,' he went on. 'When we get the go-ahead, we'll check out the flat and the car. You'd better get somebody organized to go through that computer, Jim. You know what we're after. Fraser, you can get onto his work. See if he's had any time off, when it was.'

'Très bien,' said Fraser.

'It'd be an idea to get a legitimate DNA sample, too,' said Ross.

'Yes, you can organize that,' said Carston. 'Now, what about the other lot?'

He looked at the whiteboard again, following the second swirl of arrows. There was nothing as solid as the evidence they had on Billy, but it was obvious that they needed to have a much longer, more serious talk with Dr Davidson.

They were nervous. I'd been sitting looking at them for ages without saying a word. I'd said nothing more about releasing them. They'd tried asking, but I ignored them. I had my back to the free pillar so I was part of their circle. In the centre there was the bucket with its smell. Around it, all the stains and splashes from the weeks they'd been using it. The floor around Campion was clean. He'd brushed up any crumbs with his hands and smoothed the surface of the carpet. The rest hadn't been so fussy. The bucket stains seemed to spread out towards and around them in three rays.

I got up, left the light on, and went upstairs. On the table in the kitchen there was a litre of Bulgarian wine. I'd got it in Sainsbury's. It was cheap crap. I also had a small vial of blood. It was a sample I'd taken from Dobie when I'd drugged them all with the coffee. With the HIV virus, of course. I'd added a drop of citrate of soda solution to stop it clotting and kept it in the fridge. Kept the temperature between two and six degrees. I picked it up, looked at it for a while then put it back on the table. I went to the bathroom, took off the filthy black clothes, showered and put on a white tee shirt, green sweater and a pair of chinos. I was on automatic pilot. My head was full of thoughts. I hardly knew what I was doing.

Back in the kitchen, I picked up the vial and shook it. It was still liquid. No lumps or clots in it. I took a syringe out of the cabinet over the sink and held it against the neck of the bottle to make sure it was long enough. Then I filled it with blood and, very gently, eased the needle through the cork into the bottle until the tip was poking through inside. I emptied the syringe and started again. There was enough blood for five refills. Each time, I used the same spot in the cork. When the blood was all gone, I gave the bottle a shake and saw that there were no lees or sediment of any sort. That's why I'd bought the cheap stuff. I put the bottle on a tray with five glasses and a corkscrew.

I didn't ask myself what I was doing or why. It was an idea I'd had some time ago. Then Jerry told me his story about the communion wine, and I loved the irony of it ... and the sort of symmetry. I bet if I'd stopped to analyze what I was doing, I'd have realized I was round the twist. Never mind irony, or symmetry. I was round the twist. I needed help. But it was too late. The spiral had me. The darkness.

'Surely we've got enough to get a warrant,' said Carston.

He and Ross were alone in the squad room, still looking at the white board.

'You know what the fiscal's like,' said Ross. 'He likes it to be cast in stone.'

'I bet it will be if he gives us a chance to look around.'

He tapped at a list of names.

'OK, he logged into the pharmacy a couple of days before Bailey was killed. Nothing sinister in that; he's a doctor. That's what they do. But this …' His finger moved to a list of telephone numbers. 'It's got to be significant.'

Ross raised his eyebrows, only half agreeing. The numbers were those collected by Spurle on his trawl through the phone company's records for calls made to Campion, Dobie, Bailey, and the pub in which Waring had been drinking the night he disappeared. There was only one number common to them all, a mobile belonging to Davidson. It had to be more than coincidence but for someone who seemed to be planning a mass extermination, it was astonishingly careless.

'We just need to find a couple of fibres like the ones we got at Campion's and Waring's, match up the DNA from that bush in Bailey's garden and it's solid bloody gold.'

'He's a doctor,' said Ross.

'So?'

'Good one, too, according to the others in the practice. He takes time with his patients. Goes to a lot of trouble. What sort of motive would make him do this? Doesn't make sense.'

Carston wandered from the board to the window. The normality of what he saw outside underlined Ross's words. But he'd been in the job a long time; he knew that normal people were capable of extraordinarily abnormal things.

'His brother was a good lawyer,' he said. 'But he still knelt on a chair and cut his throat. Maybe it's a family thing.'

He turned back to face Ross again.

'Remember the photo?' he said. 'The wee girls?'

Ross nodded.

'Lots of folk would think that was motive enough,' said Carston. 'So let's give him a ring. See if he's gone yet. You try his home phone and the mobile. I'll ring the practice.'

They dialled the respective numbers. Ross waited but

Carston got the engaged tone and had to keep trying.

'Answering machine,' said Ross, dialling the second number.

Carston nodded and dialled again. At last, the receptionist answered with her sing-song 'Doctors' surgery, Alison speaking. How can I help you?'

'Can I speak to Dr Davidson please?'

'I'm sorry, Dr Davidson's on leave. He won't be back until next month. Can one of the other doctors help?'

'No, I knew he was going to America but I was just hoping to …'

'No, he didn't go to America in the end.'

'Oh, where is he then?'

'He didn't say. Down south somewhere, I think.'

'I see. OK, thank you.'

He put the phone back. Ross had had no luck with the mobile either.

'He's still around,' said Carston.

'What, here?'

Carston shrugged.

'Don't know. First thing to do is phone round the airlines. Find out when he booked, when he cancelled, whether he changed flights for somewhere else.'

'D'you think your visit spooked him?' said Ross.

'Maybe,' said Carston. 'If it did and he's running, it could have done us a favour. I'm off to see the fiscal.'

The minute I opened the door and carried the tray in, they knew they were in trouble. Only McPhee and Waring knew my face, but the fact that I'd left off the mask and the black jumper and jeans told them that the rules had changed. Maybe they wouldn't be getting released after all. I put down the tray, went to my usual pillar and sat looking at them, letting them stare at me.

Eventually, I pointed at the tray and glasses.

'Well, d'you want any of that or not?'

I felt surprisingly cold but my pulse was pounding. I thought about your visit, the questions you'd asked, the strange understanding there'd been between us. I don't think you knew anything then, otherwise you'd have dug deeper. But I knew you'd be back. By then, though, it'd make no difference. I had to make a real effort to remember where I'd been before you arrived.

The silence crept back. Dobie's eyes were flicking back and forth, Waring was shaking his head. Campion looked at me. So did McPhee.

'I suppose this is our last supper, isn't it?' I said. 'Any of you Catholics?'

Silence.

I pulled out the cork and poured the wine into the five glasses.

'You'll be drinking yours first,' said McPhee.

'If you like,' I said.

I handed them their drinks one by one. They waited. I wasn't interested in the wine. I wanted to say something, find some appropriate words, take away the futility. I remembered Jerry's story about being sick outside the church. I was so fucking stupid. Trying to justify what I was doing by mixing real blood with the wine. Communion wasn't a word that belonged here. And the blood wasn't intended for them. It was for me. I was the one who needed purification. And then, Christ knows why, I suddenly remembered Jessie. I raised my glass.

'Tell you what,' I said. 'A friend of mine's been killed. I'd like us to drink to her.'

'Listen, pal,' said Waring, 'I'll drink to anybody, even a fucking woman. Let's get on with it.'

I just looked at him.

'She had cancer. And she had a husband who beat the shit out of her. Not even for fun, just because she was there. And you know what? She died because somebody put a match to her.'

They were silent. I think that, now that he knew he was being held by Tommy's brother, Waring was desperate to get the wine inside him. I thought of Tommy, Tara, their wee girls, Jimmy Roach's daughter Anne in the falling cable car. I thought of how she'd been treated by 'respectable' people. I thought of all the poor losers like Jessie who'd never been given a chance. And I thought of Bailey's agonies.

And me.

I lifted my glass and drained it in one. It burned down inside me, warmed my throat and stomach. It tasted good enough, but sour. Not sour from tannin or acid but from what it meant. And, immediately, as if it really were communion wine, I felt better. Relieved. I looked around at them. Waring's glass was empty and he was wiping his mouth. McPhee had swallowed half of his, and Dobie and Campion were sipping at it, trying to make it last. I watched them, and that weird bloody feeling ... of peace, absolution ... just got stronger. Made no sense at all.

In the end, only Campion had any left. When he noticed that the others had finished and were all watching him, he lifted his glass to me and tipped the last drop from it onto his tongue. The ceremony was over. They'd drunk the wine and, with it, the HIV positive blood from Dobie. Oh, I knew it'd do them no harm. For all the publicity it gets, the virus is still fragile. It would never survive in wine.

But it wasn't that. It was what it all meant. That's why I did it.

THIRTY-THREE

The procurator fiscal wanted to see all the documentation before deciding on the warrant for Davidson but was ready to issue what they needed to check Billy's flat. On the morning of the 29th, Carston phoned Rhona to say that she should go out and stay away for as much of the day as she could. It fitted very well with her plans because an Edinburgh punter had been in touch and wanted her to meet him in Stirling.

Carston and Ross went to fetch Billy from his work and drove him home, where the team was waiting.

'What's it all about?' asked Billy as they drove along.

'I see you missed three days work in June,' said Carston.

'So what?'

'Oh, just routine enquiries. One of my officers was asking around.' He looked at his notebook, checking the dates Fraser had come up with. 'Twenty-second, third and fourth, Monday, Tuesday, Wednesday.'

'I don't remember.'

'Often take time off, do you?'

'Why?'

Carston shrugged and looked out at the people on the pavements. His silence worried Billy more than the questions.

'Is this about Rhona again?' he asked.

'Why d'you say that?' said Carston.

'It was last time.'

'Well, it's not this time.'

'What is it, then?'

'It's about you.'

Once again, Carston turned away, ignoring the questions Billy kept on asking and saying nothing else until they pulled up outside his tenement. When he saw the other two cars waiting there, Billy paled.

'Fuck, this looks serious,' he said.

'It is, Billy,' said Ross.

'Tell you what,' said Carston, 'I'm going to caution you now, so that we all know where we are. I've never liked being pissed about. I expect you're the same.'

His tone was warm, friendly, and it disorientated Billy even further. He listened as Carston recited the familiar words, ending with a big smile and an 'OK?'

Billy just nodded.

'Good,' said Carston. 'Now I'll tell you what we're going to do. We're going to ask about you renting a black VW Golf in Dundee.'

'I've never …'

'Ssssh,' said Carston. 'We've got photographs. And we're going to ask you about a lay-by on the A90. And Sergeant Ross here, with some of the clever buggers we've got down at the station, is going to have a look at your computer to see if we can find out if you've been playing games. Phone games, stalking, stuff like that.'

'I'm not a stalker,' said Billy.

'Good. There's nothing to worry about then,' said Carston. 'Come on, let's go in and see what's what.'

Inside, Billy sat with Carston and watched as the team set up two of their computers beside his own array.

'Right,' said Carston. 'Now, I've cautioned you, but I'd rather keep it friendly. Better for both of us. So remember that I could use anything you say as evidence. But let's keep it off the record for a while. There may be things I don't know about. Things that may explain what's been going on. What d'you say?'

'I've got nothing to say,' said Billy.

'Fair enough. Let me tell you the problem I've got, though. See, you've got a car, so why did you need to hire one in Dundee? I mean, you only had it for a day. Not even that.' He looked at his notebook. 'You took it back just after lunch. And one of your neighbours saw you parking your own car back here later on the same day.'

Billy sat shaking his head.

'You think a lot of Rhona, don't you?' said Carston.

Billy looked at him. Carston nodded.

'Yes, I thought so. I expect you get jealous, too. Good looking girl like that. Everybody must be after her.'

He saw the flush in Billy's cheeks and the muscles in his jaw tightening.

'Bastard, isn't it?' went on Carston. 'I know. I used to be like that.'

Billy said nothing.

'It's true. Once you get the idea into your head, you can't think of anything else, can you? You imagine all sorts of things. Think of her in bed with other guys. Other women, too, nowadays.'

'OK, OK,' said Billy. 'It's not like that, though.'

'Really? You're lucky. Used to be bloody murder. What a prick I was. Anyway, it's you we're talking about.'

'No, we're not.'

'Oh, we are. That's what happened in Dundee, wasn't it? You knew she was there with that rep. How'd you know that, by the way? Did she tell you?'

'Don't know what you're talking about.'

'You knew, though. He stayed the night so you got rid of him, didn't you? Hired the car so that we wouldn't know it was you. How'd you get him to stop in that lay-by?'

'What lay-by?'

'I don't see why you had to bother Rhona with those phone calls, though. What was the point of upsetting her? Getting your own back, was it?'

Without waiting for an answer, he turned towards the team working on the computers.

'How's it going, Jim?' he said.

Ross looked up from his keyboard and nodded.

'Just copying some audio files.'

The shifts of focus were confusing Billy but it was the confidence of Ross and his hackers that bothered him most.

'How long have you known Rhona?' asked Carston, turning back to him.

'A while,' said Billy.

'Yeah. I can imagine what it must've felt like when that bastard Davies raped her. How'd you get him down to the golf course?'

It was all so chatty, so friendly, as if they were discussing the match over a pint. Billy had no idea what to say, but Carston carried on at the same level, switching from subject to subject, talking about golf, computers, Rhona and the size of the boot on a Ford Focus.

'What d'you think of Laura's website?' he asked at one point.

Billy's hesitation and expression confirmed what Carston suspected.

'Wonder who designed it for her,' he went on. 'It's not bad. Too many bangs and flashes, just like the rest of them. Good photos, though. What d'you think?'

'Why're you saying all this?' said Billy.

'Prices seem a bit steep to me,' said Carston, ignoring the question. 'Is that the going rate?'

Before Billy could answer, Ross called Carston across to the computers.

'Here's one,' he said.

He pressed a key and a voice came from the loudspeakers. He'd kept them low while he was looking but now he turned the volume up.

'Laura,' said the voice. 'It's been too long since we had a wee chat. Are you on your own?' There was a short pause, then the voice continued, 'There's a few things I'd like to talk about. I think you'll be interested. Nothing bad. Well, not really. You see, I was wondering about the guy who gave you a lift to Dundee. Remember? He stayed the night with you? Ended up in a ditch.'

If it was Billy's voice, it was heavily disguised. He'd got rid of all traces of his north east accent and turned it into a vague Scottish mixture.

'There's more,' said Ross.

Carston turned to look at Billy. He'd heard the voice and was staring at the two of them.

'Later,' said Carston. 'See what else there is.'

He went and sat with Billy again.

'What's that doing in your computer?' he asked.

'Nothing to do with me, 'said Billy. 'Somebody must've hacked in, you can …'

'We can get a voice print from it,' Carston broke in. 'Check it against yours.'

Billy looked down at his lap.

'I know. We'll play it to Rhona. Get her to ID it for us,' said Carston.

'No,' said Billy, suddenly afraid.

'We've got to,' said Carston.

Billy's hands were shaking now. He clasped them together and leaned forward, resting them on his knees.

'She'll leave,' he said, his voice small, fearful.

'Probably,' said Carston. 'Why don't you tell me about it. We'll see what we can do.'

Billy said nothing as he rocked slowly back and forward, his fingers clasping and unclasping.

'I love her. That's the trouble,' he said.

'It always is,' said Carston. 'Come on, let's go down to the station.'

I was up and down to the cellar all morning. I emptied the bucket, refilled it with fresh chemicals and put another one beside it. I left the light on all the time and they watched me. I brought down all the provisions I had left. Biscuits, bars of chocolate, tins of beans and frankfurters – all stuff that didn't need any sort of preparation. I stacked some around each pillar. Then I got two dozen litre bottles of water and two big packs of toilet rolls to add to each heap. It scared them. I mean, stocking up like that obviously had nothing to do with the idea of them being released. That's what I'd promised them. But each one of them now had this individual pile of food and stuff. They knew I wouldn't be coming up and down to feed them every night and morning. I was going to leave them there. From now on, it was self-service. At first, they'd tried asking questions but I didn't take any notice of them. In fact, I was on automatic. It was as if I was the only one down there.

What a difference when I'd finished. For the weeks they'd been there, they'd got just the bare minimum each day. Now, they had piles of grub. If they hadn't been so scared, it would've been like winning the lottery. But they were waiting. Waiting for me to turn out the light, shut the door and leave them there. In the darkness.

I sat down by the spare pillar again and looked round at them.

'Please don't do it,' said Dobie.

'What?' I said.

He was crying.

'Leave us here,' he said.

I shook my head.

'Bastard,' said McPhee.

'Aye,' I said.

I got up and walked to the door. Dobie's sobbing got louder. All their faces were following me. Panic in all of them. Begging me, sort of. But I left the light on and the door open. I went upstairs and had a long, hot shower. Then I dressed and went to the cupboard under the kitchen sink where I'd hung the keys to their handcuffs. I took them out, went into the hall, looked around and went back down the steps.

Dobie had stopped sobbing. In fact, there wasn't a sound from any of them. I closed the door behind me. Had another walk round them to check on their supplies. They must've heard the keys jingling in my hand. Thought I was just messing them about and was going to let them off the hook.

'You're going to let us go, aren't you?' said Waring. He tapped a carton of food beside him. 'This is one of your gags, isn't it? Christ, what a guy you are.' But there was still panic in his voice.

'Aye, I am,' I said.

I went back to the door, reached for the switch and turned out the light. The deep, dark silence was back. I could hear their breathing; short, scared again. I clinked the keys again as I took out the torch I'd brought with me. I clicked it on and turned the beam onto each of them, one by one. It made them squint. Then I pointed it at the empty pillar and walked over to it. I propped the torch against the stack of food there and sat down. I couldn't see them very well now, but they could see me. It was on my right side, leaving my left side in shadow. Picking out the edges of the tins and boxes, too.

I clicked the anklets round my legs and the other set around my wrists. The noise of the ratchets sounded bloody loud. Then I just sat there.

After a while, I took out the keys and held them up to look at them. Dangled them in my fingers. Little sparks of light came off them. Sounds daft but they looked ... well, beautiful. Then I turned and threw them behind me. As far as I could, right over into the corner. Out of reach of any of us. Just heard a muffled clink as they hit the wall, another noise as they fell, and then ... nothing.

I picked up the torch and shone it on them again. First, McPhee. He squeezed up his eyes in the glare. After a while, I moved onto Dobie, then Campion, then Waring. I looked at each one of them for ages. Studied them. They must've done the same, looking at whoever the torch was picking out. And, you know, in each one you could see terror. No other word for it.

In the end, I'd seen enough. I switched off the torch and threw it into the corner with the keys.

Darkness.

THIRTY-FOUR

Carston was patient, even gentle with Billy. He knew that they had a cast-iron case. The car hire linked him to Stride. His DNA, when they got a legitimate sample, would tie him into the murders of both Stride and Davies. And the computer files brought into the equation Rhona, who was connected with both victims and with Billy. Gradually, as the day went on and he heard the evidence they'd accumulated, Billy's resistance weakened. That had been inevitable from the moment he realized that, however this turned out, he'd lose Rhona. Without her, there seemed no point in anything. He searched for another way of seeing it all, another way of telling her, but he found nothing. Nevertheless, he still held out, refusing to recognize any of the scenarios that Carston put to him and admitting nothing.

The change came when Ross called Carston late in the afternoon from Billy's flat with news of another file which Billy had erased but which they'd managed to retrieve. Carston stepped outside the interview room to take the call. Ross explained the significance of the find and Carston told him to get back to the station and join him in the interview room. He put his mobile away, opened the door, looked around it and said, 'I just heard how you got Stride to meet you in that lay-by. Very clever.'

Then, without waiting for Billy's response, he shut the door again and went to get a coffee.

Ross arrived as he was pouring his second mug.

'Nice one, Jim,' said Carston. 'I don't think it'll take long. He keeps coming back to Rhona. That's what'll do it in the end. Come on, let's see how he takes it. You start.'

Ross poured himself a coffee and they took their mugs down to the interview room, nodding to one of the constables standing inside the door that he could take a break. The other one closed the door behind his colleague and stood beside it.

When the tape recorder was running, Ross put down his mug and leaned towards Billy with his arms on the table.

'I'm impressed,' he said. 'very neat job. Where'd you get the original file?'

'I don't know what you're talking about.'

'The BMW. That sub-routine you wrote. It's good.'

Billy was unimpressed by the compliment. His mind was on other things, mainly living without Rhona.

'It's on your machine, Billy. You can't duck it. It's not exactly a useful program for anything else, is it?'

Billy shook his head.

'OK,' said Ross. 'You tell me then, why write a program that tells an in-car computer to shut down the fuel supply when it gets ten more miles on the odometer? I'm not as good as you are, but I can only see one use for that.'

'I was trying something out,' said Billy.

'What?' asked Ross.

'Just something. I was going to adapt it to … other things.'

'So you didn't log in to the computer in Stride's car?'

'No.'

'You didn't re-program it?'

'No.'

'Tayside have still got the car, you know. It won't take long to check.'

Billy shrugged.

'It's more evidence, Billy,' said Carston. 'It's mounting up. However good your brief is, he can't explain all this away. We know your DNA's on the body, you hired the car that people saw with Stride's, your computer's got a program that would force him to stop along the A90 just outside Dundee, we've got your voice saying things about Stride and Davies that only the killer could know. As soon as Rhona confirms that it's the same voice, that's it.'

Billy listened to it all, hunched in his chair.

'Does she have to hear it?' he said at last.

'Well, that's up to you,' said Carston. 'We need to get a positive identity for the stalker.'

Billy was quiet again.

'How long d'you get for murder?' he asked, his voice

hardly audible.

Carston and Ross looked at one another.

'Depends,' said Ross. 'Motive, mitigating circumstances, state of mind when you did it – all sorts of things come into it.'

'Whether you co-operated or not, too,' added Carston.

Billy looked at him.

'I mean, if you help us, it'll be in your favour. Could help you.'

'What about doing deals?' asked Billy.

'That's America,' said Carston. 'They do some funny things over there.'

They knew that he was ready to talk, but waited so that the impetus would come from him.

'She went off to see her mum today,' he said. 'I won't see her again, will I?'

'Maybe. Who knows?' said Carston.

There was another long silence.

'I did it for her,' said Billy.

Carston allowed a little pause then, keeping his voice gentle, said, 'Why not tell us about it? It'll help you to get it all straight in your mind.'

They had to wait again but, at last, Billy started to tell the story. At first, he talked about Rhona, how long he'd known her, how much she meant to him. It was clear that, without her knowing it, he'd been tormented by his love for her for well over a year, cruelly victimized by her work.

'I knew her before she started that,' he said. 'This old guy from work used to go and see her mother. He took a few of us with him one day. Said she wouldn't mind. He'd seen her with four or five at a time, he said. I went, but I didn't do anything. Couldn't. The other guys did, though. All of them.'

'Where was Rhona?' asked Carston.

'She was there. Up in her room. Her mother made her come down. Get beers for them and that. She was like a servant.'

'Is that the first time you saw her?'

'Aye. She didn't notice me. Her mum treated her like

284

shit. So did the guys.'

'Did you go back again?'

Billy shook his head.

'Not in the house. Used to go back sometimes and just sit in my car. In case she came out.'

'Did she?'

'A few times, yes.'

'What did you do?'

Billy looked up at them, a puzzled look on his face as if he found it a strange question.

'Nothing,' he said. 'I just wanted to see her.'

'So she wasn't your girl-friend then?'

Billy shook his head again.

'Only in here,' he said, tapping his forehead. 'I felt sorry for her. I knew what she had to put up with. You could see it when she walked along. She never looked up, always looked sort of … afraid.'

Carston couldn't help thinking that this was only a truth in Billy's perceptions. Rhona could look after herself. She had a basic resilience that doesn't get learned. It must always have been there.

'How about Bob Davies? Did you know him?'

'Bastard,' said Billy. 'He used to laugh about it.'

'What, the rape?'

'Aye. Got away with it. He was always in the pub, saying she was a slag. Asking for it. Just like her mother, he said.'

'Must've been hard for you, listening to stuff like that,' said Ross.

Billy nodded.

'He said she enjoyed it. Said she'd asked him to do it again. That's what happened that night.'

They waited but Billy was lost in the memory.

'What, Billy?' said Carston.

'He'd had a skinful as usual. Said he fancied a … Said he was going over to have her and her mother together.'

'What did you do?'

There was a shimmer on Billy's lower lids. This was hurting him.

'He went out looking for a taxi. I caught up with him, said I'd go with him, give him a lift.'

'What happened?' said Carston.

Billy looked straight at him, his face that of a young boy.

'I drove down to the woods by the golf course. I was going to … beat him up, I suppose. Teach him a lesson. Just went too far.'

'Sorry, Billy, but I've got to get this straight. Are you telling us you killed Bob Davies?'

Billy nodded.

'Can you say it? For the tape?'

Billy bunched his fists and pushed them together.

'We had a fight. I killed him. Didn't mean to, but I just grabbed this bit of branch that was there and … started hitting him… He had his arms up at first, then I got him on the head. He didn't get up. I checked, but he was gone.'

'What then?'

'I got a shovel out of the car and buried him. I was panicking, didn't know what to do. I expected somebody to come along any minute, but … I was surprised nobody found him before.'

'You did too good a job,' said Carston, with a smile.

Billy saw it and smiled back. There was no humour in either expression but it made the conversation easier. Billy told them that it was not long after that that he found out that Rhona had started working as an escort. It took him a while but eventually, he found the courage to contact her. They met, the sex was good, and he became a regular.

'Not a boy-friend, then?' said Ross.

'No. Just one of her punters,' said Billy. 'One of the crowd.'

Carston, who, as he'd said, had felt all the agonies of jealousy as a teenager, sensed the havoc that such knowledge must have caused in Billy's mind. It would be like living a nightmare, the only respite being the times he was actually with her and she belonged to him. If you're jealous, you want to own your lover; Billy had only ever been able to rent his.

'Tell us about Stride, the rep,' said Ross.

'He was unlucky,' said Billy. 'I was coming back from Montrose. I'd done a job down there. Set up a network. I saw her near the filling station on the Stonehaven road. You know, just up the hill. She was dragging a suitcase. I sounded the horn but she didn't hear. I wondered where she was off to. Decided to give her a lift but you know what that roundabout's like. There were road works there, too. Took me ages to get round it and back up the hill again.'

Carston nodded. He'd been caught there often enough himself to know what Billy meant.

'Did you catch her?' he asked.

'No. That guy was driving off with her just as I pulled in.'

'So you followed them?'

'Aye. Don't know why. Just seeing her, thinking I had the chance of giving her a lift. I couldn't just drive home. He might've only been taking her part of the way.'

'And you'd have taken her the rest of it.'

'Yes. I'd have driven her to Penzance if she wanted me to.'

'But they just went to Dundee.'

'Yes. They stopped at this block of flats. He went in with her. Didn't even carry her case. Let her lug it up the steps. Bastard.'

'What did you do?' asked Carston.

The pain he'd gone through pinched into Billy's face as he remembered.

'Sat there. Waiting for him to come out.'

'So that you could go up and see her?'

'Yes. Christ, she had a suitcase. I needed to know what she was up to, where she was going.'

'But he didn't come out?'

Billy shook his head.

'I went up after a while. Listened at doors. Like a bloody kid.'

He punched himself hard on the thigh.

'I wish I'd just gone home,' he said.

'Did you find where they were?' asked Carston.

'Oh yes,' said Billy with a hard little laugh. 'You couldn't miss it. He was hurting her. She wasn't screaming or anything but you could hear it, the way she was telling him not to be so rough. He was laughing.'

'So you went in?'

'No.'

'Why not?'

Billy took a deep breath.

'None of my business. It's her job.'

'All the same, if he was treating her …'

Billy didn't let him finish.

'Look, if I'd gone in with another punter there, she'd've been really pissed off with me. Probably wouldn't see me again.'

'So what did you do?'

'Went back to the car and just sat there. The trouble is, it was just like that bastard Davies all over again. It just kept coming back into my head. I couldn't shake it off. It sounded like he was raping her, too.'

'Is that when you programmed that sub-routine?' said Ross.

'Yes. I logged on with my mobile, checked a few sites, got a schematic of the BMW fuel management system. It's a simple enough bit of programming. I by-passed his alarm, got into his computer and dumped the sub-routine in it. I gave it ten miles so I knew more or less where he'd be stopping.'

'You were planning to kill him then?' said Carston, the gentleness still in his tone.

'I don't know,' said Billy, wrinkling his brow as he asked himself the question. 'Maybe I must have been. I think I was just going to frighten him, tell him to stay away from her. Dunno.'

'What time did he come out?'

'He didn't. When it got past eight, I knew he wouldn't. That's when I went to hire the car. Left mine in a street near the rental place.'

'So you were planning to kill him?'

'No.'

'Why hire a car then?'

'I don't know. In case something happened and Rhona got to hear about it. That's the sort of thing I was thinking.'

'OK, so you've got the hire car. What then?'

'I slept in it. He came out just after half seven.'

'And you followed him.'

'Yes. I saw his car slowing and I was lucky. He just managed to roll to the lay-by. I pulled in, offered to help. Said I'd take him to a garage in the village. That was that.'

He stopped.

'You'll have to tell us, Billy,' said Carston.

'You know what happened.'

'Tell us.'

With another sigh, Billy told them he'd stopped, told Stride to stay away from Rhona. Stride got angry, said she was 'only a fucking whore, for Christ's sake' and Billy had hit him. It was the Davies story all over again.

'But I found it easier,' said Billy. 'Maybe 'cause it was the second time.'

'But it was no accident, was it?' said Carston. 'Not this time.'

'No,' said Billy. 'No, I lost my temper, punched him, kicked, then I started pulling his tie and … I s'pose that was what did it.'

'And you took his clothes off.'

'I had to get rid of his car. He'd told me where he was staying in Edinburgh so I thought it'd buy me some time if I drove it down and left it there. I put his coat and trousers on in case there were any cameras about.'

'There were. We've got footage of you.'

Billy nodded.

'Thought so. They're everywhere, aren't they? That's why I wore a hat.'

His tone had flattened, become monotonous, as if unloading all this had drained the emotion from him. He told them, in short simple sentences, how he'd walked back along Princes Street to Waverley station, got the train back to Dundee, a country bus to near where he'd left the hire car, then picked up his own car and driven home.

'What about the stalker calls?' asked Carston. 'What were they for?'

'I wasn't stalking her,' said Billy. 'I don't know, I had some stupid idea in my head that I'd just scare her. So that she'd come back home. If she finds out it was me … she'll never …'

He stopped, unwilling to acknowledge that Rhona wouldn't be part of his life again for a very long time, if ever.

'And you set up the computer to call while you were with her,' said Ross. 'Why was that?'

'So she wouldn't know it was me,' said Billy. 'I wanted her to be scared. I wanted her to know she could trust me. I could've looked after her.'

He stopped and Carston indicated with a nod of his head that he and Ross should leave. As they stood up, Billy said, 'I felt sorry for her.'

Carston ended the recording session and touched Billy on the shoulder.

'We'll talk some more later, Billy,' he said. 'Thanks for being so helpful.'

He and Ross went out. There was no elation in them. In a strange way, Billy had combined confessing to a double murderer with a touching innocence.

'He feels sorry for her,' said Ross, shaking his head.

'Yes, and she's earning more money than he'll ever see,' said Carston. 'Come on, let's start the paperwork.'

THIRTY-FIVE

They transcribed the interview but they needed to bring Tayside into it because Stride was their case. Carston arranged for a tighter, more formal session to be held. Ross would be in charge of it and two of the Tayside team would come along. It freed Carston to concentrate on Davidson.

He was still waiting for a decision from the procurator fiscal who didn't seem to be treating the request for a warrant with any urgency. The only extra information they'd got had come from British Airways. They quickly found his booking for Boston. It hadn't been cancelled; he just hadn't shown up.

Carston was surprised when he read this and rang back to confirm it.

'Yes, that's correct,' said the woman who answered the call.

'How much was the ticket?' asked Carston.

'There were two. With airport taxes, the total was £870.'

'And he just kissed it goodbye?'

'Seems like it.'

'And the second ticket was in the name of Mrs. Gayla Campbell, is that right?' asked Carston, reading from the report.

There was a pause while the woman checked her screen.

'That's right,' she said.

'Have you got an address for her? A phone number?'

'No, sorry. It was all booked by Dr Davidson. He just gave the one address.'

'And you've got no records of him booking any alternative flights?'

'No,' said the woman.

The telephone directory had lots of G. Campbells so Carston gave the job of finding the right one to DC Bellman, who, unfortunately for him, happened to be in the squad room when Carston looked round the door. In fact, it didn't take too long because the name Gayla was unusual enough to produce only two matches. One of them was a seventy-two year old

New Zealander who gave piano lessons; the other, at thirty-eight, seemed a much more likely candidate for a transatlantic jaunt. Carston drove to her house and was impressed by both the place and the things she'd gathered in it. It had none of the uniformity of so many designer interiors but was a home with taste, comfort and character. She was an attractive woman, too, and, as she made tea for them, Carston allowed himself a little fantasy about flying to America with her and joining the mile-high club.

She brought the cups through and they sat on two armchairs in the bay window.

'He was very keen on the trip,' she said. 'So was I. He'd booked some nice hotels for us. Good food places.'

'The best sort,' said Carston.

'Yes. Andrew's a bit of a gourmet. Good cook, too.'

'What made him change his mind?' asked Carston.

'About the trip? I've no idea. It came right out of the blue. Phoned me one evening last week, Monday, I think. Wanted to come over and talk. Bit of a surprise, actually.'

'Why's that?'

'It's not the sort of thing he does. He's not the impulsive type. He tends to work things out, organize things.'

'Like your trip.'

'Exactly.'

'Is that when he told you it was off?' said Carston.

'Yes. He said something had come up.'

'Did he say what it was?'

'No. He said he had to go away.'

'Where?'

'No idea. Just 'away' he said. I knew there was something wrong.'

'Oh?'

'Yes. He was … different. Seemed preoccupied. Something must have happened.'

'Any idea what?'

Gayla shook her head.

'None. He wasn't himself, though. I think it was his brother.'

'Oh?'

'Yes. He'd never really got over it, I think. I told him so. He even agreed with me. He was remembering all sorts of little things about him. I think he was comparing himself with Tommy, and Tommy always won.'

'What do you mean, won?'

'Andrew thought he was nicer, better, I don't know, more successful … at living, I suppose.'

'Difficult to come to terms with his suicide if that's the way he was thinking.'

'Yes,' said Gayla. 'Poor Tommy.'

'And you say this … change in him was recent?'

'Yes, the last few weeks really.'

'You know him well, do you?' asked Carston.

'I've got to know him better this summer,' she said, with a little smile to herself. 'We've been … friends, I suppose, for a couple of years but recently, well it's been a bit more than friendship.'

The smile faded from her lips. It was true; Andrew had been different. When she'd first known him, he was more predictable. He'd get fixated on something and stick to it, but he'd always been amusing and never forced his opinions on others. His attitude to life was relaxed, he was fun to be with. Since the dinner party when he'd driven her home, though, there'd been a change. He'd sometimes be out of reach, for no reason that she could fathom. All the outward signs showed that he was fond of her but there was a core she could never touch.

'Is he in trouble?' she asked suddenly.

'I don't know, said Carston. 'He could be. I need to talk to him to find out.'

She put her cup in its saucer and leaned back. Carston's eyes couldn't help sliding across her breasts as she did so. They were good.

'Only, he said he'd done some bad things,' she said.

'Like what?'

'That's all he said. Bad things. I got the feeling they were something to do with Tommy.'

294

Carston had plenty more questions but Gayla wasn't able to add anything of any substance. She talked of Davidson's moods and what they might signify, expressed concern that he might be in trouble and offered to help in any way she could.

'D'you think he'll get in touch with you?' asked Carston.

Gayla thought for a moment.

'You know, I have no idea,' she said.

'If he does, will you tell him I need to speak to him?'

'Of course.'

'And will you tell me if you hear from him?'

Gayla considered the question.

'It depends whether he asks me not to,' she replied.

'Your honesty could get you in trouble, said Carston, with a smile.

She smiled back.

'I'll do what I can to help,' she said.

The worst part was the need for light. I don't suppose twenty-four hours had gone by before I started regretting that I'd thrown the torch away. I didn't regret chaining myself up. I needed to do that. I had to try to share Tommy's pain. Feel there was no way out, just like he had. Now, though, the black hours dragged by and I realized what a prick I'd been. How futile everything was. All the plans, the cellar, catching them, killing Bailey. And then this. I did have other choices. I could've gone with other impulses, the ones that made me care about my patients. I started wondering about Jerry and what team his legs had decided to support now. But I'd abandoned him. I'd killed Bailey, dehumanized my prisoners and myself. I was no better than McPhee and the rest. I belonged with them.

As soon as they'd heard the torch hit the wall, they'd started screaming at me, calling me mad, threatening to tear me to pieces when they caught me at the buckets. But, after a few hours – or maybe days, who knows? – the silence came back. I listened to them sleeping and, for the first time really, I realized what I'd done. Maybe it was just that the normal, sane me took over. Whatever it was, it was appalling. It wasn't a surprise; I'd thought hard about it, imagined what it might be like, but I could never have guessed at the reality of it. So fucking intense. It frightened me more than any of their threats. It's hard to explain but ... it was as if I'd become ... everything. The only reference points I had were the pillar, the chains and the boxes of food. The streets and fields outside the house were irrelevant. As inaccessible as the moon. I'd become a huge ... surface. And outside that, this immense something that would always be invisible.

Billy had been charged but the bureaucrats were still working out how the conflicting claims of Tayside and West Grampian could be resolved. With his usual efficiency, Ross had collated the evidence, indexed it all and handed it over to the procurator fiscal. In the end, it was his office that would decide.

'I wish he'd get his bloody finger out with that warrant for Davidson,' said Carston.

They were in the pub after a long day's paperwork. For Ross, it was a quick pint because it was his turn to baby-sit while his wife went to her yoga class.

'I can't get my head around it,' Carston went on. 'What's he done? Frightened them all away? He phones them up, and they vanish.'

'Not Bailey,' said Ross.

'No, there you are, see? And if he's killed him ...'

'Big 'if'.'

'I know, but if he has, he could've killed the others. So where the fuck are the bodies? And where's he?'

'OK, let's say it is him,' said Ross. 'Maybe he's warned the others off and they've been scared enough to go away. But Bailey was too pig-headed.'

Carston nodded.

'But why's he left now?' he said. 'Why pay eight hundred odd quid for flights and then just not use them?'

'Maybe it's somebody else. Somebody setting him up, then getting rid of him.'

'Fair enough. But his girl-friend says he more or less confessed.'

'To what?'

'Just … being bad.'

'Bit vague,' said Ross.

'Anything come up from the boats, railways, traffic guys?' said Carston.

'No. No sign of him.'

The barmaid came to their table to fetch their empty glasses.

'Same again?' she asked.

Ross shook his head.

'No thanks, Jenny. Baby-sitting tonight.'

'I'll have a half,' said Carston.

He watched her as she walked away. It was worth it.

'We've got to get round to his place. There must be something there,' he said, as she disappeared behind the bar.

'Aye, and we'd better make sure we keep it legal,' said Ross.

'You're worse than Ridley,' said Carston.

'D'you want Freddy Reismann having a go at you? If you step an inch outside the …'

'I know, you're right. It's bloody frustrating, though, not getting that warrant. I mean, we've got fibres to look for, the DNA from Bailey's garden, that glue from the phone. I don't know what the guy's been up to but I bet his place is crawling with contact traces.'

'You've made up your mind it's him, haven't you?' said Ross.

Carston thought about the question, remembered the phone calls, his two brief chats with Davidson, and Gayla Campbell's description of the last time she saw him.

'He's in it somewhere,' he said.

Ross stood up as Jenny came towards them with Carston's drink.

'Just be careful,' he said.

'Nag, nag, nag,' said Carston.

Ross said goodbye to Jenny and went out as she put

Carston's glass on the table. Carston handed over the money.

'I'm all on my own, Jen,' he said. 'Want to keep me company?'

'Think you're man enough for me?' said Jenny.

'Funny, that's what my wife says,' he said.

She laughed and went away, hips swinging.

As he sipped at his beer, the puzzle of Davidson came back to him. It was frustrating having so many pieces of evidence but being prevented from matching them up. Ross had no need to worry; there'd be no point in going to Davidson's house without a proper forensic team. He knew better than to trample all over the place destroying evidence. Better to forget about it and take the evening off.

He took out his mobile and phoned Kath.

'I'm in the pub,' he said when she answered.

'So you're not coming home then?'

'Yes I am. The barmaid's rejected me.'

'So've I.'

'That's what I told her. What's for dinner?'

'Salad, lamb, flageolets, dauphinoises, Brie, pineapple.'

'Is that all?'

'Then there's the main course.'

'Shall I get a video on the way home?'

'Good idea. Get a thriller. One of those with real policemen in it.'

'Cheeky bitch. See you soon.'

'Bye, love.'

Carston put the mobile away. He always felt better after talking to Kath.

Rhona was back in Dundee. The news that Billy was not only a murderer but also the man responsible for pestering her with the phone calls had really scared her. Given her line of business, she'd always been confident that she'd be able to handle any rough stuff if it came up, but this was a real wake-up call. Billy had been gentle and loving. She'd trusted him, told him secrets. And he'd deliberately hurt her, brought fear into her life. Carston had tried to soften it all by telling her that, although Billy's crimes were bad, his motives weren't. He was misguided but not evil.

'I don't know how you can say that,' she said.

'He loved you,' said Carston. 'He wanted to protect you, punish people who hurt you.'

'And scare the living daylights out of me.'

'I know. But it was to be with you. That's all he wanted.'

'He didn't think much about what I wanted, though, did he?'

'No,' said Carston. 'But he's going to have helluva long time to think about that now.'

'How long?'

'Double murder? Life.'

'Doesn't mean life, though, does it?' she said.

'It'll seem like it to him. Will you go and see him?'

'You're joking,' she said.

'No. It was all for you.'

'Wrong. It was all for him. Control. You love it.'

'Me?'

'Men. Half what I do's not about sex, it's about control. Rape's the same.'

Carston knew that she was right. He'd wished her good luck and reminded her that she'd be a witness and that she should let them have her address. She'd packed up the same evening and gone back to her Dundee flat.

Her voice mail was buzzing with messages from punters and she was glad to get back into the normality of working again. Her first few clients got more than their money's worth as she threw herself into the simplicity of spending a few hours with men for whom the time with her was just a transaction. These were people who certainly wanted sex but who often wanted friendship even more. With her, they could be relaxed. There was no need to pretend. The only danger was that one of them would turn out to be the husband or father of one of her friends. With Billy gone, Rhona felt she had nothing to fear but embarrassment.

Tonight's punter liked PVC. She looked at herself in the mirror before leaving for his hotel. She was wearing tight shorts and a bustier. The shiny black material clung to her. The bustier was open all along its length at the front, held in place by thongs which criss-crossed her soft flesh from just below her navel up between her breasts. The ends were tied around the back of her neck. She was wearing her favourite black choker, the one with a single blue stone at its centre. Her boots reached half way up her thighs. Her lips shone, her eyes sparkled and she liked what she saw. This was Laura. She pulled on a dark overcoat, turned up the collar to become Rhona again. Laura wouldn't resurface until the door of the hotel room closed behind her.

THIRTY-SIX

When I'd brought them their food every day, there'd been a stirring of the air. Some of the cleaner air from the hall had got in, but the door had been shut for ages now. None of the stench could get out. I must've stopped noticing it, though. But it was hard to keep hold of who I was. I didn't move away from my pillar much and I only used the bucket when I was sure McPhee was asleep. I tried counting to 3,600, to get an idea of what an hour felt like, but I couldn't get the feel of anything lasting. I was just always at the centre of this blackness. The only relief, the only structure came from my contact with the others. I started to understand why they'd always been talking when I came down the steps. Their voices pushed aside the vastness; created shapes in the darkness. In the end, I joined in, answered their questions. It scared them shitless when I told them there was no 'Plan B'. The keys and torch were out of reach. That was that. No release. No survival.

But, you know, the one most affected by it all was me. They didn't like the idea that they'd soon be dying of hunger one by one, but the time they'd already spent in this perpetual night must've shaped their expectations. Probably, as far as they were concerned, it was all so unreal, so unlikely, that anything could still happen. I rationed my food but they just scoffed it back. It must've made them feel better than they had for ages. And the strange thing was, as they screamed their stupid threats at me I agreed with them. They were right. I was mad. And I blamed them for it. I'd caught it from them. And I wanted to be outside, back in the air, back in a cell or a courtroom, I didn't care. Back where there was light.

And behind me, in the corner, perhaps a metre and a half beyond the furthest point my fingertips could reach, were the keys and the torch.

Whatever case he was working on, when Carston got home, it was like dividing his day in two. His evenings with Kath drew out any stresses and restored a softer perspective. It wasn't that he forgot his work entirely or put it out of his mind; it was just that the familiarity linked him with all the time they'd had together and reminded him that most of his life was good. Tonight, the magic started working the moment he opened the door. A hot smell of lamb and garlic filled the hallway. Kath was already halfway through a glass of Villa Maria, a Sauvignon Blanc from New Zealand. Carston kissed her, poured himself a glass and listened as she told him about her day. She'd spent most of it driving and walking along the river Dee, taking photographs to illustrate an article on fishing that a neighbour was writing for an Edinburgh-based magazine.

He laid the kitchen table as they talked and opened a bottle of red which some friends had brought back as a gift from Gaillac.

'It's like being married to Nigella Lawson, only better,' he said, as she took the lamb out of the oven and set it aside to rest.

'Better?' she said.

'Yep. She wouldn't let me touch her.'

'What makes you think I will?'

'My charisma.'

'I've got news for you,' she said.

The wine, the food, and the nonsense they spoke were all part of the therapeutic process for him. The two of them eased through more chat, serious and light-hearted, and Carston ate more than he should. As they talked, however, he was aware of something unresolved going on in his head. He listened to Kath, said as much as she did, but another part of him, a slightly fretful part, kept intruding. When Kath eventually went through to watch the news, leaving him to wash up, he tried to tease it out. But it was elusive. He knew it involved himself and Davidson, but he couldn't understand why it had started digging at him here at home with Kath. It kept coming back as they watched the video he'd brought home and, later, in bed, with Kath breathing slowly and deeply beside him and the lights out, it still nudged at him, keeping his thoughts churning and getting in the way of sleep.

It was after midnight when he eventually did drop off. Then, suddenly, with the clock showing 4.12, he was wide awake, and he knew what the problem was. It lay in the smell of garlic and the fact that the New Zealand wine cost a couple of pounds more than the one they usually drank. As his suspicions and excitement grew, he couldn't understand why it had taken him so long to make the connections. He got up and went down to the kitchen to make some coffee. There was no point in trying to sleep now. Equally, there was nothing he could do until the day started, so he drank the coffee, scribbled notes and was both fascinated by and appalled at the possibility that he might be right.

He was in his office before eight and Ross, whom he'd rung on his way there, arrived twenty minutes later.

'What's the fuss?' he said as he came in.

Carston pointed to the newly made coffee.

'Get some of that. I think we're going to need it today,' he said.

Ross poured a cup and sat down.

'Right, no bodies have turned up,' said Carston. 'So where are they?'

'They've gone away.'

'Or?'

'I don't know.'

'Or they're being kept somewhere.'

'By Davidson?'

'Yes.'

'OK, where?'

'I don't know,' said Carston. 'But Gayla Campbell told me that he's a bit of a gourmet.'

'So? They're in a larder?'

'Ha, ha. When I was there last week, he said he was cooking dinner. But there was no smell of food. In fact, it smelt as if it needed a bit of a clean-up.'

Ross waited, not yet seeing the connection.

'If he's as good a cook as she said, I'd've noticed

something.'

Ross shrugged.

'Maybe he was only preparing things,' he said.

'OK, but he had empty wine bottles and boxes in his kitchen, too,' said Carston. 'Big bottles. Litre bottles.'

'So what?'

'It was Bulgarian shite. He's supposed to be a wine buff. He's not going to drink cheap plonk like that. And he lives on his own. Why would he choose litre bottles?'

'Maybe he had a party.'

'And the boxes of food,' Carston went on, ignoring him. 'They were bulk buys, processed stuff. He'd never eat that.'

Now Ross saw where he was going.

'No. Can't be,' he said.

'OK, give me an alternative. What's the food for?'

'But he's not going to be giving them booze, is he?'

It was Carston's turn to shrug.

'Who knows?' he said. 'The trouble is, if he's done a runner, what's happening to them?'

'Lots of ifs there,' said Ross.

'I know, but s'pose I'm right. Who's feeding the buggers?'

Ross thought about the question for a while. It was all too speculative for him.

'We're talking about a family GP and you're saying he's keeping a menagerie of people somewhere?' he said. 'That's pretty thin.'

'Put it with the phone calls, the poison, the motive. That's plenty of circumstantial stuff. Anyway, what else have we got? We've got to check it out. And if he's away, we can't risk leaving it.'

'So what are you saying?'

'We'll do it by the book, but somebody's got to get the bloody thing moving. You get round to the fiscal's office, spell it all out for him, lay it on as thick as you can.'

'What about you?'

'I'll be busy.'

Ross looked at him and was about to ask a question.

'Don't ask,' said Carston. 'Just get the warrant and organize a forensic team for Davidson's place.'

'I hope you …'

Carston interrupted him.

'Good. That's good,' he said. 'It's good to hope.'

Dobie's stomach couldn't cope with the amounts he'd stuffed himself with since he'd had his own private pile of food. I heard him vomiting over near his pillar. He didn't try or didn't have time, to get to the buckets. I caught the smell of bile cutting through the stench of our sweat and faeces. It surprised me in a way. My normal medic's responses had vanished. I felt no urge to give Dobie any help or advice. I couldn't even remember what to suggest anyway.

All the time, I only thought about Tommy, kneeling in the sunshine in his room and sliding a razor across his throat. I had images of the two of us in sailing boats, building dams across burns, climbing trees, sitting at the top of Lochnagar. I was finding it difficult to remember colours. So I suppose I wasn't so much seeing the images as feeling them. Weird. Tommy was helping me. Still. I mean, I'd locked myself in with these bastards but it didn't seem to matter any more whether I was punishing them, or whether I'd redressed any balance. Everybody was a victim. Everybody thought they knew who was responsible for persecuting them. It wasn't that easy. Tommy's blood had dripped onto the carpet but his true substance wasn't in the flesh that he'd destroyed; it was in all the things – the love, the intuitions – that bound him to his three girls. Waring had fucked his family up, but he hadn't been able to touch that love.

Carston realized how little he'd used the squad over the past couple of months. They'd been busy enough, and they'd brought together the evidence needed to charge Billy and to make Davidson a target, but he'd been relying more than was healthy on his own intuitions. It had started when he realized that he almost approved of the various disappearances. Recognizing that he secretly shared the apparent motives behind the abductions, if that's what they were, had made him even more introspective than usual. Fraser's bad French would have been an easy distraction. But more and more in this investigation Carston had been aware of the impulses he shared with Spurle.

As the names of McPhee, Dobie, Campion, Bailey and Waring had cropped up, his reaction to their disappearance had been visceral. Basically, he'd hoped they were either dead or suffering. It was an uncivilised attitude and each time he felt those satisfactions, they were accompanied by anger at his own capacity for malevolence.

It was partly to counter that self-disgust that he was taking a chance by pre-empting the response of the procurator fiscal. He phoned the surgery to ask whether they had a key to Davidson's house. They did and so urgent and persuasive were his explanations that they agreed to let him take it. He was anxious to disturb things as little as possible so he decided to go on his own. With luck, Ross would soon be bringing the official team along with a warrant, so he was only preparing their arrival. As he got out of the car, he put on plastic overshoes, gloves and a white forensic suit before unlocking the front door and walking carefully into the hall.

We heard you arrive. They made some noises, tried to attract your attention, but I knew you wouldn't hear them. Their voices were too feeble anyway. I didn't bother trying. I was already too far gone. I heard their chains clink a bit, but not much. I don't know whether I wanted you to come down and find us or not.

The damp residual smell still hung in the air. Carston looked into the kitchen and sitting room. Nothing had changed. The bottles and boxes were still stacked neatly together and he noticed the film of dust which had settled on them and on the tables in the hall and the sitting room. No-one had used the rooms for several days. He moved towards the stairs, looking closely at the carpet before stepping slowly and carefully forward. He noticed the door at the end of the hall and, instead of climbing the stairs, he moved towards it. Within a few steps, he knew that this was where he should start. As he got nearer, the smell thickened and caught not just his nostrils but the back of his throat. He pushed the door open and went down the steps. When he opened the door at the bottom, he was hit by the full force of a sharp, animal stench that made him gag and step back. He took out a handkerchief, held it over his mouth and nose and went into the cellar. He put his hand to the wall, searched for a light switch and flicked it on.

The five men lay on the filthy floor, four of them ragged skeletal individuals, their skins grey and greasy, with dry, flaking patches amongst weeping sores on their forearms and shins. Davidson was sitting with his back to a pillar, his hands clasped over his eyes to keep out the hard light. Pieces of food were lying on the ground beside them amongst torn packaging and the stains of spilled drinks and urine. Two chemical toilet buckets stood open in the central area, the floor around them sticky with the substances that had spilled from them. And the smell was relentless; harsh, feral, reeking its way straight to his stomach. He recognized McPhee, Campion and Waring and guessed that the other was Dobie. Dobie was barely conscious and Davidson sat very still. But the other three started babbling all at once, mixing prayers, thanks, threats and a whole jumble of things which made little sense.

He took out his mobile, risked taking the handkerchief from his mouth and rang the station. He ordered ambulances and told the sergeant to get on to Ross to bring the scene of crime team right away.

'Make sure they bring masks with them,' he said, before ringing off.

There was nothing he could do until the team arrived. They'd need photographs and video of everything and releasing the men would create problems of what to do with them until the ambulances arrived. He left the light on, told them he'd soon be back with help, and went upstairs and out into the fresh air. As he waited for Ross, he heard them calling after him, then swearing and shouting at Davidson. In each voice, there was still fear.

The ambulances began to arrive within minutes and, before the crews took their stretchers down to the cellar, he warned them what to expect. He went back down with them.

'We'll need bolt cutters for these chains,' said the first medic as he bent over Dobie.

'No. The keys are in the corner.'

It was Davidson's voice; thin, barely more than a croak. Carston turned to look at him, and Davidson pointed behind him to the torch and the keys lying in the corner. An ambulance man fetched them and began freeing the pathetic wrecks from their respective pillars. Carston went and squatted beside Davidson.

'Why?' he said.

Davidson said nothing.

'Walking around with all this inside you all the time,' said Carston. 'Coming home to it every evening. How the hell did you manage that?'

Davidson had no interest in the observations or the question. Dobie seemed too weak to know what was happening and was stretchered out without a word.

Waring was spitting imprecations at Davidson all the time.

'Listen,' he said to Carston, as he was taken away. 'That psycho's a bloody murderer. He told us. Make sure you do him for that, too. Serves the bastard right. He's round the fucking bend.'

As the last two were carried out, McPhee was silent but Campion, in a quiet, reasonable voice, said, 'I understand, you know. It's not your fault.'

When they unlocked his own cuffs, Davidson stood up, refused their offers of help and said, 'I don't need an ambulance.'

Carston looked at him. His eyes were empty, the muscles of his face loose, and somewhere in his expression there was a vast sorrow.

'Why?' asked Carston again, trying to ignite some sort of spark in him.

Davidson shook his head slowly.

'Was it me? The questions I asked?'

'No,' said Davidson. 'I don't know what it was.' He spoke slowly, seeming to think hard about what he was saying. 'I think that, once you start, it takes over. You know what I'm talking about. You said so.'

'Did I?'

'You said they deserved whatever they were getting,' said Davidson.

'Yes, but ...' Carston stopped.

'Well, I gave it to them. Tried, anyway. But in the end, I couldn't. You just can't. You touch them, and your hands are as dirty as theirs. It doesn't solve a thing.' He rubbed at his wrists as he spoke and looked around the cellar. 'No, that's not right,' he went on. 'I did all this before I touched them. Got it all ready. I was guilty before McPhee came and banged on the door.'

He gestured at the pillars, the buckets, the filth.

'This is me. This is what I'm like inside. It was my idea, my plan. No better than what Bailey did to Marion, or Dobie to his girl, or Campion.' He pushed his hand against his chest. 'It comes from here – all of it.'

'It'd probably be better if you didn't say anything about it just now,' said Carston. 'We'll be asking you questions soon enough.'

'Oh, don't worry. I'll tell you all about it. It was premeditated. I won't be doing anything to deny it.' He made a sound like a short laugh. 'You know, in a way, I ... I think it's done me good. You can't fight it, can you? It's there. Always will be there. If you do try to ... destroy it, you're just adding to it. Best to leave it. Accept it.'

He nodded, speaking now for himself rather than for Carston.

'The best I could've done for Tommy was to look after my patients. Do some good. But I ...'

Suddenly, he was crying. The scene of crime officers looked quickly at him then continued with their various tasks. Carston waited, letting him unload some of the tension. At last, with a few deep sighs, he sniffed back the last of the tears.

'Thanks,' he said, and held out his wrists.

'What's that for?' asked Carston.

'Don't you want to cuff me?'

Carston pointed at the chains beside the pillar.

'I think you've probably had enough of that for a while,' he said.

Davidson looked around again.

'What a difference the light makes,' he said.

Outside, the sun was bright on the garden and in the big Grampian sky. Davidson looked everywhere, his eyes greedy for the things he thought he'd never see again. He was driven away in a patrol car as Carston and Ross walked back to their own car in silence. Each was appalled by the discovery and trying to come to terms with what Davidson must have been feeling. Back at the station, before starting on the paperwork, Carston consulted a telephone directory and dialled a number. It was some minutes before Reismann answered.

'Mr. Reismann? Jack Carston here. I'm sorry to disturb you, but I thought you'd appreciate me telling you we've sorted out the business about Bailey and McPhee.'

'What's the story then?'

Carston told him everything. The lawyer was as disturbed by it all as Carston and Ross had been. Like Carston, one of his first thoughts was of the torment through which Davidson must have been going to conceive of and sustain such a thing.

'God, the pain that people have in them,' he said, his voice soft, slow.

'Yes,' said Carston, echoing his tone. 'Endless, isn't it?'

They had nothing to say to one another. There were no words for the things that filled their minds.

'Just one thing,' said Carston into the silence.

'Yes?'

'The doctor's going to need legal help. Do you think you would ...?'

He had no need to finish the question. Reismann

interrupted him.

'Of course. I'll be over right away.'

I couldn't stop crying. I was glad you'd saved me. Not me, not for myself, but saved me from ultimately being guilty for five deaths instead of just the one. Bailey was my payment to Tommy. It should've been Waring. If I'd had the choice, it would've been. See? The impulse is still there. No point pretending any more. I don't know if I'll ever get out but, even if I do, I'll still want to have my fingers around Waring's throat. It's who I am.

Ross shrugged on his coat the door and stood for a moment. There'd been silence in the office as they tidied up the loose ends, but the silence was introverted, reflective, for both of them. They'd talk about it in due course but, for now, the awfulness of what Davidson had suffered and perpetrated was too close.

'Bastard, eh?' said Ross.

Carston nodded.

'We should get a proper job,' he said.

'Who'd have us?' said Ross.

Carston smiled.

'See you tomorrow, Jim.'

Ross nodded and left.

Carston looked around and felt again the sadness of events that couldn't be changed. The image of the cellar, with its reeking darkness, had lodged in his mind, together with Davidson's words. And he agreed with him. All the time, the job brought him into contact with it – the degradations of which people were capable. But he knew it was in himself too. Like Spurle, he was carrying those base impulses, a primitive urge for vengeance, an instinctive tendency always to see women through a little stirring of lust, and the equally instinctive desire to meet evil with evil.

He sat for a while longer, trying without much success to will himself out of a sort of self-disgust. He needed to be home with Kath to ground himself once more. On his way out

312

of the station, he lingered for a moment beside the front desk. The phone started to ring and he left. He didn't want to hear any more problems or pain. Not today.

Rhona's punter was young, maybe twenty-four or twenty-five. He was tall, good-looking and he obviously worked out a lot. With people like that, she always wondered why they needed to buy their sex. Perhaps it was just to avoid complications. Whatever the reason, she got no pleasure from the fact that they were very presentable studs. She actually preferred older men. But this one was being kind, considerate, even thoughtful as he poured her a glass of wine in his nondescript room in the Travelodge.

'Shall I get changed?' she asked, taking a sip. It was warm, sugary, cheap.

'In a minute,' he said.

She looked around at the mainly beige décor.

'Romantic, isn't it?' she said, with a smile intended to relax the tension she could see in him.

He didn't smile back.

'We're not here for romance, are we?' he said.

She shrugged and forced down another mouthful of the wine. He was standing with his back to the window, watching her.

'Well, what sort of things do it for you?,' she asked. 'How can we ...'

Her question was interrupted by a knock at the door. Quickly, he crossed and opened it. One by one, six other men came in, all the same sort of age as her punter.

'I asked some friends along,' he said. 'I hope you don't mind.'

The friends laughed.

When the final paperwork had been cleared up, Carston took a few days off. He needed very badly to spend away from the station. On the third evening, Kath was out on a commission and he was surprised to get a visit from Freddy Reismann. He invited him in but the lawyer shook his head.

'No. I've just come to give you this,' he said.

He handed over a small padded envelope.

'What is it?' said Carston.

'Self-explanatory,' said Reismann. 'He wanted you to have it.'

Carston nodded.

'How is he?' he asked.

Reismann made a so-so gesture with his hand.

'Well, let me know if there's anything I can do,' said Carston.

Reismann nodded, walked back to his car and drove away. Carston went back in, tore open the flap of the envelope and looked inside. There was no note, just an audio cassette. He pushed it into his cassette player and pressed 'Play'. It was Davidson's voice. Carston sat down and listened.

'Listen to this. Listen properly, I mean. To all of it. Maybe your psychiatrists can make something of it. I certainly can't.

I suppose it started when I was doing that house call. Jerry Donald. He's only fifty, but his circulation's so bad it's a miracle his blood moves more than a foot away from his heart.'

Printed in the United States
210247BV00005B/115/P

9 781849 232975